YELLOWSTONE REDEMPTION

YELLOWSTONE ROMANCE SERIES

PEGGY L HENDERSON

ISBN: 9781096685166

INTRODUCTION

City boy Chase Russell is on the fast track to self-destruction. A star athlete, he gets into trouble with drugs and alcohol. Fulfilling a community service sentence in Yellowstone National Park is the last thing he wants to do. After a night of drinking in the park, he wakes up to find his new friends gone, and everything around him has changed.

Sarah Osborne grew up in the rugged Yellowstone wilderness. She can hunt and track right alongside the most experienced men. When some Indians drop a near-dead man off on her doorstep, she doesn't know what to think. He's convinced he's from the future, and wants to find a way home.

Chase has no idea how he ended up time traveling to the past. He doesn't know the first thing about surviving without modern conveniences. Finding your own food means a quick trip to the nearest fast food joint, not hunting and foraging for it. Time and again, his will is tested to stay alive in this untamed land. Is his growing love for a brave woman who shows him what it truly means to be a man strong enough to keep him in the past, or is he still determined to return to the ease and comforts of the future?

CHAPTER ONE

*M*adison Valley on the Yellowstone Plateau, 1835

"Please, Mama, why can't I go?" Sarah Osborne implored in a high-pitched voice. She followed close on the heels of her mother, who stormed through the front door of the cabin. Although her legs were much longer than the older woman's, she almost ran to keep up with her strides.

Her petite mother ignored the question, threw her hands in the air in an overly exaggerated movement, then quickly brought them back to her sides, and balled them into fists at her hips. She turned more fully toward the man sitting at the table in the middle of the room. The thick long braid of her blonde hair swung like a whip behind her back. The man finished tying an obsidian arrowhead to a long wooden shaft, biting off the end of the sinew strings. He set it aside and raised a questioning brow in her mother's direction. Her eyes glowered, and she took a step toward him.

"Daniel, talk to her. She's your daughter."

Sarah watched her father push the chair away from the table. He didn't look at her. Instead, his brown eyes met her mother's stare unflinching, and he raked a hand through his black hair to sweep back some unruly strands that had fallen into his eyes. Threads of silver mixed in with the black and reflected like icicles off the bright sunlight streaming into the room from the glass-paned window on the wall to the right. A lazy grin spread across his face, creasing the lines in the corners of his eyes. Her mother's features appeared to relax. His hand shot out, and he grabbed her wrist, pulling her onto his lap in one swift move. She gave a little squeal, and placed her hands on his shoulders.

Good grief! Not now! Why did they always have to act this way? Heat rose up Sarah's neck into her cheeks, watching her parents' display of affection.

Her father nuzzled her mother's neck, and whispered in a low growl, "No, *gediki*. She's most definitely your daughter." Her mother turned her neck to give him better access, and reached a hand up to caress his cheek. His arms tightened around her waist.

Sarah stood just inside the front door, arms around her waist, and shifted her weight from one foot to the other. She rolled her eyes, and let out an exasperated snort. Her parents always acted like a newly wed couple, even though they had been married for twenty-five years. Time to put a stop to this outlandish display.

"Would you two stop it already," she cried out. "Honestly, Mama. The way you and Papa carry on is downright embarrassing."

Sarah watched her mother sit up on her husband's lap, then turn blue eyes on her. A warm smile brightened her features, the annoyance from a moment ago apparently forgotten.

"Sarah, one day you'll meet a man and fall in love. Time

will stand still whenever he's near, and the outside world forgotten when you're with him."

Sarah laughed and let out a most unfeminine snort. "I can ride, track, and hunt better than any man in these mountains, including my brothers." She lifted her chin, then paused and met her father's amused gaze. "Well, maybe with the exception of you, Papa." She flashed him a smile she knew always won him over. "So what would I need a man for?"

With his eyebrows raised and lips drawn up in a boyish grin, he shot his wife an unmistakable *I told you so* look. Sarah's insides swelled with satisfaction, and she gloated silently, her chin raised high in a defiant gesture toward her mother. Too late, she realized she should have approached her father with her request first.

"I recall words like those coming from you at one time." Daniel swiped a finger down his wife's nose, a devilish grin on his face.

"Yes, well, a girl has the right to change her mind," Sarah's mother replied haughtily and patted his cheek, then pushed herself off his lap. She turned to face her daughter. "But I'm not changing my mind about this."

Sarah groaned silently at the stern look in her mother's eyes. "Why not?" she challenged.

"Do you remember what happened last year?" Her hands were back on her hips.

Daniel rose from the table, his size dwarfing his wife. He stood next to her, and put a hand around her shoulders, pulling her up next to him

"What's going on?" Her father directed his gaze on her.

Sarah's shoulders drooped. His dark eyes stared right through her. Trying to convince him might not be so easy after all.

"Mama says I can't go to the rendezvous this year," she

blurted out. "She doesn't think it's appropriate for me anymore."

"Darn right it's not," her mother's voice sounded adamant. "You're nearly nineteen years old, Sarah, and not married. You know what sort of riffraff shows up at those gatherings. Last year, your dad, Matthew, and Sam spent all their time fending off your wannabe suitors. You have no idea what effect you have on men. And most of those characters have questionable morals." She took a few steps forward.

Even though Sarah was a couple inches taller than her mother, the woman had an imposing presence, and didn't leave much question as to who was in charge. She stood no chance once her mother was this unyielding. Worse, her mother had her father completely wrapped around her fingers.

Sarah didn't begrudge them their happiness. She'd met other trappers' wives before, mostly Indian women, and had to listen to complaints of how unhappy some of them were, and how badly their men treated them. The way some made it sound, they were nothing more than a commodity to their husbands.

Not so with her parents. Daniel and Aimee Osborne were equal partners in everything. Neither did anything without the other's knowledge or approval. The love between them was unmistakable in the way they looked at each other and touched whenever they were within reach. Sarah was proud to be their daughter. What would life be like with a father who beat her mother, or made his woman work from dawn to dusk with little regard for her well-being. Without a doubt, both her parents would lay their lives down for each other without hesitation, as well as for their children.

Along with her three older brothers, she'd been raised here in the wilds of the Rocky Mountains, a place her mother called the Madison Valley on the Yellowstone Plateau. No one else she knew used these words. It was a man's world, and she had learned early on to adapt. Her father had taught her how to survive in this harsh environment right alongside her brothers, and Sarah loved him dearly for it.

She had the best of both worlds. She could go out into the woods and hunt and foray like a man, but she also enjoyed the chores more associated with her gender, such as cooking, tanning hides, and making pottery. Her Tukudeka aunt and cousins had certainly never let her forget that she was female. Her mother encouraged her to follow whatever made her happy, and also taught her in the art of healing. That was her mother's special gift, and Sarah was an eager student.

Just the idea of being tied down to a man made her shudder. It would have to be quite an exceptional man to draw her attention. Her father had set a pretty high standard of how a man should treat his woman. Over the last few years, she'd become more curious about men, she had to admit. She'd watch some of the Tukudeka hunters discreetly, especially in the summer months when they wore no shirts, fascinated by the movements of the muscles on their chests and arms. However, no man she'd met thus far had made her heart beat faster, or sent her mind spinning. That's what her mother told her love for a man was like. Sarah doubted she would ever find a man who could elicit such a response from her.

"Sarah Marie Osborne. Are you listening?"

"Huh?" Her mother's adamant voice in her ear pulled Sarah out of her thoughts.

"I also need you here to take care of Snow Bird. She's due to have her baby while we're gone, and she needs you to midwife for her. We've already discussed this."

"There are other midwives," Sarah mumbled.

"I agree with your mother." Daniel's deep voice brought Sarah to full attention, and she looked to her father. "With your brothers gone to St. Louis this year, it's too dangerous for you. And I don't wish for you to be exposed to the sort of men - or women - who attend the rendezvous. Understand this is for your own good. We trust you to be safe here by yourself while we are gone."

"But no doubt you'll have Elk Runner or one of my cousins checking up on me regularly." Sarah tried to keep her eyes from twitching. She swallowed her disappointment. She had lost the argument. Once her father sided with her mother, it was all over. She ventured a glance at him. His dark eyes glowed warmly at her. His slow smile melted her anger.

"I understand your disappointment, *bai'de*. But I intend to keep you out of harm's way. No matter how much you may fight it, you have become a grown woman, and men take notice of such things."

Sarah swallowed, lowered her eyes, and nodded in defeat. The annual trapper rendezvous held to the south amongst the Teewinots drew mountain men and trappers from all over the Rocky Mountains. It was an event that lasted for weeks, a time for men to gather and trade furs, supplies, and adventure stories. She looked forward to these meetings every year, which her parents attended to trade necessities to other trappers.

Her father hadn't trapped for beaver in years. At her mother's suggestion, they had set up a trading post to supply other trappers in this remote wilderness. Her mother had predicted a decade ago that the beaver would be trapped out in the mountains soon, and demand in the east would cease. Her prediction had come true. Now, along with offering supplies to the dwindling number of fur trappers, the family supplied the ever-increasing number of westward explorers.

"Your mother will be busy tending to the sick and injured." Sarah's father continued.

"But I've always helped her with that," Sarah tried one more time. At this point, she had nothing to lose. She glanced from one parent to the other. Her mother strode toward her and wrapped her arms around her shoulders in a warm embrace, then held her at arm's length.

"Sarah, I know this is disappointing, but you're a beautiful young woman, and you don't have a husband's protection. Where I grew up -" She turned to glance at her husband. Sarah wondered at the conspiratorial look that passed between them. "That wasn't such an issue. But here, an unmarried woman is fair game. You know that."

Yeah, Sarah sighed inwardly. She did know that. Her mother was right, as usual. She'd been revolted and alarmed at some of the ways men tried to fawn themselves at her during last year's rendezvous. It had gotten worse each year. And she had caught the hungry looks of some of the men who came to trade here with her father.

She was well aware that the only reason none of them had ever acted on their obvious intentions was her father's reputation. Daniel Osborne was known throughout the mountains as a man who protected his family fiercely and without mercy. There wasn't a trapper who had heard his name who dared make rude comments or suggestions toward his wife. And the services and goods her parents provided to the mountain men in this remote wilderness were highly valued. No one wanted to get on Daniel Osborne's bad side. But at the rendezvous, trappers came from all over the Rockies. Her safety, and virtue, may not be ensured simply based on her name.

Sarah nodded in defeat, hanging her head. She resigned herself that she was stuck here in the valley this summer, doing . . . what? She'd be bored out of her mind for the six or so weeks while her parents were gone.

CHAPTER TWO

*C*hase Russell groaned. The pounding in his head increased when he tried to lift it off the hard ground. He squinted his eyes into the bright sun overhead, then closed them again, fighting off the dizziness. The loud roar of the nearby waterfall drowned out all other sound. A shadow, then a sudden unexpected gush of hot air on his cheek made him flinch. It happened again, and this time it was accompanied by the sensation of sandpaper scraping across his face.

Chase forced his eyes open, and hauled himself off the ground. He stumbled over the slippery rocks and landed several feet in the frigid river. A cold wave slammed into him like a lineman's tackle, and threatened to push him further into the rushing current. He gasped in surprise and shock. Quickly, he scrambled on hands and feet over the jagged rocks, back to the safety of dry land. The icy water jolted him fully awake. A couple more feet, and the tremendous current of the river would have swept him away.

A creature with pointy horns and tan-colored fur that hung in thick tufts off its shoulders and back stood where he lay moments ago. Dripping wet and shaking from the cold, he hauled himself off the ground, keeping a wary eye on the . . . what was that? Hell if he knew one animal from another. It wasn't a bison, he was sure of that. He'd already seen plenty of those. Luckily, it wasn't a bear. It looked more like a goat on steroids. It didn't look intimidating anymore, now that he was a safe distance away, out from underneath its coarse tongue. He remembered seeing goats at the fair one year when he was little. His mother had encouraged him to enter the goat-milking contest, but he'd scoffed at her. Touch one of those things? Hell no. The closest he let himself come to animal skin was the pigskin covering of a football.

The creature stared back at him, its mouth moving in a rhythmic, circular motion. It appeared to gloat at him.

"Shoo! Get out of here!" He waved his hands in the air and took a step toward the stupid thing. Alarmed, the walking cheese factory jumped away, and gracefully sprang up the steep incline of yellow and red colored rocks about twenty yards from the river.

His gaze followed the effortless movements of the animal, as it darted up the sides of the canyon. Shit. It was going to be a long haul back up. The top was barely visible, some nine hundred feet from where he stood. His feet were still blistered from the hike down.

Damn those guys anyway! Why the hell did he go along with their idiotic schemes? Just to prove he wasn't some namby-pamby city boy? They all wanted to be here, had volunteered for this. He didn't have a choice. He was here to keep his nose clean, not get in more trouble. But trouble always had a way of finding him. At least it had the last four years.

It hadn't been his idea to come to Montana to do the community service portion of his drug conviction. He'd finished rehab. Montana was his mother's suggestion. Her sister's husband had connections in Yellowstone, and he'd pulled some strings with the Department of Corrections. Now he was stuck here for the summer, part of the trail maintenance crew that cleared the popular hiking trails of downed trees, controlled erosion, and other crap. It was hard physical work, but it beat picking up trash along an L.A. freeway. At least he'd stay in shape, since there was no workout gym close by.

A quick glance in all directions told him he was alone. Where the hell had they all gone? His sleeping bag wasn't where he'd laid it out the night before, either. Those assholes took everything, and left him. There'd be hell to pay when he got out of this canyon and back to the barracks. He only hoped his crew leader didn't catch wind of where he'd been. No doubt he'd be arrested again. Hiking in the canyon was illegal. He knew that. That had been made clear during the pep talk they all received when they started the season. Just as hot-potting – swimming in the thermal features - was illegal, but they'd done that, too. He remembered Todd suggesting they sneak out one night and piss into Old Faithful's cone. But no one had been brave enough to try that. Not yet, anyway.

He pulled his soaked t-shirt over his head and gave it a hard twist to wring out as much water as possible. How long had he been passed out? Judging by the sun directly overhead, it was noon or a little later. At least he'd dry faster. The last thing he remembered from the night before was stumbling from his sleeping bag to the river to hurl his stomach contents. Not enough food and too much alcohol had been to blame for that. Apparently he never made it back to his sleeping bag, and passed out right here. Good thing he hadn't rolled sideways, or he'd have gone for his first and only wild plume ride. Watching the water rush past, even he knew that this was one whitewater trip no one would survive.

A renewed wave of bile threatened to rise from his stomach. He smacked his dry lips together, and realized how parched and swollen his tongue and throat were. He didn't have enough spit in his mouth to even swallow. He glanced at the river. *Why the hell not?* He shrugged. It was the only water available. He dropped to his knees on the rocky bank and stuck his head in the water. The icy liquid felt good going down his throat. Chase hoped he didn't catch giardia or something. Oh well, he'd know soon enough. There was medication for that.

Chase pulled himself to a standing position again. He picked his shirt up off the ground and tied it, turban style, around his head. He looked up the jagged face of the canyon again, then squared his shoulders. *No pain, no gain.* He could hear his football coach yelling in his ear, driving him to greater effort.

His stomach grumbled and churned, but he ignored it, and picked his way up the yellow rocks. Once he'd reach the top, it was just a short walk to the parking lot, not that he expected his newfound so-called friends to be waiting for him. He'd most likely have to walk a couple miles back to the Canyon Village barracks, but at least the road was paved and flat. Maybe some tourist would take pity on his soul, and give him a lift.

He cursed Todd, Jimmy, Phil, and all the other guys with every step he took. His knuckles scraped against the jagged brittle rocks, his bare knees scuffed and bleeding. The blisters on his heels burned like hell whenever they rubbed against his barely-broken in hiking boots. Gritting his teeth, Chase pushed on, taking advantage of every gnarled tree root that jutted out of the rocks to pull himself upward. It hadn't been this hard climbing down into the canyon, and it sure as hell didn't seem as long. But the same drive that had earned him All Star Quarterback his senior year in high school pushed him forward now. Too bad that intense desire to be the best hadn't carried over to college.

Riding on a full football scholarship, he'd started partying more and more, and eventually pledged a fraternity. From there, the all night drinking escalated to drug use. His grades and game had suffered, and he was kicked off the team during his junior year. The arrest for possession followed, and now he was here.

With a quick glance up, Chase fingered the dog tags that dangled from a chain around his neck. They were the only things his loser father had ever given him. Why he wore them, he didn't know. Hell, if he had any sense, he'd toss them down into the canyon right now. His thumb rubbed the tags out of habit, then he let go and reached for the next rock jutting out of the canyon wall above him. With one final pull and grunt, he hauled himself over the edge and collapsed to the ground, emitting a long sigh of relief. Endless pull-ups in the gym had finally paid off.

Man up, Russell. Just a few more miles, and you can get some chow. Right before you knock the shit out of Todd and the rest of those idiots. His fists bunched at his sides at the thought. With an impatient swipe of his hands, he brushed away the gravel that stuck to his sweat-soaked chest and abdomen. A mosquito landed on his leg, and he slapped it away, hitting his knee in the process. He hissed and inhaled sharply. His knees looked like freshly ground beef. Cursing, he plucked some pebbles from the open sores. It had been a hot day yesterday, and he'd worn cargo shorts instead of long pants. Hindsight wasn't helping him now.

He glanced down into the canyon one final time, then turned. The gravel path that led to the parking lot should be just beyond that line of trees. They seemed denser than he remembered from yesterday. He pushed and weaved his way through the forest. His shirt caught in one of the lower branches and was yanked off his head. His forward momentum jerked his neck back.

"Shit." Chase wrestled his shirt out of the branch's grasp, and pulled it on over his head. He cringed when the fabric scraped the skin on his back. Damn, he hadn't realized he'd gotten sunburned. The tingle of his skin became more intense with each passing minute, exacerbated by his movements. The soft cotton shirt felt like sandpaper across his tender flesh.

"I'm going to kill you, Todd," he ground out between clenched teeth, and shoved his way between more trees. Where the hell was that path? He should have reached it by now. The hiking path led parallel along the canyon rim. There was no way he could have missed it. The further he walked, the darker the forest closed in around him, the sun obscured by towering lodgepole pines. The air chilled, replacing the heat from the shadeless canyon. His boots squished loudly in his efforts to trample through the moist and soggy ground.

Water trickled nearby and Chase followed the rippling sounds. He dropped to his knees at the edge of a shallow creek that snaked through the underbrush. Giardia be damned. He cupped his hands in the cool water, and splashed it on his face and neck. He refilled his hands repeatedly, gulping the water as fast as he could. With his hands on his thighs, he inhaled sharply and tilted his head back to stare beyond the canopy of the trees.

Where the hell am I? I couldn't have missed the path.

Was it his imagination, or had the blue patches of sky that peered through the trees turned an ominous dark gray? It happened so fast, it was as if someone had turned out the lights around him. Before the thought had barely formed in his mind, he heard the rumble of thunder in the distance. This day couldn't get any worse, could it?

Rain pelted him without mercy. Ferocious wind forced the lodgepoles to swing and bend ominously in its wake.

One downed tree on your head, and it's all over, Russell.

He wrapped his arms tightly around his middle, and trudged on through the forest. He kept his head bent into his chest, and only glanced up every so often in hopes of spotting the parking lot. He had no idea how long he walked, but the rain and wind were relentless.

Darkness swallowed up the trees in front of him, and Chase's body shook violently. He could barely move. His boot caught on something. A tree root, maybe? He stumbled forward and yanked his foot free of the protruding obstacle. Before he could catch his balance, he fell to the soggy ground. He spit the mud out of his mouth and wiped at his eyes.

You need to find shelter, man. No, just a little further. The parking lot is just a little further. He tried to stand, but the world around him tilted, and he sagged back to the ground. Crawling on hands and knees, he forced himself forward. His body refused to listen to his brain. The muscles wouldn't obey.

I have to get to the parking lot. Find shelter. No, everything will be okay once I get to the parking lot.

He couldn't feel the ground beneath him anymore. Couldn't tell if he was crawling on rocks or soft earth. Was he still in the forest? He willed his head to move so he could look up, but the darkness hindered his vision. *Shit. I'm going to . . . kill . . . those guys. Right after I rest here for a minute . . . so tired.*

Voices! He definitely heard voices. His body no longer felt cold. He wasn't shivering anymore. He was so damn tired, he couldn't move. Someone was hauling him off the ground. He tried to open his eyes, but his lids felt like one-ton anchors. He caught a quick glimpse of movement, but it was blurry.

He tried to blink, tried to open his eyes, but it was no use. He was floating through the air. Something slammed into his gut and his breath rushed from his lungs. His world tilted upside down.

His head floated freely, swinging from side to side. He had lost all control over his body. He forced his eyes open again. The ground moved underneath him. It was like looking at the road while riding a bike. Only, instead of smooth pavement, dirt and rocks and tufts of grass moved beneath him at surreal speeds. The ride jolted and churned him like a puppet without a master.

Soft melodious sounds of a woman's voice mingled with deeper voices, penetrated his mind. They sounded far away. Someone hurled his body through the air and whatever had pressed so hard into his gut was gone. His back made contact with hard ground, and all nerve endings caught on fire. He willed his eyelids open one more time. Through the haze and fuzziness, the vision of a dark-haired angel stared back at him. Chase drowned in the pools of her deep blue eyes.

CHAPTER THREE

Sarah stared at the man on the ground. His lids fluttered open for a mere second, and she caught a glimpse of emerald green eyes. The hint of a smile formed on his lips, and he groaned weakly before drifting back into unconsciousness.

"We found him wandering alone in the woods near the canyon of the *E-chee-dick-karsh-ah-shay*. The cold has made him sick in the mind." The deep voice of the Absaroka warrior standing behind her tore Sarah's gaze away from the man. She turned to look at the three Indians.

"*Dosa haiwi* will know what to do with him," a second man added.

Yes, Mama would know what to do, but she's not here.

Sarah wasn't about to let these men know that her parents were gone. The man they brought suffered from exposure. Even she knew that. She could help him without her mother's presence. But that meant he had to stay here. She was alone. Her father would be furious if he found out if she had kept a strange man in the house in their absence.

What choice do I have? He's almost dead already. Mama wouldn't let that happen.

"Can you carry him into the cabin," Sarah asked the men. "My mother will return shortly. I can care for him until she returns."

The undecided look that passed between the warriors didn't go unnoticed. She didn't trust these men. The Absarokas weren't exactly hostile, but they had a reputation to steal whatever they could. Having them in her parents' home was not the wisest course of action, but she saw no alternative. Looking at the man on the ground again, she knew she'd never be able to move him on her own.

"What happened to his britches, and the rest of his clothing?" Sarah asked before she could recall her words. She hoped the warriors didn't think she was accusing them of stealing. The man's dirt-caked britches fell barely to his knees, and his shirt was torn in several places.

"This is what he wore when we found him," the first man spoke. Sarah caught the distinct note of annoyance in his tone. The other two picked him up, one man hoisting him up by the shoulders, the other by his legs. She rushed ahead to open the door to the cabin.

Her parents' home was a spacious three-room dwelling with a loft. The front door opened to a large main room. A huge hearth and fireplace took up almost an entire wall. Shelves and a workbench that served as the kitchen area covered the rest of the wall. A rocking chair stood in the corner. The center of the room held a large table with six handcrafted chairs. Doors on opposite sides led to two bedrooms. One belonged to her parents, the other was hers. The loft had served as sleeping quarters for her brothers, as well as extra storage.

Making a hasty decision, Sarah led the Indians to her bedroom. She flipped back the covers on her bed, and the warriors dropped the man not too softly onto the mattress, then turned quickly to leave.

"Thank you for bringing him," she called lamely. She followed the two men outside and watched them mount their horses. They took off at a fast gallop. She caught the angry stare of the one man who'd lingered outside. She hadn't meant to insult him with her question. Shrugging it off, she rushed back to the stranger in her bed. This was not a good idea. Why couldn't this have happened two days ago, while her parents were still here?

The man was covered in dried mud, but cleaning him would have to wait. She needed to warm him first. Sarah unlaced and pulled his odd boots off his feet with some difficulty, and set them on the ground, spraying dirt all over the floor in the process. She covered him with the blankets on her bed, then left her room and rushed up the ladder to the loft to retrieve a buffalo robe and a bighorn sheep hide. She threw these over him as well, tucking them in at the sides.

Her mother had taught her how to read a person's heartbeat by feeling the throat. What she felt now alarmed her. His pulse was weak. His skin was like ice to her touch. She rushed to the main room and stoked the fire in the hearth. Next she poured water into the kettle over the flames. She reached for the three water bladders hanging on the wall by the front door, and filled them once the water was hot enough. She hastened back to her room, and placed one of the bags under each of the man's armpits, and the third under his neck. It was all she could do for now. His body would have to do the rest.

Sarah stared at the man. Only his head was visible under all the blankets and furs she'd piled on him. His hair struck her as odd. It was caked with mud, so she couldn't even tell what color it was, but she suspected it would be a lot lighter once clean. She'd never seen such short hair on a man before.

Curious, she reached out a tentative hand and touched it. It felt stiff with dirt. The man moved and groaned in his sleep, and she quickly pulled her hand away. She waited for any other movement, but he remained quiet.

A scraping sound and a whine brought her head around to the bedroom door. Something pushed it open from the outside.

"Come in, Grizzly," Sarah said with a smile. "Where have you been?" She knelt down to hug the huge dog that padded into the room. His tail wagged furiously and he licked at her face. She buried her head in the dog's shaggy gray coat. He looked more like a wolf than a dog, and was at least as big.

Sarah stood, watching her dog's nose twitch while he sniffed the air. A deep low growl emanated from his throat.

"It's all right, Grizzly. He's no threat to me." *At least not for the moment.* She patted the dog between the ears for reassurance. Grizzly cautiously walked up to the bed and sniffed the man's face. Then her dog ran his tongue across his cheek. The man stirred again, and seemed to cringe, but he didn't wake.

"All right, boy, that's enough. Come on, let's see if we can find something to eat." She slapped her hand against her leg, and the dog immediately turned and followed her out of the room.

The kettle still hung over the fire, and Sarah poured more water into it. She'd have to head to the river to refill the bucket soon. After adding more wood to build up the flame, she grabbed a slab of dried venison from a rack by the workbench, and pulled her knife from its sheath on her hip. The sharp blade sliced through the meat like butter, and she dropped small chunks of it into the water. She added a few onions that she had gathered the day before. If he was to regain his strength, the man would have to eat. She tossed several large pieces of meat to the eagerly waiting dog.

That's when she remembered something else her mother had taught her.

She scooped a cupful of the hot water, and added a few spoonfuls of sugar to it. The man's body needed fuel, and sugar was the simplest, quickest form. She stirred the cup with a wooden spoon to dissolve the white granules, then headed back to her room. She eased the door open tentatively and peered in.

The man hadn't moved. Was he dead? She held a hand above his nose. No, she could feel warm breath on her hand. She knelt beside her bed, and dipped the spoon in the sugar water. She pried his dry lips apart with the spoon, and let the liquid flow into his mouth. Most of it dribbled out the side. This wasn't going to work.

Sarah contemplated what to do. Taking a deep breath, she sat on the edge of the bed and scooted as close to him as she dared. Then she lifted his head into her lap. He emitted a low moan. His head rested heavily on her thighs. Her pulse quickened. With a trembling hand, she spooned more water into his mouth. Most of it remained, but she didn't notice him swallow. She rubbed his Adam's apple. There! Success. She repeated her actions several times, until a good half of the cup was empty.

The man squirmed. His eyelids fluttered, and slowly he raised them. Sarah stared down into green eyes again. His mouth moved, but only incoherent sounds came from his throat. Sarah smiled in encouragement.

"Angel."

Sarah barely heard the raspy word. She lifted his head off her lap and scooted away. His eyes looked dull and tired, and he obviously had a hard time keeping them open. She readjusted the covers around his neck, and left the room.

For the better part of the morning, she completed mundane chores around the cabin. She finished tanning the hide she'd been working on for several days. She needed a new pair of britches. For hours, she sat outside in the sun, rubbing sheep and elk brains into the hide to make it soft as silk and very pliable. Her Tukudeka aunt, Little Bird, had taught the skill to her. After letting it cure in the sun for a day, she would soak it in the river, and in a couple of days, she could begin sewing her new clothing. She had also planned to forage in the woods for some bitterroot and camas, but she wouldn't leave the unconscious man alone.

Late in the afternoon, she ladled some soup that had been simmering all day into a bowl, and sat at the table to eat. Her thoughts drifted back to earlier in the day. *Angel.* Something had stirred in her, like having her heart tickled by a feather, when he'd said that. Had he meant her? He was probably hallucinating. She finished her simple meal and placed the bowl on the ground. Grizzly eagerly lapped up the leftovers. She patted him affectionately on the head, then returned to her room to check on the man.

She found him shivering under the covers. It was a good sign. His body was responding again, working to warm itself up. When a person suffered from exposure and didn't shiver, it was always a bad sign.

He'd worked his arms loose of the covers, and Sarah was about to readjust them. A glimpse at his dirty shirt gave her another thought. Should she dare? Oh, this was ridiculous! This man needed care, and propriety be damned. She'd helped her mother plenty of times with injured men. She certainly had seen plenty of bare chests.

She hastily went back to the main room and set more water over the fire to heat, and found some clean washrags. When she returned, his shivering had slowed. She carefully pulled the covers further down. How would she be able to remove his shirt? He was a big man, probably taller than her father.

Sarah inhaled deeply and pulled his shirt up, rotating his heavy body from side to side to work it up his back. The sun had burned the skin on his back. She worked the shirt over his head. A thin silver chain hung around his neck, with a couple of rectangular pendants. She lifted the chain and fingered the light metals. They appeared plain, nothing anyone she knew would wear as an adornment. Something that looked like a long row of numbers was etched into them. Carefully, she laid the pendants back on his chest.

Remembering her task, she finished removing his shirt, setting the now-cold water bags aside. His long muscular arms were solid and heavy as she worked them through the sleeves. She hurried to retrieve her hot water and rags, then began washing the man's chest and arms with gentle strokes. She tried not to stare, but he was beautiful to look at. His muscles were well defined, his shoulders wide. She was about to scrub harder at what she thought was stubborn dirt caked to his chest just above his heart, then realized it was a marking. She wiped at it, and the black image of a scorpion emerged.

Sarah stared anew. She'd seen tattoos before, but nothing that looked as real as this. The image was a perfect depiction of a scorpion, its pincers held wide open, and the tail curved over the body, ready to strike. Tentatively, she touched it with her hand. His skin still felt cool, but the man was definitely warming up.

"Stared enough?"

The raspy voice sent her leaping off the edge of the bed, sloshing the water in her bowl over the floor.

"I . . . I didn't realize you were awake," she said awkwardly, averting her eyes. She heard the blankets scrape against each other and the mattress on her bed creak. She glanced up to see him push himself to a sitting position. He grimaced from the effort.

"Damn." He touched his forehead. "What the hell happened?"

"You must have been caught in the storm two days ago. You were lucky the Absarokas found you and brought you here." Sarah bent and reached for the bowl on the ground. The water had already seeped through the cracks in the wooden slats.

She kept a wary eye on the man in the bed. He was still too weak to be a threat, but Sarah's hand instinctively felt for her knife, reassured that it was securely strapped to her hip.

"Two days ago? Shit. Where am I?"

"The Madison River Valley," she answered.

The man shot her a perplexed look. "Madison? Why the hell there? Why not just take me to Canyon? They have a medical clinic."

It was Sarah's turn to look perplexed. This man must not be right in his head yet. Unsure what else to say, she asked, "Would you like some food? Some strong meat broth will help you warm up."

"Yeah. Sure," he answered absently.

Sarah hurried from the room, eager to put some space between herself and this strange man.

CHAPTER FOUR

*C*hase sat up, leaning his head back against the wooden logs that made up the walls in this room. He glanced around. Where the hell was he? This was definitely not a medical clinic. It looked like a scene out of an old west movie. The dim room had one small glass-paned window, and from what he could tell, it was getting dark outside. A simple wooden dresser stood against the wall opposite the bed. Was that a bearskin rug on the ground? Chase shook his head. The coverings on the bed were mostly hides and furs as well. A bunch of Native American-looking knick-knacks hung on the wall.

A slow smile spread across his face. Okay. He'd bite. Todd and the other boys were trying to pull one over on him again. Complete with a cute little Indian nurse. The dark-haired beauty certainly completed the scene. Her mahogany hair was braided in one long rope down her back, and her pants looked like fringed buckskins, complete with moccasins. Her cream-colored shirt fit loosely and was held together at her waist with a belt. Was that a real knife he'd noticed hanging at her hip? Shit, this could get mighty interesting. She looked vaguely familiar to him. She probably worked at one of the concession stores at Canyon.

You're losing it, Russell. A cute little chick like that, and you didn't take a closer look before? Well, maybe they could get better acquainted now.

He pulled himself further into a sitting position. The room began to spin. Damn. He hadn't felt weak like this since that one year he caught the flu. It had been a nasty strain, and Chase had been laid up in the hospital for a week. That was during his freshman year in high school, and he'd missed almost a month of football practice. He'd been surprised the coach had kept him on the team. But Coach Beckman had always believed in him. Always told him to strive to be better. He'd been more of a father figure than his old man. Right after the end of senior year, after Chase was announced All-Star Quarterback, the coach had had a massive heart attack. It had been quite a shock. Chase sure missed him. Maybe he wouldn't be here right now if Coach Beckman was still alive.

Chase heard a squeaking at the door, and looked up. His cute little nurse was back. She held a steaming wooden bowl and spoon in one hand, and a rustic-looking lamp in the other. Their eyes met. She didn't smile. Her eyes were large and round, but damn, if they weren't the bluest eyes he'd ever seen. A vague memory tapped his brain of a dark-haired, blue-eyed angel staring intently at him while he was flat on his back.

She set the lamp on the little table next to the bed, and held the bowl out to him. "This might be a little hot. But it will warm you."

"Thanks." He took the bowl from her, and set it on his lap. She was about to turn and walk away. Without even thinking, his hand snaked out and grabbed her around the wrist, pulling her down on the bed.

"What's the rush, Pocahontas? Stay and keep me company. I'll let you feed me, if you'd like." He flashed a grin that he knew worked on girls every time.

He had no idea how it happened, but the next thing he knew, he was staring at the pointy tip of a huge hunting knife. And it looked razor sharp. The girl had it pointed inches from his jugular. Chase scooted back in surprise. The fast movement caused the bowl on his lap to spill.

"Holy shit!" He jumped to the side and tumbled off the bed on the opposite side, landing on the floor with a loud thud. Damn, that soup was hot. And it had spilled all over his pants, scalding his family jewels. He hastily unbuttoned and unzipped his shorts, hoping to minimize the damage. Kicking the shorts off his legs, he pulled himself off the ground. His boxers were wet, but at least not hot where it counted. He peered up and over the bed. The girl was gone.

"Damn, Russell. What the hell was that about?" He'd certainly never gotten a reaction like that from a girl. One of the benefits of being a star athlete. All the chicks wanted to go out with you. He was used to girls – cute or otherwise – flaunting themselves at him. Having a knife pointed at his throat was an entirely new experience.

Can you blame her, Russell? She helps you out and you act like you want to get it on with her between the sheets.

Well, maybe that thought had crossed his mind, but he was in no condition to follow through with such a thought. At least not at the moment. Hell, his balls had been nearly frozen off, and now he'd almost cooked them. Maybe he wouldn't be in any condition for quite a while.

He ran his hand over his face. The two-day-old stubble felt rough against his hand. He had to look like hell. What he needed was a good long soak in a hot shower. He bent down and picked up his shorts. They were still wet, but at least the moisture was cold now. He pulled them back on, since it was all he had to wear.

Time to go make nice with the little Indian princess. Guilt nagged him. His actions had been rather rude, he admitted. He didn't know what made him do something stupid like that. Her deep blue eyes flashed before him, the look of concern on her face when he'd been barely conscious. *Angel.* Yeah. Hell's Angel.

Chase walked to the door on unsteady legs. He hated this weak feeling. His stomach growled. How long had he not eaten anything?

You could have had something to eat, you jerk. There was food right in front of you, but you had to act like an ass.

He slowly opened the door and peered into the next room. It was more or less a larger version of the one he was in now, except for the huge fireplace to his right. Everything looked old fashioned and rustic. Any minute now, Hoss and Little Joe Cartwright would walk through that front door. A lantern glowed on the large table in the middle of the room, casting large shadows on the wall, and another lamp sat on a smaller table by the front door. The last light of day was visible through the large glass-paned window to his left.

His angel was nowhere to be seen. A board of the wooden floor creaked when he stepped on it. The fire crackled warmly in the fireplace. The scene gave him an odd homey feeling. How had Todd found this place? Was this one of the tourist cabins? The ones he'd seen looked nothing like this. They weren't even cabins, really. This place felt like a . . . home.

The front door opened, and a huge shaggy dog padded in, followed closely by his angel. The dog walked up to him eagerly, and licked his hand. Chase backed up. Those teeth looked like they could do some serious damage.

He glanced up at the girl. She carried a wooden bucket

sloshing with water to the bench against the back wall. She heaved the bucket up onto the bench, her arms trembling from the effort. It had to be pretty heavy.

"Can I help?" he asked lamely after the bucket was already on the bench, and took a slow step in her direction.

She wheeled around to face him, the knife drawn from her belt so fast, he'd barely seen the movement. She held it out protectively in front of her. He stopped in his tracks, and held his hands out in front of him.

"Look. Sorry about back there." He gestured with his head toward the bedroom. "I thought you were part of the setup."

She said nothing, merely staring at him with her eyes ablaze. Her small hand didn't waver, the knife held in a firm grasp. She didn't appear nervous. In fact, she looked pretty confident with that weapon in her hand.

Chase sized her up. He could tackle her easily. Of course, she'd probably do some damage to him in the process. He wasn't about to risk getting sliced open on top of everything else that had happened to him in the last couple of days. Man, what did he do to deserve all this? Something cold and wet brushed against his leg, and Chase peered at the shaggy dog, which was intent on sniffing his pants. He must smell like that soup he'd dumped all over himself.

"Listen," he tried again. "Can I just use your phone, and I'll have someone pick me up." Why the hell did she look at him like he was from another planet? It was getting rather annoying. "You can cut the act, all right? I'll be out of your hair as soon as someone picks me up. Or would you like me to walk back to Canyon in the dark?" Somehow he figured that's exactly what she'd tell him. Was she daft? She'd sounded normal earlier. But she hadn't made a sound since coming in from outdoors.

Chase lifted his arm and cupped the back of his throbbing

head with his hand. Her eyes widened, and she pointed the knife at him.

Okay. Wrong move. He slowly lowered his arm again.

"What's your deal? I wish you'd say something." Girls usually chatted his ear off. And now he actually wanted one to talk.

She moved sideways, circling him. He realized she was giving herself an opening. Where she'd stood this entire time, he effectively had her cornered. Jeez! She moved like a lithe ballet dancer. Her feet barely touched the ground.

"You have companions nearby?" Finally, she spoke.

"Yeah, they'll come and get me. I thought Todd playing a joke on me, but it looks like I was wrong. You mentioned someone found me and brought me here. Is this place part of the park service?"

Her eyes narrowed. "You lie," she stated firmly. "The Absaroka warriors said you were alone. There was no one else."

Chase's brows furrowed, and he shook his head. "Absaroka war . . . what?"

"White trappers call them Crows," she stated as if he was the idiot who didn't know anything. He raised his eyebrows.

"Okay." He inhaled deeply, and rubbed at the back of his neck. "Could you cut the Indian maiden act? I don't know if you're part of some tourist attraction or what, but I need to get back to the barracks. Hell, I'm probably already in some serious shit." As an afterthought, he added, "Mind if I sit down?" he pointed to one of the chairs at the table. "I'm still not feeling a hundred percent." She nodded slowly, and moved to the opposite side of the table.

He pulled out a chair and eased himself into it. His head spun like a top on a slick surface. The smell of soup lingered in the room, and his stomach rumbled noisily in response.

"You can put that little butter knife away. I told you I

made the wrong assumption." *And the wrong impression.* He watched her as she appeared to be trying to come to a decision. Finally, she lowered the knife and stuck it back in the sheath at her hip. God, she was cute.

"Grizzly won't hesitate to attack if I tell him to," she said, her voice full of warning.

Grizzly? Oh, she must mean the mutt.

"I'll keep it in mind." He flashed her a smile, and for a second her eyes widened again. Yeah, he knew he had that effect on chicks. This one wasn't any different.

"So, can I use your phone?" he asked again. The silence was unnerving.

Her forehead crinkled, and she shook her head.

"Come on, you've got to have a telephone around here? How about a payphone? Madison has a campground. Are we anywhere near that?"

"The Tukudeka are camped a half day's ride from here."

"The what?" Okay, this was getting a bit ridiculous. He didn't mind a little game, but she was carrying her act a bit too far. "Look, Angel, my head is pounding, I haven't eaten in two or more days, apparently I almost froze to death, and, as you can see," he gestured at his nude torso, "I barely have any clothes on. Can we just skip the act? How much is Todd paying you for this? I'll double it."

She shot him a defiant look, her chin raised. Finally, maybe they were getting somewhere. "I know nothing of what you're asking me. Three warriors brought you here this morning. They could have left you for dead. I'm sure they will be back to extract payment for their kindness."

Chase pinched the top of his nose and squeezed his eyes shut. He wished for daylight so he could walk out of here. In the dark, he'd only get lost again before he reached the highway. He definitely didn't want a repeat of the day before.

"Okay, fine." He inhaled deeply. "Can I at least use the bathroom and clean up?"

The look on her face made him groan. "Let me guess. There's no bathroom."

"We usually bathe in the river," she answered. "There is no special room for that."

The honest, down to earth way she spoke to him couldn't be acted, could it? They stared at each other from across the table, and Chase felt his insides tighten. He was lost in her blue eyes. There was nothing pretentious about this girl. Her simple outfit, her braided hair, her radiant face devoid of any make-up – all of it added to her beauty. She was natural and wholesome, unlike any girl he'd ever met before. Something about her stirred a deep longing within him, something he couldn't quite define.

"You have never been in these mountains before, have you?" She was perceptive, too.

Chase shook his head. "I'm from L.A. I had no idea people still live like this, even in Montana." That still didn't explain her reference to warriors. Was she talking about actual Indians? Or some sort of road warriors, like a motorcycle gang.

"L . . . A?"

A wide smile spread across his face. Boy, was she backwoods.

"Yeah. Los Angeles. Big city. No mountains and rivers. I'm definitely out of my element here."

"How did you get lost along the *E-chee-dick-karsh-ah-shay*?"

"The what?"

"The Roche Jaune . . . Yellow Rock River."

Comprehension dawned. "You mean the Yellowstone River? Some buddies and I were camping in the canyon. The next morning, they were gone. I climbed out and apparently got lost looking for the road back to Canyon." No need to go into detail with her that he was drunk out of his mind the night before, or that his buddies had deliberately pulled a vanishing act on him.

"You climbed out from the canyon? How did you get down there?" Her eyes grew round in disbelief.

"Same way I came up, Angel. I know that wasn't the smartest thing to do. I'll probably get in a heap of trouble for it."

Chase's stomach growled loudly. The little angel must have heard it. She made a wide arc around him to the workbench along the wall, and reached for a bowl on a wooden shelf above her head, giving him an enticing view of her backside. *Knock it off, Russell. Get your mind out of the gutter.*

She ladled soup into the bowl from the kettle in the fireplace, and set it in front of him along with a spoon. He looked up and met her eyes.

"Do you have a name?" she asked softly.

"I'm sorry. My name's Chase."

A smile spread across her pretty face, and he suppressed a groan. Then she giggled. "That's an odd name. What do you chase?"

He couldn't help but smile in return. "Uh . . . I don't know. No one's ever asked me that before."

"I'm Sarah. I will forgive your behavior earlier. Now eat, before it gets cold . . . Chase."

He stared after her dumbfounded when she turned and headed up that ladder into the loft.

"Thank you," he said quietly to the empty space she had occupied moments before, and spooned broth into his mouth. It tasted as simple and earthy as everything around him, but he'd never eaten anything better in his life.

CHAPTER FIVE

Sarah rummaged through the heavy wooden trunk in the corner of the loft. Her brother Samuel wouldn't mind if she loaned some of his clothing to this stranger. They were probably close enough in size. Samuel had always been bigger than her twin brothers, Zach and Matt.

Chase. What an odd name. But she liked the way it sounded when he said it. For his size, he didn't seem so intimidating after all. True, he had been extremely rude earlier when he pulled her onto the bed, but she'd had no trouble fending him off, and he certainly hadn't put up any kind of fight. Perhaps he was still too weak. Something told her that she had nothing to fear from this man.

His strange words and the way he spoke was peculiar. Sarah only knew one other person who used words no one else seemed to know. Her mother. But this man had said he was from a big city. Her mother had grown up in a big city as well. Sarah had never been further east than St. Louis, and that suited her just fine. Her parents had suggested they travel to New York one year, to see her mother's place of birth. If New York was anything like St. Louis or Fort Raymond, she had no interest in going. She enjoyed her life in the mountains. She had enough friends among the Tukudeka women that she never felt lonely. She did miss her brothers, though. It seemed as if they stayed away longer each year.

Sarah heard a scraping noise below. Chase must have gotten up from the table.

"Uh . . . Sarah," he called.

"Just a moment." She grabbed a blue flannel shirt from the trunk and climbed back down the ladder. When she turned, he was standing next to the table, his face rather devoid of color.

"You should lie down," she said. Walking up to him, she reached her hand up and placed it against his forehead. "You're not hot, but you need time for your body to recover. You've been through quite an ordeal."

His green eyes stared down at her. Sarah willed her breathing to stay steady. What was it about him that brought on such warm feelings?

He rubbed the back of his head. The gesture only emphasized his strong arms, making the muscles bulge in a way that beckoned her to touch them. Sarah took a step back.

"Yeah, my head's spinning like crazy," he said. His voice sounded strangled and forced.

"Here." She thrust the shirt out to him. "One of my brothers' shirts. It should fit you well enough. You should sleep." She tilted her head to look at him. He really didn't look well. "Would you like some tea for the pain?"

"How do you know I have a headache?" His eyes narrowed.

"Your eyes are glazed, and you're holding the back of your head. I can make you some willow bark tea. It will take the pain away."

"Thanks for letting me crash here tonight," he said. "I'll get a ride to Canyon tomorrow."

She pointed a finger in the direction of her room. "Go lie down. I will bring you some tea. Tomorrow you will feel better." She didn't understand his strange phrases. Where was her mother when she needed her?

Chase shuffled off to the bedroom, and Sarah couldn't help but stare after him. She watched the muscles move on either side of his spine. He was a beautiful man. He was tall and lean, and looked strong. His face was nice to look at, although he did need to wash. He had a strong, firm jaw, and intelligent eyes. How did such a man get himself lost in the middle of a thunderstorm?

After he disappeared inside her room, Sarah rummaged through her mother's jars and pouches for some willow bark. Finding it in a leather pouch, she removed a handful and put it in a tin cup. She stoked the fire in the hearth and set more water to boil.

"What are we going to do with him, Grizzly?" Sarah took a seat in the rocking chair while she waited for the water to heat up. Her dog laid his huge head in her lap, and she stroked him between the ears. "He wants to return to the canyon, but I'm not sure he's fit enough for such a long walk." Grizzly's ears twitched, and his black eyes stared up at her. He whined in apparent sympathy. Chase's mention of companions left her with an uneasy feeling. One man she could handle on her own. More than one might be a problem.

Sarah quietly opened the door to her bedroom with the hot cup in her hand. A slow smile formed on her face. Chase was sprawled face-down in her bed, one long leg dangling over the sides. He hadn't bothered putting the shirt on. He didn't move, except for his quiet, rhythmic breathing. She set the cup on her little table next to the bed, and pulled the buffalo hide over him, then quietly left the room.

~

Sarah stretched and yawned, then opened her eyes. For a second, she wondered why she was lying in Samuel's bed. Then she remembered. Chase! How had he managed through the night? Bright ribbons of light from the early morning sun reached the loft from the window below. She hastily pulled her britches on, and strapped her belt around her waist. Her hair cascaded in disheveled waves down her back and over her face. She ran her hand through it to push it back. Then she climbed down the ladder.

The first thing that caught her eye was the open door to her bedroom. She remembered closing it the night before. Grizzly was standing by the front door, whining softly. His head turned in her direction, his almond eyes sending her a pleading look. Sarah peered into her room. The bed was empty. Chase must have gone outside. Had he left already? Her heart beat faster at the thought. Was that disappointment she felt?

She opened the cabin door and stepped out into the bright morning, scanning the meadow that spanned in front of the cabin, all the way to the Madison River about fifty yards away. Chase was standing at the river's edge, staring into the distance. He wore his odd half-britches, and the shirt she had given him the night before. He turned at that moment, then trotted toward her.

"Sarah, where are we?" He stopped so close in front of her, she thought he intended to knock her down. Her hand reached instinctively for her knife. He stared at her, his emerald eyes blazing with anger.

"The . . . Madison River Valley. I told you that yesterday," Sarah stammered. What was going on?

"This is the Madison River?" he asked, and pointed behind him.

"Yes." She shook her head, confused by his behavior.

"And that's National Park Mountain?" He pointed at the nearly vertical mountain that rose out of the earth across the river.

"I . . . I don't know. I've never heard it have a name."

Sarah had no time to react when he grabbed her by the shoulders.

"I was here a week ago, digging new steps in a trail on that hillside over there that should lead to the campground behind those trees." He gestured to the sloping hill behind her parents' home. "We re-enforced it with split logs. I busted my ass on that project. It took an entire day."

"I don't understand what you're saying," Sarah said, squirming for release from his strong grip.

"Where the hell's the campground?" he roared. "And the trail, and the ranger station over there?" His chin jutted in an easterly direction, across the meadow.

"Release your hold on me," Sarah said firmly. Chase's face sobered. He dropped his arms.

"I want to know what the hell's going on here." His eyes scanned into the distance. "There should be a road, right over there." He pointed beyond the river to the east, "And a bridge over the Gibbon River."

Gibbon River? How did he know that name? Her father called it the Little Buffalo River. She'd only heard her mother refer to it as the Gibbon River from time to time.

"There's no road, and no bridge," Sarah said. "I've lived here all my life. No one is camped in the hills behind the cabin."

Had he injured his head as well? He was talking like a

37

crazy person. She took a step back to put some distance between them. Chase held his hands to his temples.

"Jesus! What the hell happened to me down in that canyon?" He stared again into the distance, looking for something that wasn't there.

"Did you perhaps fall and hit your head?" Sarah offered tentatively. "I can take a closer look to see if there is an injury." She reached her hand up to touch his head. He brushed it away impatiently.

"I didn't hit my goddamn head!" he roared. Grizzly ran up to him and barked. Chase's loud and angry tone had startled the dog. "Call off the damn mutt," he growled.

"Come here, Grizzly. It's okay." Sarah slapped the side of her leg, and the dog quit barking instantly, and lowered his head. She looked at the irate man now pacing the yard in front of the cabin. He looked nearly crazed.

"If you can calm yourself, perhaps we can figure out what it is you are searching for," Sarah offered in a quiet voice.

Chase stopped his pacing and turned toward her. His eyes rested on her. He inhaled deeply. "Okay. All right," he said, his voice sounding calmer.

Sarah waited another moment. He appeared to be quieting down. "Come inside and sit. I will make coffee, and we can talk."

Chase nodded. He followed her back into the cabin, and sat at the table, his head cradled in his hands. The shocked look on his face puzzled her. She rekindled the fire. When the flames burned large enough, she poured fresh water into the kettle to heat. Then she turned and sat across from him at the table.

"Something happened in that canyon, Sarah," he said. "Everything's different. That's why I couldn't find the road."

"Everything has been the same here. There are no roads." She tried to reason with him.

He stared up at her. "Who's the president of the United States?" he asked suddenly.

What an odd question. She had to think for a moment, trying to remember any news she'd heard about the Americans. Here in the territories, news was slow to reach them. "I believe his name is Andrew Jackson. Why do you ask?"

Chase unleashed a string of curse words, causing the blood to rush to Sarah's face, and her cheeks burned.

"Would you please explain to me what is going on?" she asked, exasperated. He had seemed rational yesterday. Right now, his behavior was that of a demented person.

"What's the date?" he demanded.

"Date?" The distraught look on his face startled her. "It's May, but I . . . I'm not sure of the day. My mother keeps records of these things."

He waved off her answer, shaking his head. "No, what year is it?"

"1835. What does it matter what--"

"How the hell did this happen?" Chase jumped out of his chair and raked his hands through his hair, holding on to his head. "How is it even possible?" He paced the length of the cabin.

Sarah sat and watched. It was better to back away from an enraged grizzly than provoke it further, her Uncle Elk Runner always said. She kept a steady hand near the hilt of her knife, just in case.

"Okay, okay, think, Russell, think." He was talking to himself in low tones, but his pacing didn't let up. Sarah rose slowly from her seat and moved to the hearth. The water in the kettle bubbled. She spooned coffee grounds into a pot and ladled the hot water into it. Then she poured two cups. Chase came up beside her and took the cups from her. She stiffened when his arm grazed hers. He stood so close, she felt the heat coming off his body.

"Here, I got this. You don't need to wait on me." His tone had definitely calmed.

"Do you wish to tell me what has you so upset?" Sarah followed him back to the table.

He laughed, then he shook his head. "I don't even know how to explain this, but," he paused and regarded her for a moment, "two days ago I climbed into the Yellowstone Canyon with five of my trail crew compadres, and it was twenty-thirty five. The next morning, they were all gone. I climbed back up the canyon, thinking it would be an easy walk back to the barracks, but I couldn't find the road. Then that storm hit."

"What do you mean 'it was twenty-thirty five'?" Sarah wasn't sure what that number meant.

"The year two thousand thirty five. Two hundred years from the date you just told me." He glared at her.

"You came here from the future? Is that even possible?" Sarah asked incredulously. Her eyes widened in disbelief.

"Well, I'm here, so I guess it is possible." Chase laughed and shook his head again. "It definitely explains this whole setup here." His eyes roamed the cabin.

Her mind raced. What should she believe? Was Chase crazy in the head? Had he fallen and just didn't know it? Her mind tried to process what he told her. He was from two hundred years in the future. Maybe his mind wanted to believe this was true, but Sarah shook her head in disbelief.

CHAPTER SIX

"Sarah, I need to get back to the canyon. The answers are there, I know it." Chase gulped his coffee, enjoying the bitter taste. It matched the bitter feelings that enveloped him. "I need to get back to where I came from."

"It's a two day walk," Sarah said softly. "Are you sure you are up for such a journey."

Shit. Where was a car when you needed one? It would take forty minutes, at most. "Two days? Are you sure it's that far?"

"On horseback it can be done in less than a day. I have no horse available, and in your condition, I don't think you could walk it in less than two days."

"But you could?" He raised his eyebrows.

"Yes, it makes for a long day, but I can walk it in less than two," she answered confidently.

The corners of his mouth rose. "You think you're pretty tough, huh Angel?"

She didn't go for his bait. Instead of a reply, she glared at him from across the table. Why couldn't he meet a girl like her at home? Her hair fell in waves down her chest and back.

The sun streaming in from the window added coppery highlights to the mahogany colors.

"I will take you to the canyon," she said slowly. "But not until tomorrow." She looked like a mother hen, staring at him.

"Why can't we leave right now?" Chase frowned. The sooner they left, the quicker her could get home.

"You need a day of rest, and good food to build your strength. And," the smile she flashed him sent his mind whirling, "you need a bath."

He laughed. She did have a point. "Yeah, I guess I do smell kinda ripe." Inhaling a long breath, he added, "Okay, we'll leave tomorrow. I guess I can spend a couple of days in the past."

The skeptical look on her face told him she didn't believe any of it. Hell, he couldn't blame her for that. He wouldn't believe it, either. But what other explanation was there? He'd already convinced himself that the answer had to be somewhere in that canyon. What if he was stuck here for good? Hell, no. He wasn't even going to think about that.

Sarah left the table and climbed the ladder up to the loft again. He heard a squeaking noise, like a hinge, and some rustling of materials. Minutes later she climbed back down, and held a pile of clothes out to him.

"These britches might be too small. I think my brother isn't as tall as you. But there is another shirt. Take these with you to the river."

He regarded her for a moment. He reached for the clothes, his hand brushing hers in the process. She jerked away, and her eyes went round. He grinned. This girl was pure as fresh snow.

"Where's your brother?" he asked.

Sarah headed for the front door, her furry mutt at her heels. The huge dog's head was higher than her waist.

"My three brothers are in St. Louis. They don't usually return before autumn."

"You live here by yourself?" Wasn't that kinda dangerous? What about those Indians she'd mentioned?

"No, my parents are at rendezvous. They will return soon." She turned and nodded with her head in the direction of the river. Then she pointed to the mountain he'd been told was called National Park Mountain. "See the river coming out of that mountain?"

Chase nodded.

"You can swim across the Madison further downstream to reach it. The water is warmer in that river."

"Yeah, I've been in the Firehole. My buddies and I did some cliff jumping a few miles south of here." *Something else we would have gotten in a heap of trouble for.*

Sarah gave him a befuddled look. She shook her head slightly, as if she was about to say something. Apparently she thought better of it. He started walking across the meadow, his feet tickled by the grass that had been moistened from the early morning dew.

"Aren't you coming with me?" he called over his shoulder when Sarah stayed behind.

She shook her head. "I will prepare some food for when you return."

Suit yourself, Angel.

Chase pulled the shirt he wore over his head, and dropped it and the clothes he carried before reaching the riverbank. With a loud whoop and running start, he jumped into the water. He had expected it to be cold. A week ago, he and the other guys on the trail maintenance crew had soaked their feet in this river after a hard day of digging. Now, as his head resurfaced, he drew in a sharp breath. The water was frigid beyond belief. Better get to where the warmer waters from the Firehole flowed further downstream.

Sarah shouted his name, and he turned his head, treading water. Her beautiful long hair flowed behind her as she loped across the meadow toward him, her arms full with some kind of bundle. Despite the cold water, his body heated at the sight of her.

"You should have a blanket to dry off with when you're done," she called to him at the river's edge. She laid the bundle next to his pile of clothing in the grass.

"Thanks." He flashed her a grin. She turned to leave. "Hey, Sarah!" He waited for her to face his way again. "Catch." Yep, she had quick reflexes. He laughed at the mortified expression on her face. Her eyes grew round as saucers, and her mouth fell open when she realized she held his soaking wet shorts and boxers in her hands. He laughed even harder when she dropped them as if they had burned her. The glare she shot him was murderous, then she whipped around and ran back toward the cabin.

Chase headed for the Firehole. He couldn't get it out of his mind how pretty she was. Her innocent behavior turned him on more than any of the girls who'd flaunted themselves at him ever had.

Chase smelled food on his way up the meadow toward the large cabin. He wondered about the smaller cabin nestled between some lodgepoles a short distance to the right. It looked like a one-room log structure with a small window cut into the logs. It looked a lot older than the big cabin. He would have checked it out, but his nose guided him in the other direction. His stomach growled.

Never in his wildest dreams had he ever thought he'd be wearing buckskin pants and a cotton shirt that looked and felt like it was sewn entirely by hand. The pants fit snug around the waist and were several inches too short. It had taken him a few minutes to figure out how and where to tie the leather strings at his hips. If his cargos hadn't been wet, he would have just put those back on.

He knocked softly on the door, and waited. The dog barked from inside.

"Come in." Sarah's melodious voice sent his heart into overdrive. What was that all about? He entered the cabin, and a new wave of food smells assaulted him.

"That smells really good," he said, glancing around to find Sarah sitting in the rocking chair in the corner. She had, what looked like, an entire animal hide draped over her lap. The dog pranced around him, wagging his tail and panting. His mouth was partially open, tongue hanging out part ways, making him appear as if he was smiling.

"He wants you to pet him," Sarah said.

"Huh?"

"Reach down and pet him between the ears. He likes that. Don't they have dogs in the future?"

Chase didn't miss the mocking tone in her voice. She rose from the chair, and set the hide on it. Chase closed the door behind him and walked further into the cabin. He slowly reached his hand out, allowing the dog to sniff. The furry mutt stood still while Chase patted it on the head.

"See? He really likes you." Sarah smiled.

"How can you tell?"

"For one, he's not growling at you. Dogs can always tell a good person from a bad one."

"So, I'm a good person?" Chase raised his eyebrows. He wasn't so sure he qualified for that distinction.

"Grizzly thinks so, and that's good enough for me." She wasn't mocking this time.

"Well, I'm glad I've got the dog in my corner," he

answered. "Something smells really good." He walked over to the pot hanging over the fire.

"I think it's ready," she said. Coming up beside him, she stirred the contents of the pot with a long wooden spoon.

"If you'll get some bowls from the shelf over there," she gestured to a spot above the workbench, "we can eat."

Chase reached for two bowls, and held them out to her while she ladled food into them. He carried both to the table, and sat. She brought spoons.

"What is this?" Chase guessed it was some sort of stew. The meat and vegetables tasted unlike anything he'd eaten before, but it was quite tasty.

"It has meat from the bighorn sheep, and several roots in it. I wanted to find bitterroot yesterday, but had to stay here."

He looked at her from across the table. "Because of me."

She shrugged. "I'll find some on the way to the canyon tomorrow."

They ate in silence. When Sarah finished her meal, she bent down to let the dog lick the bowl clean.

"Please tell me that's not how you wash these bowls," Chase said, and glanced at his food. Sarah laughed, and he couldn't help but stare at her. She was beautiful. Her face lit up, and her blue eyes shone like the summer sky. His stomach tightened. Her smile faltered when their eyes met. Abruptly, she got up from the table. She turned her back to him, and picked up the huge piece of hide on the rocking chair.

"My brother's britches don't fit you. I was afraid of that." She didn't turn to look at him.

"It's okay. When my shorts are dry, I'll wear those again." Chase pushed his chair away from the table. The dog gave him an expectant look.

"You've got to be kidding me." He and the dog stared at

each other. With an exasperated shake of his head, Chase placed his empty bowl at the dog's feet.

"I will make you a pair of britches that will fit you." Sarah came up to him. "I just need to . . . measure you." She avoided looking at him.

"You don't have to do that. I said I'll wear my shorts."

"Long britches will keep your legs from getting injured. We will be traveling through forests and over mountains. You will be glad for leg protection."

Chase took a tentative step closer. "Angel," he said, his voice deep and raspy, "you've done enough for me already." He lifted her chin so she'd look at him. The sensation of drowning swept over him as he stared into her blue eyes. He inhaled deeply, then he stepped back and left the cabin.

CHAPTER SEVEN

*S*arah woke to Grizzly's wet tongue on her face. She turned her stiff neck, opened her eyes slowly, and groaned. She must have fallen asleep in the rocking chair. Gray light from the impending dawn filtered through the window. It was time to get moving if they were to reach the canyon before nightfall. She glanced down at her lap. A new pair of large moccasins still rested on her thighs. She hoped they would fit him.

Chase had wandered the riverbank for most of the day yesterday, which had been fine with her. She kept busy sewing him a pair of britches and moccasins, keeping her work hidden when he came back. She'd taken measurements from his short pants, and guessed at the remainder of the length. It had been the perfect solution. It avoided having to touch him almost intimately, trying to measure his waist and legs. His close proximity that morning, and the looks he'd sent her way left her with a disturbing feeling she'd never had before. Her heart seemed to do flip flops, and she couldn't draw a full breath in his presence.

After their supper of fresh bread and rabbit, he had gone

to bed. She'd sat up late into the night, and finished her sewing. She still had reservations about him walking so far in such a short amount of time, but he'd been adamant about going. She knew the shortest way, but it was also the most strenuous. Chase looked to be physically capable of such a trip, but Sarah had doubts that his body was fully recovered from his ordeal with exposure.

She'd been to the canyon many times with her family. On a few occasions, her father had allowed her to accompany him and her brothers when they hunted bighorn near the canyon with their Tukudeka relatives.

Sarah stoked the fire, bringing the smoldering coals back to life. She set water to boil for coffee, then quietly entered her bedroom to retrieve her traveling pouch and bighorn bow from the wall. Stealing a glance at the bed, she gasped and quickly averted her eyes. He slept in the nude! She didn't see anything she shouldn't have, but he must have kicked the covers off himself during the night. Only a small part of his backside was left unexposed.

Sarah's face burned. Her stomach seemed to have traded places with her heart. She was grateful that he slept on his stomach. With trembling hands, she reached for her bow and quiver, the solid feel of the sheep horn giving her an odd comfort. Thankfully, she faced away from the bed to retrieve her items. Her pouch hung off a hook by the door. She snatched it up and left the room.

Sarah sat at the table, cradling her head between trembling hands. If her parents ever found out that she'd let a strange man stay in the house while they were gone . . . She shook her head. She didn't even want to think about what her father would do. What would he do? She sat up straighter, wondering. This topic of discussion had never come up. There had never been a reason for it. Her parents trusted her, and she was proud that they thought her capable enough to live on her own while they were away.

And then *he* had to show up! She glanced toward the door to her bedroom, frowning. Hopefully, once she delivered him to the canyon, and he found his companions, all would be well again. Her parents need not find out about this.

Relieved by that thought, Sarah set to work packing some bread and dried meat in her pouch. She retrieved the spare flintlock rifle and powder horn from her parents' room. The sun began to climb over the tops of the eastern mountains, the direction they would be heading. She braided her hair, securing the ends with a strip of leather. She pulled another weapon belt from her brother's trunk along with an old hunting knife and tomahawk for Chase, since he had no weapons of his own. She didn't need to check if they were sharp. Her father had taught every member of the family to never let a weapon become dull. Two blankets rolled up and tied with leather straps and a couple of water bags completed her packing.

She poured two cups of coffee, and sliced some bread and meat so Chase could eat before they headed out. She set the coffee pot on the counter with a loud bang, and dropped a tin plate on the floor. Grizzly's head shot up from his sleeping place by the hearth at the clatter, and when the plate rolled toward him. Sarah hoped her deliberate attempt at making noise would awaken Chase. *How can any man sleep this soundly?*

"Grizzly, go wake him up." Sarah pointed at the door to her room. The dog leapt from his place, and wagged his tail happily. He gave Sarah a quizzical look, and she pointed toward her room again. "Go on," she encouraged. With a single bark, Grizzly trotted into her bedroom. Her mattress creaked, and Sarah surmised Grizzly had jumped on her bed.

Her faithful friend barked again, and then a man cursed loudly. Sarah smiled, waiting by the hearth.

"Get off me, you hairy monster."

Grizzly barked an enthusiastic reply, followed by Chase's sleepy growls.

Sarah glanced toward her bedroom, then thought better of it and quickly wheeled around. He wouldn't walk out to the main room without getting dressed first, would he? Footsteps shuffled on the wooden floor, but she didn't dare turn around.

"Why'd you have to send that mangy mutt in there to wake me?" His voice was close behind her, still raspy from sleep. She glanced tentatively over her shoulder. He wore his short britches. With a sigh of relief, she turned fully toward him. Sarah's gaze lingered on the tattoo on his chest. She wondered at its significance, but didn't want to appear forward by asking him about it.

"It's getting late, and we should leave." She pulled her eyes away from the scorpion and stared up at him.

Chase ran a hand over his sleepy face. "The sun's not even up yet," he protested, and yawned.

Sarah held out a cup of coffee to him. "It's a long walk, remember? Unless you've changed your mind, and want to stay here." She raised her eyebrows.

"No. You're right." He took a seat at the table and held the tin cup to his mouth.

Sarah's heart sped up. Nervousness flooded her, thinking about giving him the clothing she'd made. It seemed like such an intimate thing for a woman to do for a man who wasn't her husband or a relative.

"Are you planning to go on the warpath?" he called. He stared at her bow and rifle on the table.

She walked over and picked up the belt, the knife and tomahawk dangling from it. "I thought you should have

51

these." She held the belt out to him. "For the journey, since you have no weapons on you. If you'd like, you can carry the rifle."

Chase raised his eyebrows. "And what exactly am I supposed to do with these?"

Sarah stared in disbelief. She didn't know a single white man who came to these mountains who didn't know how to use a knife or rifle. She laughed. "You mean to tell me you don't know what a knife is for? Can you shoot a rifle?"

"I told you, I'm not from here, Angel," he whispered in a low tone.

Sarah nodded. She didn't know what to think. She turned away from him and picked up the britches and moccasins off the floor by the rocking chair. Hopefully he would accept her peace offering for laughing at him.

"Here. I made these. They should fit better than my brother's britches." She thrust the items at him. Her heart pounded so hard, she was sure he could hear it.

Chase rose from his seat, and took what she offered. He glanced at what he held in his hands, then at her. She quickly lowered her head. He closed the distance between them, and lifted her chin with his thumb and forefinger.

"When did you do this?" His green eyes stared right into her.

"Yesterday." She blinked. He held to her chin, keeping her gaze on him.

"You were up all night, weren't you?" he asked softly. She shrugged. "No one's ever made something for me before."

"Well, are you going to put them on? We do need to be on our way," Sarah said haughtily when he simply looked at the bundle in his hands.

"Yeah, sure," he said absently. He still held her chin. Before she realized his intent, he bent his head and kissed her squarely on the mouth. An intense ripple of adrenaline shot through her. She jumped back, and stared at him, her eyes wide.

"I'll go put these on, and we can get going," he said casually, as if kissing a woman he'd only met was something he did frequently.

Chase turned, and disappeared into her room. She willed her racing heart to slow. No man had ever kissed her on the mouth before. Plenty had tried, but her father or one of her brothers had always been there to protect her from such unwanted advances.

Sarah touched her fingers to her tingling lips. The contact had been quick and gentle, and not at all unpleasant. She finally understood a little better why her parents enjoyed kissing each other so much. The visions of her parents, and the way they caressed and touched when they thought no one was looking, sent heat into her face.

Stop this thinking, Sarah. This man will be gone tomorrow. Don't allow him any liberties. It was bad enough how intimately they'd been living together for the past two days.

Sarah banked the coals in the hearth. She hurried outside and broke three tender, thin branches from one of the lodgepole pines behind the cabin. Back inside, she laid these in a row on the table, facing east. If Elk Runner or one of her cousins stopped by while she was gone, they'd know which direction she had gone, and that she'd be back within three days. They would know what day she'd left by the moisture in the sticks.

CHASE PULLED the new buckskins on over his boxers. Any notion he might have had of animal hide as tough and stiff went out the window. These pants were as soft and pliable as any fabric he'd worn. The length was perfect, and so was the waist. Sarah even adorned them with fringe on the outside of both legs. The moccasins might take some getting used to, but the blisters on his heels didn't rub painfully against the material the way they did in the boots. He pulled the blue cotton shirt on over his head, and for a moment he felt like he was dressing for a costume party.

It was true what he'd said to Sarah about no one ever making anything for him. His mother had always been too busy with her job to do some of the special things moms did for their kids. He'd always been jealous of his friends when he was little. Their parents went out of their way to throw elaborate birthday parties with extravagant homemade birthday cakes, and made their kids' Halloween costumes rather than buying a last-minute clearance costume at the store. Birthdays for him were usually a stop at the closest fast food joint, and a store-bought generic cake.

He didn't blame his mother. It wasn't her fault that his old man had walked out on them when he was five. She had to work two jobs most of the time to make ends meet. The best thing she'd ever done for him was sign him up for football when he was eight. That had been expensive, and he knew she had put in long hours to pay for the uniforms and equipment. Football had earned him a full scholarship to college, and he'd blown that. *Russell, you're such a screw-up.*

Chase pulled his thoughts back to the present. Sarah. That kiss was purely on impulse, but the second his lips touched hers, he'd been on fire. It scared the hell out of him. Her reaction confirmed what an innocent she was. Had she not jumped back, there was no telling how far he might have taken it. Girls were a casual distraction, not something to take seriously, just like the rest of his life. What was it about Sarah that made him want to act all gallant and noble? Jeez! He really did step back in time. It was high time he got himself out of here and back to where he belonged.

Dressed the part of the mountain man, he left the bedroom. Sarah stood by the door, decked out looking like an Indian ready to go on the warpath. She had a bunch of pouches and a blanket roll slung over her shoulders, and on her back was a holder for arrows – whatever the heck that was called. In her hands, she held a bow and the rifle. Her knife was strapped to the belt around her waist.

She met his gaze, her face unreadable.

"Take the blanket and water bag, and put on the belt with the knife and tomahawk," she said, gesturing with her chin to the items on the table.

"That's all you want me to carry? Can I take some of the things from you?" She looked weighted down with stuff.

"No, I can manage." She turned and opened the door.

Chase raised his eyebrows, and grabbed the items off the table. She walked briskly across the meadow, and he jogged to catch up to her. The furry mutt jumped eagerly between their feet, his tail held high, swaying like plumage in the air.

"We will cross the Little Buffalo River. From there I will set a fast pace. I hope you can keep up," she said when he walked beside her. Her voice held an edge to it that hadn't been there before. Chase suspected it had to do with that kiss, but he wasn't going to ask. He grinned at her bold statement.

"Maybe you should worry more about keeping up with me, Angel."

She shot him a dark look, and his grin widened. Abruptly, she took off at a fast jog. No problem. This was far easier than spring training.

She barely slowed down as she splashed through the knee-high water of the Gibbon River, picking up the pace once across. The meadow quickly turned to forest. She didn't slow her pace, even as she navigated around countless downed logs. He wondered why she didn't keep to a straight line, but seemed to zigzag through the trees.

"Wouldn't it be easier just to climb over these logs?" he finally asked. He stopped and swiped his arm across his damp forehead.

"No."

Well, fine! What the hell was she trying to prove? He inhaled deeply, and sprinted after her. Chasing a girl through a forest in the middle of nowhere was an entirely new experience. Grinning, he caught up with her, but was soon forced to fall back as the forest closed in around them.

"Aren't we going in the wrong direction?" he called, watching her dark braid sway seductively back and forth as she ran. He tried to keep his eyes above her belt line.

"You want the fastest route to the canyon. This is it," she shouted over her shoulder.

Chase shook his head. His lungs started to burn. He definitely wasn't used to the thin high altitude air. Hell would freeze over before he conceded to her, though. Thankfully, the dense forest forced her to slow down to a jog rather than the blistering pace she'd been setting. He completely lost all sense of direction. He sure hoped she knew where she was going.

Chase guessed they had been running through the forest for at least an hour when the trees cleared and gave way to what looked like a thermal area. Sarah slowed to a walk.

"Step only where I do," she warned. He stayed close behind her. How did she know where to safely walk? The ground took on a moon-like appearance, the dirt gray or almost white as snow, and steam rose from vents in the ground all around them. The air was thick with the smell of sulfur, and the ground bubbled and hissed all around. It took the better part of half an hour to cross the basin, and then the landscape opened up to a lush meadow. Bison roamed everywhere. To the right, a wide creek flowed.

"What now?" Chase asked, his eyes scanning the distance. He leaned forward and rested his hands on his thighs. She shot him a puzzled look, so he pointed at the bison.

"We go around."

He rolled his eyes. Of course, why didn't he think of that? She resumed her fast jog, skirting the outer reaches of the bison herd. The lactic acid build-up in his legs burned with every step he took. The landscape began a gradual uphill climb, back into forest. There seemed to be no end to Sarah's endurance. Jeez! This girl was tough. She wasn't even breathing hard. He gritted his teeth as sweat ran down his face.

Finally reaching the top of the plateau, she slowed to a walk. She had no choice. The forest was endless and dense. The trees suddenly gave way to a small lake, and Chase's eyes widened in surprise.

"Fill your water bag here," Sarah said. She knelt at the lakeshore to fill her own water bag. The mutt lapped up water, churning up the mud as he traipsed along the shore. Chase came up beside Sarah and splashed water on his face. He sighed loudly at the refreshing coolness on his hot face. He watched Sarah out of the corner of his eyes, looking as fresh as she had when they left the cabin. She had just corked her bag, when he flicked some water at her. He grinned when she shot him an angry look, and stormed off into the trees.

"Come on, Angel, lighten up. Where's your sense of humor?" he called after her.

"Don't follow me. I'll be right back," she replied. He got the message. He walked along the lakeshore a ways and veered off into the trees, too. When he returned, she was waiting, sitting on a large boulder. Chase headed toward her, his eyes to the ground. He stopped suddenly. Large animal tracks imprinted in the earth around him caught his eye. Chase stepped into one. The print was longer than his foot. These had to be bear tracks.

"Hey, Sarah, look at this. Are these grizzly bear tracks?" He was suddenly glad for her mini arsenal of weaponry.

Sarah hopped off her perch, and strode over to him, looking where he pointed. "Black bear," she answered confidently after a quick glance.

"How do you know?"

"The claw marks are too small to be grizzly." She knelt down and touched one of the prints. "The toes have gaps between them, see? Grizzly toes are closer together, and their long claws leave an impression."

She rose to her feet, and their eyes met briefly. The familiar tightening in his gut whenever he looked at her tugged at him again. She turned away. Chase clenched his jaw, fighting the urge to pull her to him and kiss her again. A real kiss, not a quick smack on the lips.

"Are you ready to continue, or do you need to rest some more?"

He could stretch out here on this lakeshore and sleep for the rest of the day, but he wasn't about to admit that to her. "Whenever you're ready, Angel."

She shot him a skeptical look, then walked ahead, keeping to the water's edge. "The terrain here will be easier for a while," she called over her back. "We are on top of a plateau. Then we will climb one more mountain before it descends into the valley of the Roche Jaune."

Chase jogged to catch up with her. She cast him a sideways glance. "From there, it will not be far to the canyon."

By the time they reached the valley, the sun sat low in the western horizon. Rolling green hills spanned before them as far as the eye could see, and more forest darkened the mountains in the distance. Chase recognized what would be called

Hayden Valley in his time. This had been one of his favorite spots in the park. The Yellowstone River lazily meandered through the valley on its northward course. The peaceful river here belied the strong forces of nature a few miles to the north, where the calm waters would suddenly plunge several hundred feet into a deep scar in the earth, not once, but two times. Conspicuously absent from here, though, was the two-lane highway that ran through this valley. More bison dotted the landscape. Chase scanned the vastness of the land, desperately searching and listening for anything modern. All he heard were insects and an occasional bird.

"We're almost there, aren't we?" he finally asked. Sarah nodded. "A few more miles to the north is the canyon. We will make camp there, and you can search for your companions in the morning."

Chase stared into the distance. He hoped climbing back into the canyon would get him home. Whatever had brought him here had to be his ticket out as well, and it had to be in that canyon. But how would he recognize what he was looking for?

CHAPTER EIGHT

*S*arah gathered an armful of kindling and tree branches for a fire. Darkness would be upon them soon, and she wanted to have camp set up before all the light disappeared. They had made good time all day, though. There had been moments when she'd doubted if Chase could keep up with the pace she set. He had stubbornly refused to tell her to slow down, so she'd pushed on even faster. He was a physically strong man, but his body had suffered a severe shock a mere two days before, and she wouldn't have expected anyone to cover more than twenty miles in one day over such rough terrain. She was silently impressed with his endurance.

She'd chosen a spot nestled amongst a grove of young lodgepoles to make camp. A small creek trickled nearby. When they'd reached the canyon and the first fall, Chase had wanted to push further ahead to the second plunge the Roche Jaune took into the ever-deeper canyon. The second fall was even taller than the first, and had always been Sarah's favorite. What did he hope to find in the morning? She'd seen no evidence of any people in the area. He was still convinced he came from the future, and that somehow descending into the canyon would send him back to his time.

She'd never actually been down in the canyon. No one she knew saw a need for it. There was nothing there but the river. And it was a dangerous descent. The rocks in this area were brittle like sandstone.

Sarah returned with her bundle of firewood to find Chase asleep on the ground. A slow smile spread across her face. She knew he had to be tired, but he also needed to eat. She silently snapped her finger in his direction, and Grizzly, ever eager to be helpful, licked at the man's face. Chase growled like a bear, trying to wrestle the dog away. Sarah laughed. When he looked her way and their eyes met, her smile froze. Was that anger, or something else, written on his face?

She dropped her gaze and sank to her knees, busily shaving kindling with her knife.

"You're worse than my football coach, you know that?" Chase grumbled a few feet away.

Sarah shook her head. She had no idea what he was talking about, and she wasn't sure she even wanted to know.

"Are you hungry?" she asked instead.

"Yeah. Starving. I haven't had anything but bread and jerky all day."

"Then you will not complain that Grizzly woke you. You can't eat if you're asleep. If you will start the fire, I will return with meat." She glanced up at him. "Or would you rather do the hunting?"

Chase's eyebrows furrowed. "I think we're both going to starve if you're asking me to do either of those things. Unless you brought some lighter fluid and matches, I have no idea how to start a fire, and if there's not a grocery store nearby, I don't know where the food is."

Sarah stared in stunned silence. This man was telling her he was incapable of a simple task like starting a fire?

"Quit looking at me like that," he snapped. "I told you I'm not from here. When are you going to believe me?"

"Here, let me show you. A fire is simple." She didn't know what else to say. If she had any sense at all, she'd simply start the fire herself, but something compelled her to teach this man this basic survival skill. She couldn't remember a time in her life when she didn't know how to start a fire.

"Why bother? I'll be back home tomorrow, and where I'm from, I don't need to know how to do this." He sounded angry. Sarah had heard this type of anger before. Her brothers were often mad when she bested them at a task her father set out for them. Her mother would tell her that a man's pride was wounded easily, and that a man's competitive nature made it difficult for them to admit wrong doing or failing at something.

"Let me show you," she coaxed gently. "What happens if you do not find your way home in the morning? A man will die here if he doesn't know how to survive." He hesitated. The frown on his handsome face deepened, but he knelt beside her.

"Fine," he grumbled. "How do you make a fire with nothing?"

Sarah almost regretted her offer. She felt his body heat, and could smell his musky male scent. Her hands trembled when she dug for her flint in the pouch around her neck.

"Take out your knife," she said, and held the flint out for him. She gathered a handful of wood shavings in a small pile on the ground.

"Now strike your knife against the flint to create a spark, just over the kindling."

On his fourth try, a tiny spark fell on the shavings, and Sarah bent her head, gently blowing air onto the pile to give the spark more life. It shone bright orange for a second, then fizzled and extinguished in a thin wisp of smoke.

"Do it again, and this time be ready to blow on it," she commanded. Chase followed her instructions. It took him several tries, but he finally succeeded in igniting the kindling, and kept it burning.

Sarah smiled brightly. "Now add small pieces of wood, slowly, until they burn. Too much wood, and you choke the flames and they will die again. Never starve a fire of air. This also prevents too much smoke."

"There," Chase said, after a sizeable campfire crackled before them. "You'll make a boy scout out of me yet." He grinned in satisfaction.

"You did well," she said, and hastily scrambled to her feet when his gaze met hers. The smoldering look in his eyes burned hotter than the flames.

Chase stared up at the brilliant night sky. He'd never before seen so many stars. He clasped his hands behind his head, and stretched his long body out next to the fire. The mangy mutt was curled up beside him, its head resting on his thigh. He could hear Sarah's soft, rhythmic breathing from the other side of the low-burning fire. She looked small and vulnerable, curled up under her blanket. Something tightened in his chest. She had to be exhausted. While he'd slept soundly the night before, she'd been up making him clothing. Today she'd practically done all the work.

After his fire-making lesson, she had gone off, and not twenty minutes later returned with some furry thing she called a whistle dog. He couldn't bring himself to watch when she skinned and gutted it. But he ate more than his share. It had tasted like chicken. She had tossed some fig-sized roots in the coals, and told him that would be breakfast the next morning.

He'd never met a girl like her. She hadn't been judgmental at his incompetence. He couldn't make a fire. He didn't know how to hunt and find food in the wilderness, but it was second nature to her. She hadn't belittled him, just matter-of-factly shown him how to do it. She was strong and as tough as nails when it came to survival, yet underneath all that was pure innocence and a vulnerable female.

What would happen come morning? What would he find in that canyon? The nagging thought that he might not find his way through whatever time portal he had come from sent an icy chill down his spine. He couldn't stay here. The last few days proved that he was way out of his element. He stared at Sarah's sleeping form. The company was enticing enough, but she was strictly hands-off. He didn't get involved with innocent girls like her. They expected things. He believed in the love 'em and leave 'em kind of relationships.

Chase rolled to his side. The mutt groaned at the disturbance, but soon settled in against him, and draped its head back over his thigh.

CHAPTER NINE

ood crackled and popped loudly, the sounds intermingling with the noisy chirping of birds. Chase stirred, the unfamiliar sounds echoing in his head. He squeezed his eyes shut tighter from the bright sunlight that filtered through the trees. Was it morning already? Hadn't he just closed his eyes?

He yawned, then stretched the rigid muscles in his arms and legs, and rolled onto his back. His eyes opened, and he shrank back for a split second. Looming over him, Sarah's mutt dangled its tongue in his face, its hot, moist breath nearly making him gag. He'd never get used to that dog hovering inches from him every time he woke up.

"Goddamn mutt," he growled, and pushed the animal's blocky head away. He raised up on his elbows and peered around the campsite. Sarah's sleeping blanket was empty, and she was nowhere to be seen. His eyes scanned the trees, and he pushed himself fully off the ground with a groan. He stretched his arms in the air, and rotated his shoulders, working the tightness out of his muscles. Yesterday had been one hell of a long day, and sleeping on hard ground didn't help.

"Where's your owner," he said to the dog, which pranced around him, tail wagging enthusiastically. He had no idea what the mutt wanted. He didn't speak canine. Heck, he didn't even like dogs. Why had this one latched on to him? Sarah couldn't have gone far, though. She wouldn't leave her pet behind.

He ran a hand over his face. The rough whiskers of a beard scraped like sandpaper across his palms. He probably looked like a mountain man at this point. He hadn't shaved in six days. Hopefully before this day was over, he'd be soaking under a hot shower.

Chase walked around camp, working the kinks from his thigh and calf muscles. Already his legs felt less tight, and he followed the sound of the trickling creek he remembered from last night. Some cold water on his face might fully wake him up.

He thought about his climb back down the canyon to the Yellowstone River. Another strenuous day lay ahead, and the sooner he got underway, the sooner he could be back to where he belonged. He glanced through the trees where the opposite rim of the canyon became visible, the brilliant yellows and reds of the rocks shining like gold in the morning sun. The roar of the Upper Falls had been a steady background noise all night.

He pushed through the undergrowth, eager for a drink of water. A cup of coffee was probably too much to hope for. The trees opened to a small clearing where the stream meandered through the forest. The sight before him stopped him like an opposing team's defensive tackle.

The creek trickled off to the right. Sitting at its banks was Sarah. He stared, rooted to the spot. She'd unstrapped the belt from around her waist, and unbuttoned the top few buttons on her shirt. Her hair spilled in wavy cascades over her shoulder and down her back. She lifted it aside and tilted her head, running a strip of wet cloth along her neck, and down the front of her shirt. The motion caused the loose shirt to slide down her arm, exposing her shoulder and the swell of her breasts. She closed her eyes, and the slight smile on her face gave off an expression of pure joy as she savored the luxury of her wash.

Chase's mouth went dry, and he groaned silently. He grabbed hold of the tree he stood beside to curtail the urge to walk up behind her and bury his face in her hair. His hands tingled, wanting to feel her silky skin, aching to caress her. The view she presented beckoned for his touch. He licked his lips, imagining her moan with pleasure while he trailed kisses up and down her neck. Visions of her beneath him with that look of ecstasy on her face caused his gut to tighten painfully.

He tore his eyes away. *Russell, you low-life piece of crap. You're acting like a teenage peeping tom.*

He was about to turn and head back the way he'd come, when she gasped. Hastily, she pulled the shirt over her shoulder and fumbled with the buttons.

"Uh...I didn't know where you were," he called lamely, clearing his throat. He scratched at the back of his head, feeling like a kid caught with his hand in the cookie jar. Rising quickly from the ground, she pulled the belt around her waist and headed toward him.

"Next time, make your presence known." Her eyes shot daggers at him, and she elbowed her way past.

"You missed a button," he called after her, and grinned when she sped up and practically ran back to camp. *There won't be a next time, Angel.* Time to get home. Chase quickly strode to the creek and splashed water on his face. He wished the stream were deeper than a few inches. He needed a cold soaking right about now.

He walked back to camp, and spied Sarah sitting by the fire. She'd braided her hair again. She didn't look up or acknowledge him, but merely pushed a piece of bark his way. Some of those roots she had roasting all night rolled around on the piece of wood. Chase eyed the food skeptically. They looked like shriveled-up prunes. He sat down across from her and pulled the makeshift plate onto his lap.

"Thanks," he mumbled. He held one of the fig-sized roots between two fingers, and tentatively bit into it. His eyebrows rose, and his mouth watered in response to the pleasant taste in his mouth. He looked over at Sarah. To his surprise, the root had a sweet flavor, similar to a yam.

"What do you call this?" he asked.

"It's root from the camas flower."

"Those blue flowers you were digging up yesterday?" He recalled her foraging through a meadow, digging up flowers with a stick the day before when they'd stopped for a rest break. He'd done nothing but sit and catch his breath.

She looked up at him from across the fire, studying his face with narrowed eyes. Her blue eyes shot icy daggers at him. He hadn't noticed the knife in her hand, which she now pointed first in his direction, then made a sweeping motion through the air with it. "You are observant, and you learn fast. You are a grown man. Yet sometimes you behave like a little boy who needs a good switching from his mother because he forgets his manners."

One eyebrow shot up in amusement, and he grinned. "My mom never used a switch on me, Angel."

"Perhaps she should have," Sarah retorted, her chin raised.

Well, well. This could get mighty interesting. Her tongue-lashing was quite a turn-on. It would be so much fun to spar with her right now. But he held back. Sarah had crawled under his skin in ways that gave him a decidedly uncomfortable feeling. He shifted his haunches on the hard ground. He never cared about other people's opinion of him. That way he wouldn't get hurt when they left. His old man sure hadn't cared enough to stick around while he was growing up. His hand automatically went to the dog tags around his neck.

Coach Beckman, the one man whose opinions had mattered, was gone. His own mother had never asked him for anything, whether it was doing well in school or on the football field. Sometimes he wished she had held him more accountable for his actions. Deep down, he suspected she was afraid she might push him away if she was a strict parent. She always blamed herself for his old man walking away. Chase often wondered if he hadn't left because of him.

He popped another camas root in his mouth. Looking up, Sarah sat, still studying his face.

"You're right, Angel. She probably should have beat me once or twice," he said slowly. He rose to his feet. "Look, I appreciate everything you've done for me. I probably would be dead right now if it weren't for you. But I need to get back to my time. I don't belong here."

He stood over her, and held out his hand to help her to her feet. She hesitated, and eyed him warily before she finally placed her small hand in his much larger one. He pulled her up easily. She stood mere inches from him, and he clenched his jaw. *No, damn it! Don't get any stupid ideas.* He pulled his hand away. "So long, Sarah." He turned and headed toward the canyon.

"Good-bye, Chase." Her soft voice carried on the morning breeze. Her mutt bounced along beside him, tail in the air.

"Go on, get back to your owner," he snarled. He kicked out at the dog. Grizzly barked, but didn't follow any further. Chase stood at the edge of the gaping canyon, staring at the river far below. He drew in a deep breath. "Okay, Russell, back down you go." He glanced over his shoulder one last time. Sarah stood leaning against a tree, watching him. He tried to burn her face into his mind, then took the first step into the deep scar in the earth.

∾

Sarah sat by the fire, waiting. He would be back. She didn't believe for a minute that something would magically transport him two hundred years into the future down in that canyon. But how had this man gotten himself lost in the mountains to begin with? His companions had obviously left him for dead in that storm. Her conscience wouldn't allow her to just walk away.

What a strange man, she pondered. To look at him, he projected strength and confidence, much like her father. But the similarity ended there. It was as if his body had matured, but in many ways, his mind hadn't followed. How could any man live that way? It was inconceivable to her how a man could act so completely without regard for responsibility, as if life was nothing but a game. Was it possible for the mind to catch up to the body? And what would it take for that to happen?

She tossed a stick in the fire, sending up embers. She couldn't explain it, but Chase had stirred something in her that had sat dormant up until now - the need to feel like a woman. No man had ever caused such feelings in her. And there were plenty of men who knew how to take care of themselves in these mountains who had shown an interest.

She laughed out loud. Hadn't she just told her parents that she didn't want or need a man? Why was she smitten with this one, who knew absolutely nothing about surviving here? And on top of that, he'd been insolent with her on more than one occasion. Her father and brothers would have done him bodily harm had any of them been witness to his brazen behavior.

Early this morning, she had taken the opportunity to steal away for a few moments of privacy. Chase had been sound asleep when she left the warmth of her blanket to indulge in a quick wash by the creek. Why had she not heard his approach? The man moved about as stealthy as a herd of bison. When she'd caught sight of him out of the corner of her eye, her heart had changed places with her stomach for a few seconds.

The smoldering look in his eyes had made her head spin, and she couldn't remember ever feeling so vulnerable. It wasn't the leering kind of look she'd received from trappers at rendezvous in years past, or those who came to trade in the valley. No. Sarah suddenly realized the look she'd seen in Chase's stare held the same kind of admiration as she had seen in her father's eyes whenever he gazed upon her mother. Warmth suddenly spread from her insides all the way to her extremities.

With a trembling hand, she reached out and scratched Grizzly's ears. The dog whined softly next to her. "You miss him, too?" she asked softly.

She looked up at the sun straight above. He'd been gone the entire morning. How long did it take to descend into the canyon? She didn't think it would take more than an hour. With a deep sigh, Sarah pushed herself off the ground and walked the short distance to the canyon rim. She peered into the chasm from an outcropping. The river flowed far below, and she scanned as far as she could see in both directions, her gaze coming to rest on a small moving object close to the river's edge at one point. Chase! He'd made it into the canyon safely. How long had he been there already, searching for his mysterious time portal?

"This is crazy, Sarah," she spoke out loud, even before the thought of following him into the canyon entered her mind. Why not? She could help him in his search. Her father's disapproving face flashed before her eyes. He would not be happy with her. Sarah laughed. Nothing she'd done these past few days would meet favorably with her parents. In an act of rebellion, Sarah took a slow step over the edge. She turned and climbed backwards on hands and feet, cautiously feeling for a foothold, or a tree root to grab on to.

Grizzly barked furiously from the rim. "Stay," she called to her dog. "I'll be back soon." The dog continued to bark and whine, as if warning her that climbing into that canyon would only lead to disaster.

* * * * *

CHASE RETRACED his steps along the river for the third time. He ventured as close to the base of the falls as was possible. The cotton shirt clung to his skin, soaked through from the heavy mist and spray of millions of gallons of water that plunged into the canyon.

Nothing. He'd neither seen nor felt anything that could possibly be his ticket home. He'd covered every inch of ground in the area he'd been in a few days ago, retracing his steps and actions as best as he could remember from that night when he and his compadres had climbed down here.

Why was he the only one who had time traveled? He'd been the only one retching in the river. That was the one time he'd been separated from the group. When he woke up the next morning, he must have already time traveled. It had to have happened while he was passed out. *The booze got you in trouble again, Russell.*

Chase worked the details over and over in his mind while he combed the river's edge. He stared at the fast-moving water, then at the ground around him. He had no idea what he was even looking for. He kicked at the loose river pebbles in frustration. He refused to believe he was stuck here. What the hell would he do? He had no place to go. He wouldn't last a week. That much was crystal clear already.

He sank down on the rocks, his knees drawn up to his chest, and his face buried in his hands. This was a nightmare. He threw rocks in the river, cursing loudly at the sky. He'd been so sure for the last couple of days that once he came back to this spot, everything would be all right.

His head suddenly snapped up. He listened. The roar of the river and waterfall drowned out most sounds, but he could have sworn he heard his name. Someone was calling him. There! He heard it again. He stumbled to his feet, and turned in all directions. He squinted his eyes, looked beyond the river, and then gazed up the canyon walls. His heart nearly stopped beating.

Sarah! What the hell was she doing? And it looked like she was in trouble. Her feet dangled precariously in the air, her hands hanging on to a root jutting out of the rocks. If he'd learned one thing from his climbs into and out of the canyon so far, it was that most roots didn't hold long in these brittle cliffs. She'd never survive a fall from her present height.

"Sarah! Hang on," he roared. He had no idea if she could hear him. He sprinted toward the steep incline, stumbling over boulders in his rush to ascend the canyon wall. He climbed faster than he ever thought he was capable of. All those years of weight training and football practice were paying off. He slipped and slid several times, but his eyes remained on the girl hanging on to a precarious tree root for her life.

"Sarah, hold on," he called when he was sure he was within earshot. Her head turned toward him.

"Chase! I lost my foothold." Her eyes were round as saucers. He'd never seen that look on her face before. The confident girl he knew was terrified.

"I'm coming, Sarah. Don't let go." His heart pounded in his chest and up his throat. Sweat ran down the side of his face. Pure adrenaline kept him going. *Don't let her fall. Please don't let her fall. If there is a God, I'm praying to you now.*

It would be impossible to reach her from below. He labored along a parallel direction until he reached an outcropping in the rocks, where he managed to get a secure enough foothold. His hands and fingers were still raw from his ascent a few days ago, but he ignored the burning and stinging. He tested the strength of a rock he held on to, then stretched his arm as far as it would reach.

"Grab my hand, and let go of the root," he called to her. Her eyes met his with uncertainty. She glanced over her shoulder down the canyon. The root moved several inches out of the rocks.

"Sarah, grab my hand. I won't let you fall," he yelled. Their eyes met. He knew the moment she made up her mind. Her mouth set in a determined line, and her hand reached over. He grabbed on, pulling her to him. For a split second, she hung in midair. With strength he didn't know he possessed, he pulled her up by one arm.

She gasped and struggled, and with her other hand reached for the security of the rock he was on. Her feet found a hold, and his arm felt lighter. She let go of his hand, and grabbed hold of the rock. He could feel her body tremble as she caught her breath.

"What the hell do you think you're doing?" he raged.

"I . . . I thought I could help you find what you were looking for," she stammered, still out of breath. She wouldn't meet his eyes. They both stood, holding on to the rock, catching their breaths.

"That's the stupidest thing I ever heard," he yelled. "Come on, let's get up to the rim before we both end up dead."

He nudged her ahead of him, and she pulled herself up the jagged incline inch by inch. He followed close behind, steadying her every once in a while when her feet slipped in the gravel. Well, at least he knew he was a better climber than she. That thought gave him little satisfaction.

Sarah's mutt barked loudly from the canyon rim. She struggled on, and managed to pull herself over the rim with a few loud grunts. Chase found his breath again when he heaved himself onto the horizontal ground next to her. He pushed off the gravel, wiping the sweat from his forehead. She sat on her knees, her hands on the front of her thighs, her head bent into her chest. The dog ran around her, then him, barking happily.

"Shut it, Grizzly," Chase reprimanded, and gave the mutt a hard stare. Its ears dropped flat against its head, its tail down. With a final whine, the dog quieted and sat on its haunches.

"Sarah," he said softly. "It's okay now. You can get up." She stared at him. He hadn't expected to see the tears in her eyes. He cleared his throat. "Come on Angel, let's move away from the rim and back to camp." He reached down and gently grabbed hold of her upper arm, tugging her to her feet.

She must have started to rise on her own at that same moment. The added momentum of his tug sent her straight against his chest. With a mind of its own, his other arm wrapped around her waist and he pulled her closer.

She gasped and pushed her hands against his chest, her eyes slowly meeting his.

"Hey, Angel, you're still shaking," he whispered. A sensation unlike anything he'd ever felt doused him from head to toe. Warmth trickled over and into his skin, through his veins and arteries, down into his stomach, and wrapped itself tightly around his heart. The urge to protect her, to keep her safe at all cost, flooded his entire being stronger than his need to find a way home at that moment.

"Please, let me go," she said, her voice as shaky as her body. It barely registered in his brain that she'd spoken. He couldn't stop staring into her shimmering blue eyes. She stiffened and pushed away from him. All he wanted to do was pull her closer. Reluctantly, he released his hold around her waist. She quickly ducked away and headed toward the trees.

What the hell just happened, Russell? He stood rooted to the ground, staring after her.

CHAPTER TEN

*S*arah caught her breath. She glanced over her shoulder. Good, he wasn't following. She stumbled to the nearest tree and leaned against it, her hand over her heart.

Hey, Angel, you're still shaking.

His tender words, so full of concern, echoed in her head. She had already composed herself from her near-mishap in the canyon. Tears of shame at her own stupidity and carelessness had almost spilled down her cheeks, and he'd seen it. Then he had to pull her up against him. The feel of his strong arms around her, holding her to his solid physique had caused her to shake. Her mind had spun out of control. Time had stopped. All she'd wanted to do was lean into his strength and forget the world around her, but it was nonsense to give in to such feelings. Chase wasn't staying. He may have come to her aid, but no doubt he intended to continue his search for a way home.

She inhaled deeply. Her feelings for this man scared her. Sarah desperately wanted her mother at this moment. She would know what to do.

"Enough, Sarah," she scolded out loud. "You don't need a man, especially this one. He can't even take care of himself."

She pushed away from the tree, and headed in the direction of camp. A dull thud echoed through the trees, and she stopped abruptly. It sounded like an ax striking wood. Moments later she heard it again. The faint smell of wood smoke wafted to her nose. She followed the sound and smell directly to her camp.

Her eyes widened in surprise. A fire crackled where she'd doused it earlier, before heading to the canyon rim. Chase stood with his back to her, the tomahawk she'd given him in his left hand. Her mouth fell open when he took aim, swung his arm out and over his head, stepped forward with his right leg, and released the handle. The blade buried itself firmly in the trunk of a narrow lodgepole some twenty feet away. The force and accuracy of his throw stunned her. The only person she'd seen do it better was her father. He strode to the tree and worked the blade free. When he turned, he stopped and met her gaze.

Sarah walked toward the fire, glancing around for her horn bow and rifle. Another stupid thing she'd done – leaving her weapons behind. She sighed in relief. They were still propped against a tree where she'd left them. Her father had taught her better than that. A weapon should always be kept within easy reach.

Chase hadn't moved from where he stood.

"I thought you didn't know how to handle a weapon," she called to him.

He moved away from the tree and strode in her direction, tossing the ax in the air repeatedly, making it do somersaults. He caught it with a sure grip each time.

"I didn't know I could." He grinned.

Sarah held her breath. Her heart sped up. He stopped several feet in front of her, his eyes staring right into her.

"I figured you needed some time to yourself, so I kept busy." He nodded toward the fire, then glanced at the ax in his hand. "This isn't much different than throwing a pigskin. A little heavier maybe." He shrugged.

Her eyebrows shot up. "You throw pigs where you come from?"

Chase laughed. "No. A pigskin is a football."

"I don't understand." Sarah shook her head. She relaxed, but clasped her hands behind her back to hide their trembling.

"Football is a game I play back home."

"Tukudeka children play a kicking game with a ball, but you are not allowed to touch it with your hands," Sarah said. "Why do you throw it if it is called foot ball?"

He shrugged. "There are a few times when you kick the ball, but usually you throw it to a teammate and run with it."

She nodded, not understanding at all. An awkward silence followed. She'd never been tongue-tied before. She heaved a sigh of relief when Grizzly chose that moment to nudge her leg with his wet nose. He barked and furiously wagged his tail. Sarah patted the dog's head. *Thank you for the diversion.*

"I think he's saying it's time to find some chow," Chase said, kneeling down and rubbing her dog's neck. She quickly removed her hand.

Sarah couldn't suppress a smile when Chase's stomach growled loudly. "Are you speaking for the dog, or for yourself?"

He stared up at her, and Sarah took an involuntary step back. The smoldering look in his green eyes sent a shiver down her spine. He blinked, and the look was gone. Her skin tingled as if she'd been scorched. She rubbed at her arms, and turned to pick up her horn bow.

"I'll see what I can find," she murmured, eager to put some distance between them.

$\sim$

CHASE DARTED AFTER HER. "Wait up, I'd like to go with you." He grinned when Sarah's eyes widened. Her mouth opened as if she wanted to say something. "You've done all the work so far. I'd like to help out," he explained.

He pondered his own words. Suddenly it seemed important to impress her. He wanted her to see him as a man capable of taking care of himself. What had she said to him earlier? She thought he acted like a little boy and needed a good switching. Those words stung now, but he knew she was right. Something had happened when he held her in his arms, something he couldn't explain. A stirring deep within him that he couldn't quite define. Sarah's impression of him mattered a whole lot all of a sudden.

"You told me you didn't need to know how to hunt where you come from," Sarah said, her eyes narrowed. "Are you giving up your search for your time portal? Obviously you haven't found it."

"No, I'm not giving up. I just don't know what it is I'm even looking for. I know I can't stay here. I'll have to figure something out."

She studied him, her head tilted slightly to the side. An overwhelming urge to pull her in his arms and hold her swept over him. He wanted to run his fingers through her hair, watch her eyes shimmer while he . . . He clenched his jaw.

You're losing your mind, Russell. Girls like her are not for the likes of you. Sarah was tough as nails when it came to living in this environment. She hadn't turned into a hysterical female, even while hanging on for her life earlier, but she was a naive young woman when it came to men.

She's the exact opposite of the type of woman you're used to, Russell. His type was the good-time, experienced party girl, the kind that didn't come with strings attached. Compliment them, pretend to listen to their problems, then walk away after a night of fun. Sarah was the forever kind of girl. And he wasn't staying here forever.

"Chase!"

"Huh?" He startled, unaware she'd even spoken to him.

"I said we can hunt for another whistle dog, but you look tired." She scrutinized his face.

"No, just something on my mind," he answered. Taking a deep breath, he added, "Ok, let's hunt some whistle dogs."

Sarah led the way to a different spot along the canyon rim. She pointed to an area where boulders of different sizes piled on top of each other.

"They live among the rocks, and they're rather easy to kill."

Chase scanned in the direction she pointed. Several small furry creatures darted around among the rocks. They were no larger than cats with brown fur, but they looked more like hamsters on growth hormones.

"Let's see how good you are with that ax," Sarah whispered. "Move slowly, and pick one. Then you can try and hit it to stun it. You might have to get closer."

Chase grinned. He could hit one of those things easily from where he stood. They were closer than that tree he'd used for target practice. Watching the creatures for a minute, he singled one out that seemed to be sunning itself on a flat rock. He reached for the tomahawk in his belt, and aimed. A split second later, the furry thing lay splayed on its side. The rest of the group made loud whistling noises and darted into the crevices among the rocks.

Sarah stared at him in silence. Her eyes opened a little wider, and he could swear that her lips curved in a slight smile. She nodded her head in apparent approval.

"Now go get it, and if you haven't killed it, use your knife and slit the throat."

Chase picked up the limp pile of fur, reasonably sure that it was dead. He stuck his tomahawk back in his belt, and together he and Sarah headed back to camp.

"You'll need to skin and clean it, and it'll be ready to put over the fire."

He glanced at her. "You're enjoying this way too much, Angel. How about I let you do that part. But I'll watch and learn."

She nodded. A slow smile lit up her face, and he couldn't take his eyes off her. This new awareness of her was going to kill him.

Sarah averted her gaze. She reached out for the fur ball in his hand, and sat a short distance away from the fire, pulling out her hunting knife. Quickly and efficiently, she slid the knife down the center of the animal's underside from neck to tail. She pulled out the insides, which she threw to her eagerly waiting dog.

This was a lot different than dissecting a frog in biology class, but Chase was not about to turn away now. He could tell she was pleased with his newfound skill. In no time, she had the skin pulled off, and the meat skewered and hung over the fire. He observed her every move, determined to do this himself next time.

Next time? What are you thinking, Russell. You need to find a way home pronto.

"So what will you do now? Do you plan to go back down the canyon tomorrow?" Sarah asked, as if reading his thoughts.

"I don't know." He shrugged. "I don't even know what I'm

looking for." He toyed with a stick, darting it at the ground, picking it back up, and repeating his actions.

She peered up at him from across the fire. "You should come back to the valley. Wait for my parents to return. They will know what to do."

He looked up at her. "Oh yeah? They've met other people who've come through here in some time portal?"

What the hell was he going to do? He couldn't sit around here by the canyon, that much was clear. But going back with Sarah to her home? That might not be such a good idea. He was still trying to sort through these crazy feelings she evoked in him. Since coming back out of that canyon, he couldn't get his mind off her. If she knew what he'd been thinking, she'd probably run for the hills.

"Chase?"

"Sorry. What did you say?" He was turning into an absent-minded fool.

Her eyebrows drew together in a frown. She held out a portion of meat to him. *"Mah-duh-k."*

"What?"

She smiled. "Eat."

"Thanks," he mumbled.

SARAH SLOWLY PICKED pieces of meat off the bones, offering Grizzly a bite for every one she took. The dog sat patiently at her side, waiting for his share. The sun had nearly disappeared behind the mountains to the west, and the clear night sky revealed countless stars. The crickets chirped their loud nocturnal song. She tried hard not to glance at Chase sitting across from her, but her eyes seemed to have a will of their own.

He sat with his head down, and ate in silence. His mind

seemed to be far away. Was he thinking about home? She'd suggested he come back with her to the valley without any forethought. What was she thinking? She had hoped to keep these last few days from her parents' knowledge, and now she'd suggested he wait for their return.

Her father would know what to do. He'd be able to find Chase's companions, she was sure of it. But it would be at least another month before her parents returned from rendezvous. And they would not be pleased with her.

I can't just leave him here, though!

His ability with the ax was definitely a surprise. Given time, would he learn the skills needed to survive in these mountains? Sarah chastised herself mentally. He doesn't want to be here. He'd already said so many times. He wants to go home.

Chase finished his meat, and threw the bones to the dog. With a loud moan he stretched out on his back on top of his blanket. He crossed his legs at the ankles, and clasped his hands behind his head, staring at the night sky.

Sarah watched him. He was such a strong man. He had managed the strenuous journey yesterday without faltering. Today he had climbed into the Yellowstone canyon, then rescued her, and climbed back out. He was a man made for this environment. A warm feeling doused her. She sighed quietly, then her eyes followed his line of vision and gazed up at the stars.

"I never tire of looking at the stars. It's a beautiful night," she said softly.

"Yeah, it sure is."

She peered over at him. He wasn't looking at the stars. He stared directly at her. Their eyes met.

Her heart must have skipped a beat, and her mouth went dry. Sarah quickly averted her gaze. Trying to divert his attention, she looked at the sky again.

"See those stars up there?" She pointed straight up. "They form almost a square, and a tail coming off one side? It looks like a pot with a handle. My mother calls it the Big Dipper."

"Big Dipper," Chase said simultaneously.

Sarah's eyes widened, and she stared at him. "How do you know this?"

Several times already, Chase had used words and phrases that only her mother would use.

"Isn't it commonly called the Big Dipper? The Greeks called it Ursa Major, the big bear. But I don't see a bear in those stars." Chase propped himself up on his elbows.

"I don't know." Sarah shook her head. "Perhaps you are from the same place my mother grew up. She also comes from a big city. She tells different stories than my Tukudeka relatives."

"You're part Indian?" Chase looked her way, his eyebrows raised.

Her own eyes narrowed. "Would it matter if I was?" She couldn't disguise the anger in her tone. Was he one of those white men who despised the Indians?

"No, I was just curious. If you call them your relatives, that implies you're related."

"My father was raised by them as one of their own. We consider the Tukudeka our relatives."

"Okay." He shrugged. There was no hint of disdain in his voice. Sarah relaxed. She added more wood to the fire.

"So, what kind of stories did your mother tell you?" He rolled to his side, facing her, his head resting in his hand.

Sarah closed her eyes for a moment, remembering the long winter nights when she and her brothers would sit in the cabin, a roaring fire blazing in the hearth. Her mother would entertain them with tales of a magical world. Sarah would snuggle on her papa's lap, rolled up in a blanket, and they all listened in fascination. Her mother had a wonderful imagination.

She smiled at the memories, then cleared her throat. "Well, she would tell us of a magical place where the sky was filled with giant birds, and people rode inside the bellies of these birds, and flew all around the world in a day. And people could speak to each other, and even see each other, even if they were great distances apart. And men walked on the moon."

On the other side of the fire, Chase jumped up suddenly. He slid down on the ground on his knees in front of her so fast, she pulled her knife in surprise. He gave it no notice, and grabbed her by the shoulders.

"Where did you say your mother is from?" His face was inches from hers, his intense stare startling her.

"New....New York," she stammered. Squirming, she tried to break away from his grip. "You're hurting me, Chase."

His mouth relaxed, and his eyes softened.

"I'm sorry." He released his hold on her, but his hands lingered on her arms, his thumbs rubbing the fabric of her shirt up and down her skin. Warmth spread throughout her body, and her skin tingled from his touch. She forced her breathing to remain steady.

Chase rocked back on his heels. "How did she end up here in the wilderness?" he asked.

"I don't know," Sarah shook her head, her eyebrows narrowing. "I think my father just . . . found her." Her voice trailed off. She'd never asked or questioned her parents about that. It was just as natural as breathing that her mother and father should be together. How that came about had never been important.

"He just found her here, in the wilderness?" Chase repeated her words.

"Why is this important?"

"Sarah." His eyes bored holes right through her. "The stories your mother told you, the magical place, it's real. The things she told you about are real. They exist in my world . . . in my time."

Her head shook more vigorously. How could that be true? She laughed. "Those are just children's stories."

"No, they're not, Sarah." He ran his hand up and down the back of his head. "Are there any other stories? Did she ever mention other magical things? Cars, maybe?"

"No."

"Okay, maybe she didn't use that word. What kind of transportation vehicles do you have in this time?" He wasn't directing the question at her. Sarah had heard him think out loud before.

"I've seen horse-drawn buckboards in St. Louis," she offered.

"Okay, has she mentioned stuff like that, only they aren't pulled by horses? People ride in them, and can go real fast. Anything like that sound familiar?"

Sarah's stomach dropped. It did sound familiar. Even her father had added to the stories and talked about colorful monsters that moved at incredible speeds on smooth roads. Her eyes met Chase's stare, her mouth slightly open.

"Your mother is from the future, Sarah. She's from my time." He sounded absolutely sure of himself.

She could only shake her head. How could this be true? Her mother knew things that no one else seemed to know. She talked differently, too. Chase used similar words.

"There's no other explanation how she could know all this stuff. You know it's true, don't you?" Chase leaned toward her. "I can see it in your eyes."

"I . . . don't know," she whispered softly.

87

CHAPTER ELEVEN

"*I* have to talk to your mother, Sarah."

Chase couldn't believe what Sarah had revealed. She was clueless, but to him it was as obvious as day and night. No one could make up stories as accurate as what Sarah described. If her mother had time traveled, perhaps she knew how it was possible, and it would get him home. But why did she stay in this time? A sinking feeling came over him. What if it was a one-way ticket? Had she been stuck here, too? Without any other recourse, had she married Sarah's father out of necessity? Chase frowned. As difficult as it was for him to be here, he couldn't imagine what it must have been like for a modern woman, stranded in the past. Marriage to a man from this time was probably her best option. Chase had to have some answers.

"Can you take me to this rendezvous place?"

Sarah's eyes widened. "No, that's not possible."

"Why not?"

"Because I am not allowed to travel there on my own."

Chase frowned. "I'm going with you. You wouldn't be alone."

"The way there leads straight through Blackfoot country. Any white man, especially one traveling alone, would be putting his life in danger. The Blackfoot are a hostile tribe."

He shook his head, and his eyebrows drew together. He didn't get it. "But your parents are white," he argued.

Sarah laughed. "My father trades with them as well as all other tribes in this region. My mother is a skilled healer. If anything happens to them, the wrath of many other nations will descend on the Blackfoot, and they know it. They would not harm my parents."

Chase sat on the hard ground, the chill of the earth seeping up into his body. The fire crackled loudly. Sarah's features danced in the shadows, illuminated by the flames.

He held his head between his hands. One month.

Somehow he had to convince Sarah to take him to her parents sooner. He didn't want to be here that long. He needed some answers now. He glanced at her. She sat quietly, stroking her dog's neck. Her fingers moved slowly through the mutt's fur. Chase pictured her hand in his hair, stroking him . . . Irrational jealousy swept over him. *You're insane, Russell. Jealous of a dog?*

These feelings for her confused, and scared, the hell out of him. All the more reason he needed to get home.

"All right. I'll go back to Madison with you," he blurted. "I hope your mother can give me some answers."

Her blue eyes stared at him from a few feet away. She nodded slightly. "Then you'd better get some sleep," she said softly. "The trip back is not any easier."

"We can take our time. I'm not in a rush now." He stood and moved to his blanket on the opposite side of the fire. For a long time, he gazed at the Big Dipper.

~

89

An animal howled in the distance, the ominous sound reverberating through the trees. Chase woke with a start. His breath created whitish swirly patterns above him each time he exhaled. The gray sky held no hint of sunshine in the early dawn. With a groan, he rolled onto his side. His back ached from lying on the hard ground. The campfire crackled loudly, and the flames eagerly consumed the wood that looked like it had been freshly added. The flames were just beginning to envelop all the branches. He raised his head. Sarah's blanket was empty. Did this girl ever sleep?

He sat up and rubbed at his stiff neck. Reluctantly, he pushed himself off the ground. How many nights had he been here in the past now? Yesterday he'd hoped to be home again. Today he would return with Sarah to her home. Memories of the day before came back to him. The way she'd trembled in his arms, and the tears in her eyes. Her vulnerability had stirred something in him unlike anything he could remember. Would it really be so bad to spend some time with her?

No, Russell. You can't get involved with her. She's not that kind of girl.

He had to figure out a way to get to this rendezvous place, and find her mother. She had to know how to get back to his own time. But what if she didn't? What if she'd come here the same way he had? It was unthinkable for him to remain here.

"Okay. Just take it one day at a time," he said out loud. He looked around between the trees. He had no intention of walking up on Sarah again the way he'd done yesterday.

"Sarah," he called. His voice traveled through the trees. A few birds chirped in the canopies of the lodgepoles, announcing the new day. Sarah's dog barked in the distance. He called her name again, and followed the sound of the barking dog. Pushing through the trees, his eyebrows rose in surprise. Sarah was perched precariously on one of the lower branches of a pine tree, a stick in her hand, swinging it at some of the higher branches above her head. What was she doing? Chase laughed.

"Is this your early morning exercise routine, or did a bear chase you up that tree?"

She glared down at him. "If you must know, I'm trying to get us some breakfast."

"We're eating pine needles?" He grinned up at her.

"I'm trying to reach that cluster of pine cones up in the higher branches. This is a white bark pine tree."

Pine cones didn't sound any more appetizing than pine needles.

"Get down before you hurt yourself, Angel."

Chase moved to stand directly under her. He sure didn't want her falling out of that tree. He reached his hand up, and grabbed her ankle to keep her steady. Apparently his intent had the opposite effect. Sarah shrieked just before she lost her balance. Her arms flailed wildly in the air as she tried to prevent a fall. It was no use. She toppled out of the tree.

Fly into my arms, Angel. Chase was ready for her below. He held his arms out and caught her, cradling her against his chest.

"What are you doing?" she gasped.

His face grew serious. "Keeping you from breaking that pretty neck of yours."

Chase swallowed, mesmerized by her blue eyes. His chest tightened while he held her up against him, until she squirmed in his arms. Reluctantly, he set her feet on the ground. Her eyes turned wide as saucers, and she drew in a sharp breath. Chase grudgingly released her completely, his hand lingering at her waist. He wanted to kiss her. She was close enough that he could, but he held back.

Russell, you're embarrassing her. The only time she acted

unsure of herself was in his presence. Hadn't she ever have a boyfriend or whatever they called it in this day?

He cleared his throat. "Which pine cones are you trying to get?" he asked, putting some distance between them, trying to act unaffected by her nearness.

Sarah stepped back, and looked up, pointing. Chase's eyes followed her line of vision. "See that branch up there? It has quite a few cones on it."

Chase pulled the tomahawk from his belt. Stepping a few paces out from the tree, he aimed and threw the ax. It sliced cleanly through the thin branch. Both branch and ax landed on the ground with a thud.

"Where did you learn to throw with such accuracy?" Sarah asked. The admiration in her eyes warmed him to the core.

"It's a quarterback's job to throw the ball to the receiver. If the throw isn't accurate, the ball could end up in the hands of the opposing team."

"Quarterback?" Her forehead wrinkled.

How could he explain football to her? "Yeah, a quarterback is sort of the leader of the team. He makes decisions to get the ball in the hands of his teammates to score points. His teammates have to defend him and the ball from the opposing team."

"I don't understand this game." Sarah shook her head. She bent down and picked the pine cones off the branch.

Chase reached out his hand. "Here, I'll take some of those."

She glanced up at him, and held his gaze for a moment. Then she handed him a half dozen cones.

"So, how do we eat these?" Chase rotated an egg-sized cone between two fingers. It was hard as a rock.

Sarah laughed. "You don't eat the cone. The pine nuts inside are what we're after."

"Oh."

"Come. I will show you an easy way to get the cones to open and release the nuts."

She headed off back to camp. Chase shook his head, and followed. Never in a million years would it have occurred to him to look for pine cones as a source of nourishment. First roots from a flower, and now this. He'd never be able to survive here.

The campfire had burned to simmering coals. She threw her pine cones on top of the hot ashes and gestured for Chase to do the same. He watched in amazement as the pine cones burst open, one by one, just like popcorn. Sarah pulled them back out with her stick, and picked the seeds out of the centers.

"It doesn't look like a lot," she said, offering him a handful, "but they are very nourishing."

Chase popped them in his mouth. He wasn't too keen on nuts, but his stomach growled loudly.

"Not bad," he said, chewing the crunchy corn-kernel sized seeds.

Sarah rolled up her blanket, kicked some dirt on the ashes to completely douse the fire, and picked up her weapons. He followed suit, shouldering his rolled up blanket.

"Will we get back to Madison today?" he asked.

"You decide," Sarah answered.

"Let's take it slow," he said, falling in step beside her when she headed out away from the canyon. He glanced over his shoulder once more at the deep scar in the earth. With a determined set of his jaw, he turned his head and stared straight ahead.

∽

Sarah led the way west. She followed a different path than the way they'd come. It would mean camping out one more night, but even she didn't want to repeat the same brutal trek from two days ago. The way led through mountainous lodgepole forest, and lush green meadows. Sometimes she had to alter course when the area became too marshy. Neither she nor Chase spoke for most of the day. Chase seemed to be absorbed with his own thoughts, and Sarah didn't wish to bother him.

She found berries along the way for them to eat, and Grizzly had stirred up several ptarmigans in the tall grasses. She'd killed two, which would make a nice supper when they stopped for the night.

Her own thoughts wandered to the man who walked tirelessly next to her. He continued to amaze her. For someone unaccustomed to the wilderness, he had taken to it remarkably well. His dismal survival skills nagged at her, but he learned fast, and seemed to remember everything she'd told him the last few days. He had no problem starting a fire when they set up camp along a shallow tributary of the Little Buffalo River, and he even plucked and cleaned one of the birds, and skewered it to hang over the fire.

It was still early, and the sun slowly descended into the western horizon. They had eaten their meal, and Chase had wandered a short distance from camp, Grizzly at his heels. Sarah smiled, watching this big man play with her dog, repeatedly throwing a stick for him. Grizzly wagged his tail, and barked happily, retrieving the stick each time to continue the game.

Sarah sat by the fire, unbraiding her hair, and ran her hands through her thick tresses. Tomorrow, when they reached home, she would need a bath. She only hoped Chase would give her the privacy she required. Apprehension filled her with the knowledge that he would be so close by. A branch snapped in the trees behind her. Sarah whirled around, her knife drawn instinctively. A man emerged from behind the forest.

"Hello the camp," he called.

Sarah stood, and darted a nervous glance toward the creek. Chase and Grizzly had wandered further downstream out of sight.

"Hello yourself," she answered, hoping her voice sounded steady. The man came closer. Recognition filled her, and her heart leapt up her throat. Jean-Luc Briard! This man had pursued her like a fly on fresh bison dung the entire four weeks at rendezvous last year. Her brother Matthew had almost gotten into a fist fight with him.

Jean-Luc scratched his stubbly black beard, and a wide grin formed on his face.

"Sarah Osborne!" he exclaimed. "What a pleasure." He licked his lips, as if in anticipation of a delicious meal. "Might I join your camp?"

What could she say? She nodded hesitantly.

The man's eyes darted around. "Surely you are not here by yourself," he said in mock outrage. "Where is your father, or one of those twin brothers of yours?" His smile brought bile to her throat.

"I am not here alone," she said, raising her chin. "My . . . my man will return shortly."

Jean Luc's eyebrows rose. "Your man? Daniel Osborne has finally found someone worthy of his daughter?"

Sarah ignored his sarcastic question. She gripped her knife with a firm hand, holding it in front of her, and dared not take her eyes off this man. He was looking at her like a coyote ready to feast on an unguarded elk carcass. She made sure she kept the fire between herself and him.

Where was Chase? He might not know how to protect her from Jean Luc, if this vile man made advances toward her, but merely his presence should be enough of a deterrent.

"I have no food to offer you," she said, hoping he would be on his way.

"Oh, just the company is enough for a man to rest here for a while," he drawled.

Sarah swallowed nervously. "I . . . I'll be back momentarily," she said, and headed toward the creek where she'd last seen Chase. Jean Luc darted in front of her. "You can entertain me while we wait for your man to return," he said in a deep voice.

Sarah could smell the stench of rotten teeth on him. She quickly raised her knife in front of her.

"Let me pass," she said firmly. She pushed at him with her elbow and moved to the right to pass, when his hand snaked out and grabbed her wrist. He twisted it and squeezed tightly, forcing her to drop her knife.

"I have dreamed of you over the long winter months, Sarah. Do you know that?" He yanked her up against his chest. Sarah turned her face and squeezed her eyes shut. The rough whiskers of his beard scraped her cheek. "The way you teased and tormented me last summer. I know you wanted me, too. But your family wouldn't give us a moment alone."

She frantically shook her head. "You are mistaken, Jean Luc. I have no such feelings for you."

"Is there a problem here?"

Sarah's knees went weak with relief, and she turned her head at the sound of Chase's voice. Grizzly growled loudly from behind her, and Chase patted the dog's head to quiet him. Jean Luc released her, and slowly moved away. Chase's heated stare darted from her to the much shorter Frenchman. Jean Luc's eyes went wide.

"You didn't tell me you were meeting your boyfriend here, Sarah," Chase said casually.

Her forehead wrinkled. She didn't know what he meant.

"You are her man?" Jean Luc asked, uncertainty in his voice. He seemed to take the big man's measure. Sarah bit her lip. What would Chase say? Would he protect her honor?

Chase raised his eyebrows at the man's question, and shot Sarah a quick look. "Yeah, I guess you could say that," he answered slowly. Then he reached his hand out, "Come here, sweetheart."

Sarah darted around Jean Luc, and took hold of Chase's hand. He pulled her up close to him and wrapped an arm around her waist. Despite the tension in the air, her body reacted to his nearness. Warm tingles surged along every nerve ending that made contact with his solid body.

"Maybe you should go and find your own spot to camp," Chase suggested unconcernedly, but his muscles tensed. "Me and the . . . little woman here like our privacy. Isn't that right, sweetheart?" He flashed her a wide grin, and she nodded her head slightly. Chase leaned over and kissed her on the mouth. Her senses overflowed. Shocked at first, she dared not pull away from him this time. She couldn't inhale a deep enough breath, and her heart hammered against her ribs. Chase's lips moved against hers, and his hold around her waist tightened. Mortified, her body seemed to have a will of its own when she leaned closer to him. Her lips parted slightly, and her hand came up to rest against his heart.

Short coughing sounds behind her brought her back to her senses. Chase loosened the hold around her waist, but maintained contact.

"My apologies," Jean Luc said, his eyes cold and twitching. Sarah tensed, and gripped Chase's arm. "I will be on my way then."

Jean Luc picked up the rifle he had dropped on the ground, and looked to head for the trees. Suddenly he wheeled around, and raised the flintlock, aiming it at Chase.

Grizzly growled deeply, and Sarah saw movement out of the corner of her eyes. Her dog leapt into action, and ran at Jean Luc. With a loud snarl, he lunged at the man. The sound of a gunshot mixed with the high-pitched whine of a dog in pain. Sarah's heart dropped.

"No!" Her eyes widened in horror. The giant dog fell on top of the Frenchman, knocking him to the ground with a loud thud, and a cracking sound like rock hitting rock. Both bodies lay limp and motionless.

Sarah ran to her dog. "Grizzly, no."

She fell to her knees, her hands buried in the dog's thick fur, combing over his body. Her vision blurred, and she wiped a hasty hand over her eyes. Chase came up beside her.

"Is he dead?" Chase's voice sounded somber.

Sarah shot a quick glance at Jean Luc, who hadn't move underneath the giant dog. His head was turned at an odd angle. Blood oozed from a spot on his head that made contact with a large rock on the ground. The man's mouth was half-open, his eyes frozen in shock.

"Yes, he's dead," she spat, not hiding the bitterness in her voice.

"Not that creep. The dog," Chase said, his voice raised.

Sarah sniffed. She continued to feel along Grizzly's ribcage. She felt a slight movement. The dog stirred, and let out a low moan, like a primordial howl, deep in his chest.

"No." She gave a quick laugh. Relief eased the tension and sinking feeling in her. "I have to find his wound." She looked up at Chase. His mouth was drawn in a tight line, and his jaw muscles moved along the sides of his face. She'd never seen him with such a serious expression.

Chase's arms reached for the dog. "Here, let me move him off that piece of shit." He ran his hands under Grizzly's body, and lifted him off Jean Luc. Gently, Chase carried the dog and placed him on his blanket by the fire. The venom in his spoken words touched her to the core.

Grizzly dog-paddled with all four legs, trying to right himself from his lateral position. He lay dazed, his tongue lolling out the side of his mouth, but he was able to remain lying in an upright position.

Sarah knelt down beside him. "There," she pointed to Grizzly's head. "The shot grazed his skull. It's only a flesh wound. It must have knocked him out momentarily." She wrapped her arms around the dog's furry neck, and he whined softly.

"He saved my life," Chase said solemnly. He knelt down beside her, and stroked the dog's back. Sarah studied him. The boyish demeanor she was used to seeing was completely replaced with that of a hardened man. Their eyes met, and she smiled softly, blinking away fresh tears. Chase's eyes darkened. His hand came up, his fingers grazing her cheek.

"Sarah," he whispered, his voice trailing off. He leaned toward her. His touch was so gentle, she wanted to give in to her body's desire to lean into him. Pulling away, she rose quickly to her feet.

"I . . . I need to get fresh water to clean Grizzly's wound." She spun around to head toward the creek.

"What are we going to do with the dead guy?" Chase called after her.

Sarah turned. "Take him downstream, and drop him in the water," she said coldly. Chase walked toward her. She braced herself, her heart rate increasing.

"You sure you want to pollute the water with him?" Chase asked.

"The current will carry him away from here. A dead body will only attract predators."

"Who was he?" His heated gaze scorched her from the inside out.

"Just a trapper." Sarah shrugged, and glanced over at the body on the ground. "He made undue advances toward me last year at rendezvous. My brothers and father kept him away from me." She looked up and met Chase's eyes. When had he moved so close to her? She could feel the heat coming off his body. "Thank you for letting him believe you were my man," she whispered.

"Any time," he said, his tone husky. "Jerks like that exist in my time, too." He clenched his jaw, then turned back to where Grizzly lay on the blanket. He touched the dog's head, and Grizzly whined softly. "Better go get that water, Angel."

CHAPTER TWELVE

*B*y mid-afternoon the following day, the Gibbon River Canyon they'd been traversing widened. Coming over a low rise into the valley, Chase spotted the log structures of Sarah's home. The large cabin sat nestled against some pines at the base of a steep incline that led to more forest. It was strategically built to offer a spectacular view of the valley, just across the bend in the Madison River, and the steep mountain rising beyond the opposite bank. The smaller cabin sat a short distance away. There was no other hint of civilization. Two weeks ago, the meadow was busy with families enjoying a few days away from their otherwise hectic lives. Fly fishermen had waded in the Madison, casting their lures in hopes of landing that big trout.

Chase groaned, and shifted the giant dog in his arms. Grizzly had survived his heroic act of protecting him from getting shot by that trapper, and his wound didn't appear all that serious. It had left him weak and dazed, however. While he was able to walk short distances, the dog stopped frequently and refused to follow Sarah any further. Chase had carried the animal most of the way here. He was glad to finally be able to lighten his load once they'd reach the cabin. The dog had to weigh a hundred pounds, if not more, but it was the least he could do for this animal that had saved his life.

"Why don't you let him walk the rest of the way?"

Sarah's softly spoken words jolted him out of his memories of last night, when he returned from the creek to find that scum touching her. Chase's first impulse had been to grab the neck of the short little weasel and knock him into next week, but he'd decided to play it cool instead. He now wished he had done the former. Then the dog wouldn't have gotten shot.

He'd been happy to play along and pretend to be Sarah's husband. He'd assumed that's what the weasel had meant when he called him Sarah's man. Never one to miss an opportunity, Chase had seized on the chance to kiss her. He had wanted to do that for days, and the opportunity had presented itself. The way she responded to him came as a complete surprise. He vowed that the next time he kissed her, it would be under different circumstances.

Chase lowered the dog to the ground. Grizzly stood on wobbly paws for a moment, then trotted off across the meadow.

"He looks like a drunken sailor." Chase grinned.

"A what?" Sarah asked, meeting his gaze when he looked down at her.

"It's an expression. When someone is drunk, he can't move too steadily on his feet, and swerves and weaves around a lot. Just like Grizzly's doing." He nodded in the dog's direction. He reached up and wiped some sweat from his forehead before his eyes caught Sarah's stare.

"What?" he asked. Did he say the wrong thing?

"Have you ever been drunk, Chase?"

He groaned silently. He didn't want to go there. For a

moment, he held her sharp stare. He couldn't lie to this girl. With a deep intake of breath, he said, "Yeah, Angel, I've been drunk." He didn't need to elaborate and tell her that his drinking and drugs were the reason, ultimately, that had brought him here.

"I have seen what alcohol does to a man's senses." The disgust in her voice was unmistakable. "Men drink themselves into a stupor, and they behave worse than animals."

He'd been the man she described plenty of times. Sweat beaded his forehead anew.

"Why do men feel the need to drink?" she asked.

Chase scratched the back of his neck. "I don't know." He shrugged. "Fun, maybe. Recreation. To be accepted socially." He stared straight ahead. They were almost at the cabin. "Maybe to forget things . . ." his voice trailed off.

"My childhood friend, Falling Rain, fell victim to a man who chose alcohol for . . . as you say, fun and recreation."

He peered over at her. With a sinking feeling, he knew what she would say next.

"You say men use alcohol to forget. I know Falling Rain has never forgotten the man who raped her and left her to die while he was in a drunken stupor. She was twelve years old."

"Shit." Chase ran his hand down his face.

Sarah stopped walking. She offered a slow smile. "I'm sorry. I overreacted. None of that has to do with you. I just get angry when I hear or see men make fools of themselves and turn into vile creatures because of alcohol. I'm sure you had good reason when you chose to consume too much."

Russell, you could use a stiff drink right now.

"Look, it's still early. I think I'll go rinse the trail dust off in the river."

He needed to get away. What would she think of him if she ever found out that drinking himself to the point of passing out had been part of his daily routine less than a year ago? Hell, it's what had landed him here in this time. She'd probably tell him to get lost, and slam the door in his face. Not that he could blame her. He headed toward the Madison without another word. He could feel her eyes on him, probably wondering if he'd ever done something as low and disgusting as what she'd just told him.

~

Chase knocked on the cabin door, pulling his shirt on over his head. Sarah didn't answer, even on his second knock. Slowly, he opened it, and peered inside. Grizzly greeted him with a weak wag of his tail, and a whine. His eyes darted around the dim main room. A warm sensation doused him, and he smiled. Sarah sat in a chair, her head resting on her arms on the table. She was sound asleep. The weapons, bedroll, and pouches she'd been carrying on their trip all lay in a heap on the ground.

He couldn't blame her. She had to be worn out. She'd barely slept in three days, and had done most of the work. Chase nudged her gently. She moaned softly, but otherwise didn't stir.

"Come on, Angel, time for bed," he whispered. He peeled her arms off the table, supporting her head as it fell back against his arm, scooped his other arm under her knees, and lifted her off the chair. She sighed and nestled her head against his chest. Chase stared at her for a moment and tightened his hold, then carried her to her bedroom. He elbowed the door open, and deposited her quietly on the bed. He was about to pull some covers over her, when his eyes fell to her belt. He unbuckled it and pulled it out from under her, laying it on the table next to the bed.

"Good night, Angel" he said, and bent over her, touching his lips to her forehead. She nestled deeper into her covers, and a gentle smile formed on her lips. Chase's stomach tightened. He brushed some loose strands of hair out of her face, his fingers lingering on her cheek, then quietly left the room.

The dog lay by the hearth, his tail thumping loudly against the floorboards.

"How about we get this place warmed up and rustle us up some chow, Grizz?"

The tail thumped more forcefully against the ground.

Chase pulled out his knife and flint, and was about to kneel in front of the hearth, when he realized the firewood box was nearly empty. He rose, groaning at the stiffness in his legs. He'd definitely gotten a good workout the last few days. Where was a gas log when you needed one? One flip of a match, a turn of the key, and a fire would be no problem. Better yet, an electric heater would be nice.

Wishful thinking wasn't going to warm this cabin up, and the sun had almost disappeared into the western horizon. Chase went outside to the enormous woodpile around the corner. Most of the wood sat in large chunks, too big to burn. He spotted a tree stump that obviously served as a chopping block, with a huge ax leaning up against it.

"Okay, how hard can this be," he said out loud. He picked up a block of wood and set it on the stump, then swung the ax. The blade buried itself in the wood and held on.

"Damn." He figured he could have split the log with one blow, but apparently he needed to swing harder. With the wood still attached to the blade, he swung again, bringing the log down onto the chopping block. This time it split with a loud crack. The two resulting pieces were still too large, so he repeated his actions to split the half pieces into quarters. With each blow, he learned and adjusted how much force to use, and within twenty minutes he had a sizeable pile of usable fire logs at his feet.

Grinning in satisfaction, he wiped the sweat off his forehead, and rotated his shoulders. Carrying the dog all day, and after that unplanned workout of chopping wood, he'd definitely be sore in the morning. There was barely any daylight left when he carried his last load into the cabin, but at least the box was full again.

Starting a fire was no longer a problem. He'd gotten the hang of that real quick. His stomach growled loudly, and he glanced around the workbench. Was there anything to eat around here? Chase lit the lantern on the table, then the one on the smaller table in the corner. The room gave off a soft glow. Still not as bright as an electric light, but it gave him a homey feeling.

The water bucket he'd seen Sarah carry from the river several days ago still stood on the workbench. It was empty now. With a heavy sigh, he picked it up and went back outside, headed down to the river, and refilled it. The night air was loud with the rhythmic cadence of crickets chirping. An occasional owl hooted in the trees. Countless swallow-like birds hovered over the river, darting up and down to feast on the millions of bugs that swarmed the water.

He'd never stopped to appreciate the peacefulness of it all. The few weeks he'd been in Yellowstone prior to his unexpected plunge into the past, he'd done his job without really looking around. He had to admit, the sights and sounds of nature held a certain appeal. Getting used to doing without modern conveniences like electricity and indoor plumbing might take a lot longer. He'd never realized how he'd taken all those modern things for granted, now that he had none of them available. Instead of hopping in his car and driving to the corner fast food joint, he had to either kill something, dig it up out of the ground, or pull it out of a tree. Then it needed to be cooked. He hoped there was an edible morsel somewhere in the cabin.

Carrying the bucket from the river, his eyes veered toward the small cabin to his right. Curiosity took hold. He set the bucket on the workbench in the main house first, then picked up the lantern off the table, and went back outside. Slowly, he opened the door to the other cabin. The hinges creaked loudly. He raised the lantern high to see better, but he still couldn't make out much.

The cabin was a simple room. There was one bunk on the wall to the right. The back wall was one large hearth and fireplace. Stacks of blankets, furs, and leather items lined the opposite wall. Several wooden trunks were stacked in a corner. His lips raised in a grin when he spotted a rack along the wall by the hearth. What looked to be dried meat hung from the rack. Chase removed a large chunk, and returned to the main cabin.

He sliced a bite-size piece off the large chunk and put it in his mouth. It was hard and dry. He'd be chewing this stuff all night just to get his fill. Glancing around, hoping an inspiration would hit him, he saw the kettle Sarah had used to cook her stew. Why not? He could cut up some of the meat and pour water over it, and cook it. That might soften it up.

"Don't look at me like that, Grizz," he said to the dog, which lay patiently by the hearth, observing his every move. "You're going to be eating this, too." The dog whined. "And no complaints about my cooking."

An hour later, Chase ladled meat and broth into two bowls. He set one in front of the dog, who lapped it up eagerly, and took his own to sit at the table. The meat had softened considerably, but it was tasteless, as was the broth.

"Sarah's going to have to do this kind of cooking, huh, Grizz? Hers definitely tastes better."

He stretched his long legs in front of him, crossing them

at the ankles. Clasping his hands behind his head, he yawned. Where was he going to sleep? The rocking chair didn't look too comfortable, and he definitely didn't want to go into that other room. He suspected that was Sarah's parents' bedroom. He shrugged and left the table. Sarah's bed was large enough for two.

He entered her room quietly. She hadn't moved from where he left her earlier. He pulled his shirt off, then his moccasins, and slowly lowered himself onto the bed on the opposite side, not wanting to disturb her. He stayed on top of her covers, and pulled a blanket over himself.

He stared at the dark ceiling. Maybe this wasn't such a good idea. He'd never actually slept, in the literal sense, in the same bed with a girl before. Sleep had never been a priority on those occasions when he shared a bed with a woman. He listened to Sarah's slow, rhythmic breathing inches from him, and ground his teeth. As exhausted as he was himself, sleep would be a long time coming.

CHAPTER THIRTEEN

Sunlight filtered in through the small window of her room, and Sarah squeezed her eyes shut tighter. She arched her back and stretched dreamily, not wanting to give in to the start of a new day. Still half-asleep, she thought vaguely that she hadn't slept this well in days. She rotated her head, and her hand moved upward. The contact with bare skin startled her fully awake. Her leg was draped over Chase's leg, and her hand rested on his nude chest, while her head was nestled in the crook of his arm.

Sarah bolted upright. Her face flamed with heat, and her heart raced wildly. Quickly, she yanked her leg back. What had she done? A quick glance down offered her some reprieve. She exhaled slowly. At least she was wearing her shirt and britches. She scrambled to the edge of the bed, and held her scorching face between her hands. Behind her, Chase stirred.

"Morning, Angel," he said, his voice raspy from sleep. Sarah bolted off the bed and yanked her door open, racing into the main room. Her breaths came in quick, shallow gasps. What had happened last night? She frantically searched her mind. She remembered entering the cabin, and Chase had gone to the river. A quick glance around the room, and she spotted her weapons and pouches where she had dropped them. She recalled sitting at the table for a moment to rest her feet. Then what happened? She shook her head. She couldn't remember.

She stiffened at the shuffling sounds behind her. Her heart rate accelerated again. Biting her lower lip, she squeezed her eyes shut.

"Nothing happened, Sarah." He stood too close. She could feel his breath in her hair as he spoke. Slowly, she turned to face him.

"Why?" Her voice squeaked like a mouse. She couldn't get the words out.

"I came back from the river, and you were asleep at the table," he calmly answered her unfinished question.

"Why didn't you wake me?" she whispered.

"I tried. You were so far gone, you barely moved. So I brought you to your bed. I figured you could use a good night's sleep."

"And you?"

"I didn't want to sleep in that rocking chair, Angel. I swear, nothing happened. I kept my pants on, and my hands to myself." He grinned, then winked at her.

She whirled around to face away from him, mortified anew that he would speak like that.

"Lighten up, Sarah. I'm not going to ravish you. Haven't you ever had a boyfriend?"

"A what?"

"A guy who pays attention to you. Not like that jacka . . . jerk from yesterday. What would you call it? A suitor?"

Sarah felt his warm hands on her shoulders. He applied pressure, coaxing her to turn around again. Slowly, she obliged, meeting his heated gaze. She swallowed repeatedly, and moved her tongue around inside her dry mouth, trying to stimulate saliva to flow.

"No." she looked up into his eyes. There was something haunting about the way he looked at her, as if he was staring straight into her soul. "Do you . . . do you have someone waiting for you at home?" she asked tentatively.

He laughed. "No. I've never been one for attachments." He dropped his hands and stepped away from her. Why did his answer bother her?

Grizzly whined at that moment. The dog padded over to the door.

"How are you this morning?" Glad for the diversion, Sarah moved away from Chase and patted the dog on the head, running her fingers over the wound. A thick scab had formed, and there was no excess heat or swelling. She opened the door and he trotted off.

"I fed him last night."

She turned, her eyebrows raised.

"He ate it, but he much prefers your cooking." Chase's boyish grin was back. She couldn't help but smile back.

"I'll fix breakfast," she said.

"Is there anything you need me to do?" he asked, sincerity in his voice. She glanced at the wood box, then raised her eyebrows in surprise.

"I filled it last night." He shrugged.

"Then, no, there's nothing I need at the moment."

"Okay. I'll . . . ah, go outside and see what that dog is up to."

Sarah watched him turn to leave. "Chase." He turned back around. "I . . . I would like to bathe later . . . " Her face flamed again.

"Understood." He smiled. "I'll be far away when you do." He headed for the door again.

"Chase."

He stopped, his hand on the door. Sarah bit her lip. "Thank you . . . for not . . . you know," she stammered. The words didn't want to come out. He faced her and raised his eyebrows. She inhaled deeply. "Thank you for being an honorable man."

His eyes darkened, and he stared at her for a long time. "Don't be so sure about that, Angel."

He left, closing the door on his way out.

SARAH RAN a brush through her wet hair, untangling the long strands with her fingers. She sat at the riverbank, and gazed across the expanse of water toward the Firehole Canyon. Her thoughts strayed to the man who was quickly taking over her heart. She couldn't help herself, but she trusted him completely. He may have told her he wasn't an honorable man, but she didn't believe it for a moment, no more than she believed that he came from the future. He'd had plenty of opportunities to take advantage of her. She was not so disillusioned that if he wanted to, he could overpower her easily. He may be unskilled with weapons, save for the tomahawk, but she was no match for his size and strength.

In his own way, he had protected her from Jean Luc. The memory of that kiss caused her lips to tingle, and she put her fingers to her mouth, a slow smile forming on her face. What would it be like to lie in the arms of a man, to be loved by a man? Her face flushed. She'd shared a bed with him the entire night, and her body had obviously sought him out, the way she'd found herself entangled with him this morning. And she had to admit, it felt nice, even if her shock hadn't left her any time to enjoy the feeling.

Sarah sighed. He'd told her he didn't want any attachments. Why was she even entertaining the notion that he might be interested in her? His heated looks told her he saw her as a woman, but he hadn't acted on it, not really. Did she want him to? She wasn't sure.

Hastily, she buttoned up the last two buttons of her clean shirt, then carefully wrapped her cake of scented soap that her brothers had brought from St. Louis last year in cloth, and grabbed her blanket off the ground. Glancing around to make sure she hadn't forgotten anything, she headed back to the cabin.

She opened the door, and gasped. Chase sat in the rocking chair, his hands in the air. An Indian stood over him, his bow drawn taut, ready to release a deadly arrow.

"Uncle, no!" Sarah called in Shoshoni, and sprang forward. The Indian turned. His features relaxed, but his bow didn't.

"*Paite.* I find this strange white man in your home, but not you. You are well?"

"Yes, Uncle. Lay down your weapon."

He did so reluctantly. "You know this man?" The Indian gestured toward Chase, who hadn't moved. His eyes shot from Sarah to her uncle.

"I know him," Sarah confirmed. Her palms began to sweat. How was she going to explain this? In the Tukudeka tradition, a man and woman living in the same lodge for more than a few days was as good as a declaration of marriage. Her uncle lowered his bow, and stepped back. He looked at her, then at Chase, but didn't say anything.

"What's going on, Sarah? Who is this guy?" Chase finally lowered his hands, but kept one near his tomahawk.

"This is my uncle. His name is Elk Runner," Sarah explained. "He won't hurt you."

"Oh yeah? From where I'm sitting, I thought he was about to blast that arrow in me. Two days ago, some clown points a rifle at me, and today I'm staring down an Indian with an arrow pointing at my gut. Forgive me for getting a bit jumpy."

Elk Runner's eyes followed the conversation. Sarah wasn't sure how much he understood. Her mother had taught him and his family some English, but mostly they spoke in the Shoshoni dialect whenever they were together.

"Walk outside with me, *paite*." Elk Runner turned and left the cabin.

"I'll be right back." Sarah shot Chase a nervous glance, and followed her uncle. She ran to catch up with him as he walked toward the Madison.

"Uncle, what brings you here?" Her pulse quickened. This was an awkward situation.

"Snow Bird has asked for you," Elk Runner replied. He turned and looked toward the cabin. "Her time is near. I have come to take you back to the village with me." After a pause, he added, "Your father has asked that I watch over you while he is away, but it appears that you've found your own guardian."

"He was brought here by some Absarokas. They found him near death. I've helped him recover."

"So I see."

Sarah groaned silently. Her uncle didn't miss anything.

"He lives in this cabin with you?"

"Please, Uncle, it's not what you think. He is lost. He can't find his companions. I believe they have left him for dead. I was hoping when my father gets home, he will help him return to his people."

"Your father will not be pleased with this." The man's tone was serious, but Sarah saw the sparkle in his eyes, and the mischievous curve of his lips.

"I have done nothing inappropriate," Sarah said firmly.

"No, I don't believe you have," he said slowly. "You are truly your father's daughter."

"What is that supposed to mean?"

Elk Runner's smile widened. "Only that your father was also honor bound at one time, and refused to act on his feelings for a woman."

Sarah's eyes narrowed, and she shook her head. "You speak in riddles, Uncle."

"Are you certain this man can be trusted?"

"He has already shown that he would protect me from men with vile intentions."

Elk Runner's face darkened. "You are in danger from someone?"

"No. Chase spoke up for me, and Grizzly actually killed the man. It was the trapper Jean Luc Briard. He remembered me from rendezvous last year."

"Yes, your father has mentioned him. That is why your parents did not want you to attend this year. An unmarried woman is like fresh meat to a starving grizzly bear." He put his hand on her shoulder. "I can see that your thoughts about uniting with a man have changed."

Sarah's face flamed, which would only serve to confirm her uncle's perceptiveness. "I have no such intentions," she stated hotly, and turned away from him, hoping he hadn't seen her face.

Elk Runner laughed. "As I have said, you are your father's daughter. I recall similar words spoken by him when he first found your mother."

Those words made her turn back and face him. "Tell me how they met."

Elk Runner studied her. A devilish grin lit up his face, and he appeared much younger all of a sudden. "I came to your father, and told him I had seen a white woman who appeared to be lost in the woods. He didn't believe me, but when we found her again, she was near death on a cliff in the canyon."

"The canyon?" Sarah's heart beat faster. "The canyon of the *E-chee-dick-karsh-ah-shay?*"

"No. The Little Buffalo River. Just beyond the falls."

"Did she ever say where she came from?"

"I never found out. It didn't matter. Your father needed a wife. He fought against it for a long time, but I could see from the start that she would be his woman. I fear he would still live a solitary life if not for her." He paused and studied her through narrowed eyes. "Why these questions about your mother? Perhaps you should ask her."

"I will," Sarah said absently.

They stood in silence by the river. Then Elk Runner said, "Pack what you need. You will want to reach the village before nightfall. Snow Bird is anxious to have you at her side."

"What am I to do about Chase?"

"Bring him along."

Sarah stared, open-mouthed at her uncle, and watched him walk away.

"Where are you going?" she called after him, not disguising the annoyance in her voice. Sometimes her uncle could be so infuriating.

"There is no need for me to wait for you. You have a man to bring you safely to the village," he called over his shoulder.

She grumbled under her breath, and stomped her foot in the dirt. Living under the same roof with Chase was one thing, as long as no one found out. What would her aunt and cousins think when she showed up with a man by her side? It would be perceived as an open declaration that they were a couple.

A ground squirrel darted back into its hole when she walked past. Right now, she wished she could make herself small enough to join the rodent in its dark, underground cavern, and hide from the world.

CHAPTER FOURTEEN

"We're going where?" Chase gaped at Sarah.

"I've been called to tend to my cousin. She is due to give birth soon, and I have agreed to act as her midwife."

He watched her dart around the cabin, collecting all the things she'd barely put away from their return yesterday. He rubbed the back of his neck with his hand.

"Maybe I should stay here," he said. He wasn't much in the mood for another hike through the wilderness. The only other hike he'd planned to make was to find Sarah's mother. And he definitely had enough of people pointing deadly weapons at him.

"Believe me, you staying here would be my preference as well," Sarah mumbled.

"Okay, then I'll stay here. How long will you be gone?"

She stopped wrapping bread in cloth to stare at him. "I said it would be my preference. But you can't stay here alone."

"Why not?"

"Many reasons."

"Can you be a bit more specific?"

She turned fully to glare at him. "You cannot fend for yourself, for one thing." She threw her hands in the air. "What will you eat? And what happens if a party of Absarokas shows up? Or worse, some Blackfoot. They will kill you before you can blink."

She shoved her way past him to pack the bread in a leather pouch on the table. She turned on her heels to head back to the workbench, her motions more agitated with each passing second.

Chase moved in front of her, deliberately blocking her way. She tried to elbow past him, so he grabbed her upper arm.

"Why the hell are you so uptight?" he asked.

He hadn't seen her like this. She was nervous about something. Chase stared down at her. She hadn't braided her hair since coming from the river and speaking with her uncle. Her mahogany waves swayed down her back and over her shoulders, and the room seemed uncomfortably warm all of a sudden. He could smell a subtle flowery fragrance in her hair. He found her feisty side quite appealing, and the way she blushed around him, but the way she fluttered around like a sparrow caught in a windowpane was new. He suspected it had something to do with her uncle's visit.

"I . . . I'm not," she stammered.

Chase's lips curled upward slowly. "Why are you blushing, Angel?"

She tried to pull her arm away, and shot him a heated look, which only served to turn him on more.

Russell, you're going to go straight to hell for this.

His right hand came up and slid along her cheek, then under her hair, until he cupped the back of her head. His left hand followed on the other side. Slowly, he lowered his face to hers. Her entire body stiffened, but it was too late. He couldn't stop now. He had to taste her lips. Her hands shot up to push against his arms just as his mouth covered hers. He groaned as white-hot heat shot through him, as if the feel of her lips had turned on an electric circuit. He couldn't remember ever having such a feeling kissing a woman. Slowly, he moved his lips against hers, coaxing, teasing her to respond. His hands massaged the back of her neck, his fingers entwined in her hair, and he stepped closer until the length of her body brushed up against his.

He wanted to plunder her mouth, ravish her senseless until she gave in, but it would only scare her away. He kept his assault gentle, his actions unthreatening. If she fought him, he'd back off. He moved his lips away from hers a fraction of an inch, giving her a tiny window to escape. When she didn't move, he covered her mouth once again and renewed the kiss.

Her resistance melted. Her hands no longer pushed against him, and her lips parted slightly. Chase slid one hand down her back and encircled her waist with his arm, pulling her up against him. She leaned into his embrace, a soft whimper escaping from her throat.

Every nerve cell urged him to intensify the kiss. In his mind, he carried her to her bed, and this time they wouldn't be sleeping. Instead of acting on those visions, he pulled back slowly, and released his hold on her. They both struggled for a normal breath. Sarah's blue pools stared up at him, and he smiled softly.

"That wasn't so bad, now was it," he said, his voice hoarse. Sarah took a step back, her eyes still round as saucers. "Angel?"

"You . . . please don't do that again," she whispered.

It was the last thing he expected her to say.

"You didn't enjoy that?" He stepped up to her again, and gently held her shoulders. Panic seeped into her eyes. He kneaded her arms with his palms and fingers. Her entire body trembled.

She feels it. She just doesn't know how to respond.

He suddenly realized he was probably the first and only man who'd ever kissed her. An overwhelming feeling of possessiveness came over him.

"I . . ." She averted her eyes and turned her face away. He brought it back with two fingers under her chin, forcing her to look at him.

"Don't be afraid of me, Sarah. If you don't want me to kiss you again, I won't."

That was going to be a difficult promise to keep. He released her arms, and stepped away from her, turning his back so she wouldn't see the evidence of her effect on him. God, she had to have felt him pressed up against her.

He exhaled slowly. Never before had he been this attracted to a girl, and definitely not to one without experience. He couldn't even explain it to himself what had come over him since he met Sarah. Her naïve ways about men, coupled with her confidence and knowledge in everything else, made him feel things he never felt before. He wanted to be the honorable man she thought he was. Her opinion of him might have changed after that kiss.

"So, when do we leave," he asked, his back still turned.

Sarah walked briskly along the banks of the Madison, heading west, her head held low. The urge to step out of her skin and run away from herself was overwhelming. These feelings inside her would drive her mad. She'd always considered herself strong and able to defend herself in any situation. Her guard had been down the other day with Jean

Luc, or he would have never gotten as close to her as he had. She'd been too content in Chase's company to see the danger.

With Chase, she had no defenses. She was embarrassed for her weakness around him, and for the things he made her feel. She hoped he'd be true to his word and not kiss her again, even though she wanted him to. God help her, she wanted him to kiss and hold her again. The way he made her feel, the way her body tingled from the inside out, was unlike anything she ever imagined.

Her face grew hot, the memory of that kiss playing itself over and over in her mind. She tried to picture Jean Luc, or any other man kissing her, and those visions conjured up nothing but disgust. But Chase, who walked silently next to her, held a power over her she couldn't explain. She didn't have the strength, or the will to fight him. If he kissed her again . . .

Sarah raked her teeth over her dry lower lip. She had to get her emotions under control before they reached the Tukudeka village. Everyone would see it on her face that she had kissed this man, wouldn't they? It would be obvious to all, and they would ask questions. Questions she couldn't answer, because Chase was not her man. He had made it clear that he didn't want to be attached to a woman, and that he wanted to find his way home. He probably had many lady friends where he came from. Was he simply used to women paying attention to him, and since she was the only woman he had contact with presently, expected her to act a certain way in the same manner as them?

She wasn't sure what to make of the looks she'd seen in his eyes. And the kiss seemed to have affected him as much as it had her.

What do you know of men, Sarah? The only ones who have paid attention to you acted vulgar and disgusting.

It seemed that men were only after one thing. That's why

it was unwise to have such silly notions about a man unless he had asked for her in marriage.

"What are those things?"

Chase's deep voice among the lulling sounds of the river and crickets in the grasses startled her out of her deep thoughts. She looked up, momentarily confused. When had they traveled this far? She almost missed the tributary where they needed to veer away from the river and head in a northerly direction.

"Are you going to act all jumpy around me now? I swear I won't touch you again." Why did he sound so angry? "I didn't realize what I did has you so repulsed. Shit."

He kicked out at a ground squirrel mound, sending dirt flying.

Sarah flinched involuntarily at his heated words. If only he knew how he affected her. She certainly didn't find him repulsive. She couldn't bring herself to say it, though.

"Forgive me," she said quietly. "I was deep in thought. Your words just startled me. What were you asking?"

Chase glared at her. He ran his hand along the back of his neck. His chest heaved in a deep sigh. "I asked, what are those things over there?" His voice had gone normal again.

He pointed toward the river at what appeared to be mounds of wood stacked along the shore, reaching into the water. "Is all of that driftwood?"

"No." Sarah shook her head, relieved that she could talk to him about things that were familiar to her. "Those are beaver lodges. Most of them are probably abandoned. There aren't a lot of beaver left in this area."

"Why do they stack up such huge amounts of wood? What's the purpose in that?"

"They live inside them. The entrance is accessible only under water. Inside it's like a dry cavern. It's where they sleep and raise their young." She laughed, and Chase looked at her with raised eyebrows. "I once hid from my brothers for an entire day inside a beaver lodge. They were so furious with me that I outsmarted them."

"Why were you hiding from your brothers?" Chase seemed more relaxed again. Perhaps he was grateful for the neutral conversation, too. She smiled brightly at the memory.

"Matthew and Samuel made a bet that they could track better than me. They had lost a deer track the day before, and I suppose I gave them a hard time about it." She glanced up at him, and shivered involuntarily. His mischievous smile and the sparkle in his eyes sent her pulse into overdrive.

"It's not a good idea to show up your brothers, Angel." His grin belied the seriousness in his tone.

"Show up?" What did that mean?

"Yeah. Boys don't like it when girls are better than them, even if it's true."

"You don't seem to mind." The teasing words escaped her mouth before she had time to think. She almost covered her mouth with her hands, as if she'd said a nasty word.

"I know when I'm defeated, Angel. With you, all I can do is roll over and play dead." His eyes turned dark as he stared at her. Sarah swallowed nervously.

She had no idea what he was talking about. Would her mother understand his unfamiliar phrases?

He cleared his throat. "So, what happened with the bet?"

Sarah stared out at the landscape. A few more miles, and they would reach the village. She would find the camp at the base of a rocky cliff, surrounded by forest. She headed away from the main river and its tributary, and entered a sparse forest.

"My brothers challenged me to act as the prey, and they would track me down. They gave me an hour's head start. I led them through the forest and over a steep mountain for a while, then covered my tracks and headed for the river. A beaver had just emerged from his lodge, and it gave me the idea to seek a hiding place there. I was successful. They never found me." She beamed at him.

He didn't say anything for a while. Had even listened to her boastful story?

"You're amazing, you know that?" He hadn't looked at her when he said the words, barely above a whisper, and kept his eyes trained straight ahead. He had his thumbs hooked through his belt where his weapons hung off on either side of his hips. His knuckles turned white with tension. Her heart skipped a beat. She had no response to his compliment.

CHAPTER FIFTEEN

What the hell, Russell. This girl isn't interested in you.

All he seemed to accomplish was to make her nervous. She acted as if he'd done more than just kiss her. Other women sure never seemed to mind. And he sure as hell didn't have to work half as hard with them.

Chase stopped himself short. What *did* he want from Sarah? His attraction to her was annoying as hell. Each time he told himself to leave it alone, words came out of his mouth that left her flustered again. He had to find a way to reach her mother. It was as simple as that. He needed to get home, back to where things were familiar. He definitely didn't have a clue about life in this time.

Living here in this environment was harsh, that much was certain. Why didn't he seem to be bothered by it, then? He did mind having his life threatened. Twice now, in less than a week. If he didn't learn to defend himself, he'd be dead soon. Sarah had spoken the truth that he'd probably end up on some Indian's platter if he stayed behind at the cabin while she visited her friends.

Is that why she's not interested in you, Russell? Because you're not a man in her eyes? She'd made it plain that she didn't think he could take care of himself. Was that the way to impress her?

Listen to yourself! One minute you want to get out of this place, the next you want to impress her. What the heck, man. He laughed out loud at the absurdity of his predicament. On the one hand, he just wanted to go home, making sure he'd never see her again. The next moment he tripped all over himself for a girl he could never have. He didn't have a clue as to how to win her over. Back home, all he had to do was mention he was a jock, and girls lined up to be with him.

"Something amuses you?" Sarah stared at him as if he'd just grown wings.

"Yeah. My situation here is pretty funny," he said flatly.

"Situation?"

Chase stopped walking. He waited for Sarah to stop, too. When she turned to look at him, he said, "How far is it to that rendezvous place, Sarah?"

Her eyes widened. "You can't be thinking of going there," she said, her voice heated.

"I just want to know where it is." He shrugged, pretending mild interest.

"You will never get there alive. The Blackfoot will kill you the moment you enter their territory."

"Stop telling me how incompetent I am, dammit," he yelled. Did everyone see him only as a failure?

"It has nothing to do with incompetence." Sarah glared at him, her hands on her hips. "No man I know travels through hostile territory alone. It is suicide. Other trappers travel in large groups. It is safer that way. Do you wish to die?"

"No, I just want to get the hell out of here." He ran a frustrated hand through his hair. She let out an audible gasp at his harsh words. "What's the matter, Angel? Why does that surprise you? There's nothing for me here," he sneered.

"I . . . I thought you were getting along here quite well," she said quietly.

Her words surprised him. No one other than Coach Beckman had believed in him, encouraged him. After he died, all desire to be the best had died along with him. Sarah thought he was doing well?

"Sorry I yelled at you," he mumbled.

She walked up to him and placed a tentative hand on his arm, looking up at him intently. He clenched his jaw. "You are a good man, Chase Russell," she said softly. He stared into her deep blue pools.

"You have the prettiest blue eyes, you know that?" His words were a mere whisper.

Since when do you spout silly compliments to women, Russell? He mentally knocked himself in the head. He was turning into a lovesick tomcat. Next he'd be spouting poetry.

"My Shoshoni name is *Aibehi Imaah ba'a.*" She smiled at him softly. "My mother named me after a particular hot water spring she calls Morning Glory Pool."

"I've seen that pool." Chase stepped closer to her. "It's nothing compared to your eyes."

Grizzly barked next to him. "Great timing, partner," Chase grumbled, reaching down to pat the dog's head. He looked up again and grinned at Sarah. She hadn't moved. "You're making it hard for me to keep that promise I made this morning, you know that, Angel?"

Her face turned scarlet. Chase smiled inwardly.

"Don't we have to be somewhere?" he said with as much cheer as he could muster. He headed off in the direction they'd been traveling. Another second of her staring at him so intently, and a herd of bison wouldn't stop him from taking her in his arms and breaking his promise.

～

Sarah stared after him. He would have kissed her again if Grizzly hadn't barked. And she'd wanted him to. She shook her head, and ran to catch up with him. They would reach the village soon. Her thoughts needed to be elsewhere other than on the tall man walking next to her.

"Where is this rendezvous, Sarah?" he asked again.

She sighed impatiently. He wouldn't know how to get there, anyway. What could it hurt to tell him? "Beneath the Teewinots, by the great lake," she finally answered.

He shot her an annoyed look, which made her smile. "Speak English, Sarah."

"Teewinots . . . it means many pinnacles. It describes the mountains." She hesitated, then added, "the French call them les trois tetons." She blushed.

Chase grinned broadly at her, his eyebrows raised. "My French is a little rusty, but did you just say the three breasts?"

Sarah buried her face in her hands. Chase laughed loudly. His light slap on her back shocked her out of hiding. His boyish grin was infectious. She began to laugh.

"Yes, that's what it means," she said between fits of laughter.

"I know that place. In my time, we call those mountains the Grand Tetons."

"Don't try and find your way there." Her face grew serious. "Wait until my parents get home. Surely you can stay here that long."

"For you, Angel, I'll stay," he answered.

Sarah couldn't react or reply to his comment. The sound of voices carried through the forest, as did the smell of wood smoke. The village came into view through the trees. She exchanged an uneasy smile with Chase. By the look on his face, she could tell he felt nervous, too.

"Most of the people don't speak English," Sarah said. "If you know French, a few can speak it. The Tukudeka tend to keep to themselves. They are mountain dwellers, and have very little contact with other tribes, or with white men."

"I'll try and behave myself, Angel. Wouldn't want to embarrass you." He shot her a devilish grin. Sarah swatted his arm with her hand, but couldn't help from smiling back at him. She turned her face when her cheeks grew hot again.

She led the way toward the village. Nine conical shaped wooden dwellings stood erected throughout the clearing, with one smaller hut further off closer to the tree line. The freestanding dwellings were tightly covered with deadfall, and thatched with dried grasses. Cooking fires burned in front of the majority of the huts. Men and women moved around, each busy with some task. Children laughed and ran around, playing with sticks and carved figures. Dogs lay about everywhere, and some raised their heads and barked a greeting at the newcomers. Grizzly's tail stood erect like a flagpole, the tip moving back and forth cautiously. People stopped their activities when they noticed Sarah and Chase.

A short, heavyset woman walked toward her when she and Chase entered the clearing, open-armed and smiling brightly.

"*Imaah*, it is good that you are here." The woman embraced her warmly.

"It is good to be here, Little Bird," Sarah replied. "How is Snow Bird?"

"She is in the birthing hut. Her time is near." The woman cocked her head up at Chase, and perused him with curious eyes.

"Chase, this is my aunt, Little Bird. She is the wife of Elk Runner. You've, ah, already met him." Turning to her aunt, she said, "This man is called Chase. He has seen to my safety in coming here."

Chase reached out a hand. Sarah put hers out and blocked him. "Just nod and say hello," she said. He nodded his head at the woman, muttering a quick hello. Little Bird continued her perusal. Sarah shifted weight from one foot to the other. She could only guess what her aunt must be thinking.

"I, ah, need to go see Snow Bird," she said to Chase.

"I'll be waiting." He shrugged.

Little Bird nodded at him. "Come," she said to him in stilted English, "you sit with . . . my . . . *kuhma*." Her eyes darted to Sarah for help.

"Husband," she supplied.

Little Bird gestured for Chase to follow her. "Sit with husband," she said.

Chase walked off after the woman, turning once to Sarah, and said, "I'll be fine. Go do what you need to do."

Sarah admired his broad shoulders as he walked away. He didn't appear to be uncomfortable here, and carried himself with confidence. With a satisfied smile, she headed off to the one wickiup that stood furthest from the rest.

SARAH STRETCHED HER BACK, and massaged her neck, groaning at the relief it brought to her tense muscles. She squinted as she stepped out of the darkened hut into the bright early afternoon sunlight. The baby had taken his sweet time in making an appearance into the world. Snow Bird had labored all through the night, and Sarah had wished her mother could have been here to help. She had feared for her cousin and her little son a few times. But nature had taken its course, and he'd simply been a slow arrival.

She needed to walk off the soreness in her muscles from sitting and squatting for long hours. Snow Bird and her baby slept peacefully, and Sarah used the opportunity to leave the hut for a while. With some trepidation, she also wondered how Chase had fared the night.

Loud and boisterous children's laughter and shouting reached her ears. She glanced around in the direction of all the noise. At the other end of the village, a group of boys clad only in breechcloths, and several girls, ran around like a flock of birds. There seemed to be two groups of kids, with one group chasing after the other.

At the periphery of the cluster of children, Sarah spotted Chase. Her mouth fell open. He was calling to a particular child, and held something in his hand. Just as she'd seen him do with the tomahawk, he raised his left arm and aimed for a throw. The object in his hand sailed through the air, into the waiting arms of the little boy, who took off running in the opposite direction after catching what Chase had thrown, whooping loudly. The rest of the children ran after him, yelling like a war party of Blackfoot in pursuit.

Chase pumped his arm in the air, rooting the boy forward. Sarah stared openly at the tall man. He wore no shirt, and his lean upper body glistened in the sunlight, a sheen of sweat covering his skin. The display of solid muscle caused her face to flush, and her pulse increased.

Spotting her aunt and a group of women sitting off to the side beneath some shady trees, Sarah headed in their direction. Grinding nuts and dried berries with round stones against flat rocks, the women watched the excitement with smiles on their faces. A few older men, her uncle included, stood on the opposite end of the play field, their heads together in heated conversation, obviously discussing the tactics of the game.

Little Bird glanced up at her when Sarah approached. She

motioned for her to take a seat next to her. Sarah eased herself to the ground, and picked up a flat rock and round stone, and reached for a handful of nuts from a woven basket that sat in front of Little Bird.

"What is going on?" Sarah asked, moving her wrist in a rhythmic motion, grinding the round rock over the nuts.

"Chase has taught the children a new game," Little Bird beamed. "It has something to do with a foot and a ball, but I was not clear. Maybe he meant to say not to use the foot, because it is obviously a throwing game. The ball doesn't look like a ball, either. He showed me what he wanted, and I sewed him the type of ball he asked for. It is more oblong in shape than round. Very interesting game, this white man plays."

"The children seem to enjoy it," one of the other women commented, leaning forward to look at Sarah. "Where does this man come from, *Imaah*?"

"First, tell us how Snow Bird is doing," Little Bird interrupted.

"She is well, and so is her son. Where is her husband?"

"He has gone hunting with a group of the young men, in celebration of the impending birth. He went to visit our neighbors to the north. Hawk Soaring is with them, too. He will probably come for a visit with the hunters when they return in a few days." Little Bird smiled brightly at Sarah.

"Hawk Soaring?" Sarah echoed. Why would her aunt mention him in particular? She had been friends with the man since childhood. Her brothers and he had often gotten into mischief together, and Sarah had usually tagged along, to her brothers' great annoyance. She hadn't seen him in several months. He lived with another Tukudeka clan who favored the higher mountain ranges to the north.

"Won't it please you to see him?" Little Bird asked.

"Well, yes, I suppose. I haven't seen him in a while." The

expectant look on her aunt's face, and a few of the other women perplexed her.

"You are not excited about the news?" Shining Water asked.

Sarah shook her head. "There is something you all know that I obviously do not." She laughed.

Little Bird shot her an incredulous stare. "Your father hasn't told you?"

"Told me what? Please stop speaking in riddles," Sarah chuckled, suddenly feeling nervous.

"Hawk Soaring has been to see your father," Shining Water said. "He has asked for you." Her face beamed, obviously pleased to be announcing this news.

Sarah's heart dropped to her stomach. A sick feeling rushed through her.

"When . . ," she choked out the words, "when did he do that?"

Little Bird looked uneasy. "We thought you knew, *Imaah*. This happened before your parents left for the rendezvous. We assumed your father had spoken to you."

"No," Sarah whispered. Her eyes darted to Chase, who was running around with the children, shouting encouragements at them. "No, he hasn't said anything."

She swallowed back the bitterness creeping up her throat. Why would her father not tell her? What could it mean? Never had she believed that he would decide on the man she would marry someday. She always assumed that decision would be left to her.

Her parents had commented often lately that she didn't have a husband, but she had said she wasn't interested in a man. Did her father believe she needed to marry, and he'd made the decision for her? She'd always liked Hawk Soaring. He was a nice man, and a very capable hunter. There was no doubt that he would be a good provider to a family, but her feelings for him did not extend beyond that of friendship. He didn't send her pulses racing like . . . Chase. Sarah blinked back the tears that threatened to spill from her eyes.

"Imaah," Little Bird said gently. "I can see that your heart lies with another. Does this white man plan to ask for you?" She patted Sarah's arm.

"No." Sarah laughed half-heartedly. Her throat constricted tightly. She couldn't even swallow. "He has no such intentions."

CHAPTER SIXTEEN

Chase spotted Sarah sitting in the shade with her aunt and several other women. How long had she been there? He hadn't noticed her coming from that hut. All morning, he'd played an improvised version of football with the village kids. He'd even been able to communicate to Little Bird about making him a football shaped ball. It was a far cry from a real pigskin, but it served its purpose.

He motioned to the kids to keep playing, then strode over to where Sarah sat. She looked worn out.

"Hey." He grinned down at her. He knelt in front of the women, and stuck his hand in the basket, scooping up a handful of nuts and berries, and flashed them all a bright smile. One of the women swatted his hand away, but she had a wide grin on her face.

His attention returned to Sarah, who sat quietly. She looked like she was about to cry. Her aunt kept darting him curious glances, and the other women leaned their heads together, whispering.

"Everything all right?" he asked. "Nothing happened to the mom and baby, did it?"

Sarah looked directly at him for the first time. "No, they're fine."

"Then why so glum?" He didn't wait for an answer, and reached his hand out to her. "Come on, Angel, I've got just the thing to cheer you up."

Her eyes widened.

"Come on," he coaxed. "The opposition is losing pretty badly. They need a wide receiver who can run fast. I think you're just what they need." His grin widened. She had no clue what he was talking about. She hesitated, then reached out and grabbed his hand. He pulled her to her feet the instant she made contact with it. She shot a nervous glance over her shoulder at the women. They smiled brightly, and Chase wondered vaguely at the reason before he led Sarah toward the group of waiting kids.

"You want me to play?" Her eyes grew round.

"Yup." Chase tugged her along when her steps began to falter.

"I don't know how," she protested, a slight note of panic in her voice.

"It's really easy, Angel. All you have to do is catch the ball that this little guy," he pointed to a young boy with a wide smile on his face, "is going to throw to you, and then you run with it." Pointing into the distance, he continued, "See that row of rocks lying on the ground over there?" She nodded. "That's your goal. If you reach those rocks and run past them, you're safe, and your team scores."

"That sounds easy," she said. "All I have to do is run with that ball?"

"Catch it and run." Chase nodded. "And don't let anyone on the other team catch you."

"Okay. If it will help, I'll try it." She smiled at the group of kids.

"Excellent." Chase beamed. He motioned for the kids to take their positions, pointing fingers at kids and showing them where they should stand. Then he handed the ball off to the boy who was his designated quarterback for the opposing team.

"Sarah, you need to stand behind this line of kids. They're going to try and prevent this guy," he pointed to the boy holding the ball, "from throwing it to you, and also to catch the ball themselves. Got it?"

She nodded affirmation.

Chase took up a position at the front of the line toward the outside to give the boy the advantage of a clean throw. He nodded, and the boy jumped back, aimed, and threw the ball. All the kids started shouting at once, and mayhem ensued. Sarah had to run forward since the throw fell short of where she stood, but she caught it at the last second before it would have hit the ground. Smiling brightly, she whirled around, and ran in the direction of the goal.

His heart beat faster at watching her. She would have been a natural at flag football or maybe softball. She had the athleticism for it. Chase darted after her. Her head turned, and he caught the surprised look in her eyes when she saw him in pursuit. Her laughter spurred him on, and it didn't take much for him to overtake her. She screeched when she realized she'd been outrun. He grabbed her around the waist and pulled her to the ground, twisting his body so she'd land on top of him, then quickly rolled her underneath him.

"You're not allowed to do that," she squealed. "That's not fair." Her face was flushed from the excitement, and his gut tightened in response to her radiant smile.

"That, Angel, is called a tackle," he said in a heated whisper, his face inches from hers. If they didn't have an entire village of Indians as spectators . . . He pushed himself off of her, and extended his hand to help her up. She shot him an indignant stare, but accepted his hand.

"You should have told me about that. You never said knocking me down was part of the game." She slapped at the dust on her pants.

He shrugged sheepishly. "For once, I wanted to have the advantage over you," he said. "You wanna try again?"

"No, I think I've had quite enough," she scoffed.

"Suit yourself." Chase grinned. "I think I've had enough for a while, too. Those kids sure have a lot of endurance. We've been going strong all morning."

"They obviously enjoy your game." She called something to the children, who responded with disappointed groans and turned down faces.

"Tell them we're taking a time out, and play again later," Chase offered. She'd obviously told them the game was over.

The children scattered when Sarah shouted to them again, several boys giving chase to one kid who carried the ball. They'd carry on their own version of the game.

"I need to check on Snow Bird," Sarah said suddenly. "I'll return shortly."

"Sure, Angel. I'll just go and chat with Elk Runner. Your uncle is a real riot, when he's not trying to kill me. Maybe he has some of that great-tasting meat left that he gave me last night."

The slow, almost evil grin on Sarah's face made him nervous.

"What?" he asked, throwing his hands up.

"My uncle gave you some meat?" she asked, her grin widening.

"Yeah," he said hesitantly.

"Did you like the taste of coyote?" she asked innocently. She laughed. The look on his face must have been quite amusing.

"I was eating dog?" He wasn't sure whether to laugh, or throw up.

"No, not dog. The Tukudeka value their dogs. But a coyote . . . my uncle has a certain liking for it. He used to try and feed it to me and my brothers, but my mother usually intervened."

"You could have warned me sooner," he grumbled, but smiled at her. "It was good, though."

Sarah's smile faded. A distant, haunting look came over her. Chase wondered at the abrupt change in her. Her body language changed, too. She no longer seemed relaxed, but stiff, and ill at ease.

"I will return," she said solemnly.

Chase wondered at her behavior. He watched her walk off toward that hut where she'd spent the entire night, then spotted Elk Runner and some men sitting around a large campfire, a shallow basket between them. When he approached, he noticed a bunch of small stones in the basket. They were obviously playing some version of a dice game.

"You want play?" Elk Runner grinned broadly, and motioned for Chase to sit down beside him.

"No thanks. I think I'll just watch." He pointed his fingers to his eyes, then at the basket. Elk Runner shrugged, then picked up the basket and gave it a toss. The stones flew in the air and landed in a scattered array in the tray. The men all shouted and laughed at once. Chase had no clue what the little symbols painted on the stones meant. Elk Runner scoffed, and tossed some kind of animal fur on the ground.

"You want more eat?" Elk Runner motioned with his fingers to his mouth. Chase held up a hand, waving it in front of him.

"Not what you're cooking, man," he said. Elk Runner's grin broadened. The other men laughed.

Chase continued to watch the men play their dice game,

but his eyes kept darting to the hut at the far end of the village, wishing Sarah would reappear. Why had she suddenly clammed up like that? They'd had a few tense moments and arguments yesterday on the way here, but she'd relaxed and turned almost playful just before they reached the village. Had she wanted him to kiss her again? He didn't know what to make of that look in her eyes when she'd stood so close to him and told him he was a good man. He chuckled at the memory of her words. *Yeah, right.*

His back straightened when he spotted Sarah ducking out of that hut again. He was about to excuse himself from the men, when Elk Runner cuffed him on the shoulder.

"*Imaah,*" he nodded toward Sarah, "beautiful woman, no?"

Was this a loaded question? Chase didn't know how to answer. Elk Runner seemed to enjoy a good laugh. It might get him in a heap of trouble if he answered the wrong way, and he didn't want to do or say anything to embarrass Sarah. Of course she was gorgeous, he wanted to shout. Any man would think so. He merely shrugged. "She saved my life," he said. "I'm very grateful to her for that."

"She marry soon," Elk Runner commented with indifference, but Chase felt the man's eyes boring into him. His stomach constricted as if he'd been sucker punched when the meaning of Elk Runner's words sank in. Sarah was getting married? Why hadn't she mentioned that to him? Was she marrying one of them? His eyes involuntarily moved through camp, as if he'd be able to single out her intended husband. The majority of the people here were older men, women, and children.

"My son . . . go hunt . . . celebrate new child," Elk Runner kept talking. Chase wasn't sure he wanted to hear more. "*Imaah's* soon husband . . . go with him. Come home, two days."

Okay, so the guy wasn't here. *What difference is it to you, Russell? You won't be here much longer anyway.*

"That's great for her," he managed to say with as much cheer as possible. At the moment, he just wanted to get the hell away from everyone and be alone. He was about to push himself off the ground, when Elk Runner's hand rested on his shoulder, applying pressure to keep him sitting. Chase raised his eyebrows at the man.

"Sometime . . . two men," he held up two fingers in front of his face, "want same woman."

Chase groaned silently. Was it that obvious that he had the hots for Sarah? Elk Runner was extremely perceptive. He didn't know what else to do, so he laughed.

"If you're thinking I'm interested in Sarah, you're wrong. I'm trying to get back home. I won't be here a whole lot longer." He sure hoped he sounded indifferent.

"You good . . . strong man," Elk Runner insisted. "You no want wife?"

"Nope." Chase shook his head. "I kinda like my freedom."

Elk Runner laughed. "My brother, White Wolf say same thing many years ago."

Chase sighed. Why was he having this conversation with this man? "Yeah, so did he ever get married?"

"Marry good woman . . . *Imaah's* mother."

"Your brother is Sarah's father?" Chase's mind reeled. "What can you tell me about her mother? How did your brother meet her?"

Elk Runner's forehead wrinkled. "*Imaah* ask same question two days ago."

She did, did she now. That was interesting. She didn't believe him that he came from the future, or that he thought her mother came from the future, but apparently he had planted a seed of doubt in her mind.

"Yeah, so what did you tell her?"

Elk Runner shook his head. "You ask *Imaah*." His tone told Chase he wouldn't be arguing the point. Then the man smiled brightly again, and slapped Chase on the back. "You go . . . I show how hunt bighorn . . . soon, no?"

"Uh, thanks, Elk Runner, but like I said, I won't be here long. I have to get home."

Elk Runner waved a hand in dismissal. "When Tukudeka lose way, find answers from spirits. You are lost man, Chase Russell."

"You can say that again." Chase inhaled deeply. "But right now, you need to excuse me." He jumped up before Elk Runner could hold him back or say anything else. He headed straight for Sarah, who sat with the group of women again.

Without saying anything, he grabbed her arm and hauled her to her feet. "We need to talk," he said gruffly, and pushed her in front of him toward the edge of the village.

"Let go of me." She squirmed, trying to loosen his hold on her arm. "What are you doing?"

"I'll let go, but you're coming with me, so we can talk in private."

Sarah glanced over her shoulder. Chase did the same. All eyes were on them. Her uncle still sat with the group of men, grinning broadly in their direction. Chase released her arm, and led the way into the forest. Only when they were out of sight of the village, did he slow down.

"What is going on?" Sarah's eyes shot daggers at him.

"Why didn't you tell me you were engaged to be married?" Chase blurted out. Why did this bother him so much? He had to get an answer from her, to find out if Elk Runner was telling the truth, or if he'd simply tried to get a reaction out of him. Sarah's face turned ashen. Apparently he had his answer. She hadn't spoken yet, and he turned away from her.

"I . . . I didn't even know myself." Her soft voice prompted him to face her again.

"Explain yourself," he demanded.

"Apparently Hawk Soaring came to see my father and asked for me before they went to rendezvous. I didn't know. My father hasn't said anything to me."

"So, you're not allowed to choose your own husband? Your father arranges the marriage?"

"I always believed he would allow me to choose."

"Do you love the guy?"

Sarah looked stunned. "I . . . he's a good friend," she stammered.

"That doesn't answer the question," Chase ground out.

Sarah took a step back. Her eyes narrowed, and anger blazed in them. "How dare you!" she scoffed. "What business is it of yours whether I like, or love, a man or not? What has gotten into you?" Her hands were on her hips now. "I don't need to tell you anything."

Chase paced back and forth in front of her, his hand behind his neck. He inhaled and exhaled long and slow a few times, trying to get his jumbled emotions in check. She was right. He had no business asking her these things.

You're jealous, Russell. What the hell? This was new to him.

"We will leave in the morning. The other women will tend to Snow Bird now. It is too late to leave today. I hope you can be civil until then," Sarah said, her tone icy. She turned and stormed off in the direction of the village.

Chase watched her march off. What did he expect? Sarah had her life to lead. If she wanted to marry this Hawk guy, then so be it, but he didn't need to stick around to watch it happen. He had to find a way back home, dammit. Sarah's mother held the answer.

The Grand Tetons. Those snow-capped mountains were pretty hard to miss. If he headed south, he'd be sure to walk

PEGGY L HENDERSON

right past them. The great lake she had talked about could only be Jackson Lake. If there was some kind of big meeting going on in that area, he would find it. He made up his mind. He'd get some rest tonight, and before anyone else woke in the morning, he'd be gone from here.

CHAPTER SEVENTEEN

"*Y*ou and your son are doing well." Sarah smiled brightly at Snow Bird. The young woman returned her smile, but her eyes looked tired.

"My husband will be back soon. He said he will bring meat as a gift to the village in celebration of the birth."

Sarah nodded. Snow Bird's husband was Elk Runner's and Little Bird's youngest son, Touch the Cloud. The love he had for his young wife was unmistakable. Sarah had often seen the way they stole glances at each other. That's how it should be between a husband and a wife. Her own parents still acted like that after many years of marriage.

Could she learn to love Hawk Soaring? They got along well together. If her father insisted on the marriage, she couldn't refuse him. Chase's smiling, handsome face flashed before her eyes. Her heart fluttered involuntarily. Her mother's words the day before they left for rendezvous unexpectedly came back to her.

One day you'll meet a man and fall in love. Time will stand still whenever he's near, and the outside world forgotten when you're with him.

Sarah inhaled sharply. Chase made her feel that way, she realized suddenly. Was she in love with him? How could that be possible? She had known him no longer than a week. Was it possible to fall in love with someone in that short amount of time?

"Your thoughts are far away, *Imaah.* " Snow Bird's softly spoken words startled Sarah out of her thoughts.

"When did you first know you loved Touch the Cloud?" she blurted out.

Snow Bird smiled. "I think I knew the moment I first set eyes on him. My family traveled to this village, and he'd just returned from a hunt. He was so proud of the bighorn he killed. His father introduced us, and I think he felt as I did right from the start." She looked down at the infant at her breast. "And here is the first of many sons I will give him as proof of our love."

Snow Bird's eyes came up and met Sarah's. "Do you have feelings of love for Hawk Soaring?"

Sarah rolled her eyes. "Does everyone know but me?"

"You didn't know he went to your father?" Snow Bird's eyes grew round.

"I just found out from Little Bird yesterday," she sighed.

Snow Bird reached out a hand to touch Sarah on the shoulder. "You do not love him." It was a statement, not a question.

"What am I to do?" Sarah bit back tears that threatened to spill. "I think my heart belongs to someone else."

"Perhaps this man will approach your father as well," Snow Bird offered. Sarah laughed.

"He doesn't know my feelings. He only arrived in the mountains a short time ago, and he wishes to return to his home. He is not looking to share his life with a woman."

Snow Bird nodded silently. "In time, the answer will come to you. Many marriages begin as only friendship.

Perhaps you can learn to love Hawk Soaring. He is a good provider."

Sarah didn't answer. After minutes of silence, she finally said, "I must be on my way home. I will visit again in one month when you are able to leave the hut. I don't want to miss when you introduce your son to his father."

"I don't like to have to wait that long," Snow Bird said. "But it is tradition, and it would be bad luck to break it. What will I do for one month in this wickiup?"

"Just what all the other new mothers do. Enjoy your son, make him a cradle, and clothing. You will be grateful for this time alone. Little Bird will no doubt spend time with you."

Sarah gathered her belongings that she'd tossed along the wall of the hut. "Farewell, Snow Bird," she said, and gave the other woman a quick hug.

"Farewell, *Imaah*. I am grateful to you for coming as my midwife."

Sarah nodded, and stepped out into the bright morning light. She sighed deeply, and glanced around at the other huts. Women were busy starting cooking fires. Men sat around, sharpening knives, or working on arrowheads. Elk Runner stood with Little Bird, watching her add meat to her cooking pot.

"Is Chase awake yet?" Sarah asked when she approached her aunt and uncle. The two shot quick glances at each other.

"He has already left the village, *paite*," Elk Runner said. "I saw him leave before dawn. When I asked him where he was going, he would not tell me, only that it is his wish for you to remain here."

Sarah's hand flew to her mouth. "No," she gasped. "I have to go. I'm sorry for leaving without a proper good-bye, but I have to find him. Please tell everyone I am sorry. And, Uncle, keep Grizzly here. He is not well enough yet to travel again."

Panic gripped her insides. Chase had no intention of

returning to the cabin. He was going to try and find the rendezvous.

~

CHASE STRAINED his wrists against the leather that bound his hands behind his back. His forehead beaded with sweat. He'd been left to stand tied to a pole for hours already, and the warm afternoon sun had beat down on him relentlessly all day. He was glad to be wearing a shirt, or his skin would be cooked. He licked his dry and cracking lips. He'd give anything for a drink of water at the moment.

Russell, you're such a flippin' idiot! Sarah had been right, of course. Amazed that he'd been able to find his way back to the cabin, Chase hadn't stopped there. He'd trekked on, heading south along the Firehole at a jog for most of the early afternoon.

That group of Indians had come at him out of nowhere. He didn't even have time to pull his ax from his belt. If they'd have offered him a good bar brawl, he might have been able to do some damage, but they'd pointed their spears and rifles at him, and tied him up like a Christmas turkey. Sarah had said they'd kill him on the spot. He wondered now why they hadn't done it. They'd forced him along through dense forest and an open meadow to their village that was set up along a wide, fast-moving river. It was quite a bit different that the Indian village he'd just left that morning.

These Blackfoot lived in teepees covered in hides, as opposed to wooden huts. This tribe was also much larger than the small clan of Tukudeka that lived together. Women and children, and more men had shouted and cheered when the six warriors had brought him in and paraded him to the center of the village. Gritting his teeth, Chase had imagined himself at the beginning of a football game, the crowd cheering as the team entered the stadium.

He hung his head. His arms throbbed from the unnatural position of having them tied behind his back all these hours. He used the tree trunk he was tied to as support to keep himself upright. Why the hell didn't they just get it over with and end his miserable life? *You've failed again, Russell. You're just a sorry-ass loser.*

At least the air seemed cooler now, with the sun beginning to set behind the mountains to the west. No one had approached him all afternoon. A few kids had thrown some dirt and sticks at him, which he had ignored.

A loud commotion startled him out of his half asleep state. His head felt heavy when he raised it to find out why the people were shouting once again. At the edge of the village, a large group had gathered, and someone was walking up from the river.

What the hell! Chase squinted to see better. Goddamn her! What was she doing? Sarah marched among the villagers, her hands raised high above her head, showing her weapons meant no harm to anyone. A few of the warriors had rifles trained on her.

"No, Sarah. Why did you have to follow me," he rasped.

No one heard him. His heart slammed in his chest, afraid of what these Indians would do to her. No one tried to stop her, however. She was speaking to them, but he couldn't hear it. Her voice didn't carry all the way to him. She stopped suddenly, and looked right at him. She was too far away yet for him to see the expression on her face. Then she walked straight toward him.

"Angel, why did you come here?" His voice sounded pathetic in his own ears. She stood in front of him, her eyes filled with fear. Wordlessly, she uncorked her water bag and lifted it to his mouth. He gulped the cool liquid as fast as he could, half of it dripping down his face. Suddenly, the bag was yanked out of her hands. Sarah shot the offender a murderous glare, but the man only sniggered at her. He grabbed her roughly by the arm and pulled her away.

"Leave her alone, you son of a bitch," Chase ground out. *What the hell are you gonna do, Russell? A man is supposed to protect the girl, not the other way around.*

Sarah didn't put up a fight when the Indian pulled her along behind him, and Chase could only watch helplessly as she disappeared inside one of the tipis. She hadn't said a word to him.

CHAPTER EIGHTEEN

*C*hase woke from dozing. He groaned at the pain in his shoulders. The sky was still gray, and an eerie mist hovered over the river. It must be early morning. He'd drifted in and out of sleep all night, wondering what was happening with Sarah. She hadn't come out of that tipi, as far as he could tell. Dammit! If anything happened to her because of his stupidity . . . He clenched his jaw.

The village came alive, as men and women milled about. His stomach growled loudly in response to the smell of food in the air when women set to work preparing their morning meals. Some of the warriors began to crowd closer around him. He stared up at them, unflinching. Let them do what they wanted to him, as long as they didn't harm Sarah. Several women stepped forward and began beating him with sticks. The men all laughed. He ground his teeth. Hell would freeze over before they'd see him cower. This was no worse than a fraternity hazing during pledge week.

Suddenly, the beatings stopped and the men and women stepped back, parting a path to one of the tipis. Sarah crawled from the opening and hurried toward him. Chase let out a sigh of relief. Thank God she was all right. She approached him, and the anguished look in her eyes alarmed him. What had they done to her?

She looked into his eyes when she stood before him. Hesitantly, she cupped his face between her hands and kissed him lightly on the mouth. Her lips lingered. The unexpected gesture sent a shock of adrenaline through him, and he leaned into her as far as his restraints allowed. At that moment, he knew he would give his life for her. The intensity of his feelings overwhelmed him.

She broke the kiss, and he leaned forward, touching his forehead to hers. He didn't want the contact to end. He cursed the bindings that prevented him from reaching out to her, aching to hold her in his arms. His breathing came fast, still basking in the sensation of her soft lips pressed to his.

"Now what did I do to deserve that?" he whispered. His raspy voice had gone husky.

"How fast can you run?" she asked, still holding his face between her hands, her eyes shimmering with unshed tears.

He gave a short laugh. "Angel, I'm not in any position to run anywhere right now. I'm kinda tied up at the moment." He hoped his grin belied the cold fear that swept over him. She wasn't planning an escape, was she? "How did the Pow Wow go in there?" He gestured with his head toward the tipi she'd come from.

"They are willing to let me go," Sarah said softly, her lips trembling. Her fingers caressed his stubbly jaw. "They know who I am, and don't want to jeopardize trading with my father."

"Then go," Chase implored without hesitation. "What are you waiting for?" There was no hope for him.

"How fast can you run?" she asked again.

Chase's brows furrowed. "I can hold my own. Why?"

"You will be given a chance to run for your freedom," she answered. "The Blackfoot enjoy making sport of white men."

"And exactly how is this game going to work?" Hell, if he was given a chance to run for his life, he'd take it.

Sarah inhaled deeply. "You will be stripped of all your clothing and your shoes. They will give you a knife, nothing else. You will be told to run, and the young warriors will then hunt you down."

Chase shrugged. "Sounds like fun." He flashed her a cocky smile.

"Why do you make jokes?" Sarah stepped away from him, her eyes blazing in sudden anger. "You will die. This is not a game they will let you win."

"Have a little faith in me, Angel. I know I've screwed up, but maybe I can prove that I'm not completely incompetent." He hoped his voice projected confidence. His insides certainly didn't feel it. His face grew serious. The blue pools in Sarah's eyes threatened to spill over.

"Kiss me again, Angel, and I'll run to hell and back," he growled and leaned his face toward hers. She hesitated before stepping up to him, then pressed her lips to his again. He strained against the leather bindings, even as they sliced through his wrists. He pulled harder, deepening the kiss, claiming Sarah's lips with an intensity of a condemned man savoring his last meal. She didn't back away. Slowly, her arms crept up and around his neck, and she stepped closer to him, molding her body to his. Chase groaned.

A sudden hard yank brought him back to his senses. He panted, even as two Indians pulled him away from Sarah. She tried to reach for him, but another set of arms prevented her. Their eyes met. Tears spilled down her face. He'd give anything at that moment to take away the pain in her eyes.

"Run north from here, across the river and meadow. The forest leads over a mountain to a valley. You will see steam rising in the distance, coming from a place my mother calls a geyser basin. Once you reach that basin, and cross the Firehole River there, you will be safe. I will wait for you."

The warrior holding Sarah's arms shoved her roughly toward the tipi. Chase watched her stumble along. Her head kept turning back toward him.

"I'll be there, Angel," he yelled out to her.

Sarah disappeared inside the tipi again. As long as she was unharmed, he didn't give a damn what happened to him. He eyed the warriors who now circled him, most leering with contempt. One man, who wore a fox fur over his head, stepped forward. He spoke directly to him. Chase didn't have a clue what he said.

Foxhead motioned to one of the other warriors, who pulled a knife from his belt and approached him. Chase didn't move. He wasn't going to cower in front of them. If they were going to kill him right now, at least he'd have the satisfaction that he wouldn't die begging for mercy.

The warrior sliced the ropes that bound him with one quick jerk of the knife, then held the sharp blade to Chase's throat with a cold smile on his face. Chase held the Indian's stare while rubbing circulation back into his raw and tingling wrists.

The man wearing the fox on his head spoke sharply to the other Indian, who backed off. Chase guessed he must be some kind of chief or leader. Foxhead motioned with his hands as he spoke again to Chase. The other warriors around him laughed. The message became clear. He was being told to strip. Slowly, Chase pulled his shirt over his head, and waited. The chief motioned to his britches and moccasins.

Chase shot him a cocky grin. Yeah. If they wanted a peep show, they'd get one. He eyed the women standing around the periphery of the circle. Leisurely, like a practiced male stripper, he pulled first one, then the other moccasin off his feet. Then he released the thongs loose at his waist, and unhurriedly slid the britches over his hips and down his legs. He raised himself to his full height, and held his arms out at his sides, like Da Vinci's Vitruvian man. The chief actually flashed him a smile. Chase was glad that Sarah wasn't here to witness his humiliation. She'd be mortified, anyway. He glanced in the direction of the tipi.

He counted about twenty young men who now stepped forward and began yelling and whooping, punching the air, holding spears and knives, or tomahawks.

So, this must be the opposing team. Okay, Russell. Scorpions against Blackfeet. The odds were not good, he realized, but he'd brought his team back to victory after things looked dismal on more than one occasion. *All you have to do now is think of your game plan. You're the quarterback. It's your responsibility to lead your team to victory.*

The trouble was, he didn't know his opposing team's tactics. This game would have to play itself out on the fly. *You weren't All Star for nothing, Russell. Prove that you haven't lost your touch.*

The chief thrust a hunting knife in Chase's hand, and pointed in the direction across the river. The shouting and hollering of every Indians in the tribe grew deafening. Chase glared at Foxhead, and tipped his index and middle fingers to his temple in a mock salute. He inhaled deeply, then expelled the air quickly through an open mouth. With a war cry of his own, he took off running.

Game plan, Russell. What's your game plan? He didn't have one yet. For the moment, it had to be wait and see tactics. He had to get to know his opposing team first. He threw a quick glance over his shoulder. The whooping and hollering continued. For a split second, he thought he'd seen Sarah, but he couldn't be sure.

The shouting increased, and Chase knew that his opponents were in pursuit. They sure didn't give him much of a head start. His one hope at the moment was to put enough distance between him and them to give him time to maneuver. If they outran him, it would be all over.

Chase plunged into the river. The cold water shocked him for a split second, but he swam underwater until he reached the opposite shore. He used the strong current to his advantage, letting it sweep him downriver quite a distance. Gasping for breath, he emerged and scrambled up the bank. His hand clutched the knife tightly. The splashing behind him told him he didn't have much of a lead.

Without turning to look for his pursuers, he sprinted on, swiping a hand at the water dripping down his face. He had to cross the open meadow to reach the forest in the distance. Perhaps there he could lose them. The grass beneath him concealed clods of dry, packed dirt and rocks, and he gritted his teeth, ignoring the pain whenever he stepped on hard earth. At least the grass itself was cool and moist, soothing the injuries to his unprotected feet.

His lungs burned, and he pumped his arms furiously, his head held high as he ran. Once he ventured a glance over his shoulders. The warriors had spread out, but he had a good twenty-five yard lead on his closest pursuer. Hopefully they weren't planning on throwing their weapons. He had no idea how far those spears could fly through the air.

Chase found a rhythm in his stride, and focused on the trees ahead. They had to be at least a mile away. *A mile sprint is nothing, Russell.* Inhaling through his nose, and exhaling through his mouth, he ran with his elbows at his sides, pumping his legs to move faster. The knife in his hand became his football, and the trees up ahead were the goal line. He was running for a touchdown. He swore he could hear the roar of the crowd.

Another hundred yards closer to the trees, and the

ground suddenly became moist. Too late, he realized he was running straight into a boggy marsh. He veered to the right, then quickly changed his mind and headed left. He had to keep going north. He splashed through the thick, soupy quagmire, the stench of rotting vegetation stinging his lungs. A swarm of mosquitos pursued him now, along with those Indians. The air became so thick with the pesky flying insects, he had to close his mouth to keep from inhaling too many.

He turned his head to venture another glance over his shoulder. Several Indians had dropped far behind. There were about six or seven that were still way too close for comfort. Chase pushed on, his pace slowing considerably as he splashed through the mud. He hit a deep spot and stumbled, almost losing his balance completely. For a moment he was grateful that he was barefoot.

Finally, he reached the first trees. The earth beneath him turned firm and dry again. He slowed his pace, darting back and forth between trees while still moving forward, like a jackrabbit. Hell, that's what he felt like - a rabbit being chased by a hungry pack of wolves.

The forest actually blanketed a steep mountainside, which hadn't been apparent from a distance. Chase scrambled up the mountain, his thigh muscles on fire from exertion, but he forced himself forward. Keeping his eyes on the ground to navigate his way up the rocky mountain, he noticed his feet bleeding from the many jagged roots that stuck out of the ground and sliced his soles. He gritted his teeth and dug into his inner reserves.

He could almost see the summit, or what he hoped was the summit, when a loud war cry behind him made him whirl around. The first of his pursuers had caught him. With a fierce grimace on his face, the warrior rushed him, a tomahawk held over his head, ready to deliver a death blow.

Chase didn't think. He merely reacted. His left arm swung back, then forward. He thrust the knife at his opponent. The man's momentum drove him directly into the sharp blade. Chase felt the drag of his knife sliding into meat. The warrior froze, his eyes bulging and wide open. Chase roared and pulled his knife back, and gave the warrior a shove with his right hand. He fell backwards down the incline, his body connecting with a tree trunk with a loud thud. He lay motionless. Chase stared at the lifeless form, stunned and struggling to fill his lungs with air.

You've just killed a man, Russell.

He gasped for breath. Bile rose to his throat. *Don't think about it. He would have killed you. This was self-defense.*

Scurrying movement between the trees further down the hill alerted him that several more of his pursuers had caught up. His eyes darted quickly around. The warrior's tomahawk lay on the ground a few feet from him. Chase grabbed for it. He now had two weapons. Without another look back, he continued up the mountain, unmindful of the burning in his legs. By the time he reached the summit, and the ground mercifully leveled out, he struggled against passing out. Black spots danced before his eyes, and his lungs burned with every breath he inhaled.

He wiped at some sweat on his face and under his nose with the back of his hand, and licked his dry lips. He tasted salt and something coppery in his mouth. When he looked down, his hand was streaked red. Had he exerted himself to the point of bleeding from his lungs?

He swallowed, which was futile, since he had no moisture in his mouth. It only caused his throat to hurt more. Glancing over his shoulders, the group that had been closest to him gathered around their dead companion. They let out a loud war whoop, and three took off up the incline.

Time to go, Russell.

Chase scanned the landscape below him. Down the sloping hill loomed a vast valley that he needed to cross. Bison grazed in the distance, and a wide stream or river cut through the meadow. Beyond the river, behind more trees, smoke plumes billowed in the wind. It had to be the geyser basin Sarah had mentioned. Once he reached that, the Fire-hole River was within his grasp. The meadow looked daunting. He had no idea how many miles across it was just to reach the river. And those bison were right in his path.

He inhaled deeply, closed his eyes, and then his mind, against the pain in his feet and lungs, and scurried down the hill. Losing his footing in the loose dirt, he fell against a large boulder, and with a cry of pain, tumbled down the mountainside amidst dirt and debris. Spitting and coughing when his descent was halted by a tree trunk, he quickly scrambled back on his feet. He shot a hasty glance up from where he'd come. Two bodies moved cautiously down the hill. He grimaced and clutched his right side where he'd hit the tree. Breathing became more painful.

He limped onward, gritting his teeth against the pain in his feet, his side, and in his lungs, until he was past the tree line on flat ground again. The open meadow loomed in front of him. Chase leaned forward, his hands on his knees, trying to catch his breath. His eyes darted to the right and left. There was no other way. He had to run straight across the open grassland. It was the fastest way to get to that geyser basin.

His head darted around over his shoulder at the sound of rustling leaves, dirt, and gravel rolling downhill. His two pursuers were relentless. Chase clutched the knife in one hand, and the ax in the other. If he was going down, it would be fighting.

Sarah's face suddenly flashed before his eyes. He closed them tightly for a mere second to see her image more clearly in his mind. Her vision smiled in encouragement, before she turned. She was walking away from him. Every few steps, she glanced over her shoulder, her long mahogany waves blowing in the breeze. She smiled seductively, and once beckoned him with her index finger.

"I'm coming, Sarah," he called. Clenching his jaw, he took off running. Sarah's image began to fade in and out of sight. He ran faster. He had to catch up to her. She wasn't going to wait for him.

"Don't leave, Sarah. I won't fail you. I'm coming."

Chase pushed himself to greater speed. His arms and legs pumped like pistons, his breathing coming in regular, rhythmic breaths. Sarah was almost out of sight.

"Wait!" he yelled. "Don't leave me, Angel. I love you! Don't leave me." His hand reached out. He tried to grab for her. The vision disappeared. Chase opened his eyes fully. He kept running. The bison materialized closer up ahead.

"I love you, Sarah," he shouted into the wind.

The truth of his words fueled him on. He loved her. Why hadn't he realized it before? *You've never been in love, Russell. How could you know?* Now that he'd said the words out loud, he knew them to be true with absolute certainty.

Nothing would stop him now from reaching the Firehole. He was running for his life, running to the woman he loved, and for the first time ever, he felt free. His lungs burned and his heart pounded in his throat. It was the most exhilarating feeling he'd ever had, and he felt alive.

He turned his head, looking over his shoulder again. Only one pursuer remained. The other had barely left the tree line. The one behind him was close enough that he could throw the spear he held in his hand.

Game time, Russell. Do something the opposition will least likely expect.

Chase stopped in his tracks. He whirled around, and

assumed a fighting stance, his legs wide apart, his knees bent, and his arms out at his sides. He clutched his weapons in his hands. Breathing hard, a wide sneer crossed his face. The maneuver had worked.

His opponent looked stunned and surprised. He tried to stop, tried to brandish his spear, but in his shocked disbelief, he tripped and fell to the ground. With a loud splintering noise, the spear broke in half. Chase gave him no chance to recover. With a loud roar he ran at the man on the ground. He dropped his weapons and grabbed for the broken lance.

The man struggled, but Chase used his size to his advantage, holding the warrior to the ground. He rammed the spearhead into the dirt, pinning the man's shirt into the dirt. He could have easily killed the warrior, but he couldn't bring himself to do it. He hoped rendering him immobile would buy enough time to put some distance between them.

Chase stood and righted himself. His other pursuer was gaining ground, and he could also see several more warriors emerge from the trees. He lunged for his weapons, and took off again, straight for the bison herd. He remembered all the warning pamphlets he'd read that the park service provided, which stated to stay at least twenty-five yards away from bison. They were dangerous and could gore a man in seconds.

To hell with that.

Chase needed another tactical surprise element. He ran straight for the herd. Several of the lumbering beasts looked up from their grazing when he approached. He didn't slow down. He ran and darted between the big beasts. Several shied away, kicking and galloping in the opposite direction – the direction his pursuers came from. Chase whooped and punched the air with one hand, sending even more bison scurrying.

He could hear the rushing sound of the river now. It was

just up ahead. He'd made it through the herd unharmed. He hoped his tactics had paid off. He couldn't run any further. Plunging head first into the cold water, he welcomed the soothing feeling on his scorched skin. He gulped mouthfuls of water even as he swam downstream, aided by the current. He was swept past a beaver lodge. What had Sarah told him?

"I once hid from my brothers for an entire day inside a beaver lodge. They were so furious with me that I outsmarted them."

"Thank you, Angel." He grinned. He pulled himself through the water, back upstream toward the beaver dam. He dove and swam under the lodge, until he found the opening. When he resurfaced, he was in a dark, muddy chamber. A beaver sat in the mud, chatting loudly at seeing the intruder. Chase ignored it.

How long would he have to stay hidden? The cold water began to chill him, and it was dank inside the lodge. He pulled himself up onto the muddy platform. The beaver abandoned his perch and dove into the water, slapping his tail in protest. Did those Indians know this little trick? He could be a sitting duck for all he knew.

He drew his legs up close to his body, shivering as the minutes turned to hours. Once, he thought he'd heard voices just above, but they'd quickly died away. His surroundings darkened even more. Chase huddled against the mud, gritting his chattering teeth. He closed his eyes. If he could sleep for a few hours, he could continue to the geyser basin in the morning. It might be best in the cover of night, but he'd get lost. In the blackness, he wouldn't be able to see anything.

He drifted in and out of sleep. Sarah's face materialized before him. Imagining her smile warmed his insides.

He was in love with her.

The realization still stunned him. Did she have feelings for him, too? Why should she? He wasn't the kind of man she needed. She needed a strong man who knew his way around the mountains and would protect her from its dangers. He couldn't even keep his own ass out of trouble.

Her father had probably already given her in marriage to that Indian guy. Anger boiled inside him when he thought of her in the arms of someone else, of another man touching her, making love to her. He shook his head. It was probably for the best. *What could she possibly see in you, Russell? You're nothing but a screw-up.*

Would her old man simply sell her to the highest bidder? Is that how marriage was arranged among the Indians? He had no idea how to barter for a woman in this time. The thought was ludicrous. He still needed to get home to his own time. He couldn't let her know how he felt about her. She'd probably just laugh in his face.

Chase woke with a start. Faint sunlight streamed in through some of the tightly-woven branches above him. He clenched his teeth and hissed when he tried to move. How long had he slept in this folded up position? He forced his legs to stretch. He was numb from the cold, his body caked in dirt. Blood splattered his chest, and his feet looked like they'd been put through a meat grinder.

You need to get moving. You can't stay here.

He scooted off the muddy ledge into the water with a soft splash, biting his lips when his raw feet touched the water. Inhaling deeply, he dove and swam under water, and resurfaced near the shoreline. He emerged slowly, grateful that the riverbank was overgrown with tall grasses. At least it would provide some cover. He glanced around. The bison had moved on. A hawk fluttered nearby, squawking loudly. Other than that, he saw nothing but wide-open meadow. He hoisted himself up out of the water, and sank back to the ground onto his back. The warmth of the early morning sun did little to stop his shivering.

Get up, Russell. You need to move.

He was so damn tired. There wasn't a spot on his body that didn't hurt. His stomach growled loudly.

Chase stood and wobbled on unsteady legs. Walking on broken glass through hot coals had to be less painful than the agony in his feet at the moment. He forced himself to walk in the direction of the smoke plumes. It couldn't be more than a couple miles. He had to at least work the stiffness out of his legs. He could deal with the pain in his feet. He swung his arms back and forth to increase the circulation in his body, and his strides lengthened.

He looked ahead, scanning the distance. Any second now, he expected his pursuers to materialize out of the forest up ahead. Had they given up? Somehow he didn't think so.

CHAPTER NINETEEN

Sarah paced along the riverbank. The horse she'd been given to return home on cropped lazily at the tall grasses. She hadn't slept all night. Was Chase dead? Surely someone would have announced their victory to her by now if he had been killed. She fought the urge to mount up and cross the Firehole, and search for him. Chief Heavy Moccasin had warned her not to interfere. If she was found on the other side of the Firehole, his warriors had permission to kill her, too.

She recalled some of the horrific tales told by other trappers of the Blackfoot toying with their captives. The games were never intended to bring victory to the unfortunate prisoner. They were designed to torture and prolong death. Chase didn't stand a chance. She had never heard of anyone surviving one of these cruel games.

She'd known there was no hope for him the moment Heavy Moccasin had told her of his intent. She had bartered and pleaded with him for Chase's life to no avail. She'd even threatened that her father would no longer trade with the tribe.

Heavy Moccasin had merely laughed at her, saying he would not bargain with a woman, and she should consider herself fortunate that she'd be allowed to return to her home unharmed. He even granted her a brief moment to speak with Chase. Out of respect for her father, he had given her the use of a horse, and allowed her to retrieve Chase's clothing. When she'd left the village, he had told her someone would send her a piece of Chase's body as a gift. It was considered a great honor. Sarah swallowed back the bitterness in her throat at the thought.

The horse suddenly popped its head up. Grass hung from its lips. Its ears were pricked and its head turned toward the river. Sarah's heart beat faster. What had the horse seen or heard? She grabbed for her rifle and scanned into the distance. She couldn't see anything except the smoke and mist from the hot water pools on the opposite side of the river.

The horse didn't resume its grazing. It moved around nervously, and Sarah was grateful that she'd remembered to hobble the mare's front legs together to keep her from running off. Something was definitely on the other side of the river. Her eyes scanned systematically up and down along the tree line far off in the distance. Suddenly she spotted two warriors. They were running toward the hot springs in her direction. What were they doing? Sarah dared not hope. Was Chase alive? Had he made it this far? It seemed impossible. Those two warriors were definitely trying to position themselves to head someone off.

Sarah continued to scan into the distance, her heart pounding as she struggled to see anything. There! To the south, a figure darted out of the trees. She dared not believe her eyes. Chase!

She laughed, tears streaming down her face. This man, this incredible man was making a mockery out of the mighty

Blackfoot warriors! Several other figures emerged from the forest in hot pursuit. She could hear their frantic war cries. All he had to do was run straight to the river, and he'd be safe. At the pace he was going, he would easily outrun his pursuers.

With a sinking heart, she remembered the two warriors who lay in waiting. Sarah didn't waste another second. She was too far away to shoot, but she could at least warn him. Running upriver toward where she'd seen the two Blackfoot, she spotted them lying on the ground, like cougars ready to spring at an unsuspecting antelope. Sarah aimed her rifle. She wouldn't hit either of them. The distance was too great. But it would alert Chase, and perhaps distract these two.

The sound of the gun echoed into the distance. The two Indians jumped up, whooping loudly.

"Cowards," Sarah yelled at them across the river in the Siksika dialect. The two stared at her from across the water. With trembling hands, she reloaded her flintlock.

"You are nothing but old women, hiding like weaklings."

She peered toward the south. Chase was almost at the river. The two warriors she'd surprised lifted their loincloths behind their backs and bent their rears toward her, laughing loudly, then dashed upriver.

"Chase! Look out!" she called frantically. He must have seen them by now. He didn't alter his speed or his course. In mid-run, he raised his arm, and threw an ax he held in his left hand at the warrior closest to him. The man dropped like a rock.

Sarah pointed her rifle at the other warrior who'd slowed his advance, probably from surprise at his companion's unexpected death. She fired off her shot. It fell short of the Indian by mere feet, sending up dirt, but it gave Chase the advantage he needed. He plunged into the river. She watched him go under, then his head popped up through the waves, and he pulled himself through the strong current to reach the other side.

He was almost to shore, and Sarah ran to meet him. Several of his pursuers reached the other bank, their war cries shrill and loud. Two of the warriors threw their spears. One landed within inches of Chase's head in the water. He scrambled up the embankment, gasping for air. He hadn't pulled himself all the way up when he collapsed onto the soft earth. Sarah dropped to her knees at his side, grabbing his arm, trying to drag him up the riverbank. He didn't budge.

"Move!" she yelled in his ear. "Just a little further."

It was impossible for her to try and pull him. Slowly, and with a long moan, he lifted his upper body and pulled himself up the soft slope. His ragged gasps for air tore at her heart.

Several more spears darted through the air. Sarah shot to her feet.

"He has defeated you all! He is a better warrior than fifty of you put together. Go home and tell your families of your defeat."

The warriors responded with shrill cries of their own at her insults, but none of them would dare cross the river. They all might be angry at their defeat, but the respect they now had for this white man would not allow for a cowardly killing.

Her attention returned to the man lying on the ground. Chase's body heaved with each painful breath. With an agonizing moan, he rolled onto his back. Sarah ran to the horse and grabbed her blanket. She averted her eyes and covered his torso. Tears streamed down her face. She knelt beside him and cradled his head between her hands. His body was covered in dirt, bruises, and blood that the quick plunge through the river did not wash off. She gasped at the condition of his feet. How had he been able to stand, much less run? Raw flesh wounds and cuts marred his soles.

Chase blinked, and opened his eyes. A smile formed on his lips. "Angel?" he rasped between gasps for breath.

"Shhh, don't talk," Sarah whispered, stroking his cheeks.

"Thank . . . God you're okay, Angel." He closed his eyes again, and his body went limp.

"Chase?" Sarah shrank back in shock. No, his chest heaved. He was still breathing. It was unthinkable that he would die after all.

Sarah glanced up and across the river. A group of warriors still stood, watching, probably hoping to claim victory after all if Chase was dead.

"He lives," she yelled. "Go home." Several raised their weapons high in the air, but none of them made a sound. Sarah knew it was a gesture of respect. Slowly, the group turned and headed in the direction from which they'd come.

Her full attention returned to Chase. She had no supplies with her to properly take care of his wounds. The slow trickle of blood from his nose alarmed her. Her mother's teachings came back to her full force. If he stayed lying on his back, he would drown in his own blood.

Sarah pulled at his arm, then shoved at his back, grunting to get him rolled at least on his side. She pulled a piece of deadfall behind him so he couldn't roll onto his back again.

Satisfied that he breathed steadily, she gathered wood for a fire. She wished he hadn't passed out. There was no shelter along the banks of the river. Twenty yards away, the trees would offer protection from wind, but here in the open it would be more difficult to stay warm. She didn't have a choice. She had to build her camp around him. He was too big and heavy for her to move.

Chase began to shiver a short while later. She'd built the fire as close to him as she dared, and added more wood. She pulled his bundle of clothes from the horse's back, unfolding his shirt. Maneuvering him as best as she could, she managed to pull it on him. The blanket would have to be enough to cover his lower half, until he woke and could pull his britches on himself.

Fresh tears welled up in her eyes when she assessed his feet. She needed to clean the dirt off of them somehow. She filled her water bag at the river, and poured the liquid over his feet, gently cleaning away the mud and debris that clung to his open wounds.

Chase flinched and moaned several times, and pulled his feet away, but Sarah kept to her task. Without a second thought to her own comfort should the weather turn cold, she pulled at the shoulder seams of her shirt until the sleeves were free. It would have to do for bandages. She wrapped these around his feet, then pushed his moccasins on to offer more warmth and protection.

All she could do now was watch and wait. She sat by his side, staring down at him while he slept. If he woke soon, there would be time to reach the cabin before the darkness of night. Should she try and rouse him? She could care for him properly in her own home.

Tentatively, she touched trembling fingers to his cheek. Her chest tightened, and she smiled slowly. She loved him. Why this man? She'd never experienced such feelings of joy and warmth in her heart. She loved her parents, and her brothers, but this was different.

She no longer had doubts that Chase could survive in these mountains. He had done what no other man had ever accomplished. All he needed was a guide, a teacher, to show him the way of life here. Chase didn't believe in himself. That much was clear to her. Something had happened to him that prevented him from seeing himself as a capable man. Would he see himself differently now? And how did he see her?

Sarah, stop fooling yourself. He doesn't want to stay in the mountains. He wants to go home. He has made this clear on many occasions.

Even if Chase stayed in the mountains, would he want to be tied to a woman? He had told her he wanted no attachments. Could he learn to care for her? He liked kissing her, she knew that much. But all men enjoyed that, and it didn't have to be with a woman they loved or cared for. She'd seen enough of that at rendezvous, Fort Raymond, and St. Louis.

Sarah sighed. She would not burden him with her thoughts. A man who wanted a wife made his intentions known. Hawk Soaring entered her mind. He had asked for her. She'd never realized he noticed her in that way. If her father insisted she marry him, what would she do? Sarah had no answers. Could she marry one man, even though she loved another?

Chase stirred, pulling her out of her thoughts. His painful moan tore at her heart. She wished she could take away his suffering. His body would need time to heal. He should not be out in the elements in the cold of night. She had to get him home.

"Chase." She touched his shoulder, giving it a gentle shake. "Please wake up." His eyelids opened slowly.

"Sarah?" His voice sounded weak and far away.

"Chase, we need to leave. We can't stay the night here. There is no shelter."

He hissed when he tried to move. "Just . . . go and leave me," he rasped.

Anger suddenly coursed through her. "I did not wait here an entire day and night just to have you die now, Chase Russell. How dare you think I would leave you behind?"

A strained smile formed on his lips. He tried to push

himself on his elbows, then grimaced. He finally managed to pull himself to a sitting position, and glanced down, then at her. "You dressed me?"

"Only your shirt." She kept her voice indifferent. His quick and shallow breaths told her how much pain he was in. If only she could comfort him. Her anger seemed to have spurred him to action, however. If it required her to be angry to get him moving, then that's what she would use.

"Here are your britches." She held them out for him. "I'll tend the horse, and I suggest you get dressed. We need to be on our way."

"You should really consider becoming a football coach, you know that, Angel?" Without warning, he pulled the blanket away from his lower half.

Sarah spun around. His chuckle turned into fits of coughing. Sarah ground her teeth. Served him right.

"Perhaps I should have left you to die." The anger in her voice this time was real.

CHAPTER TWENTY

*C*hase coughed and spat blood on the ground. *Dammit, Russell. Why'd you have to act like such a jerk again?*

Still sitting on the ground, he slowly worked his britches up his legs. Even the slightest movement in every one of his limbs sent currents of pain through his system. Sarah had put his moccasins on for him, too, he noticed, and at closer inspection, bandages were wrapped around his feet. He glanced over at her. She stood some ten yards away, talking quietly to a horse. Her soft voice carried on the breeze, and he strained to listen. He couldn't understand what she said. She must be speaking in Shoshone, but the melody of her voice had a soothing effect not only on the horse, but on him as well.

She lifted a hand to pat the animal on the head. Her olive complexion was in stark contrast against the horse's white face, her raised arm enhancing her slim, toned upper limbs. The sleeves of her shirt were missing, he realized suddenly. Chase looked at the bandages on his feet again.

It's because of her that your sorry ass is even alive, Russell.

Thoughts and visions of Sarah had gotten him through this ordeal, and now she'd used whatever resource was available to help him again.

"I love you, Angel," he muttered under his breath, and watched her stroke the horse's long neck. She turned her head toward him, and he stiffened. She couldn't have heard him. He wanted to say the words out loud, tell her what she meant to him. He couldn't bring himself to do it.

"Are you dressed?" she called.

"Yeah," he managed to reply in a normal voice. She walked over to him, her face set in stone.

"Can you try to stand?"

"Sure," he answered with a bitter laugh. "And then I'll walk back to the cabin, no sweat."

"We have a horse," Sarah stated matter-of-factly.

"I've never sat on a horse in my life. How the hell am I even supposed to get on that thing?"

God, he felt like an invalid. He knew what condition his feet were in. This morning, when those damn Indians had found him, he'd been going on pure adrenaline. That had worn off now, leaving him exhausted and feeling every cut and scrape. Each time he moved, the sensation of needles jabbing into his soles made him want to give in and scream like a girl. If there was ever a good time to get drunk, now was it.

"If you can stand, and climb on that boulder over there," she pointed toward the trees, "you can get on her back."

Chase stared up into Sarah's expectant eyes. He inhaled deeply, his lungs and ribs protesting the expansion. That boulder was no more than twenty yards away, but the distance looked daunting at the moment.

"Sure Angel. No problem." How the hell was he supposed to sit on a horse and stay on? Reluctantly, Chase realized there were no other modes of transportation, and he'd have to endure this inconvenience as well as everything else he'd put up with so far.

Sarah knelt down beside him. She placed her palm on his chest, a frown forming on her face. She darted a nervous glance at him. "Continue to take deep breaths. I worry you will get lung sickness. You should not lie flat on your back anymore, either."

The feel of her hand on him was like heaven, soothing among all the aches and pains. Chase closed his eyes for a moment. Then he clenched his jaw. He heaved himself off the ground, clutching at his side, and grimaced. All he needed now was to cry out in pain in front of her. He inhaled sharply when his feet supported his full weight. His legs shook, even as he stood hunched over.

Sarah rushed to his side, and put her arm around his waist, trying to support him. That would be futile. He had to outweigh her by fifty pounds or more.

"Angel, what are you doing?" he said between gritted teeth. "Don't get me wrong. Your hands and arms all over me feels wonderful, but I'll just crush you."

She must have realized what he said was true, or maybe he'd just managed to get her all flustered again. Wordlessly, she released him, and hurried off to the horse, leading the animal back toward him. He'd never been this close to a horse before. Sarah brought it right up alongside him.

"Here, put your arm over her back just behind her neck, and she'll support you to get to the boulder."

He reluctantly followed Sarah's instructions. Raising his arm was pure agony. Not only did his muscles burn like hell, but his ribs were killing him as well.

"Ready?" Sarah asked, standing at the front of the horse.

"Yeah, sure." He couldn't produce more words. The horse stepped forward, and he followed. It did support him like crutches, and he managed to take a lot of weight off his feet, but the sensation of hot blades slicing through his soles remained.

"When we get back to the cabin, I will make you some willow bark tea. It will help with the pain," Sarah called over her shoulder.

"Is it that obvious?" he ground out. Sweat beaded on his forehead, and his shirt clung to his back. He squeezed his eyes shut, hoping to dispel the dizziness that came over him. He leaned heavier on the horse for support.

"Yes," Sarah answered. She stopped, and the horse did, too, in front of the granite boulder. Chase wondered vaguely why this boulder seemed so out of place along the lush green banks this side of the river. None of the mountains around here were carved from granite.

Sarah turned and faced him. "You have nothing to be ashamed of. You don't need to hide the pain you are in, Chase. Your pride can remain intact, I assure you." Her icy stare and sharp words were in stark contrast with the way she'd spoken to the horse earlier.

He tore his eyes away from her, and assessed the huge rock. He reached up and put his hands flat on the near level top, and heaved himself up. It was the most excruciating pull-up he'd ever had to do. His shoulders might be on fire, but at least he didn't have to use his feet at the moment. Years of weight training were paying off for him now. He hadn't lost any of his upper body strength, even if it did hurt like hell. Using his knees rather than his feet to bear some of his weight, he managed to pull and push himself to the top. He rested on his stomach for a moment to catch his breath, then twisted his body and hips to a sitting position, his feet dangling over the edge. He wiped an impatient arm across his sweaty forehead.

"Now what?" he asked between gritted teeth. He hated

this helpless feeling, and that Sarah had to see him so inca-pacitated.

"Swing your right leg over her back."

The horse's back was a few inches below. Chase inched forward. He reached down and put his hands on the horse's neck, grabbing a handful of mane, then swung his leg over. The horse shifted her feet, and he leaned forward for balance, his thighs instinctively tightening around the animal's sides to maintain centered.

"Scoot back and give me some room," Sarah ordered.

"We're riding double?" Was there enough room for two?

"I can walk if you prefer," she retorted.

Chase grinned, despite the pain. Anything to have her close to him. "Hop on, Angel."

"Here, hold this." She thrust her rifle in his hand. Chase stared at it. He seriously needed to learn how to shoot one of these things. The next Blackfoot Indian he met had better watch out.

Sarah climbed on the boulder with the grace and agility of a gymnast, and swung her leg forward over the horse's neck. She adjusted her seat, and picked up the reins. Mere inches separated them. Chase's hands involuntarily reached for Sarah's waist when the horse began to walk. She stiffened under his hands. Leaning forward, his head inches from her ear, he whispered, "It was your idea to ride double, Angel."

What did she expect? A changed man? Sarah inhaled deeply, trying to concentrate on the route home. Her back muscles ached from the stiff way she'd been sitting on the mare. She should have realized how close their bodies would touch if they rode double, but she'd only thought about getting Chase home as quickly as possible. If she chose to walk now, he'd only have more fuel for rude comments.

His body heat radiated into her back, and strands of her hair clung to the nape of her neck. Thankfully, he'd moved his hands, and hadn't spoken in a while. His breathing told her the ride wasn't comfortable for him. With the way she'd seen him clutch at his sides, she worried that he might have some broken ribs. Sarah questioned her sanity. Why did she care for this man, when his behavior and manners were so infuriating at times?

She wouldn't allow him to get to her, she told herself firmly, and tried to focus on the path ahead. A man's wounded pride was sometimes more difficult to heal than physical injuries. Her brothers had been good examples of that over the years. Chase had nothing to be ashamed of. He had survived impossible odds. Wasn't he aware of that?

The well-traveled deer trail along the Firehole River allowed the mare to extend her walking strides, and she glided smoothly along. The forest wasn't as dense in this area, but Sarah saw the mountains closing in on them, and knew they'd soon reach the Firehole Canyon. It was the quickest way home if they traveled on foot. The rocky terrain would be impossible for a horse to traverse, however.

The rushing sound of the water increased in volume, announcing the first cascades up ahead as the river journeyed on its way through the narrow canyon now only a short distance away. She turned the mare away from its banks, and headed east.

"How much further?" Chase's words sounded strained.

Despite her annoyance, she hurt for him, wishing there was something she could do to ease his pain, but until they reached the cabin, he would have to suffer through the discomfort.

"At least one more hour," she answered. "Lean . . . lean forward against me, if it will help," she offered in a quiet tone.

He didn't reply. Minutes passed, then his arms slowly encircle her waist, and his chest leaned into her back. He rested his head on her shoulder.

"Thanks, Angel," he whispered.

Warmth radiated from her center throughout her body and into her limbs. She savored the sensation of his strong arms around her. She could pretend it was a loving embrace, although she knew he didn't have anywhere else to put his arms, and it helped him stay balanced. She had to brace her back to stay upright from his heavy bulk leaning into her.

The forest grew dark around them, and Sarah maneuvered the mare around deadfall and between trees. There was a definite chill in the air. If not for Chase's heat, she might be cold. He was so hot, she feared he had developed a fever. His even breathing told her he'd fallen asleep, but his body involuntarily jerked every once in a while. She hoped he stayed asleep until they reached the cabin.

His arms had not lessened their grip around her waist, and her stomach and leg muscles clenched, trying to keep both of them balanced on the horse. She was thankful that the mare had a smooth gait, and was well trained.

By the time the woods finally gave way to meadow, Sarah's body was sore and tired from Chase leaning on her. The Little Buffalo River was just up ahead, and beyond that, home. She nudged the mare with her knees to walk faster, and the horse obediently splashed through the water.

"Chase, wake up," Sarah said. Her shoulder ached. His head rested heavily against her neck. "Chase," she said louder. She reached her hand around and tapped his arm.

"Huh?" He woke with a start. His body swayed to the side, and his hold around her waist tightened.

"Wake up. You're going to make both of us fall to the ground. Don't grip me so tight."

"We're back?" he asked, his voice raspy again.

"Yes. I need to get off the horse. You need to release me."

He removed his arms, and Sarah shivered at the sudden cold around her waist. She swung her right leg forward over the horse's neck and slid off the mare's back.

"I'll bring her right up to the cabin door, but I'm afraid you'll have to walk to the bedroom." She glanced up at him.

His eyes were glazed over and his face was covered in sweat. He definitely had a fever. She had to get him in bed and covered before he became chilled. The late afternoon sun no longer provided warmth, and thunder clouds rolled toward them from the west. She was glad she'd decided to make the trip home rather than stay camped by the river.

She led the horse right up to the door, then dropped the reins to the ground. Like a well-trained Indian pony, the mare stood still. Sarah rushed into the cabin, and opened her door wide. She hastily flipped some covers back on her bed, and stacked a few at the head. She didn't want Chase lying flat. He needed to stay as upright as possible to ease his breathing.

He swayed on the mare's back when she returned moments later.

"Chase, don't pass out. Stay awake," she yelled. The last thing he needed was to fall from the horse's back.

"How do I get off?" he asked weakly.

"Lean forward, then pull your left leg over her back, and slide down. I'm sorry, there's no other way. You will have to walk inside."

"I'll manage," he grumbled, and did what she'd instructed. He hissed when his feet touched the ground. Sarah reached out and held his arm, trying her best to support him. This time he accepted her help and leaned heavily on her as she guided him into the cabin to the bedroom. With a heavy moan, he fell onto the bed.

"No, you have to lie upright on your back," Sarah commanded.

He would have simply passed out on his stomach the way he'd fallen onto the bed. He didn't move.

"Come on, move," Sarah yelled. It hurt her to be this cruel. She could only imagine the pain his body was in, but it was necessary or the Blackfoot might be entitled to claim victory after all. Sarah had no intention of letting that happen.

"Get up, Chase Russell. Be a man," Sarah barked. "Don't let them defeat you now. You're stronger and better than they are."

Her words must have reached him. He pulled himself fully onto the bed.

"Roll on your back," she commanded, tugging on his arm. Slowly, he complied. When she finally had him positioned the way she wanted him, she was drenched in sweat herself. Sarah felt his forehead. He was hot to the touch, and clammy. She pulled some covers over him. For the moment, he could rest. With a final concerned glance over her shoulder, she left the room to see to the mare, and prepare some medicines that she hoped would ease Chase's pain.

CHAPTER TWENTY-ONE

*S*arah woke from a restless sleep. Two long days and nights of tending to Chase had started taking their toll. She was worn out, no question about it. But her condition was far better than his. His fever had raged on and off since bringing him home. He hadn't fully regained consciousness, and often mumbled incoherently, or said words and phrases that made no sense to her. Thankfully, his breathing had returned to normal within a day, and Sarah heard no more raspiness to indicate fluid in his lungs, nor was there any more blood coming from his nose.

She bathed and dressed his feet in fresh bandages daily, checking for any signs of infection. She was pleased to see that the wounds all appeared to be healing well. She wasn't nearly as proficient as her mother at assessing internal injuries, but she couldn't feel any abnormal give to his ribs, and convinced herself that none were broken. Only a large bruise marred his right side. She'd removed his shirt and washed the dirt, blood, and sweat off his chest, arms, and face.

Sarah raised herself out of Samuel's bed. Chase was

muttering in his sleep again. She quickly pulled her britches on and climbed barefoot down the ladder to her room. The cabin was completely dark. She had no idea what time it was, but definitely not time to start the day yet. Quietly, she pushed her bedroom door fully open. Chase's panicked voice startled her.

"No, please don't leave. Stay with me. I love you, don't you understand? Don't go, please. I'll try harder. I'm sorry for all the drinking."

Sarah could hear the shifting of covers, and his limbs moving. What had he said? *I love you.* Who was he talking to in his sleep? And what did he mean by he was sorry for all the drinking? He'd told her he'd been drunk. Had he meant more than once? Sarah couldn't recall the specifics of that conversation. Had he been drinking to forget a woman he was in love with? He was begging her to stay. Had she rejected him?

Sarah, do you really want the answers? Her heart pounded faster. It would explain his desire to return home, wanting to return to the woman he loved. But he had told her he didn't want attachments. Was that a lie to end her question? Her eyes began to sting. She blinked several times, trying to fight back tears.

Slowly, she walked closer to the bed. He hadn't said any more. Sarah sat on the edge, and felt for his face. He was drenched in sweat, but his skin felt cool. His fever had broken.

Despite her trepidation, she smiled. He would live. He had beaten all the odds, defeated a village of Blackfoot, and he would live to tell about it. He was an incredible man, and she loved him. Sarah caressed his cheek.

His hand shot up suddenly, and he grabbed her wrist, the strong grip biting painfully into her skin. She nearly fell off the bed from the shock.

"Chase. Let go. You're hurting me," she gasped, and pulled against his tight hold.

"Sarah?" he answered weakly out of the dark. He released her immediately. "I'm . . . sorry. I couldn't see. I didn't know it was you."

"Let me light the lamp," she said, and scooted off the bed, rubbing her wrist as she fumbled in the dark through the cabin for the lantern.

She returned to her room, finding him sitting propped up against the wall.

"I feel as weak as a newborn baby," he said. "What time did we get back to the cabin?"

"Two days ago," she said, setting the lamp on the table beside the bed. His eyes no longer looked glazed. He was definitely better.

"Two days! I've been out for two days?"

"You've been battling a fever."

He pushed himself further up. "Hell, I need to get out of bed," he grumbled.

"Can it wait until the sun rises?" Sarah asked, a smile on her face. After two days of worrying whether he would live or die, she was elated to have him conscious again.

"It's good to see you smiling, Angel," he said. His voice sent shivers down her spine. "I do need to get out of bed, though."

"Surely it can wait."

"Ah . . . no it can't. Nature calls."

Sarah's face grew hot. Hopefully the shadows cast by the lantern would conceal it. Why hadn't she thought of that? She darted for his moccasins at the foot of the bed, hoping for a distraction.

With a loud groan, Chase pulled his legs over the edge of the bed, holding the right side of his ribcage. "God, I feel like I've been hit by a freight train."

Sarah knelt before him on the ground, and gently slipped his shoes on his feet. She glanced up. She could swear her heart stopped beating when her eyes met his. There was something different in the way he looked at her. She couldn't define what it was, but the boyish silliness was gone, replaced with the seriousness of a grown man's face. His eyes held a certain intensity that took her breath away.

"Get up, Sarah," he said quietly. "You're not my servant."

"I . . . I just wanted to help. Your feet should be covered when you go outside." She sat back on her haunches, and finished putting the shoe on his foot. She felt his hand under her arm, pulling her up.

"You have done more for me than I can ever repay, Angel." He stood, his face contorting in a grimace. He hadn't released her arm yet. She'd forgotten how big he was when she stood right next to him. The last few days, she'd looked down at him. Now she had to look up.

Her eyes swept over him. His stomach looked sunken in, and no wonder. He hadn't eaten in four days. The little bit of broth she'd been able to give him had not provided enough nourishment to sustain a man his size. His skin pulled tightly over his muscled arms and chest. He'd definitely lost weight. Nothing a few good meals wouldn't bring back, though.

"Do you need assistance to walk outside?" she asked tentatively.

"I'll manage," he answered. He released her arm, and took a first slow step. "My feet feel better already," he said. "I'm just weak as hell."

It took him several minutes to get to the door of the cabin. Sarah watched him. There was nothing she could do but let time heal his wounds. The weakness would go away once he could move around more again, and his feet seemed to be healing well. She'd do whatever she could to help restore his strength. The question was, would he accept her help.

Sarah glanced around. It was too late now to think about going back to sleep. She built up the fire in the hearth, and pulled the kettle over it to reheat the stew she'd cooked the day before. He'd no doubt be hungry when he returned. She sliced thick pieces of bread, setting them on a plate at the table. Measuring out more willow bark into the coffee pot, she added water to it, and set the pot near the fire to heat.

When he returned from outside, his meal sat waiting. He glanced at the table, then looked at her. The warmth in his eyes made her want to melt into the floorboards.

"Sarah, you've got to be tired. I hate for you go through all this trouble for me."

"Oh? So you were going to prepare your own meal, were you?" she said haughtily. "You've had no food in four days. Pretty soon even the wolves and bears won't find any meat on you."

"Well, since you put it like that." He grinned at her, and pulled a chair from beneath the table. "You're right, I could eat a horse. But this will do just fine."

Sarah turned away from him to conceal the wide smile on her face. Why did he act so different? So . . . nice.

Chase's health improved with each passing day. Sarah insisted on tending to the wounds on his feet daily, amidst all his protests that he could do it himself, and she was pleased with the healing progress. He was able to walk longer and with less pain. The bruise on his ribs had turned various shades of yellow, a good indication that it was healing.

She still couldn't explain the change that had come over him. He was kind and polite, and his rude comments had stopped completely. Was this his way of showing his gratitude to her? Sarah had thought herself in love with him before his encounter with the Blackfoot. The man he was now melted her heart faster than snow falling into a hot spring.

While he treated her with nothing but respect, there was a certain ferocious resolve about him that she couldn't explain. She sometimes caught him looking off into the distant mountains, gripping his tomahawk with such intensity, she'd see the sinewy tendons and muscles on his forearms stretch taunt. His easy-going expressions she'd come to love, and found infuriating at the same time, were absent. While his outer wounds healed with each day, the invisible scars in his mind seemed to fester and grow worse.

Sarah didn't know what to do. She had learned over many years of dealing with her brothers that a man did not like sharing his inner thoughts. Her father seemed to be the exception. There was nothing he didn't communicate to her mother. But she did not share the closeness her parents had with Chase. She didn't know how to approach him about his inner demons. The battle for his life with the Blackfoot must have left a deeper scar within him than any physical wounds ever could.

With concern, she watched him push his physical limits every day. He carried fresh buckets of water from the river, whether she needed them or not. The wood box was never empty. Sarah had argued with him, and lost, that chopping wood wasn't something he should be doing yet. She caught him practicing his throwing skills with the tomahawk with fierce tenacity, sometimes for hours at a time. Many trees in the vicinity bore the scars of his persistence.

"Would you like some water?" she called, walking up

behind him during one of his practice sessions. His back glistened with sweat in the noontime sun. He turned to face her, accepting the water bag she held out to him. He wiped his hand across his forehead and took a long drink.

Sarah couldn't help but watch the muscles move along his chest and arm, and how his scorpion tattoo moved as if it were alive. His body had grown stronger, his muscles leaner and firmer with each passing day.

"What are you staring at, Angel?" he asked, his voice teasing. He handed the water bag back to her. She hadn't been aware she'd been watching him so intently. Her face flushed, embarrassed at being caught openly staring at him.

"I . . . was just wondering about the tattoo you have. I've never seen one so perfect."

"No? This one's a real simple one."

Encouraged that he remained polite, she couldn't help herself from asking the question that had been on her mind since she'd first seen the tattoo. "What is the meaning of the scorpion?"

"My high school football team was called the Scorpions. We all had this done at the beginning of our senior year."

Sarah shook her head, not understanding.

"I know you probably don't know what I'm saying. It's kind of like a mascot. Do you know what that is?"

"A good luck symbol?" she ventured a guess.

"Yeah, something like that." He smiled.

Sarah looked up at him. His green eyes had turned dark like the forest around them. His face grew serious.

"Why did you kiss me that day in that Indian village, Sarah?" His words were spoken in a low, quiet voice. It was a question she was not prepared for.

"I . . . I thought you would die." She lowered her head. He chuckled.

"Last meal for a condemned man?" he asked, his tone strained. She directed her gaze at him once more.

"Chase, you have done what no man has ever done before. I have never heard of anyone, especially a white man, survive what you have. Men will talk of your deed for many years. You defeated the best young warriors of their tribe. This is not a feat to be taken lightly." She tentatively put a hand on his forearm. "You will be remembered in many lodges as a great hero to those who count the Blackfoot as their enemies."

Chase scoffed. "Some hero. If I had listened to you, or if I knew how to defend myself in this godforsaken wilderness, this wouldn't have happened. I can't even take care of myself. Every time I turn around, someone's trying to kill me." The fierce look in his eyes, the angry set in his jaw, made her back away.

"No man can say you are incapable, Chase. Your ways may be different, but you still bested them. A man does not survive here by chance. You may be unfamiliar with the ways of the people here, but this can all be learned in time." She smiled encouragingly at him. Why couldn't he understand that he had not failed?

Chase took a step closer to her. She held her breath. His eyes were locked onto hers with such intensity, she thought he stared right through her. Suddenly his features softened, and his hand reached up to touch her arm, sliding slowly upward.

"I'm glad you're here to believe in me, Angel," he said softly. His touch, and the way he spoke to her, sent delicious ripples down her spine. In the distance, a dog barked. Sarah turned her head.

"Grizzly?" she called. The warm sensation of Chase's hand remained on her arm, even as she spun to look into the distance. To the west, heading toward the cabin along the

Madison, she spotted three figures walking along the river-bank. Her dog bounded through the grass in front of them. He'd obviously healed from his ordeal as well.

"It's my uncle," Sarah said. Chase stiffened visibly next to her. She gave him a searching look. "Would you come with me to greet him?"

"You go ahead." He motioned with his head. All softness had left his eyes. "I can say hello when he gets here."

"Chase, these men are not Blackfoot." Did she have to remind him? "The Tukudeka are hunters, not warriors. They avoid conflict."

His cheek muscles worked while he clenched and unclenched his jaw. He forced a smile. "I know, Angel. Go out and meet your uncle. And, Sarah . . . don't say anything to them about what's happened."

Sarah searched his face. Reluctantly, she turned and headed out to meet her relatives. They were still quite a distance away, too far to recognize individual people. Who else traveled with her uncle? She glanced over her shoulder. Chase hadn't moved. She headed out across the meadow. Grizzly's barks grew in their intensity, and he ran to her at full speed when she whistled to him. The giant dog leapt at her, knocking her to the ground.

"Easy, you big beast", Sarah laughed. "I'm glad to see you, too." She wrapped her arms around the dog's neck, while he attempted to lick every inch of her face. She still sat in the moist grass when the three men drew near.

"Your dog was anxious to return to you," she heard her uncle's voice. Looking up from wrestling with Grizzly, the smile froze on her face. She quickly jumped to her feet, wiping her hands on the seat of her britches. Standing next to her uncle was his son, Touch the Cloud, and next to him stood Hawk Soaring. Her cousin smiled brightly at her, much like Elk Runner. Hawk's face remained passive. He nodded politely at her, then focused his eyes further into the distance.

"*Imaah*, it is good to see you are well," Touch the Cloud said.

"And you, *tangumpua*. You must be proud that you have a son." She swiped some stray hair out of her face.

"It will not be soon enough when I can meet him and hold him in my arms," Touch the Cloud said proudly.

Sarah's eyes darted to the man standing next to her cousin. He stood tall and proud, his hand firmly around his horn bow. He wore a simple buckskin shirt and fringed pants. Around his waist hung his weapons belt, with tomahawk and hunting knife hanging on either side of his hips. His moccasins were plain and unadorned with quills or beads. A single hawk feather was tied in his long black hair. A quiver full of arrows hung over his shoulders, as well as a large leather pouch.

Sarah forced a smile. "I see you are well, *Kwiyoo Natukunto'eh*. It has been a while since we last met." She'd always been so at ease around him. Now, she didn't know what to say.

His eyes turned to her, and he bowed his head. "*Imaah*. I have brought you a gift." He stepped forward and offered her the leather pouch. "Meat from a successful hunt," he added. "You will not need to find your own for the remainder of the time your parents are away."

Sarah took the offered pouch. It was heavy. "Thank you, *Kwiyoo*." Her eyes darted to her uncle, who smiled smugly. Her eyes narrowed in annoyance.

"Will you come to the cabin for some food? I have fresh huckleberry pie. I know you like that, Uncle. I thank you for bringing my dog to me."

Elk Runner's face lit up. "I will not say no to that," he said, a wide smile on his face. He rubbed at his stomach. Sarah nodded and headed back in the direction of her cabin. Her uncle walked beside her, and the two young hunters brought up the rear.

Sarah's heart beat faster. Behind her walked the man who wanted her for his wife. Ahead somewhere was the man she wished would ask her to be his wife. And her uncle was well aware of this fact. Why would he bring Hawk Soaring, other than to toy with her? He had to know that Chase was still here. She shot him a heated sideways look. He smiled brightly at her, shrugging. She wanted to give her uncle a piece of her mind. Looking up ahead, Chase stood by the woodpile, waiting on their arrival. Sarah wondered if he would be civil, or if his anger with the Blackfoot carried to her relatives as well.

CHAPTER TWENTY-TWO

*C*hase stood by the woodpile and watched the group approach. Unexplainable anger welled up inside him. *They're a different tribe of Indians, Russell. You can't be mad at all of them now because of what you had to go through.* The Shoshone people that Sarah considered her relatives lived completely different from those Blackfeet. He'd always pictured Indians as living in tipis, riding horses, shooting guns and arrows. The Blackfoot matched that description, but not these Sheep Eaters.

From what Sarah had told him, the Tukudeka were the only tribe that lived in these mountains permanently. The other tribes, like the Crow and Blackfoot, traveled through here, but didn't stay the winter. He'd experienced first-hand how they lived in close-knit little family units, not in a large tribe. None of them had rifles. They hunted with bows they made from bighorn sheep and elk antler horn, and utilized their dogs as helpers in the hunt.

Chase watched the four people approach. He knew Elk Runner. He'd never seen the other two. He could almost guess who one of them was. He didn't recognize either of them from the village. They were much younger than the older men he'd seen there, probably close to his own age. He clenched and unclenched his jaw, gnashing his teeth together.

How was he going to act around the guy who wanted to marry Sarah? He hadn't asked her again how she felt about the arrangement. He had gotten the impression that she wasn't too happy about it, which suited him just fine. But what if her father had already sold her off to this Hawk guy?

You're a real coward, you know that, Russell? Why can't you tell her how you feel about her? He could just picture himself walking up to her father, asking for his daughter's hand. He'd probably get shot, and he hadn't even met the man. He couldn't even take care of himself here, how would he convince someone he could take care of a wife.

Wife! What the hell are you thinking! You haven't even asked her out on a date yet. What are you going to do, take her with you when you go home? Yeah, he could just picture Sarah living in the twenty-first century. She'd never fit in to modern society. Heck, she'd only been to a city a few times from what she'd told him. Her whole life was built around her family and Indian friends.

Chase pulled his shirt on over his head. If he had any sense, he'd be happy for her to marry this Hawk person. She'd no doubt be well taken care of. Images of her living in one of those wooden wickiups, surrounded by a cluster of little black-haired kids wearing nothing but loincloths flooded his mind. Damn!

Just be polite and don't make a scene. Elk Runner already suspected that he was in love with Sarah. He'd made comments even before Chase had realized it himself. It was time to put on a smile and a poker face, and be civil to the guy who would get the girl he wanted for himself.

He recognized Sarah's nervousness immediately when

she and Elk Runner and company approached. Her smile didn't reach her eyes, and she clasped and unclasped her hands in front of her. A large pouch was draped over her shoulder. He hadn't seen that before. Her eyes were round as saucers when she met his gaze. She was probably hoping he wouldn't say or do anything to embarrass her.

Chase plastered, what he hoped, was a welcoming look on his face. The only one with a genuine smile was her uncle. The younger men walked silently, their facial expressions not giving away any inner thoughts they might have as to his presence. Did Elk Runner even mention him? Their looks showed mild interest, more like curiosity. Chase didn't see anything he could consider hostile.

Elk Runner extended his arm and opened his hand. "Chase Russell, you still lost?"

What the hell kind of question was that? "As lost as ever." Chase clasped the older man's hand.

Elk Runner pulled him to the side. He turned to Sarah, and she nodded when he spoke to her. Chase met her nervous glance. "I will have some pie ready in a moment." Obviously Elk Runner had sent her away. He didn't want her to listen in? Chase eyed the other men.

"This my son, *Sungkwa'ah Pakuunappuh*, and friend, *Kwiyoo Natukunto'eh.*"

Chase shook both their hands. The Indians nodded respectfully, but Chase could tell he was being sized up. That was fine by him. He was taking their measure as well. Both of them were considerably shorter than he, but their proud and confident stance made them appear much larger. He and the guy Chase suspected to be Hawk held each other's stare longer than necessary.

"You need go on spirit journey."

Chase broke eye contact to look at Elk Runner. "The only

spirit journey I've ever been on came from a bottle. And look where that landed me."

Elk Runner looked him up and down. Why was this crazy Indian staring at him like that? He nodded, then said, "When you ready, I will teach."

"Teach me what?" Chase asked impatiently.

Elk Runner draped an arm around Chase's shoulder, and walked off with him, leaving the others standing by the woodpile.

"You want live like mountain man? Need learn much things."

Who the hell said he wanted to be a mountain man? Chase laughed. "I need to talk to Sarah's mother, then I'm hoping to go home. I'm definitely not a mountain man." If he were, he wouldn't have gotten himself caught by those Blackfoot.

Elk Runner's eyebrows rose. "You know *Dosa haiwi?*"

"What's that?" His own brows furrowed in confusion.

"Dosa haiwi . . . Imaah mother."

Now he understood. It was someone's name. "What is her white name?"

"Aimee Osborne." The English name sounded strange with the stiff way he pronounced it.

"No, I don't know her. I just need to talk to her. She might be able to help me get home." Chase stared at the ground.

"Chase Russell no realize he already home." Elk Runner placed his hand on Chase's upper arm. He seemed genuinely sincere.

Chase laughed nervously. The man was insane. He didn't belonged here anymore than Elk Runner belonged in twenty first century Los Angeles.

"Are you all just going to stand around talking all day?" Sarah's impatient voice called from the cabin. All heads turned in her direction. Chase watched the way Hawk's eyes fell on her. The man's unreadable expression from a moment ago softened. Yeah, he was definitely in love with her. Anger and jealousy welled up inside him, and the urge to hit the guy surprised him.

"We were just on our way to the cabin," Chase called, and headed toward her, hoping this conversation with Elk Runner was over.

"That smells really good," Chase said, sniffing the air when he stepped through the door. Sarah had set out four plates around the table, each piled high with thick slices of golden-crusted pie. "When did you make that?"

"While you were busy chopping down that tree out by the woodpile." Sarah smiled. "I have to warn you, my mother is quite fond of that tree. She told me once that it was just a sapling when she met my father."

"I guess I'll find something else to use for target practice then."

The Indians filed into the cabin, and by the looks of things, they seemed familiar being here. They took their seats around the table. Hawk's eyes followed Sarah, who had her back turned as she wiped crumbs off the workbench. Chase could tell he was trying to be discreet about it, the way he had his head lowered, but glanced upward in her direction.

"Aren't you coming to sit down?" There was no place set for her.

"Oh, no." She shook her head. "I prefer to eat later."

He wanted to argue with her, but then he'd only embarrass her again, so he let it go. Before he sat, he touched her between her shoulder blades, and ran his hand down to the small of her back. He let his palm linger for a moment. Her spine stiffened under his touch.

"Suit yourself, Angel," he said, and turned to take his seat at the table, gloating silently. He didn't have to look at Hawk to know the man's glare was murderous.

~

SARAH BUSIED herself cleaning invisible dirt off the work-bench. If it had just been her uncle, she would have joined them at the table, but etiquette decreed that she not be in close proximity with Hawk Soaring. Everyone knew he had asked for her. She only needed to give her answer. If she sought out his company, it would appear as if she consented to the match. She needed to speak to her father first.

The feel of Chase's hand on her back still tingled. Why had he done that in front of everyone? He'd been polite the last few weeks. He hadn't made any rude remarks, nor had he done anything inappropriate. Earlier, by the woodpile, his hand had rested on her arm. She was sure he'd meant to kiss her, but Grizzly had interrupted them, announcing his homecoming. What did it all mean?

Chase's ways were so different from anyone else's. Her emotions seemed to constantly wage war inside her lately. On the one hand, she was pleased by the changes in him. But then, she admitted shamefully, that she missed some of his remarks that made her face turn scarlet.

Chair legs scraped against the wooden floor. The men had eaten in silence, and the meal was apparently over. Sarah turned, intending to collect the plates off the table. Hawk Soaring stood before her.

"*Imaah*, I wish to speak with you." She glanced up into his brown eyes. Warmth and affection was directed at her. "Will you walk with me outside?"

Her eyes darted to the other men in the room. Elk Runner spoke with his son, and the two men headed out the door. Chase hadn't left the table. Her eyes held his longer than she should have, and she swallowed involuntarily. His expression was unreadable. She turned her attention back to Hawk and nodded. "Lead the way," she said.

She followed him outside, and he headed for the river-bank, staying in plain view of her uncle and cousin. Hawk's hands were clasped behind his back. Sarah caught up to walk beside him, but kept a respectable gap between them.

"What is on your mind, *Kwyioo?*" she asked, when he didn't speak.

He stopped to face her. "This white man. He lives in your house?"

Sarah nodded. She knew where this was heading. It was best brought out into the open now.

"Have you taken him as your husband?"

"No, *Kwyioo*, I have not." She concentrated her eyes on the grasses at her feet, rather than look at him.

"You are aware that I have spoken with your father."

"I am aware. What did my father tell you when you saw him?" Sarah had to know. She stopped counting blades of grass to look at Hawk.

"He told me the decision would be yours to make. He would not speak for you."

Sarah expelled the breath she'd been holding. Her arms and legs tingled in relief.

"Do you have an answer for me?" His expression told her he already knew the answer.

"*Kwyioo*, you and I have known each other since we were children. I have great affection for you, but not in the ways a woman has affection for a husband. I'm sorry." Sarah reached out to touch his arm. She knew she'd hurt him, but his facial expression remained passive.

"Perhaps in time, you could learn to love me," he said hopefully.

Sarah took a deep breath. "Will you give me more time to think on this?"

His face brightened in a smile. "As long as you need. And whatever decision you make, I will respect your wishes."

"Thank you, *Kwyioo*. You are an honorable man."

They walked in silence back toward Elk Runner and Touch the Cloud.

"We must be on our way," Elk Runner said. "Your pie is as good as the ones your mother makes. I wish I could convince Little Bird to make this also."

"If she did, you wouldn't have an excuse to come visit so often." Sarah laughed. "Good-bye, Uncle. Until we meet again."

Sarah said her good-byes to her cousin, and Hawk Soaring. His gaze lingered, and Sarah had the feeling that he wanted to say something, but then he abruptly turned and followed his companions.

"Remind Chase of what I have told him," Elk Runner called over his shoulder.

Sarah's eyebrows furrowed. What had her uncle told Chase? Perhaps she'd ask him later. Her eyes darted around. Where was Chase?

The thought had barely occurred to her, when the door opened and he walked out. Their eyes met and held.

"Are they gone?" he asked. There was a definite edge to his voice.

"They wanted to get home before dark, I think," Sarah answered, and skirted around him. "I'd best clean the dishes."

Chase's hand reached out, and held her arm, preventing her from walking past him. Her eyebrows raised in surprise.

"What did you and Hawk talk about?" Why did he look so angry again? Her own temper flared.

"I don't believe it is any of your business what he and I discuss," she answered, her words clipped.

"I can't understand a word of what you say when you speak with them, Sarah."

"The feeling is mutual, I'm sure. Elk Runner is the only one who speaks a little English. Touch the Cloud and Hawk Soaring do not. They could not understand when you and I spoke, but they certainly weren't angry about it."

"What did he say to you, Sarah?" Chase asked again, his voice strained. His grip on her arm tightened.

"He told me he'd spoken to my father. Then he asked if I had an answer for him." Sarah refused to cower, and matched his heated stare.

"And did you give him an answer?"

"Yes, I did." She pulled her arm away. "Now release me and let me pass." She could see Chase's jaw working. After a moment, he finally released her. Sarah rubbed at the sore spot on her arm, and headed for the cabin, slamming the door shut behind her. She leaned against it momentarily, her hand held to her chest. What was that all about? He acted almost like . . . like what? A jealous suitor? She had no experience with that. And why would he be jealous? Not once had he said that he intended to speak to her father.

She inhaled deeply, then pushed away from the door, and collected the tin plates and forks off the table. She tossed them into the wooden bucket, and grabbed for the rope handle. She was about to head back out the door to the river, when Chase barged in.

"Where's your rifle?" He sounded urgent, his eyes darting around the room. "And grab your bow and arrows, too."

Sarah didn't move. "Why?"

"There's a bunch of Indians on horses coming this way. I'm going to be prepared this time."

Sarah walked to the window, peering out. From the east, she counted seven riders, their long black hair blowing in the breeze.

"They're not Blackfoot," she said calmly.

"How do you know?"

"For one, they come from the east. The Blackfoot live to the south, remember? And their hair is much longer than the Blackfoot keep theirs. The men out there are Absarokas . . . Crow. The only thing you need to worry about with them is that they don't steal your belongings. They are notorious thieves."

Sarah calmly walked to the door, and stepped outside. She could understand Chase's apprehension. After what he had to endure, his hatred for the Blackfoot was valid. He hadn't spoken directly about his ordeal, and she suddenly realized that she hadn't asked him, either. She hoped he would see that not all Indians behaved in the same way as the Blackfoot. They made war with almost every other tribe they encountered. It was part of their culture. What a shame it would be if he now felt hatred toward all the other tribes who lived in peace.

She held up a hand in greeting when the group of warriors pulled their horses up in front of the cabin. One man threw his leg over his mount's neck and leaped lightly from its back. Without hesitation, he walked up to her.

"We have come for the man with the scorpion on his chest."

CHAPTER TWENTY-THREE

*S*arah caught herself from letting her mouth drop open.

"Why do you believe to find such a man here?" she asked, hiding her surprise at the warrior's request, spoken in English. There had been no greeting. Her eyes darted briefly to the rifle in his hand. His forehead was painted red. This wasn't a raiding party, was it? Had she been too careless in her assumption that these men meant no harm? The Crow had never given her family any problems.

"Word travels quickly through the mountains. We bring gifts to the man who made old women out of young Black-foot warriors. Such a man deserves our praise and honor."

Sarah felt Chase's presence behind her. The skin on her neck tingled inexplicable, and the air was suddenly warmer. She suppressed a gasp when his hand rested at her waist. He gently moved her aside and put himself between her and the Crow, holding her rifle in front of him. What was he doing? He didn't even know how to shoot.

"What do you want from me?" Chase stared at the shorter man in front of him.

The warrior appraised him boldly from head to foot, and a slow smile formed on his face. "You are the man who made fools of our enemies?"

"If you're referring to me running for my life, then yeah, I did that." There was no boastfulness in Chase's tone, only disdain and a hint of anger.

The six Indians on horseback murmured, and nodded their heads in approval. The warrior standing in front of Chase smiled brightly. He reached his hand out to him. Chase hesitantly shook it.

"You come and travel with us to our village. We will sing praise, and honor you as a great warrior among our people. Your victory will be remembered in our lodges."

"I don't think so. I'm not looking for praise and honor. I ran to save my life, not to give you guys something to gloat about."

"You are a humble man. That is good. You refuse to travel to our village. So be it." The warrior sliced his hand through the air in front of him. "We will hold a feast in your honor here, and tell our families that we have met you."

Sarah quickly put her hand on Chase's arm before he said anything more to the Crow. If he declined their offer, he would insult them. He turned to her, his eyebrows raised in a silent question.

"Allow them to do this for you, Chase." She hoped he would understand.

"All right," he said, turning back to the Crow. "Why not?" He shrugged.

"We bring meat and, what the white trappers call awerdenty." He smiled broadly.

Sarah inhaled sharply. She hadn't expected that. Chase had to accept their offer. It would be a great insult to them if he didn't. But why did they have to bring whiskey?

"Your woman will cook the meat." She barely heard the

Crow's words. Her mind was still wrapped around the fact that these men would be drinking alcohol, and no doubt consume enough to alter their minds and judgment.

"No, she won't." Chase said firmly. Turning to her, he reached for her hand, giving it a light squeeze. "Sarah, stay in the cabin. My, ah . . . guests and I will be out here. We can roast whatever meat they brought in the fire pit."

"Chase, do you know what awerdenty is?" she asked hesitantly.

"Not a clue, Angel. Some kind of disgusting meat, like coyote?' He grinned at her.

"No. It's . . . alcohol."

His eyes twitched in the corners, but there was no other reaction from him. His facial expression didn't give away his thoughts. He slowly released her hand. Handing her the rifle, he turned and walked away with the Crow warrior, leaving her standing by the door.

The rest of the men dismounted their horses, and followed him to the fire pit, which was dug into the earth near the small cabin. Sarah watched them quickly build a large fire, and huge slabs of meat soon sizzled over the flames. She headed into the cabin, bolting the door behind her. Perhaps they hadn't brought enough liquor with them to make them all drunk. She could only hope.

SARAH SAT AT THE TABLE, her head cradled between her hands. The sun was slowly sinking into the western horizon, throwing the interior of the cabin into darkness. The flickering lights from the enormous fire in the yard cast large moving shadows on the walls. Sarah refrained from lighting a lantern. She didn't want to draw attention to the cabin. She had occupied her time reading *The Last of the Mohicans*, a book she had read on more than one occasion. The pages of the leather-bound edition were well-worn. Although she enjoyed the story each time she read it, she had found it difficult to concentrate this time.

The men's boisterous laughter had grown louder as the afternoon wore on. Chase's jovial voice reached her ears, and she wanted to cry. How much longer would they carry on out there? The liquor had to have run dry by now. Sarah's glance fell to her dog, sleeping contently near the hearth, his muzzle twitching occasionally. Sarah wondered what dogs dreamed about. She wished she could find the kind of peace that her furry friend enjoyed at the moment.

She nearly jumped out of her skin at the sound of gunshot. Even Grizzly raised his head, a quiet growl coming from deep in his throat. Anger welled up inside her. This was her home! She should have sent Chase to go with the Crow to their village. Let them shoot each other there. She left the table, stretching her stiff back, and peered out the window.

Several warriors danced around the fire, kicking their legs in the air, and flaying their arms about wildly. With those clearly exaggerated movements, it wouldn't surprise her if one of them fell in the flames. Chase sat on the ground with the warrior who was clearly the leader of the group, the man who had first approached her about Chase. They were both talking animatedly, laughing at whatever the other said. They held water bags in their hands, as did each of the other warriors. Sarah knew it wasn't water they were drinking.

She turned away, disgusted by what she saw. Tears stung her eyes. She wiped them away impatiently, and paced the cabin with her arms wrapped around her middle. She thought he had changed. In his fevered state, he had apologized to the woman he loved for his drinking habit. Sarah had never brought it up to him. Apparently those had been the words of a sick man. Now that he was well again, he no longer had feelings of remorse. The first opportunity to drink had presented itself, and he was obviously taking full advantage of it.

The sound of several more gunshots resonated through the cabin. *Enough's enough! Go out there and give them a piece of your mind.*

Sarah grabbed for her own rifle, and unbolted the door. Grizzly sprang up from his sleeping place.

"You stay here." She held up her hand to signal the dog to sit. *I might get shot.* Mentally, she counted how many gunshots she'd heard. It had to have been at least five, if not six. These men were too inebriated to reload their weapons. She felt reasonably safe to go out there and not get hit by a bullet.

Slowly, she opened the cabin door. The rowdy noise grew louder. Sarah squared her shoulders, raised her chin, and marched toward the fire pit, her hands firmly gripping her rifle. No one seemed to take notice of her when she approached.

"Don't you all have women and children waiting for you?" she yelled. "Return home to your lodges. This celebration must end now."

A few of the men stared open-mouthed at her, swaying on their feet. Two of the dancers had stopped. The other one continued his wild body movements. Sarah stepped closer. Chase and the other warrior stared at her.

"I said, it's time to go home," she repeated.

She raised her rifle slightly for emphasis. The men started to laugh. Without warning, someone grabbed her from behind around the waist. Sarah gasped. She hadn't noticed anyone moving behind her. The stench of alcohol wafted to her nose. Her assailant spun her around, and she faced a leering Crow warrior, his red face paint contorting his features in an evil-looking twist.

She struggled for release, but the man only held on to her with greater force. An instant later, his arms were torn away from her. Her head spun around. Chase was there, towering over her assailant. He grabbed hold of the front of the man's shirt with both fists, and almost lifted him off the ground.

"If you touch her again, I'll kill you," Chase growled in a menacing tone.

He threw the warrior away from him. The drunk Indian fell to the ground. Silence ensued, the only sound coming from the crackling of the fire. Sarah spun around and ran to the safety of the cabin, her heart beating wildly in her chest. Her breaths came in short, quick gasps. She slammed the door shut, darting to the back of the room. Leaning over the workbench, she braced her hands against the counter for support. Tears ran down her face.

How long she stood there, she didn't know. The touch of a warm hand on her shoulder startled her. She'd forgotten to bolt the door!

"Sarah." Chase's voice was close to her ear, sending shivers of apprehension down her spine.

"Please leave," she whispered, trying to control her erratic breathing.

"They left. I sent them away."

"You should have gone with them," she said, her tone bitter.

"I didn't drink, Sarah." Both his hands were on her shoulder now. He slid them slowly down her arms, and applied pressure to turn her around.

She looked up at him through blurry eyes, trying to make out his features in the darkness. "You could have fooled me," she spat.

"I didn't touch a drop, I swear, Angel." The hands caressing her arms sent renewed shivers through her body.

"Can you smell any alcohol on my breath?" He leaned in closer.

Sarah forgot to breathe. She tried to back up, but her backside bumped into the workbench. Chase slid his hands to her shoulders, then up her neck, his thumbs caressing her cheeks, swiping away her tears. Her knees went weak at his touch.

"Sarah . . ." he whispered, then covered her mouth with his. Lightning currents swept through her system. The slow movement of his lips against hers melted her resolve. Her arms reached up of their own will, sliding around his waist and up his back, until she gripped his shoulders. His kiss grew more demanding, and he pressed his body to hers with a throaty moan.

Sarah's head spun in a dizzying spiral. It felt so natural, so right, and so good to be in this man's arms. His hands seemed to be everywhere. She hadn't even realized his arm had gone around her waist, until he pulled her tightly to him. He abandoned her mouth to trail kisses down her face. He nuzzled her neck, rooting with his face in her hair. Sarah gasped. She shuddered at the delicious chills that shot up and down her spine.

His hands trembled as they traveled up along her waist and arms, cupping her face again. He leaned into her, pressing her back against the workbench. Her own hands had somehow moved up along his chest, and his heart drummed strong and fast against her right hand. His mouth claimed hers again, and his hands slid down her front. She gasped a second time and stiffened when he covered her breasts, his palms hot to the touch through the fabric of her shirt.

His hands continued their exploration of her body, traveling down along her ribcage and settled at her waist, and he pulled his head back. In the darkness of the cabin, Sarah couldn't see his face, but his breathing was as shallow and sporadic as her own.

"Now do you believe me? I only drank water," he whispered.

Sarah couldn't speak. She only nodded, not sure if he could even see her.

"I'm sorry I broke my promise." He cleared his throat.

"Promise?" she managed to utter.

"That I wouldn't kiss you again," Chase reminded her. "You're the one who kissed me when I was tied up, remember?"

Sarah sniffed, and laughed nervously.

"It's a lot better when I can put my arms around you," he said, his voice deeper than usual, and pulled her close to him. Her hands were still pressed to his chest, and she sighed at the multitude of feelings that assaulted her. She wished she could hold on to this moment forever.

"Angel? Say something. I can't see your face."

"Please . . . will you . . . would you kiss me again, Chase?" Had she actually spoken the words or only thought them? Chase hadn't moved. She shifted her weight from foot to foot, suddenly embarrassed by her bold request. She pushed against him, intending to scurry out of his embrace before she humiliated herself any more.

His hold around her waist tightened. "How would you like me to kiss you, Angel? Like this?" He brushed his lips across hers lightly. "Or like this?" His mouth crushed down on hers, one hand behind her head, holding her to him, his other arm pulling her tightly against his lower half.

Sarah moaned. Adrenaline rushed through her, and she thought she would melt. The world spiraled out of control. Her arms crept up around his neck, her hands entwining behind his head. Her own mouth parted, and she moved her lips in response to his assault.

Chase raked his fingers through her hair, then his hand caressed her cheek. In the next instant, it slid down along her ribcage, and back up again. Abruptly, he broke away.

"If we don't stop now, Angel," he panted, "I'm going to do something you'll regret in the morning."

His hands lifted away from her. She tightened her hold around his neck, leaning into him, and put her head against his chest. He drew in a deep breath, and his arms wrapped around her waist again.

"Sarah, you have no idea what you're doing to me," he whispered. Sarah listened to his rapid heartbeat, relishing the feel of his solid strength.

"Will you please just hold me?" she asked into his shirt. Her face flamed, both from the rush of feelings flooding her, and from embarrassment at her boldness. His chest expanded in a long sigh. He stepped away from the work-bench, pulling her along with him. He stroked her back, lightly kissed the top of her head, and caressed her cheek with his warm hand.

"Anything you want, Angel."

She raised her head from his chest, looking up in the direction of his face. "I'm ashamed of my behavior," she said slowly. His hand tightened at her waist. "I have no right to ask you these things, and I'm sorry. I know about the woman you're in love with."

Chase stiffened. He released her waist and drew away from her. Sarah's eyes burned, and her heart rate accelerated. *Here it comes, Sarah.*

He chuckled.

"I need to light the lantern, Angel. I need to see you." He released her completely and moved away. Sarah heard him shuffling around in the darkness, until the soft glow of the lantern on the table illuminated the center of the room. He turned and met her eyes.

PEGGY L HENDERSON

"Come here, Angel." He held out his hand to her. She took a hesitant step forward, then another. He took hold of her hand and pulled her to him.

"What do you know about the woman I'm in love with?" he asked, staring intently down at her, stroking the palm of her hand with his thumb.

"You were talking in your sleep when you were feverish."

"And what did I say?"

"You kept saying you were sorry for the drinking, and begged her not to leave you, and that you loved her." Sarah couldn't help the tears from flowing. The words were painful enough to say.

"Did I mention a name?" Why was he smiling at her like that? Couldn't he see this was tearing her apart?

"No." She shook her head, lowering her gaze to the ground.

"Look at me, Sarah," he commanded softly. She didn't comply. "Look at me," he repeated. Slowly, she forced her head up.

"Sarah, the woman I'm in love with," he paused and his left hand came up to caress her cheek, "is you."

CHAPTER TWENTY-FOUR

*S*arah stared at him in stunned silence. Her heart pounded in her ears.

"Angel?"

Chase's hands cupped her face, tilting her head up. His image became a blur as her eyes filled with new tears.

"Sarah, I love you."

She heard the words again.

"Can you please say something?" He laughed nervously. "I've never said those words to anyone before." He ran a trembling hand through his hair.

"You . . . you love me?" She barely managed to produce the sounds. She wanted to hear it again, to make sure she hadn't misunderstood. Chase loved her. Her mind reeled. She dared not believe it was actually true.

"Come here, you silly woman. Yes, I love you." His smile lit up his face, and he pulled her into a tight embrace.

Sarah's arms wrapped around his back, and she sobbed into his chest. "I love you, too, Chase."

His hold tightened until she could barely breathe. His

arms trembled. The sensation of weightlessness, of floating through the air swept over her. Chase pulled back abruptly.

"Why are you crying, Angel?" His hand swept loose stands of hair from her face. His expression grew serious. "It's Hawk, isn't it? You have to marry him, don't you?"

Sarah shook her head. "No, I told him that I needed more time to think."

Chase stepped away and rested his backside against the table. He pulled her to stand in front of him, his fingers entwined with hers. "What about your father? Does he decide whether you marry Hawk or not?"

"I believe he will let me have my say," Sarah answered. "If another man asks for me, he may have to make a decision, but I'm certain he will let me choose. I won't know until I speak to him. I still don't understand why he didn't tell me before rendezvous that Hawk Soaring came to him."

She looked hopefully into Chase's eyes. His jaw tightened, and his hands loosened around hers. Her heart sank to her stomach. He had no intention of asking for her.

"You still want to go home. You still believe you come from the future, don't you?" She stepped away from him.

He reached for her hand again, holding her fingers lightly. "I do come from the future, Sarah," he said solemnly. "This world here, it's not what I'm used to."

"But you can learn, can't you? You have proven yourself over and over again since you came here." Sarah cringed at the sound of her pleading voice. He'd just told her he loved her, yet he wanted to leave. Her eyes met his. "Take me with you when you find your way home."

Chase let out a short laugh. "You don't belong in my world any more than I belong in yours, Angel."

"At least I would be willing to learn, Chase Russell." Anger welled up inside her, concealing her anguish. "You say you love me, but you don't want to be with me." She pulled away from him and spun around. Taking a deep breath, she squeezed her eyes together. Perhaps it would have been easier on her heart if he'd never told her of his feelings for her.

"I'm still trying to figure out what it is I want, Angel." His warm breath against her neck sent chills down her spine. His hands slid around her waist from behind, and he pulled her up against him, and he rested his chin on top of her head. "Let's just go one day at a time, okay?"

～

His eyes followed her as she climbed the ladder up to the loft. Chase still couldn't believe how easy it had been to say those words to her. He couldn't even describe the feeling that came over him when she told him she loved him, too. He had no right to ask her about Hawk. The guy was in love with her, and no doubt he would make a good husband. Chase wanted to see her well taken care of. Leaving would be much easier, knowing she'd be protected.

After everything he'd experienced so far, he knew that this wilderness was a harsh place to carve out a living. A woman could not survive here without a man. Sarah was highly capable at finding food and shelter, and all the basics needed to live in the woods so far away from civilization. But, she was still a woman in a man's world, and she had no defenses against a stronger, determined man. It was a husband's job to protect his wife and family.

He was not that kind of man. How could he possibly offer her his protection if he couldn't protect himself? Why couldn't she understand that? He ran a frustrated hand through his hair. Why did everything have to be so complicated? For the first time in his life, he found someone he truly cared about. Sarah brought out the best in him. How could he let her go? But he couldn't take her home with him. That was out of the question.

Russell, how do you know you can even get home? Maybe Aimee Osborne had faced the same dilemma, and was stuck here for good, and married a man who offered protection. That thought had occurred to him more than once already, but it had been different for her. She had married a woodsman, one who already knew how to survive here. Chase could not offer that to Sarah. With a heavy sigh, he turned down the lantern, and shuffled to the bedroom.

He pulled his shirt off over his head and sank down onto the mattress. Sarah had insisted he remain in her room, even though he'd told her days ago that his injuries were all healed and he experienced no more pain when walking. He could easily climb up that ladder and sleep in one of her brothers' beds. That way she could have her room again.

He lay on his back, his hands behind his head, staring at the dark ceiling.

"One day at a time, Chase," she'd agreed before he sent her off to bed. Turning her around in his arms, he'd kissed her again, struggling to maintain control. He couldn't get enough of holding her, of feeling her cling to him. He grinned and shook his head. He'd never stopped at just a kiss before. Kissing a woman had always ended with both of them in the bedroom.

He wanted Sarah that way, too. God, how he wanted her. She was like butter in his arms. It would have been easy to just sweep her up and carry her to her bed, and make love to her. But, he had more respect for her than that, and she'd regret her actions the next day.

"When did you turn into such a noble soul, Russell," he wondered aloud. He knew the answer to that. The day a dark-haired, blue-eyed angel stood over him when he was frozen half to death, and claimed his heart.

He woke to the delicious smells of fresh baked bread, and the sizzling sound of meat cooking in the skillet. With a groan, he forced himself out of bed. He'd lain awake through the long hours of the night, thinking about Sarah and his ultimate dilemma. He must have dozed off some time before dawn. His head felt like it would split open any second.

Chase stretched, and rubbed the back of his neck. The door to the room creaked open slowly. He smiled when Sarah's head poked through the crack.

"I'm decent, Angel. Come on in."

Sarah's bright smile when she stepped into the room caused his heart to skip a beat. His gut tightened. Her hair spilled loose around her face, falling down her shoulders in wavy cascades.

"I have coffee waiting for you," she said tentatively. "Breakfast is almost ready."

He stepped up to her, and wrapped his arms around her waist. Why did this feel so natural, so right? Her big blue eyes gazed up at him, and her hands rested against his bare chest. He groaned at the ripples of pleasure her touch created. He raked his hands through her hair, tucking long strands behind her ears. His head bent and he kissed her neck where her pulse throbbed strong. She inhaled sharply, and shuddered. Her hands wrapped around his neck.

"Good morning, Angel," he whispered, and pulled back.

"Good morning." Her soft voice resonated through his system, dousing him in hot liquid.

Chase released her. He didn't know how long he'd be able

to maintain his self-control before his resolve at nobility crumbled.

"I could sure go for some coffee," he said, and led her out into the main room. That bed was much too close and tempting.

He rubbed at his temples, hoping some caffeine would take care of the pounding in his head. Sarah brought him a steaming cup, and motioned for him to sit at the table.

"You are in pain?"

He smiled at the concerned look on her face. "Just a headache. I didn't sleep well."

"I could make you some willow bark tea," she offered.

"I think coffee will take care of it. I might just lie back down for a while, unless there's something you need me to do today."

Sarah set a plate of fried meat and bread in front of him. "I was going to dig for camas roots today. You should take the time and rest. You've done way too much work as it is. Your body is still recovering."

"I think my body's just fine, Sarah," he said huskily. He chuckled when her face turned crimson. She'd obviously understood his implied double meaning. She smiled, and turned away from him, finding something to do at the workbench while he ate. He hadn't teased or antagonized her since his ordeal with the Blackfoot, since he realized he was in love with her. A little teasing right now seemed appropriate. She didn't appear to be too flustered over his remark.

Chase stood after finishing his meal, and swallowed the last of his coffee. He carried his dishes to the workbench.

"That table looks mighty clean," he said, inspecting the smooth wooded surface that Sarah was busily scrubbing with a rag. He stopped her motion with his hand, and tugged on her arm, turning her to face him.

Their eyes met.

"I will be gone a few hours." Sarah's voice was unsteady. "You get your rest. I will wake you when I return."

"Not before I do this," he murmured, and stepped up close to her, bending his head toward her. He claimed her mouth, and his hands settled at her waist. Her response was immediate. She wrapped her arms around his neck and leaned into him. Chase kissed her long and slow. His insides were on fire. He'd never get tired of holding her.

"I love you, Angel," he whispered when he broke the kiss.

"I love you, too, Chase," she answered, and leaned her head against his chest. Chase wrapped his arms around her, and squeezed his eyes shut. How could he let her go when the time came? He had no answers.

A CHOKING SENSATION startled him awake. Something cold and sharp pressed into his throat. His eyes shot open as he tried to back away, but the pressure increased. Startled, Chase stared into the darkest, most ferocious eyes he had ever seen. A black-haired man leaned over him, his forearm pressed across his throat, the cold blade of a large hunting knife grazing his jugular.

"Where's Sarah," the dark man growled in a low voice.

Chase couldn't speak. He couldn't breathe. He struggled against the restraint, which only encouraged his tormentor to increase the pressure. This wasn't happening again, was it? A little over two weeks had passed since his run for his life against the Blackfoot, and now he was staring death in the face again.

"Where's my daughter?" the man growled again. Although menacing, he spoke so calmly, he could have been simply shooting the breeze, as if this was a normal way for him to have a conversation.

Wait! Daughter?

Chase tried to speak. Only gurgling sounds escaped his throat from the man's tight hold. Sarah's father must have realized he was trying to communicate. His hold lessened. Chase gasped for air. Abruptly, the large man grabbed him by the neck and pulled him off the bed. Chase scrambled to get a foothold on the ground. Sarah's father slammed him face first against the wall, twisting his arm behind his back.

"Calm down, man," Chase ground out. "Sarah's fine. This isn't what it looks like."

The older man released his hold and took a step back. Chase breathed a sigh of relief. Slowly, he turned to face Sarah's father. The man was a good inch shorter than he, but there was no question who would come out the victor in a fight. At least twice his age, the man projected strength and confidence. Chase could hold his own in a good bar brawl, but he had no intention of going head to head with this man.

"Tell me what you've done with my daughter," he said in the same eerily calm voice as before.

"She told me she was going out to collect roots," Chase said, rubbing the back of his neck, still feeling the bite of the other man's fingers. "I've been asleep all morning."

"Then answer this: Who are you, and more important, why are you sleeping in her bed?" His eyes seemed to darken even more. Chase held up his hands and shook his head.

"Hold on, man, this isn't what you think. I haven't done anything inappropriate." *Not that you haven't wanted to, Russell.*

"Explain yourself."

"Sarah nursed me back to health several weeks ago."

The dark eyes looked him up and down. "You look healthy now. Why are you still here?"

"Because I . . . I don't know where else to go."

The deep frown on the man's face was unnerving.

"Daniel, I could use some help out here. Is Sarah . . .? Oh!"

A petite blonde materialized in the doorway. She stopped in her tracks. Her eyes widened in surprise and disbelief, darting between him and the imposing man who still had his knife pointed at him.

Chase could only stare at the woman. There was no question this was Sarah's mother. They had the same sparkling blue eyes.

"Who . . . who are you?" She seemed to be at a loss for words. At least she wasn't attacking him with a knife.

Chase glanced at the man in front of him before turning his attention to the woman. "My name is Chase Russell. I was trying to explain to your husband that this isn't what it looks like."

She shot him an odd look. Her eyes lingered on his head, then moved to the tattoo on his naked chest. *She knows! She can tell you don't belong here, Russell.* He smiled. The day had arrived when he would finally get some answers.

CHAPTER TWENTY-FIVE

"*M*rs. Osborne?" Chase directed his question at the blonde.

"Aimee," the woman corrected him, nodding.

Chase's eyes darted back to the man before addressing the woman again. "I need to talk to you."

"Why don't we all go out front," she said, looking pointedly at her husband. He didn't move. His scowl was still directed at Chase. "Daniel? Let's hear what this young man has to say."

Reluctantly, the scowling man lowered his weapon, and motioned with his arm for Chase to move out of the room. Chase grabbed his shirt up off the floor where he'd dropped it the night before, and led the way. He stood by the main table and turned to face Sarah's parents. This was worse than staring down a village of Blackfoot. He took a deep calming breath, rubbing the back of his neck again, and pulled the shirt on over his head.

Aimee Osborne motioned for him to sit. Her husband stood stoically, his impenetrable dark eyes staring holes into him. Aimee nudged him in the arm, indicating for him to sit down, too, and she took a seat across from Chase.

"Okay, Chase Russell. Let's hear your story," Aimee said, resting her arms on the table. She leaned forward. Her stare was unwavering. Chase caught the split second perplexed look her husband shot her when she spoke. Her voice, her speaking mannerism, had changed. While her few words from a moment ago were spoken in the almost formal way he'd become accustomed to hearing from Sarah, now she sounded different. Her manner of speech was modern. He cleared his throat.

"Some Indians brought me here about a month ago. Apparently I was hypothermic." He paused for a reaction. Her facial features remained unchanged, but she had obviously understood his word. Sarah had never used the word *hypothermic*. She'd called it *exposure*.

"Sarah took care of me. She's been . . . great."

"I ask again, why are you still here after all this time?" Daniel Osborne interrupted. He slammed his open palm on the table with a loud crack. Aimee's hand reached out to cover her husband's.

"Let him speak, Daniel," she said softly. She seemed to be the only one in the room whose nerves weren't on edge.

Chase met the older man's stare. He sure as hell didn't want to antagonize Sarah's father, but he wasn't going to cower, either.

"I can't seem to find my way home," he answered contritely, and his eyes moved back to Aimee, giving her a meaningful look. "One minute I'm passed . . . asleep, the next, I . . ." He couldn't finish.

The cabin door flew open, and Sarah stormed in. All eyes at the table darted to her. She shot hasty looks at her parents, before her eyes lingered on him. Her face was flushed, and her chest heaved as if she'd been running. The only sound in the cabin was Grizzly's panting and enthusiastic tail thumping against furniture as the big dog rushed through the door to greet the new arrivals.

"Mama . . . Papa . . . you're home." She didn't sound happy to see her parents. Her voice was tense, her words clipped.

Chase almost laughed out loud at her obvious statement. He gripped the table to keep from pulling her into his arms.

Aimee smiled at her daughter, then glanced toward her husband. Daniel's face turned murderous. He wouldn't harm his own daughter, would he?

"Sarah, I see you stayed busy while we were gone," Aimee remarked, her eyebrows raised. Daniel's body catapulted out of his seat. His chair toppled to the floor with a loud thud. He raked a hand through his hair. His lips were drawn in a tight line, and the muscles in his jaw clenched and unclenched. His dark eyed fell on his daughter. His features softened slightly, but only for a moment.

"Walk with me outside, *bai'de*."

Without waiting for her, the big man left the cabin. Sarah darted a nervous glance at her mother. She forced a smile, her wide eyes moving to Chase, where they lingered. She swallowed repeatedly, and her teeth raked along her lower lip.

It's okay, Angel. I can handle this. Chase wanted to speak to her, but he needed to get a better feel for the situation first. He hoped his reassuring smile communicated that to her. She nodded slightly, then turned and followed her father out the door.

Chase expelled a deep breath, then turned his attention back to the petite woman facing him from across the table. She folded her hands in front of her, and stared directly at him.

"Okay, Chase. Let's not beat around the bush. What year are you from, and how did you get here?"

Chase cocked an eyebrow. He smiled. "The year is 2035. I was hoping you could fill me in on the how," he said slowly. His heart sped up. All these weeks, he'd lived with the hope that his hunch was correct, that Sarah's mother had time traveled, too. His chest felt much lighter all of a sudden, knowing he'd been right.

Aimee's eyes narrowed, a perplexed look on her face. "You don't know how you time traveled?"

His smile faltered. "Not a clue. Some buddies and I hiked down into the Yellowstone Canyon, and--"

"They allow that in 2035?" she interrupted.

"Well . . . no, not exactly." He rubbed the back of his neck. A knowing smile lit up her face. Her blue eyes sparkled. *So like Sarah . . .*

Chase cleared his throat. "We, ah, got to drinking too much, and I must have passed out. I woke up the next morning by the river, and everyone was gone. When I climbed back out of the canyon, everything was changed . . . different. All signs of civilization were gone. I got caught in a storm, and some Indians must have found me." He shrugged.

He could see her mind spinning.

"How did you know I wasn't from this time?" she asked.

"I guessed. Sarah mentioned some stories you used to tell her, and it became pretty obvious to me." He paused, leaned forward over the table, and asked the question most on his mind. "Is there a way for me to get back home?"

Aimee Osborne searched his face. What was she think-ing? She was as unreadable as her husband.

"Yes, and no," she finally said.

"What does that mean?" His stomach dropped. The reality of his situation hit him again full force, and his chest tightened. He watched her tap the tips of her fingers on the surface of the table.

"You really have no idea how you came here? Do you

remember touching anything, a strange object?" Her forehead wrinkled. Apparently, something wasn't making sense to her. Did she know how she had traveled back in time?

"No, nothing." He shook his head, grinding his teeth in frustration. "I don't remember anything about that night. How is this time traveling even possible?" He ran his hand over his face, and rubbed at his temples. His headache from earlier was back, stronger than ever.

"I'm only familiar with an object that looks like a snake head that makes time travel possible. I have no explanation how it works."

"So where is this object?" At least it was a start. She did know how it was possible.

"Daniel and I got rid of it twenty-five years ago," she said softly.

Chase groaned.

∾

"Walk with me, *bai'de*."

Sarah's heart rate increased. Her father didn't need to raise his voice in anger. His softly spoken words had a greater effect than any shouting or yelling ever could.

She swallowed, even though her mouth was completely dry. Her heart beat drummed in her ears. Sarah nodded, and they walked side by side through the trees, following a familiar trail up the gentle slope of the hills behind their home. Her apprehension increased. She rubbed her sweaty palms together. Her father hadn't said a word. She glanced over at him. He walked erect, his eyes focused straight ahead.

"You are angry with me?" she asked tentatively, unable to bear his silence any longer.

He stopped abruptly, and faced her.

"We return from rendezvous to find a strange man sleeping in your bed. You tell me what emotion I should be feeling." He swept his hand in front of him, and pointed toward the cabin. His brows drew together, and he leaned toward her.

Sarah's chin dropped to her chest. She wished he'd yell, or lash out at her in anger. His stoic way was unbearable.

"He was in need of help, Papa. I couldn't just turn him away. He was near death when three Absarokas brought him here." She blinked away the tears in her eyes. She didn't want to appear weak in her father's eyes.

"He is well now. Why is he still here?"

Sarah took a deep breath. "He . . . he had no place to go." She laughed nervously. "He thinks he's from another time, that something unexplainable brought him here." Sarah watched her father's expression change. His jaw clenched visibly, and something changed in his eyes. He knew! Was Chase correct all along about his belief that her mother was from the future?

Sarah cocked her head. It was her turn to stare hard at her father. "He says Mama is from the future," she said slowly, watching him closely. Her father ran his hand through his hair, a sure sign that he was frustrated about something.

"It is true, isn't it?" Her voice rose, and her eyes widened. Why had no one ever mentioned this before? What other secrets did her parents keep? "Do my brothers know this?" she nearly shouted at him.

He inhaled deeply. Her strong and always self-assured father looked tired all of a sudden. He half-closed his eyes, as if something pained him.

"Your mother abandoned her former life to live here with me. We didn't think it was something our children needed to know. It was something we chose to bury."

"How did she get here?" Sarah couldn't believe what she was hearing. Chase had been correct all along. Her heart pounded up into her throat. She took a step forward to steady herself. Her head whirled so fast, she thought she might lose her balance. Nothing made sense any more.

"Perhaps we should speak of this in your mother's presence," he said somberly. Sarah whirled around and ran back down the trail. She didn't stop running until she reached the cabin. Wiping at her wet face, she threw open the door. Chase and her mother still sat at the table, apparently deep in conversation.

"Why didn't you ever tell us you come from the future?" Sarah glared at her mother. Her vision blurred, and she blinked impatiently. Chase stood and headed her way. She turned on him, her hands on her hips. "Are you happy now? Will you finally get to go home?"

His hands reached out and he gently took hold of her arms, and drew her into an embrace. Sarah stood stiffly in his arms before giving in. She leaned into him, sobbing uncontrollably. His hands stroked her back, his fingers massaging her tense muscles.

"Why don't you two come sit down before your father walks in."

Her mother's gentle words barely reached her ears. Chase pulled back. He smiled down reassuringly at her, and led her to the table. Sarah wiped her face on her shirt sleeve, and sniffed. She sat when Chase offered her a chair, and met her mother's eyes.

"What do you want to know, Sarah?" Her mother reached a hand across the table, and took hold of hers, squeezing gently. Sarah wanted to be angry, but the look of sadness and anguish in her mother's usually sparkling eyes unsettled her.

"Did you come here, and couldn't return?" Sarah asked slowly. The cabin door creak open and close behind her. Her father did not come to the table. She merely felt his presence, and Chase's glance over his shoulder told her he was watching them intently.

Sarah's mother took a deep breath, and her eyes lifted to look past Sarah as well. Then her gaze settled on her again.

"Twenty-five years ago, your grandfather sent me here from the year 2010. His is a long story, and one I'll save for another time. He offered me a chance to come here to this time, because I loved these mountains in my own time. I met your father, and we fell in love."

Her eyes sought her husband's before she continued. "I could have returned home, but I chose to stay with him. I knew I was meant to be here." She paused, an unsure smile on her face. She glanced first at Sarah, then at Chase. "The device that made all this possible caused your grandfather a lot of anguish. Before he died, he wanted it destroyed. Daniel and I agreed. I buried my past life. There was no reason to tell you or your brothers. We never expected . . . this to happen." She looked at Chase.

"How did you destroy the device?" Chase asked slowly.

"It's not exactly destroyed."

There was a noticeable hesitation in her mother's voice. Sarah's eyes darted to Chase. The hopeful look on his face made her bite back fresh tears. He was intent on finding a way home. Sarah stood abruptly from the table. She glared at him in silence, then turned and headed out the door, pausing to dare her father to block her way. He stood with his arms folded across his chest, his face unreadable. He didn't stop her from leaving.

EVERY NERVE CELL in Chase's body screamed at him to go after her. The high he'd been on since yesterday evening when he confessed his love to Sarah came crashing down worse than a nasty hangover. Why did it have to be so short-lived? Not even twenty-four hours of happiness with her, and his world crumbled. He rubbed the back of his neck, and glanced up at Aimee. She was watching him with knowing eyes. Chase hadn't even noticed that Daniel had moved to stand behind his wife. The man moved as silently as a church mouse. He suddenly felt small, sitting at the table while this fierce woodsman glared down at him.

"You have feelings for my daughter." It wasn't a question. The man's stare was unnerving, his voice low and even.

Chase swallowed. "Yes, sir," he finally said, taking a deep breath.

"Have you acted on those feelings?" His eyes narrowed.

That depends . . . "No, sir."

Suddenly, being tied up in the middle of a village of hostile Indians didn't seem so daunting anymore. No wonder the Blackfoot left this man alone. He would kill them with his stare alone.

"Good. And you never will. It is not possible for you to remain here." Daniel moved away from the table. Sarah's mother sat quietly, her eyes darting back and forth between him and her husband.

"I will go in search of the time travel device," Daniel spoke again. "You will return to your time." There was a definite finality in his tone.

It's what you wanted all this time, Russell.

Sarah's father made it plain that he didn't think he was good enough for his daughter. Chase knew he was right.

Aimee Osborne cleared her throat. She stood, and pushed her chair away from the table.

"Daniel. A word with you, please," she said, facing her husband. Chase had to smile to himself. This little woman seemed to be the only person who didn't cower in front of Daniel Osborne. He could see where Sarah got her feistiness.

"I . . . ah . . . I'll just go outside, then," Chase ran his hand up and down the back of his neck, and stood. He was anxious to find Sarah and talk to her.

"You will remain here." Daniel shot him a dark glare that dared him to challenge his authority. He left the cabin. Aimee smiled tentatively at him, then followed her husband out the door.

CHAPTER TWENTY-SIX

*A*imee inhaled deeply, and stepped out of the cabin. She quietly closed the door behind her, and scanned the meadow. There was no need, really. She knew Daniel would be down by the river. Whenever he had something on his mind that required alone time, that's where he went. She smiled softly. Sure enough, her husband stood at the riverbank, looking beyond the Madison. Aimee wasted no time, and hurried to his side. She reached up and placed her hand on Daniel's shoulder.

"Weren't you a bit harsh?" she asked gently. Daniel was usually reserved and quiet, and he never passed judgment in haste. He turned to face her, his eyebrows raised in a silent question.

"He's confused, Daniel. He was thrown back here without his knowledge, to a time and place he's completely unfamiliar with, and—"

"Exactly," Daniel interrupted her, his voice firm. "That's why he needs to go back to his time as quickly as possible." He avoided her eyes, and focused on something along the opposite riverbank.

"He's in love with Sarah," Aimee said softly. How well she understood that feeling.

"I can see that," Daniel's voice raised uncharacteristically. His body tensed, and he continued to stare off into the distance. Aimee moved in front of him. She wasn't tall enough to obstruct his view, so she wound her arms around his neck and pulled his face down to meet her gaze. Still tense, his arms wrapped around her waist.

"And she's in love with him," Aimee added, staring into his dark eyes.

Daniel's jaw clenched and unclenched.

"You know it's going to be near impossible to find that time travel device. It's been twenty-five years. We never thought we'd use it again, remember? That's why we disposed of it the way we did. What happens if you can't find it?" She wrapped her fingers around some strand of hair at his nape, and one hand caressed his jaw. His tension eased, but only slightly.

Daniel didn't answer. He moved his hands away from her waist, and took a step back. She dropped her arms. Daniel had his stubborn moments, but she usually succeeded in swaying him to see reason. He turned away from her and walked along the riverbank. She followed, and slipped her hand in his. Finally, he gave it a tight squeeze. It was a start. At least he wasn't shutting her out completely, and there were things that needed to be said. Aimee had her suspicions for the cause of his behavior, and it was best all brought out now.

"You have to teach him," she said, pulling him to a stop. He turned, and stared down at her. She almost laughed. He looked at her in stunned silence, much like the man she fell in love with twenty-five years ago, when she proposed the same challenge.

"If you think you know everything, then why don't you teach me?"

"He needs to return to his time," Daniel stated adamantly. The gentle afternoon breeze lifted strands of Daniel's hair from his neck.

"He needs to learn to survive here, in case he can't go back," she argued.

"Impossible." He shook his head.

"Why?" Aimee glared at him, and threw her free hand in the air. "You taught me. You taught our children."

"That's different," he said quickly. He looked past her shoulders into the distance, avoiding eye contact. What was he thinking? Did he remember standing along this path so many years ago, when she had dared him to teach her to survival skills?

"How so? How is it different?"

"A man needs to be able to protect his family, and provide for them. This young buck can do neither." He gestured with his chin toward the cabin.

"That's why you need to teach him." Why couldn't he see the logic here?

Daniel released Aimee's hand, and ran it through his tousled hair. He inhaled deeply before he spoke again. "Hawk Soaring came to me, before we left for rendezvous. He has asked for Sarah."

Aimee tilted her head at him and studied his face. "And what did you tell him, Daniel? You could never give your daughter in marriage to someone she doesn't want."

"Perhaps I will. He is a good man. He will be a good provider."

Aimee laughed. "I know she and Hawk Soaring have been friends, but has she ever said she is interested in him as a potential husband?"

Daniel didn't answer. The scowl on his face sent most men into hiding.

"You want to know what I think?" Unperturbed by his dark look, she stood to face him and put her hand on his chest.

Daniel's scowl turned into a frown, and he inhaled sharply. His lips were drawn in a tight line. "No, but I'm sure you will tell me anyway," he growled.

"I think you are afraid to lose your little girl . . . to any man."

Daniel continued to avoid eye contact. She reached up and cupped his face in her hands, forcing him to look at her.

"Teach him. He might surprise you. I'm sure you noticed the tattoo on his chest." She waited for his response.

Daniel scoffed. "He can't be the same man we've heard about. A man completely out of his element, defeating an entire village of Blackfoot? Impossible."

"So the obvious explanation is that there has to be another white man in these mountains somewhere with that kind of tattoo. Is that what you're saying?" She laughed before her face grew serious again. "Daniel, he looks highly capable to me. He might be out of his element, but he's had certain training in his own time that requires similar skills that are needed to survive here."

Daniel sighed, and stared intently at her. Had he forgotten all the pain and anguish they'd both endured when they were torn apart from each other all those years ago? Surely he could see that his daughter loved this man. And by the look on Chase's face, he was deeply in love with her.

There was a difference, however, Aimee had to concede. Chase seemed to want to return to the future. Aimee remembered how she had fought against being returned to 2010. She had wanted to remain here. She'd been told she'd be time traveling to the past. It was still a mystery to her how Chase had ended up here.

Chase was a confused young man. He needed more time to figure out exactly what was important to him. From what he had told her so far, he had made some bad choices and gotten into a lot of trouble. Maybe he just needed to see that he could make a fresh start here.

Aimee had liked him immediately. She could tell he was torn between his love for Sarah, and for feeling out of place here. That seemed to be the only reason he'd want to return home. If he got a good foothold here, learned about the mountains and how to survive, he would see that this was where he could truly become a man.

All he needed was the confidence, the belief in himself, to survive on his own, which he seemed to lack. Besting a village of Blackfoot didn't come by sheer luck. Daniel had been ambushed, and nearly died at the hands of a war party twenty-five years ago. If he'd been taken hostage instead, and given the same chance that Chase had been given, could her own husband have accomplished such a feat when he was that age?

Daniel pulled her in his arms and kissed her. "I will teach him. But, I do so only because you ask."

Aimee wound her arms around his neck. "Your daughter will thank you for it," she smiled into his warm eyes.

"I still plan to search for the snake head," Daniel said sternly. "In the meantime, I will do as you wish. But, he cannot sleep in our house any longer. He will move to the old cabin."

Aimee nodded in agreement. "When do you plan to look for the device? We have lots to do here."

"I will decide when the time is right. We've just returned home."

"You'd best go unpack the horses. Those poor things are

still standing around with their loads. I think I need to find our daughter and have a woman to woman talk with her."

"When has our daughter become a woman," he mumbled.

Aimee smiled at the frown on her husband's face. "Ask Chase to help you with the horses," she called over her shoulder as she walked away.

She found Sarah sitting on a downed log at the top of the rise behind the cabin. The area was concealed by lodgepoles, yet provided a panoramic view of the valley. Sarah's shoulders slumped, and she stared at her hands in her lap.

"Can I sit with you?" Aimee asked quietly. Sarah's tear stained face tore at her heart. She remembered that feeling of losing the man she loved all too well. For a young woman, it was a devastating feeling. Sarah nodded, and Aimee sat down next to her.

"Do you want to talk about it?" she asked, wrapping her arm around Sarah's shoulder. Her daughter's body shuddered when she took in a deep breath.

"Why does he say he loves me, but wants to go home?" Sarah sobbed.

Aimee closed her eyes and inhaled deeply.

"It's complicated for him, Sarah. He comes from a world that is very different from here. He doesn't know how he fits in."

"But you wanted to stay here with Papa. How did you fit in?"

"I sort of knew what I was getting into when I got sent here. I wanted to be here. Chase has no prior experience with the wilderness. He told me he's never been away from the city in his time, until he came to this area shortly before he was sent back in time."

"He has no confidence in his abilities, Mama." Sarah wiped her face on her sleeve, and sniffed. "You should see him. He throws a tomahawk as good as Papa, and he

237

defeated twenty Blackfoot warriors, but he still doesn't believe he can survive here."

"Right now, I'm sure all he remembers is what a struggle it was to defeat those warriors. He can't see it for the accomplishment it truly is." She chuckled. "Perhaps he thinks it is a common thing for a man in this time to run barefoot and nude over mountainous terrain for the many miles he covered."

Sarah stared at her. "I told him I'd never heard of anyone accomplishing such a feat."

"He must have been hurt badly during that ordeal." Aimee's face grew serious.

"He could barely walk. He was feverish for days. I thought he would die." Fresh tears pooled in her daughter's eyes.

"I'm proud of you, Sarah." Aimee rested a hand on Sarah's shoulder, giving it a light squeeze. "Your healing skills are getting very good." After a moment's silence, she added, "I asked your father to teach him."

Sarah's face lit up, then the smile froze. "Papa doesn't seem to like him very much."

Aimee smiled smugly. "Your father needs to come to terms with a few things. He'll warm up to him."

"Why didn't he tell me that Hawk Soaring spoke to him before rendezvous?"

"You know about that?" Aimee raised her eyebrows in surprise.

"I found out when I tended to Snow Bird. She has a healthy son."

Aimee nodded. She looked down into the valley from their perch high above. Chase emerged from the cabin behind Daniel. The two walked to where the horses were tethered by the woodpile. Daniel appeared to be instructing him on what to do. He'd always been a patient teacher. She hoped he wouldn't deviate from his ways with his newest pupil.

"Looks like they're getting along just fine," Aimee said cheerfully, pointing toward the cabin. Sarah watched in silence. Her shoulders slumped forward, and she twisted a blade of grass between her fingers. There was no hint of joy on her face.

"Your father can't see you as a grown woman yet, Sarah. It's hard for him. In his eyes, he still sees the little girl who fell asleep on his lap every night. It's hard for him to give you over to another man. I think Hawk Soaring's request took him by surprise. Imagine his shock now." Aimee laughed. "He comes home, and the last thing he expects to find is a man in the house who is obviously quite taken with you, and you with him. And," she paused and leaned forward to see her daughter's face, "we never expected to have this time travel device come up again. That was something we've both put behind us."

Sarah stared into the valley, her eyes trained on the man unloading blankets and furs off one of the horses. Her hand plucked at some grasses in the dirt.

"Chase has no intention of asking for me. He wants to go home," Sarah said solemnly. Aimee didn't know how to console her.

"Sarah. The man is in love with you. That is a powerful thing. It probably scares him. He doesn't know what to do. All I can say is, give him time."

"Papa wants to find the thing that brought Chase . . . and you, here. Will he find it?"

"Chances are, he won't."

"Good," Sarah said firmly.

Aimee smiled softly. "Sarah, do you love him enough to let him go?"

"What do you mean?" She looked up, confusion evident on her face.

"Sometimes, you have to let the person you love be free. You can't force him to stay if he doesn't want to. Would you rather that he be miserable if he truly doesn't want to stay here? If your father does find that device, you have to be strong enough to let Chase go if he chooses."

Sarah nodded. She wiped her hand across her face, and stood. "May I speak with him?" she asked softly.

"Of course," Aimee answered. "Just because we're home doesn't mean you two can't interact."

"Papa won't allow it, I know it."

"You let me deal with your father, okay?"

Aimee rose from the log, and patted Sarah on the shoulder. She led the way down the hill. The Tukudeka had strict rules about courting, and it must have been difficult for her daughter to go against all the customs she'd grown up with, to have a man live under the same roof with her for over a month. And Chase's modern ways no doubt added to the confusion. She smiled to herself. Hadn't it been similar with her and Daniel so many years ago? Her unconventional ways had perplexed him at the start of their relationship. Fond memories came flooding back, warming her insides.

Sarah opened the door to the little cabin, the hinges squeaking loudly, and walked in. Her mother had told her she'd keep her father occupied in the house so she could speak with Chase. Mama understood the need for the two of them to talk, after all that had happened this day. Sarah hadn't expected to find such a strong advocate in her mother.

More often than not over the last few years, they'd argued over the most trivial things.

Chase was busy shoving trunks against the wall opposite the bunk. He turned when she walked in. His tightly drawn lips relaxed, and wide smile lit up his face. He covered the space between them in two strides, and grabbed her around the waist, pulling her to him.

"I thought I'd never get you alone again," he said in a husky tone. His hand swept loose hair away from her face, and he brought his lips down on hers.

Sarah stood stiffly for a moment. Her parents were home. She shouldn't be this close to Chase. His lips on hers quickly made her forget about her parents. Her body relaxed, and her arms crept around his neck. She leaned into him and let the warm sensations of being in his arms wash over her.

"I missed you, Angel," he murmured against her ear, then pulled back.

"I missed you, too. If my father finds me here . . ." she let her words trail off.

Chase grinned. "Yeah, I'd better watch my manners. I already got the lecture from him. He's not one to mess with, is he?" His warm hands at her waist sent shivers through her. "The trouble is, I'm willing to take the risk. I can't stay away from you." He bent and nuzzled her neck.

Sarah wrapped her arms around him. She leaned her head against his chest, his strong heart beating against her ear. *Then why don't you want to stay with me?*

Her mother had said to give him time. How much time would he need? And would she really be strong enough to let him go if her father found the device? Would he choose to leave?

CHAPTER TWENTY-SEVEN

*C*hase walked up to the cabin and knocked on the door. His first night spent in the old cabin had felt odd. He missed Sarah's scent on her bed, but it was better this way. It would feel even worse living under the same roof with her parents.

He recognized Aimee's voice inside, inviting him to enter. His eyes swept the room when he stepped in. Sarah stood with her back to him at the workbench. She turned, and their eyes met. An imperceptible current seemed to flow between them. His gut tightened. The urge to rush to her, pull her in his arms, and kiss her senseless was overwhelming. His toes curled in his moccasins, as if they would root him to the ground and prevent him from moving toward her.

"Sit down, Chase. Breakfast is ready."

Aimee's soft voice broke the invisible tie between him and Sarah. She ladled food out of the skillet onto plates, and Chase took a seat at the table. He glanced around, wondering why Daniel wasn't in the room. He hoped he hadn't sat in the man's chair, but no one told him to move. Sarah brought him a steaming cup of coffee. His hand darted out and touched hers when she set the cup in front of him. She didn't move, and the longing in her eyes when she met his gaze was almost his undoing.

"Thanks," he said, clearing his throat. He pulled his hand away when Aimee set a plate in front of him. Sarah turned and headed back to the workbench.

"Sleep well?" Aimee asked cheerfully.

"I guess so." He shrugged, taking a bite of the pancake-looking things on his plate.

"Sarah and I are headed to the Tukudeka village after breakfast. We should be home before dark."

His eyes lingered on Sarah's turned back. He wouldn't see her all day. The thought left an odd empty feeling in him. He almost groaned at the thought of spending the day with Daniel. If he got lucky, maybe the man would have things of his own to do. Chase would simply have to make himself scarce somehow.

"Is there anything you'd like me to do while you're gone?" he asked.

Aimee didn't have a chance to answer. The door to the bedroom opened, and Daniel walked into the main room, a rifle in each hand. Without warning, he threw one toward Chase, who caught it in his left hand, looking at the older man in surprise. Daniel's expression was unreadable.

Score one for you, Russell. You passed the reflex test. It was hard to maintain a poker face. He stared at the flintlock in his hand, and all smugness left him. What was he supposed to do with that?

Daniel's eyes assessed him without a hint of what he was thinking behind that dark stare. Abruptly, he turned toward his wife. "We're headed north. We may not be back before dark."

Chase watched the man's hard face turn suddenly soft when he looked at Aimee. His hand rested on the small of her back, and she smiled warmly up at him. The love between Sarah's parents was quite obvious. He didn't have a single memory of his mother and father ever sharing a tender moment. He recalled plenty of yelling and door slamming, before his old man walked out on them for good.

His eyes wandered to where Sarah stood by the workbench. She was watching him. *I love you, Angel.* He formed the words with his mouth. She smiled before darting a glance at her father.

"Have you finished eating?"

Daniel's voice startled him. His focus had been on the dark-haired beauty standing in the corner. Knowing her smile was only for him gave him an almost euphoric feeling. Why didn't he tell her weeks ago how he felt about her? Then they could have explored their relationship without the constant presence of her parents. Aimee seemed more open-minded. But then, she'd grown up in a time where open display of affection between unmarried couples was socially acceptable. Daniel seemed to be the stereotypical old-fashioned father, who would rather shoot him than let him within a hundred yards of his daughter.

Chase hastily stuffed the rest of the food in his mouth, and washed it down with coffee. He pushed his chair back from the table, still holding the rifle in his hand.

"Ah, what am I doing with this?" he asked, raising the rifle slightly, hoping he didn't sound too stupid.

"Where's your weapon belt?" Daniel asked, instead of offering an answer.

"I left it in the other cabin." Chase shrugged.

"First rule in the mountains. You never leave your weapons unguarded. Always carry them with you." The impatience had left his voice. He sounded more like an authoritative teacher. "Let's go." He motioned with his chin toward the door.

Chase shot him a questioning look, his eyebrows raised.

"We're going hunting," Daniel said, as if that was obvious. He motioned again toward the door.

Chase's eyes sought Sarah's. He couldn't help it. An invisible magnet drew him to her, and he couldn't just walk out the door without one last look. Her eyes were wide as saucers, and she wore an almost panicked expression on her face. They both smiled at the same time. He wished he could have five minutes alone with her, but knew that wouldn't happen, at least not for the rest of today.

"Chase." Daniel's stern voice prompted him to finally turn and head out the door.

After Chase retrieved his belt, Daniel led him through the forest behind the cabin, heading into the hills to the north. He cut through the dense growth of lodgepoles, following some imperceptible path. It had to be some kind of trail, since they seemed to avoid most of the downfall that lay about everywhere. At times, the older man picked up the pace, then he'd slow to a brisk walk. He didn't speak for, what seemed like hours.

Perspiration beaded Chase's forehead, even in the crisp early morning air. The sun's rays didn't quite reach the forest floor. He hadn't done this much walking and jogging since that day . . . Anger welled up in him anew. He gripped the rifle he held in his hand. Perhaps if Daniel taught him to shoot this thing, he'd feel more confident the next time he came across some Indian. The tomahawk hanging off his belt felt more familiar. At least he knew how to use that.

"Are you paying attention to your surroundings?" Daniel's voice broke into his thoughts. Without warning, he had stopped, and Chase nearly ran into him.

"What am I supposed to be paying attention to? There's nothing here but trees. I figured you had a plan on where we're going."

Daniel cocked an eyebrow, and Chase knew that he'd given the wrong answer. What was he supposed to say? Daniel hadn't said two words to him since leaving the cabin. What did he expect? At least if he'd tell him what to look for, or what they were doing, he could focus on the task at hand.

Having an attitude with Daniel was probably not a good idea. Chase inhaled a deep breath, trying to curb his annoyance.

"Can you find your way back to the cabin from here, alone?" Daniel turned and raised both eyebrows at him.

Chase looked around. The forest was as dense as ever. Everything looked the same to him. His sense of direction was nonexistent.

"No," he reluctantly conceded, working his jaw. He felt like a kid who hadn't studied for his algebra exam. He'd found his way back to the valley from the Tukudeka village that ill-fated day he left, but he'd had a river to follow then. The middle of the forest was completely different.

"How did you outrun twenty Blackfoot warriors, yet you cannot focus on what is in front of you right now? The spirits must have smiled on you that day."

More like a dark-haired angel.

"I had help. Sarah gave me some pretty good directions."

Daniel's face darkened. "My daughter gambled with her life that day. I hope you know that."

Chase met his stare, his annoyance growing. "Yes, sir, I do know that, and not a day goes by that I don't feel guilt over what happened." He threw his hands in the air. "Maybe you should try coming to the twenty-first century, and see how well you get around when you don't have a clue about your environment." His voice raised in anger. Wheeling around, he kicked at the dirt. Shit! He felt bad enough as it was. He didn't need a constant reminder as to his incompetence.

"I have been to the twenty-first century, and I understand about not knowing your environment."

Chase had to strain his ears to hear Daniel's quietly spoken words. Slowly, he turned around.

"You've been to the future?" he asked. He couldn't picture Daniel Osborne in a modern city.

"I went in search of my wife, after she was taken from me." Daniel nodded. "I didn't know what to expect. I had very little information to go by in order to find her, and to this day I believe it was by sheer luck that I managed to track her down." He paused, and put his hand on Chase's shoulder. "But I was determined. Never lose sight of what is important to you once you figure out what that is. Then focus to achieve your goal."

Chase could only stare at the man, dumbfounded. His high school football coach had said those same things to him. Back then, he had been focused. But after Coach Beckman died, he'd lost that inner drive. What did he have to focus on now? His sole motivation since coming here was finding a way back home.

Sarah.

She'd become the most important thing to him, he realized with sudden clarity. The elated feeling that had swept over him that day, running for his life, when Sarah's vision had spurred him on and he'd realized he loved her, suddenly came flooding back. He had to focus on her, doing what was right for her. *Is she more important than going home, Russell?*

Daniel smiled suddenly. "I see you are understanding what I say."

Was the man a mind reader, too?

"I've been intent on finding a way home," Chase said slowly. "It's all that's been on my mind. That, and . . . Sarah." He rubbed the back of his neck. Daniel dropped his hand, and Chase looked him in the eye. "Teach me how to shoot this rifle." He moved his arm in front of him in a sweeping motion. "Show me how to find my way out of this forest."

Daniel nodded. "There will come a day when you will be faced with making a choice, Chase Russell. And it will be a choice only you can make."

SARAH LISTENED to the rhythmic chirping of crickets in the evening air. She sat by the woodpile on an overturned log, stroking Grizzly's fur. The dog lay faithfully at her feet. The sun had long gone down, and there was no moon to give off even a little light in the distance. How long were they going to be gone? She and her mother had returned hours ago from visiting Little Bird and Snow Bird. The baby had grown in the nearly three weeks since his birth.

Her cousin Touch the Cloud had hovered outside the birthing hut most of the day, bringing water and firewood when Snow Bird requested it. Another week and he would finally get to meet his son. Sarah could tell he was anxious to be reunited with his wife as well. Hawk Soaring had, thankfully, not been in the village. Elk Runner made sure he informed her that he would be coming for a visit soon, then in the same breath, had inquired about Chase.

Grizzly's head suddenly jerked up from its resting place on his huge front paws. His tail thumped the dirt. Sarah strained her eyes into the darkness. Her father's familiar form emerged from the darkness, and several paces behind him, a taller figure that sent her heart beats racing.

She rose from her perch on the log. The light from the window in the main cabin softly illuminated the approaching figures. Her father moved with his usual confident stride. There was a noticeable difference in Chase's gait. Sarah squinted her eyes. Chase was definitely limping. She rushed up to meet them, and her father's hand prevented her from reaching the man she wanted to throw her arms around.

"It's late. Go inside, Sarah," her father's firm voice commanded.

"Please, Papa, just a minute," she asked softly. He slowly removed his hand from her arm.

"You have five minutes." She caught the reluctance in his tone.

Chase hadn't stopped walking. Without a glance her way, he headed for his cabin.

"Chase," she called out, catching up with him when he reached his door.

"Do what your father says, Sarah. Go back to the main house."

"What . . . what happened? Are you hurt?" She reached out her hand to touch his arm. She noticed him clutching his side. Had he somehow reinjured his ribs?

"I'll be fine in the morning," he grumbled. "It's been a long day. I just need to get to bed."

"What about some food? You must be hungry." Why was he acting so strange?

Chase inhaled loudly. "Sarah, I appreciate your concern. I'll be fine." Sarah could feel his eyes on her, but his body stood rigid. She ran her hand up his arm. He pulled away. "Good night, Sarah," he said, opening the cabin door.

"Chase?" He stopped in his tracks. The tension in his muscles lessened.

"I had a run in with a deer, okay. Your dad can fill you in about my incompetence. I can't seem to get anything right." His voice was filled with self-loathing. He kicked at the door when it wouldn't stay open. "Good night, Angel." He disappeared inside the dark cabin, the door closing swiftly in her face.

Sarah stood rooted to the spot momentarily. Reluctantly,

she turned and headed toward the house. She needed to find out what had happened.

Her mother set a plate of stew in front of her father when she walked in. Her eyes met his.

"Is Chase hurt?" she asked.

"Only his pride," her father said, a smile softening his features.

"You didn't bring back any meat," her mother remarked.

"No, we didn't." He grinned broadly now. "It seems the deer had other plans. Chase decided he was more proficient with his ax than the rifle, and took it upon himself to surprise the doe. His stalking skills are to be commended, but he neglected to stay down wind, or watch his surroundings. Another deer darted out of the thicket, knocking him to the ground."

Sarah's mother began to laugh, and her father joined in.

"Why didn't you warn him not to do that?" Sarah asked, her hands on her hips, glaring at her parents.

"He learned his lesson today. He will not be making that mistake again."

Sarah conceded that her father was probably correct.

CHAPTER TWENTY-EIGHT

*A*imee stepped out of the bedroom, and spotted Daniel standing by the window, staring out into the distance. The gray early morning light held no hint of sunshine. July brought varied weather to her beloved mountains, and the sunshine they had enjoyed for weeks now seemed to want a day of rest. The fire in the hearth had already been brought to life, and water was set to boil for coffee. She walked up behind her husband, and wrapped her arms around his waist.

"What's on your mind," she purred, sliding her hands up his chest. He covered her hands with his own, and inhaled deeply.

"We made a grave mistake when we threw that device over the waterfall that day," Daniel said solemnly. "We never expected it to resurface, did we?"

"No. I don't see how that could have happened. We both thought it would lie at the bottom of those falls forever. I guess fate sometimes has its own plans. It must have somehow moved downstream and beached itself at the river's edge. That's the only way Chase could have inadvertently touched it in his time."

"I have to find it. It has to be removed. Something like this can never happen again." He turned toward her.

"You're right," Aimee sighed. "But what do we do about our immediate problem?"

"Chase?"

"And Sarah." Aimee nodded. "They remind me of us, Daniel. Two young people in love, from different worlds, each unsure of what to make of the other."

"You wanted to be here." Daniel stroked her cheek, smiling down at her.

"Your daughter has handled herself well. I can only imagine what had to be going on in her mind. She felt obligated to take care of him, but it went against all the customs she's grown up with." Aimee laughed. "I remember you barely setting foot in your own cabin when I arrived. You acted like such an honorable Tukudeka. Of course, I didn't know your reasons back then."

"You scared me to death." He grinned.

Aimee rested her head against his shoulder.

"How do you feel about Chase now? You've spent practically every waking moment with him for the last three days. Is that because you prefer his company to mine, or is it to keep him away from Sarah?"

Daniel held her close and stroked her hair. "He has much to learn. He is young and impulsive. I believe he has not had much guidance in his life. When he finds his true path, he will be a great man."

"As great as you?" Aimee raised herself on tip toes and kissed his cheek.

"In our daughter's eyes, he already is."

"I'm glad you won't deny your daughter a chance to find

love, Daniel. I guess time will tell where these two are headed."

"If I find the device, he may choose to go home." Daniel's expression turned serious.

"True," Aimee sighed. "I fear what this might do to Sarah."

She pulled out of Daniel's embrace, and stood next to him, in front of the window. She laughed softly, shaking her head.

"She hasn't been interested in a man, ever, that I can think of. Then Chase shows up, a man completely unfamiliar with the ways she knows, and sweeps her off her feet. I'm telling you, Daniel, there are stronger forces at work here than you and I will ever comprehend."

Her eyes scanned the distance across the meadow, and she raised herself on her toes to see better.

"Is that Elk Runner?" she asked, pointing to the west.

Daniel looked to where she pointed. "And it looks like he's brought company."

Aimee turned her head and looked at her husband. A slow smile formed on his lips. Aimee's eyes narrowed.

She turned back to watch her brother-in-law and another man approach. Her hands shot to her hips. "One of these days I'm going to have a serious talk with your brother. Him with his shenanigans." She threw her arm out in the general direction of the approaching men, pointing a finger their way. "That's Hawk Soaring he's brought with him."

"Why should that bother you?" Daniel raised his eyebrows.

Aimee glared at him. "He knows, Daniel. He knows about Chase, and how Sarah feels about him. Three days ago while we were visiting Snow Bird, he kept asking Sarah how Chase was doing. And apparently he also found out from some Crow about Chase's run with the Blackfoot. I wonder if that's why he's here." Her voice rose, and her speech became faster with each word.

"You're getting too upset, wife," Daniel pulled her up against him. "Perhaps he merely comes to visit with me. I haven't seen him since before rendezvous."

"You don't believe that any more than I do," Aimee scoffed. "He's up to something." She paused and angled her head at her husband. "And what are you going to say to Hawk?"

"There is nothing to say." Daniel shrugged. "The decision rests with Sarah."

Aimee pulled away from him and headed for the hearth. She busied herself pouring hot water in the coffee pot. Daniel went out to greet his brother. Loud voices and laughter outside drew nearer, and she plastered a smile on her face when the men walked through the door.

"You sure didn't waste any time when you said you were coming for a visit." She glared at her brother-in-law. Elk Runner smiled brightly.

"White Wolf, your wife is as disrespectful as ever. When will you teach her how to properly address a hunter of the Tukudeka?"

Daniel winked at Aimee from across the room. She greeted Hawk Soaring, then said, "If you'd like to sit, I'll have some breakfast ready in a while."

Elk Runner held a passel of freshly caught trout, already cleaned and gutted, out to her. "I bring the food, if you will cook it." He took a seat at the table. "Perhaps this will placate your disposition, woman."

Aimee stood glaring at him, her hands on her hips. Then she broke into a wide smile. Staying mad with him was impossible.

Hawk Soaring remained standing near the door, a stoic look on his face.

"We've come to ask if you," Elk Runner looked at Daniel, "and Chase would accompany us on a bighorn hunt. We are headed to the Sheepeater Mountains. The hunting is good there."

Aimee shot a suspicious look at her husband, who tried to avoid her stare.

"I'd be happy to go, but I have not seen Chase yet."

"I'll wake Sarah. She can help me with fixing breakfast." Aimee headed toward her daughter's room.

"She's already up and gone." Daniel said, stopping her.

Aimee was about to ask where Sarah had gone, when the cabin door opened. Everyone's head turned when Chase walked in. He stood rooted to the spot for a moment, his eyes darting from one person to the next. They lingered particularly long on Hawk Soaring, whose own stare didn't waver.

"Sit down, Chase. We're going to have fried trout for breakfast. Elk Runner's treat," Aimee said cheerfully. "You have already met him, I believe."

Chase walked to the table and held out his hand in greeting. "Yeah, we've met." He sneaked a glance toward Sarah's closed bedroom door before he took a seat opposite Elk Runner.

Aimee turned her back to the room full of men. She laid the trout out on the workbench, and sliced a knife along the sides of the fish. It would be interesting to see how Chase and Hawk interacted with each other. Jealousy was as powerful an emotion as love. Both of these young men cared for her daughter. She wondered how this would all play out. Finished fileting the fish, she coated each with some cornmeal and flour, and tossed them in a sizzling hot skillet over the fire. The cabin quickly filled with the delicious smell of fried fish.

"White Wolf, may I speak?" Hawk Soaring's even voice asked. Aimee's head turned. She glanced from Hawk to her husband, then to Chase. She realized how disadvantaged he was. Everyone in the room spoke in Shoshoni. Chase probably didn't understand any of it.

Daniel left the table, and walked toward Aimee. He reached for the coffee pot, and filled five cups.

"Speak, Kwiyoo," he said, picking up two cups and setting them at the table. He returned for the rest without looking at the young hunter.

"Might you permit me to find *Imaah?* I wish to speak with her."

Aimee's eyes volleyed to each man in the room. Elk Runner wore his usual silly grin. Chase's attention was on Hawk, his jaw clenched. He couldn't know what Hawk had asked.

"She went in search of eggs. She mentioned a fresh goose nest about a mile to the east along the Little Buffalo River. You will probably find her there." Daniel waved him off.

Hawk nodded respectfully, then turned to leave. Chase's body tensed, his palms on the table as if he was about to spring out of his seat. His arm and shoulder muscles tightened.

"Shouldn't someone wake Sarah?" he asked casually.

"She's already up, collecting goose eggs, I think" Aimee smiled at him. "Maybe she's planning to bake something today."

Elk Runner bent toward the floor, and picked up a horn-bow. It looked newly made. When he held it out to Chase, Aimee's eyes widened. The Tukudeka were known for their excellent bows, which they fashioned from elk antlers or mountain sheep horn. It was a painstaking and long process to make one of these bows, and it was a hunter's most prized possession. Seldom did they trade or otherwise part with them.

Chase gave him a questioning look.

"For you, Chase Russell," Elk Runner said. "A hunter need good bow."

Chase reluctantly accepted the gift. "I . . . don't know what to say." His eyes darted to Aimee and Daniel. Daniel's eyebrows furrowed, a questioning look directed at his brother.

"Someday, I teach you make own bow. Now, you use this. We go hunt *wasuppin*." He looked at Daniel for help.

"Mountain sheep. Bighorn," he supplied the English translation.

Chase stood abruptly. "Will you all excuse me? I forgot to wash up." He set the bow on the table, then quickly darted out of the cabin.

The three remaining people looked at each other.

"He needs a good weapon to hunt." Elk Runner shrugged, when both Aimee and Daniel glared at him.

"What is your interest in Chase?" Aimee asked. She removed the trout from the skillet, scraping the meat onto plates, and set them in front of the men. Daniel returned to his place at the table.

"If he is to be my future nephew, I can surely present him with a gift," Elk Runner said, taking a bite of trout.

"I fear my daughter has two suitors," Daniel said, pushing the food around on his plate. "What am I to do with that?"

Aimee hadn't sat down. She stood by the workbench, her arms crossed over her chest, watching the conversation like a tennis match.

Elk Runner shrugged. "What do bull elk or bison do when two want the same cow?"

Aimee's mouth dropped open at his words.

"You're suggesting I let them fight over her?" Daniel's fork stopped in mid-air, the trout falling back onto the plate.

"Oh stop it, you two," Aimee scoffed, throwing her hands in the air. She glared at her husband and brother-in-law.

"Listen to yourselves. Sarah is not a cow, and neither are Chase nor Hawk bulls. These are three young people we are talking about, not elk or bison. Someone is going to get hurt by all this."

"Sarah will have to decide which man she chooses," Daniel said, reaching a hand out to Aimee. She took it, and he pulled her up to stand beside him while he sat at the table. His arm snaked around her waist. "The trouble is, only one of them has asked for her."

"Chase is not ready yet, but he will be." Elk Runner said confidently, shoveling more food in his mouth.

"Maybe he wants to return home to the place he came from," Daniel suggested. "He is still unsure of himself. His skills at tracking are improving, but these things take a long time to learn. It is not like learning from childhood. Chase is a grown man, and has no experience."

"Why are you so intent on Chase and Sarah?" Aimee asked suspiciously. "Wouldn't you want to see her with Hawk Soaring?"

Elk Runner shook his head. "Hawk Soaring is a good man, but he is not a good match for your daughter."

"Why do you say that?" Aimee asked, curious as to why he would think that. After all, they were both Shoshone, and Chase was a white man, a mere stranger.

Elk Runner's face lit up. "To begin with, your daughter is too much like you, *Dosa haiwi*. Her ways are not the ways of a proper Tukudeka wife. Hawk Soaring would have difficulty with her. And also," his face grew more serious, "he has relatives among the Akaideka to the north who have had problems with some whites. I would not wish my niece to be shunned by her husband's family because of the color of her skin."

"Sarah's in love with Chase. I don't see that she will choose to marry Hawk, even if Chase doesn't ask her," Aimee said. "I can't see her marrying just any man. She's been so adamant about not needing a husband, and now all she wants is for Chase to make her his wife." She sighed deeply. "Young love can be so complicated."

She moved to stand behind Daniel, her hands rubbing his shoulders. She remembered all too well all the misunderstandings between herself and Daniel before they finally realized they loved each other.

Sarah walked through the thick tall grasses along the riverbank, searching for goose nests. She had already found one, but it had only contained shells. A fox or coyote must have gotten to the eggs before her. A flock of Canada geese honked loudly as she approached, and several took to the water. A few others charged her, their long necks lowered and their beaks open, their wings spread wide and flapping loudly. It was a good indication that they were protecting a nest.

She used the long stick she'd brought with her to ward off the angry gander's charges. She didn't want to hurt the bird, but she also knew that their bite could be quite painful.

"Can I be of some help, *Imaah*?"

Sarah whirled around. Hawk Soaring was the last person she expected to see here this early in the day. And what was he doing, coming to her without the benefit of a chaperone this far from other people? It was highly unconventional. It was something Chase would do, but not Hawk.

She hadn't seen much of Chase since her parents' return. The last time they had been close was right after he'd moved into the small cabin, when he told her he couldn't stay away from her. He sure seemed to have had a change of heart.

Since the night he and her father returned from their first foray into the woods, he had been polite with her, but he never sought out her company alone. She saw the longing in his eyes when he looked at her across the table during shared meals, and sometimes he'd touch her hand when her parents weren't looking. Other than that, he'd remained distant.

Sarah had wondered hopefully if he was courting her in the proper way. Perhaps her father had warned him to keep his distance. Chase didn't seem to be the type of man who would be afraid of such a warning. She missed his touch, his strong arms around her, and his heated kisses.

Other times she considered if he had a change of heart. Had he changed his mind about her, and was getting ready to return home? There had been no talk of finding the time travel device, at least not in her presence.

"*Imaah.*"

Hawk Soaring approached, covering the ground with long strides. He wore a bright smile on his face. The presence of a second human caused even the bravest gander to take refuge in the river.

"*Kwyioo*, what a surprise," Sarah stammered. She shifted the basket she carried from her left to her right hip. "What brings you here?"

"Your uncle and I have come to ask your father to go hunting." He stopped a few feet in front of her, much too close to be considered proper. A slight smell of fish wafted through the air. Sarah backed up a few steps.

"I think of you often, *Imaah*," he said in a low voice. "Perhaps the traditions of the Tukudeka do not suit you. I am wondering if I behaved more like a white man, you would find me more acceptable."

Sarah drew her eyes together. "I don't understand what you mean, *Kwyioo.*"

Before she could react, he stepped up to her, his hands

holding her upper arms, and he pressed his lips to hers. Sarah stiffened, nearly dropping her basket. Her heart didn't pound faster, her lips didn't tingle, there were no chills running down her spine. She was merely shocked at his boldness.

She tried to pull away, when suddenly his hands were torn away from her. A spilt second later, Chase's fist connected with Hawk's face, sending him to the ground. Shocked, Sarah stood rooted to the earth. Like an agile cat, Hawk Soaring jumped to his feet, his knife in his hand. Blood trickled from the split in his upper lip.

Chase's hand went to his belt, gripping his tomahawk. The two men circled each other slowly, looks of contempt on both their faces.

Sarah dropped her basket. "Stop it! Both of you! *Yingka!*" She ran between them, holding out her arms, palms out, to prevent them from stepping closer to each other. Her head whipped from side to side, looking at each of them.

"Why is he kissing you, Sarah?" Chase growled, directing his glare at her, then back at Hawk.

Her temper ignited. He acted as if he owned her. He had no right to ask such a question. If he'd declared himself, wanted her for his wife, but he didn't. He wanted to go home. So why would he behave as though she belonged to him?

"Maybe because he wants something you don't," she spat at him. His eyebrows shot up. "Me for his wife," she clarified. "Perhaps that gives him more of a right to kiss me than it does you."

She grabbed for her basket on the ground, and shot both of them a heated glare. Then she ran across the meadow, her vision blurred by the tears streaming down her face.

CHAPTER TWENTY-NINE

*C*hase eyed Hawk wearily. The other man wiped at the blood on his lip. Both turned at the same time to watch Sarah run toward her home. Hell. She was mad at both of them. He knew he'd acted like an impulsive jerk.

Elk Runner's gift had touched him more than he wanted to admit. The cabin walls had closed in on him, and he definitely hadn't wanted to cry like a baby in front of Daniel, so he'd hightailed it out of there. He'd caught the word *Imaah* when Hawk spoke to Daniel, which was part of Sarah's Indian name.

Following the Indian seemed like the right thing to do, but Chase hadn't expected to see Hawk in a lip lock with Sarah. Intense jealously like he'd never experienced before had swept over him, and he punched the guy on impulse. Now he felt like an ass.

He'd hardly spoken to Sarah over the last several days. Her dad was running him ragged through the hills, drilling him on tracking animals, identifying spoors and plants, and stalking game. He'd barely been awake each night when they returned back to the cabins, and had dragged his butt to bed from pure exhaustion. It left no opportunity to talk to her, much less hold and kiss her like he'd wanted to.

Daniel had hinted to him about proper courting rituals of the Indian tribe he grew up with. No wonder Sarah had been so nervous about having him live under the same roof with her after her uncle had shown up that first time. Chase had never given it much thought. Guys and girls lived together as roommates all the time without a second thought, but apparently among the Shoshone, a couple intent on marriage only had to live together for a few days, and be seen together in public to be considered wed.

Chase wasn't sure if Daniel had been trying to warn him to keep his hands to himself, or was just instructing him on the proper ways to court his daughter. He'd told him in no uncertain terms that first day that nothing could ever come of his feelings for Sarah. Did the man have a change of heart? He obviously saw that Sarah had feelings for him, as well.

What are you going to do about your problem, Russell?

The less he saw of her, the more he wanted to be with her. No one had brought up the time travel device. Chase wasn't sure if Daniel still planned to look for it or not. He'd have to ask him about it soon. He hated this feeling of being stuck in limbo, between worlds with no real foothold. His skills were definitely improving under Daniel's guidance, but did he really want to stay here? Was this the kind of life he wanted?

Chase glanced sideways at Hawk. "Come on, buddy. We might as well head back, too," he grumbled. He held out his hand to Hawk, who looked at it suspiciously. Chase took a step toward him, and thrust his hand out for emphasis. Hawk finally took it, and they clasped hands.

Chase nodded. Hawk's features softened, and his lips actually curved in a slight smile. He cut his hand through the air in a firm movement. Chase took it to mean that all was forgiven. He slapped the shorter man on the back, and together they set out in the same direction as their girl.

Chase caught sight of Sarah sitting under a tree by the woodpile when he and Hawk reached the cabin. Hawk had seen her, too. He gave Chase a searching look, then headed for the house. Chase strode over to her. Her knees were drawn up to her chest, her hands clasped around her ankles.

"Hey," he said, and lowered himself to the ground next to her. She didn't say anything, nor did she look at him. Her face had dirt smudges from tear stains. He reached for one of her hands, pulling it free of the other one.

"I apologized to Hawk for my behavior." He brought her hand to his mouth and kissed it, peering up at her. Her eyes turned round when she met his gaze. "You're right," he said. "I had no call to do what I did."

Fresh tears welled up in her eyes.

"Why are you crying, Angel?" He swiped his fingers under her eyes.

"Why did you have to tell me you love me, Chase? It would have been so much easier when you go home if I hadn't known."

He inhaled sharply. "Do you think this is easy for me, Sarah? I don't have the skills necessary to take care of you. I couldn't live with myself if something happened to you because of something I did, or didn't know how to do to protect you."

She stared at him blankly. "But you're learning."

He shook his head in frustration. "I don't know if I can even get home. The assumption right now is that I can't, that I won't be going home, ever. I'm trying to live my life here with that thought. We were going to take it one day at a time, remember?" He gave her a reassuring smile, and squeezed her hand.

She nodded slowly.

"I'm supposed to go on a hunt for mountain sheep with your dad and uncle, and . . . Hawk. I don't know when I'll be back."

Sarah searched his face, her eyes finally locked onto his. "Those hunts can last a few days."

"So, can I have a good-bye kiss, since I won't see you for a while?"

She lowered her head.

"Come on," he coaxed. "Then you can compare who kisses better."

He grinned, then laughed at Sarah's outraged look. He leaned over and kissed her lightly on the lips. She wrapped her arms around his neck and pressed her mouth to his. Her response was unexpected. His resolve to keep the kiss light crumbled. He pulled her up against him, groaning as he claimed her mouth. His fingers entwined in her hair, his other hand massaging her back. Abruptly, he pulled back.

"Angel, I'm trying to behave myself, but you're making it really hard."

"I love you, Chase," she whispered.

"I love you, Sarah." His hand swiped at the tear streaks on her cheek. He stood and reached for her hand to pull her up. He gave it another squeeze.

"Be good while I'm gone." He tore his eyes from her beautiful face, then turned and headed for the cabin.

"Bighorn sheep are difficult to approach. They are extremely flighty and alert to any danger. When stalked, they move to higher ground. It's where they feel safe," Daniel explained when Chase inquired about the hunt. After a long hike through the usual terrain of meadows and forests, they stopped for the night along a fast-moving creek.

"The strategy of the hunt is simple. You and Hawk Soaring will move up hill and lie in wait. Elk Runner and I, with the dog's help, will drive the sheep your way."

Chase nodded. It all sounded easy enough. All he needed to learn now was how to shoot an arrow from that bow Elk Runner had gifted him. He marveled at how the three men efficiently set up camp. No one spoke. Each individual knew what to do; everyone except him. Daniel put him to task collecting wood and build a fire. At least he could manage that. Hawk went off and brought back several birds.

Elk Runner took it upon himself to pull Chase aside and instruct him in stringing his bow, the amount of force to use in his draw, and releasing the arrow.

Chase quickly realized what a powerful weapon the bow was. He'd never expected such force and speed from an arrow. His aim improved with each practice pull. Whether he would be able to hit a moving target remained to be seen.

He noticed Hawk watching him like a . . . hawk. Chase couldn't be sure what the other man was thinking when he looked at him from across the camp. Chase only hoped he didn't look as inept as he felt.

But it's your kisses she prefers, Russell. He smiled smugly. He conceded that Hawk was a nice and likable guy, and under different circumstances, if they weren't both after the same girl, they might have even been friends.

If you leave, she'll be well taken care of. Hawk would make a good husband, he was sure of it. Could he leave this place, and Sarah, with that knowledge? That she could choose to marry Hawk? An idea had begun to form in his mind over the course of the last week, but Chase wasn't sure how he would be able to go through with it. He'd have to do a lot more thinking. All he knew was that he couldn't go on living like this indefinitely, like a man torn between two worlds.

The terrain they traversed the next morning became rocky and steep. Chase focused on the climb ahead, the mountains looming ever taller in front of him. No one spoke. There was no need. Everyone knew what his job was. He had a pretty good idea of what was expected of him. Grizzly bounded ahead of them. He seemed to know he would play a crucial role in a short time. The dog would help herd the sheep to a designated area, where two of the hunters would lie in wait.

Elk Runner stopped abruptly, halfway up a mountain pass. Silently, he pointed to a flat area covered in sparse grasses and short pine trees that looked more like bushes than trees. Three sheep stood grazing in the distance, their rumps pointed at the men. Daniel hand-signaled to Grizzly, and the dog obediently remained with the group, although his eyes and ears were trained on the sheep.

Daniel translated when Elk Runner gave his instructions.

"Chase, you and Hawk Soaring will climb up to that ridge, and take cover." He pointed into the distance. "Elk Runner and I will alert the sheep to our presence, and start driving them your way. With any luck, you should be able to bring down one, if not two of them, as they pass by."

Chase glanced at Hawk, who nodded at him. Staying downwind from the sheep, they slowly climbed up the steep cliff, Hawk ahead of him. When they reached the top of the ridge, the Indian motioned for him to take cover behind a rocky outcropping. More cliff walls loomed behind them. Hawk moved some twenty yards further along, and found cover behind some boulders. It was a waiting game from here on. If the sheep ran straight up the pass, they would run right past them. Chase hoped he could get off a clean shot.

He stayed crouched behind the rocks, listening intently

for any sound of hooves on hard ground. All he heard was the wind whistling at this high elevation, an occasional hawk screeching as it soared through the air, or the clucking sounds of the ever-present ravens. How long would it be before Daniel and Elk Runner chased that group of sheep up this incline? He adjusted the arrow he had strung to his bow in anticipation.

He was determined not to look like a fool in front of Hawk, who'd no doubt been on countless hunts like these. Chase glanced up the slope to where Hawk lay in wait. The man stayed as motionless as his surroundings, focused intently on the narrow pass leading downhill. His bow was strung taut, ready to release his arrow at a second's notice. Chase wondered if he could ever look as confident and able as this Tukudeka hunter appeared. Hawk had a lifetime of training. There was no comparison between them. If this were a football match, the tables would be turned.

Hawk turned his head slightly, and his eyes met Chase's. His features turned hard. Apparently, they were both thinking the same thing. While they'd been cordial with each other in the older men's presence, this was a competition. Chase had no doubt that Hawk believed whoever brought down a sheep would gain favor with Sarah. He smiled to himself. *Sarah loves you, not him.* Would it really matter to her if he came back with a sheep kill?

It should matter to her, Russell. If he couldn't bring down game, which he hadn't been successful at yet, how could he ever hope to care for a wife in this environment?

A rock on the cliff above Hawk Soaring suddenly moved, or had Chase imagined it. Was there a sheep up there above them? He strained his ears to listen, but couldn't hear anything. He glanced upward, squinting into the bright sunlight. He didn't see anything at first. Then he noticed the movement again, behind some rocks, directly above Hawk. With a sinking feeling, he realized what it was.

While they were lying in wait for their quarry, a different predator was stalking them. A mountain lion was crouched low, its body hugging the rocks, ready to spring at its unsuspecting prey. The cat inched slowly forward, its haunches and forelegs bunched. Its ears lay flat against its head.

Chase's heart leapt to his stomach. Adrenaline coursed through his veins, leaving his knees rubbery and weak. With a sinking feeling, he knew what was about to happen.

"Hawk, look out!" Chase yelled, and shot up from his position behind the rocks. At the exact same moment, the cougar leapt through the air, landing on top of Hawk, who had barely had the chance to react to Chase's warning. He whipped his body around, looking up. His hands shot forward in an act of self-defense, as the cat knocked him to the ground. Hawk's bow fell to the ground several feet away.

"Dammit!" Chase yelled.

He raised his bow and aimed, but hesitated. His hands trembled, and he couldn't hold the weapon steady. There was no way he could get off a clean shot. He wasn't confident with the weapon, and might hit Hawk instead. Sweat beaded his forehead. He sprinted up the slope.

The cougar had Hawk on the ground, tearing into the man's neck. Hawk struggled underneath the animal, a grimace on his face. His hands wrapped around the cat's neck, trying in vain to keep the sharp teeth from biting into his flesh. The predator outmatched him in strength. He'd had no chance to defend himself.

"Dammit." With time slipping away, Chase no longer thought consciously of his actions. His body seemed to move on its own. He yanked his tomahawk from his belt and took aim, sprinting up the slope. He knew he couldn't run up the hill fast enough. His only hope was to put the cat out of commission for a moment to buy him a few seconds. His well-aimed throw hit the animal squarely on the head. The cougar dropped to the side, but wasn't dead.

Chase ripped his knife from his belt, clutching the handle. He roared and lunged at the cat. Not giving the predator a chance to recover from the hit with the tomahawk, Chase threw himself on top of the cougar and plunged his knife into its neck. He pulled the knife back, and repeated his action. Sweat ran into his eyes, and he could barely see. The animal thrashed its huge paws through air, raking Chase's thigh. Pain shot through his leg, but he ignored it. With renewed effort, he threw his entire weight into the cat, twisting the knife into the animal's throat. After several more violent jerks, the cougar's body finally went limp.

Chase leapt off the cat. His breath came in short, quick gasps. He turned his head in a frantic motion to find Hawk. He sank to his knees beside the man on the ground. Hawk was covered in blood. A deep tear marred the side of his neck. Blood spewed from the wound with every beat of his heart. His breathing was ragged and shallow. A sheen of sweat covered his face and neck. With trembling hands, Chase hastily pulled his cotton shirt over his head, and pressed it against Hawk's neck in desperation, hoping to slow the bleeding.

"Come on, buddy, stay with me," Chase said through clenched teeth.

With an impatient swipe of his arm, he wiped the sweat from his forehead. He looked up, his eyes darting around the rocks, and down the trail. Where the hell was Daniel or Elk Runner? If the mountain sheep had come this way, he hadn't noticed. He groaned in frustration, mumbling swear words under his breath. He didn't know what to do. Other than trying to stop the bleeding, there was nothing he could do.

"Arghh."

Chase looked skyward, imploring the heavens for a sign, anything that would help him save Hawk's life. He knew it was futile. He kept a firm hand on Hawk's wound, his shirt already soaked through with blood. His own hand looked as if he'd dunked it in a bowl of red paint. Chase's entire body shook. He swallowed hard, inhaling the stench of blood and sweat. The dead cat mere feet away emitted a foul and sour odor, reminding Chase of rotten meat.

Why the hell was this happening? Nothing could have prepared him for something like this. This primitive world bested him again. Hawk's eyes were open wide, a glazed look to them. His hand shot up and he grabbed hold of Chase's wrist.

"*Namaappa'i Imaah*," he said through short gasps for air. "*Namaappa'i Imaah*." His grip on Chase's arm tightened, a frantic look in his eyes.

Chase nodded. He had no idea what Hawk was saying, but it had something to do with Sarah. Hawk's body stiffened suddenly, and he groaned. A split second later, he went limp, and his hand fell away from Chase's arm.

"No, dammit!" Chase yelled. "Don't die." He shook the lifeless body. Jumping to his feet, he let out a loud roar in frustration. His own trembling body was drenched in sweat. Chase sank back to the ground on his knees beside Hawk. He bent his head to his chest, his shoulders slumped, and placed a hand over the man's heart.

"I'm sorry," he whispered, squeezing his eyes shut. "I'm sorry I wasn't fast enough."

CHAPTER THIRTY

a heavy hand pressed down on Chase's shoulder. He jerked, trying to dislodge the pressure. He'd been on his knees beside Hawk Soaring's body for . . . how long? Time had no meaning anymore. He had no feeling in his legs. His entire body was numb.

The hand remained. Finally, Chase stared unseeing into Daniel's somber eyes. The older man tightened his grip.

"I didn't react fast enough," Chase whispered, his voice hoarse. "I didn't see the cougar until it was too late." His head dropped again. He didn't want to face Daniel or Elk Runner's accusations.

"I see what has happened here. No one is to blame," Daniel said. "This was a tragic accident." His voice sounded like an echo through a tunnel.

Chase rose to his feet at Elk Runner's urging. He turned away from the older men, kicking at rocks, and holding his hands to his temples.

"What the hell am I doing here?" he roared, his voice reverberating off the mountains. He turned to the cliff wall, pounding his fists into the hard rock, until fresh blood from his fingers and knuckles mixed with the dried blood on his hands.

He fought against the hands pulling him back. Daniel grabbed both his arms and locked them behind his back. The harder Chase jerked and struggled, the firmer the other man's grip became. Daniel finally wrestled him to the ground.

"I can't go on like this," Chase said between clenched teeth, breathing hard. He relaxed his muscles, finally daring to look up into the faces of Daniel and Elk Runner. There was no anger, no contempt, only silent compassion.

"Chase Russell have many evil spirits inside," Elk Runner said. "Must find way to fight."

Chase gave a short laugh. "Yeah," he said in a defeated tone, glancing at the lifeless body of Hawk Soaring a few feet away.

He ran a trembling hand over his face, inhaling deeply. "He said . . . something to me before he died." His voice quivered unsteadily. He furrowed his eyebrows, trying to remember the words. "It had something to do with Sarah. I recognized her name. It sounded like . . . nampi . . . namapee?" His eyes darted from one man to the other, hoping they might understand.

Daniel and Elk Runner exchanged quick glances.

"*Namaappa'i?*" Daniel offered.

"Yeah, I think that was it, and then *Imaah*. That's Sarah's name, right?"

Daniel's lips were drawn in a tight line. His jaw was set firmly, his eyebrows furrowed.

"He asked you to take care of Sarah," he said quietly, finality in his voice.

Chase closed his eyes and exhaled slowly, the weight of the world descending on his shoulders.

～

Sarah knelt at the river's edge, dipping a shirt into the water and pulling it back out. She spread it on a rock, and ran a bar of hard lye soap over the material. With vigorous hand motions, she rubbed the fabric together to scrub it clean. Then she dipped it in the water again to rinse. Her mother sat beside her, performing the same task.

A basket piled high with clothing sat between her and her mother. Sarah wrung the water from the shirt, and picked up another one. She held it up. It was one of Samuel's shirts that Chase had been wearing. Without thought, she held it to her face, inhaling the strong masculine scent of the man who was constantly in her thoughts. They had been gone for a week already. Sheep hunting usually took many days, but a week was about as long as her father and brothers had ever been away.

Realizing what she was doing, she dropped the shirt from her hands. Her cheeks flushed. Her mother wore a soft smile on her face when Sarah darted a quick glance her way.

"Can I ask something, Mama?" She turned to look fully at her mother. The older woman laid the shirt she held on the ground, and turned to her daughter.

"What's on your mind, Sarah?"

"Chase," Sarah said softly, her gaze dropping to the ground.

"I know that." Her mother chuckled softly. "What about him do you want to know?"

"Tell me of the traditions in his time concerning a man and woman."

"Oh . . . well." She expelled a long breath. "Things are a lot different in his time than here. You've grown up knowing only the tribal customs of the Shoshone."

"Yes, but in his time. How does a woman express her love for a man? Or how does a man ask for a woman he wants to make his wife?"

Sarah wondered at the almost uncomfortable look on her mother's face. Why was she reluctant to answer?

"A man will usually ask the woman to marry him," she finally said. "A couple often will live together openly before declaring themselves. Sometimes they part ways if they realize they are not a good match."

She paused, and looked Sarah straight in the eyes. "Relationships between unmarried couples are common in his time, Sarah. Chase doesn't have the belief that he needs to be married to you in order to kiss you, or . . . do other things. In his time, a man and woman don't need to be married to act on their feelings for each other. To him, this is perfectly acceptable. This is why you are confused by his behavior."

"He tells me he loves me, but he doesn't say whether he wants me for his wife. He says he can't provide for me."

"It sounds like he wants to do the right thing, Sarah. I think he realizes how harsh life here is, and taking care of a wife requires certain skills. According to your father, he is making great progress. He comes from a time when men don't go hunting for food anymore. It's just always available. Providing for a family is different in his time than it is now. Learning all these new skills is very hard."

"So, it is okay that he says he loves me?" Sarah tried to understand. "It is acceptable that he kisses me, even if he hasn't asked for me?"

"To his way of thinking, yes. Just make sure it is acceptable to you."

"Did you kiss Papa before you were married to him?"

"Yes, I did." Her mother smiled. "It was complicated for him. He grew up with all the same traditions as you. He struggled, because he couldn't go to anyone to ask for me."

"So what did he do?"

"Well, he . . . ah, we just took it upon ourselves."

Comprehension dawned. "Oh," Sarah said, her face flaming again. She picked up Chase's shirt, and absently dipped it in the water.

"Has Chase mentioned anything more about finding the device to send him home?" she asked after a long silence.

"Not to my knowledge." Her mother reached her hand out and placed it on Sarah's shoulder. "Like I said, he's been trying really hard to fit in here. I can see the love in his eyes for you, Sarah." She smiled warmly.

Sarah smiled back. This conversation had been very informative.

"Do you ever miss your old life?" Sarah asked after more minutes of silence.

Her mother took a deep breath. She stared out across the expanse of the river. "There are times I miss certain things, certain people I left behind." She looked at Sarah. "But I've never regretted my decision. I was meant to be here. I knew that early on."

Sarah nodded. Chase didn't feel the same. He didn't believe he belonged here. In silence, they finished their laundry. Sarah carried the basket to the clothesline behind the cabin. Rope had been strung between two trees, and Sarah hung the clothing up to dry.

She went over the things her mother had told her. It gave her a better understanding of Chase's behavior. In his time, it wasn't shameful for men and women to kiss when they loved each other. Her mother had even hinted that more than kissing was acceptable behavior. Chase had mentioned he was trying to behave himself. Is that what he had meant? He was trying to stay within the boundaries she had grown up with? Would it be so bad if she acted more like a woman he might be accustomed to?

Sarah's hands trembled at the thought. She had limited knowledge of these things. It wasn't something that was openly discussed. Of course, she knew what the act of mating entailed. As it applied to people, she only knew that it was a husband's responsibility to teach his wife. Chase could teach her. Where he came from, it was accepted that a man and woman didn't need to be married to carry out the act. He was making an effort to behave in ways she was accustomed to. She could do the same for him, couldn't she?

Sarah sighed and picked up the empty clothes basket. She would have to give it some more thought. She headed back toward the cabin. Two figures walked side by side along the riverbank from the west. The blonde-haired man was taller than the other, whose raven hair waved gently in the breeze. It was her father and Chase! She smiled brightly, and her heart sped up. The cabin door opened and her mother emerged. She must have seen them from the window.

"They're home, Mama," Sarah called and ran to her mother's side.

"I would have expected them to come from the other direction," her mother remarked. "They must have gone to the village first, since Elk Runner and Hawk aren't with them."

Something was wrong. Both her father and Chase had somber looks on their faces when they approached. The hunt must not have been a success. They weren't carrying any meat.

"Welcome home," her mother called and headed out to meet her father. Sarah stayed by the door, watching her parents embrace when they met across the yard.

Chase kept walking, his eyes on her. The hard expression on his face softened. Without hesitation, he strode up to her and wordlessly pulled her into a fierce embrace. His body trembled. Her arms reached around his waist.

"You feel so good," he whispered against her ear. Slowly, he pulled away, and stared into her eyes. He didn't smile.

"What's wrong?" Sarah asked, looking up at his subdued face.

Chase turned his head when her parents reached the cabin. There was no hint of joy on her father's face, either. She hastily stepped away from Chase.

"Let's go inside," her father said, and motioned with his head to the door. "We have things to tell you."

Sarah followed her parents into the cabin. Chase brought up the rear.

'What happened, Daniel?" her mother asked the moment everyone stood in the room. Her eyes darted from him to Chase. Chase sat at the table, his head between his hands, his back to them.

"Hawk Soaring is dead," her father said in his quiet voice.

Sarah gasped, and her hand flew to her mouth. Her mother quietly said, "Oh, no."

"A cougar," her father continued. "We returned his body to his family. We stayed for the burial. That is why we are back so late."

Chase stood abruptly and left the cabin. Sarah moved to follow him, but her father's hand reached out and held her back.

"He blames himself," he said. "Leave him. He wants to be alone. He has much to think about."

"Why does he blame himself?" Sarah asked.

Her father moved to sit at the table.

"Would you like some tea or coffee, or something to eat?" her mother asked, standing behind him and rubbing his shoulders.

"Some coffee," he answered, before he looked at Sarah. "He was with Hawk Soaring when the cougar attacked. Chase was brave and acted selflessly. He killed the cat, but it was too late. He believes he didn't act quick enough." He sighed. "He continues to only see his failures, not his successes. He has told me much about his past . . . in the future."

"What did he tell you?" Sarah asked tentatively. Chase hadn't told her anything about his past.

"If he wishes for you to know, he will tell you himself, Sarah. I cannot speak for him. I can only say that he has suffered the loss of a person close to him, a man who guided him. After his death, Chase struggled and lost his way. He needs to find his path again." He looked directly at her. "You have given him a purpose, Sarah, a way to get back on the right track, but his fear of loss and failure is still holding him back."

Sarah stared at her father, not knowing what to say. She wanted to go to Chase, comfort him, and tell him he was a good man. All the things he had accomplished since his arrival spoke of greatness. Guilt consumed her. Hawk Soaring's tragic death should be foremost on her mind. Although she felt sad, she couldn't bring herself to properly mourn his death.

CHAPTER THIRTY-ONE

*S*arah watched Chase. His back was to her, a sheen of sweat covering his muscular shoulders and back as he repeatedly swung the ax. Each log split in two with a single blow. Two weeks had gone by since his return from the sheep hunt. Most days, Chase roamed the woods with her father, leaving early and sometimes returning well after dark. She often wondered what they did all day, but never asked.

Chase ate his evening meals with them, and then invited Sarah to sit with him outside for a while before he retired to his cabin. Those were the times she looked forward to the most. He would hold her in his arms, tell her how much she meant to him, and that he loved her. His kisses were restrained most of the time. Sarah could tell he wanted to kiss her like he'd done on a few occasions in the past, when their bodies clung to each other, leaving them both breathless. He always stopped himself before he let it get to that point.

Sarah wondered at her father's complete tolerance of Chase's attentions. He had to know they kissed and touched.

Her father knew everything that went on around here. Not that she would bring it up with him and, as her mother would say, stir the pot. Her mother only shrugged when she asked her about it, and said she didn't know.

Chase refused to talk about Hawk Soaring's death. She'd tried to get him to tell her about the accident, but he only said he'd get over it. She took that to mean he had accepted the fact that it wasn't his fault or lack of ability that caused his death.

Chase split the last log, and set the ax against the chopping block, wiping the back of his hand across his forehead. Sarah approached him.

"I have water for you," she said, holding out a cup. He smiled at her and accepted the drink.

"Thanks." He drank and handed the empty cup back to her.

"You aren't out in the woods with my father today," she remarked when he didn't speak.

"No. I thought I'd spend the afternoon with you."

"Really?" she smiled brightly.

"Really," he said, running the back of his fingers across her cheek. "Unless you have something better to do."

"No." She shook her head quickly. "What did you want to do?"

He shrugged. "Nothing. Just spend some time with you. We can go for a walk, or something."

"That . . . that would be nice."

"Let me clean up. I'll be back in a bit." He disappeared inside his cabin, only to reappear a moment later, a clean shirt slung over his shoulders, and headed for the river.

Warmth spread through her. Chase hadn't said a word in weeks about wanting to go home, or finding the time travel device. For all outward appearances, he behaved as if he was settled in. Her warm feeling faded. He also hadn't indicated he intended to ask for her. *Give him time.* Her mother's advice came back to her. She didn't know how long she should wait, but time seemed to be all they had.

Sarah paced by the woodpile. She couldn't help but wonder why he'd want to suddenly spend the day with her. Looking up when he returned from the river, she wouldn't question it, and simply enjoy his company. Water droplets beaded in his sandy-colored hair. She realized how much it had grown in the weeks since his arrival, and decided she liked his shorter hair better.

"Where would you like to go?" he asked cheerfully, strapping on his weapon belt.

Sarah shrugged. "It doesn't matter."

He grabbed her hand, entwining his fingers with hers. "Okay, let's go this way then." He led the way up the slope into the trees behind the cabin. They reached the top of the incline, the spot that Sarah often visited to be alone, before he spoke.

"Wow, you can see the entire valley from here." His eyes scanned the distance.

"This is one of my favorite spots," Sarah remarked.

"I can see why." Chase turned to her, and pulled her up against him. He looked into her eyes for a long time, and Sarah suddenly felt nervous.

"You mean the world to me, Sarah. I just want you to know that."

He bent and kissed her gently on the lips. His hands at her waist sent shivers up and down her spine. She longed for him to kiss her with the intensity of that night when he first told her he loved her. He didn't. He pulled away from her, and took her hand again.

They continued through the forest, and Sarah was pleasantly surprised how well he navigated along almost imperceptible deer trails, avoiding most deadfall. Neither one spoke. Chase led her out of the forest, heading down a grassy incline toward the Madison River. The cabin was visible as only a small dot to the east. He eased her to the ground at the river's edge, and they sat in silence, watching the slow current pass by. Chase tossed countless rocks into the water, making them skip across the surface.

Sarah glanced over at him. Why was he so quiet? Should she speak first? Chase suddenly turned to her. The intense look of yearning and desire in his eyes startled her. He cupped her face, and scooted closer.

"I love you, Sarah," he said huskily, and finally claimed her mouth in a way she'd longed for. She wrapped her arms around his neck and clung to him. Ripples of desire swept through her. He eased her onto the carpet of soft grasses, keeping his weight off of her as he wrapped her in his arms. His lips nuzzled her neck, while his hands swept up and down along her hips and torso. Finally, he rolled onto his back and pulled her up close, his breathing ragged.

"Would you like to head back to the cabin now?" he asked after a while.

Sarah lay there, her head resting in the crook of his arm, as happiness enveloped her. "Can we stay just a little longer?" she whispered.

"Anything you want, Angel," he said, his hold on her tightening.

The door of the cabin groaned slowly. Chase was instantly alert. Quietly, he reached for the tomahawk lying beside his furs. Who was in his cabin in the middle of the night? His heart rate sped up as he lay still, listening. The door creaked again, then the sound of soft rustling. Someone was definitely in here.

"Chase?"

A woman's soft voice. Sarah's voice! He bolted upright on his pallet.

"Sarah? Hold on."

Straining his eyes in the dark, he fumbled his way to the hearth and stoked the coals. Breathing air onto them, he fed some kindling to the glowing embers, and a small fire sprang to life. He added some larger pieces of wood, and the room gave off a soft glow.

Turning around, he noticed Sarah standing a few feet behind him, her eyes large and round as the flames illuminated her silhouette.

"Is everything all right? What are you doing here in the middle of the night?" Chase put his hands on her shoulders, looking down at her, trying to interpret the expression on her face. She seemed unsure of something.

"I . . . I came to see you," she said, a nervous hitch in her voice. She took several steps back, and he dropped his hands.

"Are you okay?" he asked.

His eyes narrowed. She wasn't in her usual cotton shirt and britches. She wore a simple buckskin dress that fell past her knees. Chase's gaze lingered on her loose hair that framed her face and cascaded down her front and back. His groin tightened. She looked so beautiful, standing there in the glow of the firelight, her features dancing in the shadows.

He watched as she slowly reached up with trembling hands and untied the leather thongs at her shoulders. Freed from its bindings, the dress fell slowly down her torso, exposing firm breasts, then slid past the curve of her hips to finally rest in a heap around her feet.

Chase could only stare. Her bold actions rendered him speechless. He'd never seen anything so beautiful. The blood began to pool in his loins. He swallowed, but his mouth had gone so dry, it only made his throat burn. Coming to his senses, he looked intently into her eyes. She held his gaze, uncertainty in her eyes.

"Sarah." He cleared his throat. "Angel, what are you doing?" His voice was raw and had a slight high pitch to it.

She raised her chin, trying to project the confidence he knew she didn't feel.

"Teach me . . ." she whispered, and took a tentative step toward him.

"Teach you what?"

"Teach me how to be a woman, Chase."

The obvious implication jolted him to the core. He had wanted her for so long, the fact that she was here, of her own will, took him a moment to comprehend. He ran a nervous hand along his jaw.

"Uh . . . Angel, I don't think this is such a good idea." He laughed nervously, and turned away from her. Another second of looking at her, and he'd be a goner.

"You don't want me?" she asked.

The hurt in her voice was unmistakable. Chase squeezed his eyes shut and inhaled deeply. Abruptly, he faced her again and closed the distance between them in a single stride, cupping her head between his hands. His mouth crushed down on hers as he pulled her to him.

The feel of her peaked breasts against his naked chest sent an electric shockwave through him. He had to have more. He couldn't get enough. He deepened the kiss, coaxing her lips apart, showing her how to respond. Her body relaxed, and she leaned into him, her arms coming up and tentatively encircling his neck. The entire length of her nude body was pressed against him. His erection pushed uncomfortably against his britches, into her stomach.

He broke the kiss, panting and trembling as he ran his

hands over her face, brushing her loose hair back. He tilted her head so she'd meet his eyes.

"Angel, I've never wanted anything the way I want you," he whispered in a husky tone. "I think you know that."

He trailed kisses across her face and claimed her mouth again. Her response was more immediate this time. Her tongue grazed his lips. He groaned, and wrapped one arm around her slender waist, the feel of her silky skin driving him mad. His other hand raked through her hair.

He had to force himself to slow down. He wouldn't be able to hold back if he kept up this wild and feverish assault on her lips.

"Do you know what you're asking? Are you absolutely sure this is what you want?" he asked, pressing his forehead to hers.

"Make me your woman, Chase." The softly spoken request pounded in his ears.

Chase pulled back. He gently removed her arms from around his neck, and took her smaller hands in his. He held them to his mouth and kissed the knuckles on each hand, never taking his eyes off of her. She inhaled sharply, her breathing faster than normal. Flashing what he hoped was a reassuring smile, he led her quietly to his pallet. He ran his hand under her hair, cupping the back of her neck. Brushing his lips softly against hers, he sat and tugged her down with him.

Go slow, Russell.

Not that he had to tell himself that. She wasn't one of his usual sorority chicks. No other girl could ever hold a candle to the beautiful angel he held in his arms at this moment.

Chase eased her onto her back, and leaned over her, just looking at her. Her blue eyes stared back at him, questioning, nervous, anticipating.

"What do I have to do?" she asked, her voice faltering.

He chuckled. "Just follow my lead, Angel," he said, his own voice raspy. "You don't have to do anything. Just feel, and let me love you." She nodded.

"If I do anything that you're not comfortable with, or if I hurt you at all, you tell me, okay?"

He stared into her eyes, trying to imitate the look he'd seen in her father's eyes when he meant business.

"You won't hurt me, Chase."

God, she was so trusting. He sure as hell hoped he could hold it together for her sake. This was uncharted territory for him, too. He'd never been with an inexperienced girl before. Most of the women in his past had taught him a trick or two. And, most importantly, it had never mattered to him before. He took what he could get. With Sarah, it mattered a whole lot. Giving her pleasure was more important than his own needs.

"Put your arms around me," he whispered. She obeyed instantly. Chase leaned down and kissed her again, slowly at first. She responded with a fever he hadn't expected. It was going to drive him mad. He draped one leg across her thighs, keeping his full weight off her. His hand slid down her shoulders, across her stomach, and up to cup her breast. She moaned and arched her back into his hand. He kneaded gently and rubbed her nipple with his thumb.

His mouth left hers, and he trailed kisses down her neck, licking with his tongue. She shuddered. She moved her hands hesitantly up and down his shoulders and arms, and Chase felt a renewed tightening in his gut. His mouth found her nipple, and he ran his tongue over it until it was hard and peaked. He suckled gently, and Sarah gasped. Her hands reached up and grabbed at his head, holding him to her.

He paid the same attention to her other breast, and ran his hand down her stomach, past the slight curve in her hip, and along her thighs. Sarah squirmed underneath him.

"Easy, Angel," he whispered. He kissed the valley between her breasts, then back up her neck, and finally found her mouth again. She wrapped her arms tightly around his neck, kissing him like she'd been doing it forever.

He pulled his leg back, and fumbled with the thongs holding his britches. Moments later his hand found her silky thighs again, and he gently nudged them apart. His hand trailed up her inner thigh, to the juncture of her legs. She stiffened slightly.

"Remember, tell me to stop, Angel," he said, his voice hoarse.

"I don't want you to stop," she whispered.

Chase groaned and claimed her lips again, while his fingers probed her intimate folds. She was ready for him. He kicked his britches off and positioned himself over her, and hesitated. What if he hurt her? He knew there was no easy way the first time. All he could hope for was that he'd readied her body enough. He entered her with one swift thrust, crushing his mouth over hers to drown out her cry. Her body went rigid. So did his. He stayed motionless so she could get used to him.

"Sarah, are you okay?" he asked.

She nodded. "Is it over?" she asked quietly. Chase hadn't expected that question.

"No, Angel, it's only just begun."

Slowly, he began to move inside her. She gasped again and her breathing increased. Chase clenched his jaw. He couldn't hold back much longer. He reached his hands down around her hips, pulling her up toward him, showing her how to move in time with him. He buried himself deep inside her, and held her hips to his. When she wrapped her legs around his waist, he nearly came undone. *Not yet, Russell. This is for her.*

"Chase," she gasped his name, and her body began to

shudder. Her legs trembled, and her breathing was fast and shallow.

"That's it, Angel, just let it happen," he whispered in her ear, holding her tightly. When the tremors slowed, Chase moved inside her, his momentum building with each stroke. He couldn't get close enough to her. She was driving him mad. He clutched at her hips, pulling her up to him as he drove into her, until he shuddered in his own release. Spent, he collapsed on top of her.

Willing his breathing to slow, he stroked the hair out of her face and kissed her. She clung to him and sobbed. He stiffened and pushed himself up on his elbows.

"Angel? Oh, God, Sarah, did I hurt you. I'm . . . I'm sorry."

"No, that's not why I'm crying. I never thought . . . it was like this. Is it always like this?"

Chase relaxed, a smile forming on his face as he looked down at his beautiful angel. What had he done to deserve her? He was nothing but a screw-up.

"It can be," he whispered. He rolled off of her onto his back, and pulled her up close to him. Sarah rested her head on his chest.

He stared up at the ceiling, one hand behind his head, the other wrapped around the sweet woman nestled up against him. His fingers lazily stroked her arm.

After what had just happened, his resolve was stronger than ever. He couldn't go on with his life in limbo the way it was, but how could he possibly go through with his plans now? Sarah deserved a better man than him, he reminded himself firmly. He gazed down at her. She hadn't moved. Her hair spilled over her shoulder and down her back, some strands tickling his stomach.

"Chase?" She raised her head to look up at him, her eyes wide.

"Yeah, Angel." he kissed her forehead.

"My father will kill us if he finds out."

He sucked in a long breath. "Then let's not tell him." He chuckled.

* * * * *

Sarah stretched slowly, trying to work the soreness out of her arms and legs. She opened her eyes. Everything was still dark, but a small stream of light shone through the burlap covering the small window of the cabin. She was suddenly wide awake, realizing she wasn't in her own bed. A dull ache spread from the junction of her thighs upward. Memories of last night came flooding back.

She smiled slowly. Chase had made her his woman. She placed her hand over her abdomen. A new awareness dawned of what all those tingling feelings and lightning jolts meant whenever Chase had touched and kissed her before. Her face flushed when she thought about her own boldness at coming to him.

She sat up and glanced around. She was alone in the cabin. She pulled her legs over the edge of the bunk, a little disappointed. Shamefully, she wished Chase were here to hold her in his arms. What was going through his mind? Did he feel the same joy and elation she felt?

Her dress still lay in a heap near the hearth. How late in the day was it? Almost panicked, she left the bed and grabbed for her dress, pulling it on with trembling hands. She could barely tie the leather thongs at the shoulders. Why had Chase let her sleep? She had planned to return to her room before dawn. How was she going to get to the main cabin without notice?

Sarah peeled the burlap aside and glanced out the window. The mountain across the Madison was still covered in shadow. The sun's rays had not reached it yet. It was still early, but not early enough. Her parents were surely awake. Slowly, she opened the cabin door. All was quiet. She darted across the yard to the main cabin, and leaned against the wall, her heart pounding. She inched along until she reached the window, and peered inside. Relief washed over her, and she exhaled slowly. The room was empty.

Quietly, she opened the door and stepped in. She was almost to her room, when her parents' bedroom door opened. She froze.

"Sarah?" Her mother's voice sounded surprised.

Sarah's heart dropped. She closed her eyes, and slowly turned to face her mother. The older woman's eyes assessed her quickly, comprehension dawning in her eyes. Sarah hung her head. What would her mother think of her now?

"Do you . . . need to talk?" her mother asked softly, and took a step closer.

Sarah glanced up, her face hot. "N . . . no," she stammered.

The last thing she wanted was to discuss her experience with her mother. She only wanted Chase at the moment, talk to him.

Her mother smiled at her and walked up to her. She put her hands on her shoulders. "Well, I'm here for you if you do."

"Okay . . . Where's Papa?" Her eyes darted to her parent's bedroom. He wouldn't be as understanding, seeing her standing here in a dress she'd never worn. A chill crept up her spine. Her father would recognize immediately what had happened. There was no telling what he might do to Chase. They had gotten along well, better than Sarah could have hoped for, but what she and Chase had done without being wed . . . her father's wrath would be merciless. "And . . . Where's Chase?"

"They left before dawn this morning. They've been planning an extended excursion for days. Chase didn't tell you?" Her mother's forehead wrinkled.

Sarah shook her head. "He . . . never mentioned it."

She swallowed back her disappointment. After what they'd shared, she just wanted him to be here, hold her, and tell her he loved her. Now it might be days before she could talk to him.

"I . . . I need to change." She turned and quickly entered her room, closing the door behind her. She squeezed her eyes together, holding back the tears that threatened. She laughed softly. All she seemed to do lately was cry.

Why had Chase left her in his bed without waking her? Why couldn't he tell her he would be gone for days? Chase was experienced when it came to women. Perhaps what they had shared wasn't as meaningful to him as it had been for her.

CHAPTER THIRTY-TWO

The familiar yellows and reds of the Yellowstone Canyon loomed before Chase. The roar of the Lower Falls grew louder by the second. It was a spectacular sight.

"I never grow tired of this view," Daniel said, pulling his horse up beside him. Coming here on horseback rather than walking had cut the travel time in half from when he'd made this same trip with Sarah all those weeks ago. Daniel swung his leg forward and over his mount's neck, and leapt lightly to the ground. Chase did the same, but he wasn't as agile as the older man. Riding a horse was still something he hadn't quite gotten used to.

"Yeah, it's quite a sight," Chase remarked.

"We've made good time," Daniel said. "Do you wish to set up camp along the rim, or head into the canyon and begin the search?"

"Let's get it over with," Chase answered. "If we don't find it today, we can camp down there and get an early start in the morning."

Daniel nodded. He hobbled the horses' legs with leather,

so they wouldn't wander too far, and removed their bridles. Chase slung his bedroll and rifle over his shoulder, and headed toward the rim. He stopped and watched the mighty falls plunge into the depths of the canyon.

Sarah had been in his thoughts the entire ride here. He still couldn't believe she'd come to him last night. Being with her had been the most incredible experience of his life. She'd fallen asleep in his arms, and he'd held her all night, finally forcing himself away as dawn approached. He'd almost reconsidered his decision, but knew it had to be this way. He and Daniel had formulated their plan weeks ago, when they returned from burying Hawk. Everything he'd done since that time led to this moment. All he had to do now was help Daniel find the time travel device.

I'm doing this for you, Angel. You deserve better.

"Are you still certain this is what you want to do?" Daniel asked, standing next to him, peering down into the deep chasm.

"Absolutely," Chase said firmly. "I can't live like this anymore, Daniel, you know that. I love your daughter, but I'm not the man she needs me to be, or the man she deserves. You can understand why I have to do this, can't you?

"Yes, I understand. But Sarah will be hurt deeply. I don't wish this on her, either."

"I would rather she be angry with me. That way, if . . . that way she can get on with her life. If she had known about this, she would have talked me out of it, or worse – asked to come with me."

"She will not be told." Daniel placed a hand on his shoulder. "Her anger will fall on me. The device will be disposed of properly this time. What happened to you cannot happen to anyone else. I will make sure it is gone for good." Daniel paused, then said, "For as often as I have been here in my life,

I never thought I would actually descend to the bottom of this canyon." He grinned.

"The view from up top is better, trust me," Chase said dryly. Inhaling deeply he stepped over the edge to begin his final descent into the canyon.

～

Sarah stood at the river's edge, watching the soft swells of the water as it meandered on its way. An occasional circular ripple broke the surface as hungry cutthroat trout snatched at insects that had foolishly hovered too close.

When would they return? Each day, with each passing hour, she became more anxious. Three days had passed since she'd been in Chase's arms, since he'd changed her forever. She ached for him to hold her, tell her that he loved her. Surely after what they had shared, he would ask for her to be his wife. She already considered him her husband.

The whinny of a horse drew her attention. She looked toward the east, where the Little Buffalo River converged with the Firehole to form the wider Madison. She smiled brightly, and her heart leapt in her chest. Her father's horse emerged from the trees, ready to cross the river. Another horse followed close behind.

Sarah's face froze. There was no second rider. Her father guided his mount through the river, leading the other animal behind. Sarah ran along the river's edge.

"Where's Chase?" she called, when she was barely within earshot. Panic filled her. Her heart raced wildly. She tried to see beyond the trees, beyond the Little Buffalo River. What had happened to him?

Tears welled up in her eyes. "Where's Chase, Papa?"

She drew alongside her father's horse. His look was hard and unreadable. Her heart sank. Something terrible had happened.

"We will talk at the cabin," he said, and nudged his horse forward.

Sarah stood frozen to the spot. Breathing became painful. Did he get killed? No. She shook her head. Her father would have returned with the body. She watched her mother meet her father near the cabin, and they embraced after he dismounted his horse. Sarah raced to catch up.

Wordlessly, she stood before him, her eyes darting to her mother and back to him.

"He's gone, *bai'de*." He said quietly, and reached for her, pulling her in his embrace. She pushed away from him.

"What do you mean, he's gone?" Comprehension filled her. "You went to the canyon." Her father's expression told her that her assumption was correct. "You made him leave. You never wanted him here in the first place."

"Chase is a man who made his own choice, Sarah," Daniel said firmly. "There was no influence from me. In time you will come to understand his decision."

"I'll never understand," she yelled, turning away from him.

"He wanted me to tell you . . . he loves you, and you will always be in his heart. And he hopes you will find it in you to forgive him someday for what he had to do."

"You found the device?" her mother asked quietly.

"Yes."

"Where is it now?"

Sarah wheeled back around. Maybe she could use it to bring him back.

"I disposed of it. For good this time. Nothing like this will ever happen again."

"How? That thing was indestructible," her mother said.

"I threw it into the Hell Mouth. It will be lost for all time now."

"The Hell Mouth?" the older woman's eyebrows furrowed. Then comprehension dawned on her face. "It's called Dragon's Mouth in the future. You're right. No one will ever be able to remove it from there." She shot an anguished look at Sarah.

A crushing sensation came over her. She gasped for breath, as if she was drowning. The images of her parents and her surroundings blurred.

"Sarah." Her mother's hand reached for her. Sarah yanked her arm away. She ran for the small cabin, stumbling as she went. Her hands trembled while she fumbled with the latch on the door. Once open, she slipped inside, and hastily closed the door behind her, welcoming the darkness of the room's interior. She threw herself on Chase's bed, clutching at the blankets that held his scent.

She cried silently until no more tears would come. A cold numbness enveloped her. This had been his plan all along. He never intended to stay. The afternoon he had spent with her, she realized now, had been his way of telling her good-bye. Their night together had meant nothing to him. She had given herself to him completely, in all ways. Sarah swore she would never surrender her heart to another man again.

Sarah's face materialized before his eyes, coming in and out of focus. He blinked, trying to bring her image into focus.

"Angel." His hand reached out to her. She smiled at him. Slowly, her fingers worked the leather bindings on her dress. It fell in slow motion down her shoulders, over her breasts, then her hips, until it landed in a heap at her feet. She reached for him. Chase groaned. He wiped at his sweat soaked face, blinking away the burning sensation when the salty fluid touched his eyes.

This was the best high he'd ever been on. He'd have to get himself some more of this stuff. Sarah wrapped her arms around his neck, rubbing her body along the length of him. Chase's breathing increased.

He was no longer inside his own body. He watched everything from above, hovering in the air just out of reach. His corporeal image was pulling her to him with fierce intensity. Suddenly, his image changed into that of a man with a hawk feather tied in his long black hair. Chase gasped, startled. *You're dead!* He wanted to scream, but no words came from his mouth. His breathing became erratic. Sarah seemed not to have noticed the change. An instant later, the image of Hawk changed into the form of a short trapper wearing a thick fur hat, his hands groping at her, laughing triumphantly.

"Sarah, no!" Chase called out. Maybe she'd hear him. She pushed away, panic in her eyes. Chase's body shook. The trapper morphed into an Indian with a cruel leer on his face, covered in war paint. His lance was poised in the air, ready for a lethal stab.

"Sarah, run!" Chase yelled. Sweat drenched him. His shirt clung to his chest and back. He bolted upright off the ground, his eyes darting around, not recognizing any of his surroundings. Strange images were painted on the walls all around him. The images began to move. They came alive. Scorpions were everywhere, crawling all over him. The images came at him in ever faster rapid-fire succession now.

Hawk Soaring appeared, telling him he wasn't to blame. He'd done what he could. Another man might not have acted so bravely and gone after the cougar. The Blackfoot warriors stood before him, hanging their heads in defeat, raising their weapons in the air to honor him as a great warrior, one to be respected. He saw his own father, handing him his military dog tags, patting him on the head.

"You're a good kid, Chase. I'm leaving your mother because we don't get along. It has nothing to do with you."

Coach Beckman yelled at him that he could do anything he set his mind to, even with him gone. "You don't need me to tell you what to do. It comes from within you."

And finally there was Daniel, pushing him, drilling animal tracks into his mind, telling him in his firm and quiet ways to have patience when stalking his prey.

The images came to an abrupt halt. Elk Runner, with his silly grin, offered his help, and suggested that he needed to fight his evil spirits with a vision quest.

Sarah stood before him once again. "Make me your woman, Chase," she said quietly.

"You are my woman, Sarah," he answered. "You always will be."

Suddenly everything went black.

CHAPTER THIRTY-THREE

*C*hase entered the stuffy building, and waited for his eyes to adjust to the dim lighting. The air was filled with smoke, making breathing difficult. Someone really needed to open a window in this place. Glancing around, he observed several of the patrons sitting around tables, drinking, smoking, and playing cards. Even for the middle of the day, this place was busy. The bar was along the far wall, and Chase headed in the general direction.

What the hell are you doing in this place, Russell?

The bartender busily wiped at a nonexistent stain on the counter when Chase leaned his elbow on the flat surface. He looked up and grinned.

"What'll you have?" he asked, tossing his rag over his shoulder.

"Beer," Chase answered. He could sure go for something stronger. He hadn't touched a drop in nearly seven months, since that fateful climb into the Yellowstone canyon. Each time the urge became too strong, visions of his dark-haired, blue-eyed angel swam before his eyes.

Sarah. Not a day went by, not even an hour, that he didn't

think of her. Keeping his focus on what he'd set out to do had been hard when thoughts of her kept entering his mind. Memories of their one time together kept him awake during the long and lonely nights. Leaving that morning had been the most difficult thing he'd ever done in his life. Harder than anything he'd endured since. But he couldn't remain where he was, stuck the way he was. He'd realized that when he held her in his arms. He had to do what was right for her.

"Forgive me, Angel," he whispered, staring into the frothy beer that sat untouched before him. He knew if he had told her of his intentions, she'd have talked him out of it, or worse, insisted that he take her with him. It was an impossible thought. The last few months had been more challenging than anything he'd ever imagined. And he missed her. Did she ever think about him? Was she too angry to be bothered?

"Hey, there he is," someone shouted from behind him. "I told you we should have checked here first."

Chase recognized the familiar voice, and whirled around. A smile formed on his lips. His friends had found him.

"We're ready to go," one of them said. "You haven't changed your mind, have you?"

"Nope. Absolutely wouldn't miss it for the world," Chase answered cheerfully. He tossed some money on the counter. Without touching the beer, he walked away from the bar, and followed his friends into the bright sunshine outside.

Sarah stared unseeing out the window. The cold December wind howled ferociously, and the cabin's eaves groaned in protest. The glass panes creaked. Behind her, the fire in the hearth crackled and popped loudly. She didn't have to turn to know her mother had added more logs. Sarah wrapped her shawl more tightly around her shoulders. One hand darted instinctively to her belly. The cold seeping in through the cracks in the windowsill matched the iciness in her heart.

"I hope your father gets back soon." Sarah's mother moved to stand beside her, peering anxiously out the window. "It looks like we're going to get more snow. With just the three of us this year, he really didn't need to go out to shoot a turkey for Christmas dinner."

Sarah caught the wistfulness in her mother's voice. This would be the first year the entire family wasn't together for Christmas. A trapper had told her parents at rendezvous that he had met her brothers in St. Louis. They had mentioned they might spend the year in the city, or at Fort Raymond, and return the following spring after the snowmelt.

Sarah sighed. She tried to swallow away the bitter taste in her mouth. Nothing was the same anymore. The summer had certainly changed her. She was no longer the naïve girl she had been. Her delight in the world and her surroundings had disappeared along with the man she thought herself in love with. No amount of coaxing from either of her parents had lifted her somber mood over the months. On some level, she still blamed her father for Chase's leaving. He'd known about Chase's plans, and he'd even helped him.

Sarah turned away from the window. The emptiness in her heart would not go away by blaming others. She knew that. Chase had made his choice. How often had he said he needed to find his way home? She still believed he loved her, just not enough to stay with her.

I hope you found your happiness, Chase. She held on to that thought. Her mother had been right. She wouldn't want him to stay with her if he truly didn't want to be here. These thoughts did nothing to lessen her feelings of loss.

Sarah rubbed at her abdomen. She'd already altered her britches several times to accommodate her expanding waist. At least her loose fitting shirts, and the way she wore her belt, could still disguise the truth. Without any clothing, the fact that she carried Chase's child was already evident.

She'd kept the pregnancy hidden from her parents all this time. Shame and humiliation held her back from telling them. What would they think of her? Her mother knew she had been intimate with Chase. Did she ever wonder if that union had created a child? Her father would be furious. Sarah didn't want to think about what he would do to her.

She sighed. A few more weeks at most, and everyone who saw her would know. What would she tell people? She would never find a husband in her condition. And who would want her for a wife now? She had lain with a man without the benefit of marriage. Now she would pay the price of her actions for the rest of her life. Not that she had any desires to marry. She would never love another man the way she had - still did - love Chase. That he didn't feel the same about her hurt deeply.

Sarah smiled softly. Despite all the shame she would have to endure, she would love this child as much, and more, as she had loved its father. Chase had given her a part of himself, and no one could take that away from her. If she had to live as an outcast for the rest of her life, she would manage somehow.

It had taken Sarah several months after Chase disappeared to realize the truth of her condition. Her monthly flow had stopped, and when the nausea took over each morning, she couldn't deny it any longer. She'd kept her sickness hidden from her parents, although it wasn't easy at times. Thankfully, it had only lasted a few weeks.

"What can I do to help prepare dinner, Mama?" Sarah asked. She headed for the workbench, picking through the heap of root vegetables on the counter.

"There's not much to do right now. The pies are ready to go into the fire, but we'll wait. If your father brings home a bird, it'll be a while before it's cooked. You can help with the plucking. You know how much I hate that."

Sarah smiled at her mother. "Sure, Mama," she said quietly.

She added more wood to the fire to stave off the cold. Rummaging through some tins on the shelves above the workbench, she found the one that contained her favorite dried nettles. Reaching for a cup, she dumped a handful in, and added hot water from the kettle hanging over the fire. Perhaps some hot tea would chase away the coldness inside her.

"Unless you're not up for plucking a bird in your condition," her mother said from behind her. Sarah spun around. Her mother looked at her, her eyes filled with concern.

"I think you've been burdened long enough, Sarah," she said softly, and placed her hand on Sarah's belly. With a gasp, Sarah jumped back. Wide-eyed, she stared at her mother.

"How . . . how long have you known?" she asked, her voice cracking.

Her mother smiled. "For months. I've suspected probably before you became aware yourself. I thought you'd have come to me by now. You won't be able to hide it much longer."

Sarah hung her head. "Does Papa know?"

"I don't think so. Men don't pay attention to these kinds of things, until it becomes obvious." She paused. "Another month, and it will be. Right now, your clothes are still disguising your growing belly."

"What will I do?" Sarah blurted, the tears flowing freely.

Her mother knew. There was no judgment, only under-standing. Sarah rushed to her mother, and fell into the older woman's arms. Relief swept over her that she didn't carry this secret bottled up inside any longer. She should have come forth with the truth right away. Her mother soothed her with quiet words and shushing sounds, just as she'd done when Sarah was a little girl.

The cabin door burst open suddenly, sending cold air rushing in.

"Daniel, you're back!" her mother exclaimed. Sarah stepped away from her and hastily swiped at the tears on her face. Her mother hurried to close the door. Her father held a huge turkey by its legs. He handed the bird to her mother, who shot Sarah a meaningful look.

"We'll talk later," her mother said with a reassuring smile, and Sarah rushed over and took the turkey from her.

Her father shook out of his heavy buffalo robe and gloves, rubbing his hands together. "A turkey's not all I brought," he said, a wide grin on his face. His eyes darted between his wife and Sarah.

The door opened again. "Merry Christmas, Mama!" Three men spoke in unison. Sarah's mother gasped and her hand flew to her mouth. The room suddenly became smaller after they all filed in.

"Oh my goodness, you're home!" She spread her arms, reaching up to hug Sarah's brothers one at a time, tears in her eyes. "How did you get here in this weather? All the way from Fort Raymond?"

The men all beamed. "We wouldn't miss Christmas here at home, now would we, Mama," Samuel said, giving his mother a warm hug. "The passes weren't that bad. It only took eight days."

Zach and Matthew, her twin brothers, approached Sarah. Matthew lifted her into his arms and spun her around. "Hey little girl. You've grown again since spring," he beamed. "Looks like you've packed on some pounds, too."

"Hi, Matt," Sarah smiled, and hastily stepped away from him.

"We're gonna have an even harder time fending off the men, Matt. She's starting to look real fine." Zach grinned, giving her a bear hug of his own. He set her away from him and gave her an approving once-over. Except for their mother's blonde hair, Sarah's brothers' features and smiles were so much like their father's.

Samuel, her older brother by two years, walked up to her, a wide boyish grin on his face. His tousled blonde hair hung in strands over his eyes, no matter how often he shook his head to fling them out of his face.

"So, Sis, what have you been up to?" He punched her lightly on the arm. Sarah swatted his hand away, and shot him an angry glare. "I thought I'd come home and be an uncle by now. *Kwyioo* sure talked about you a lot this past spring. We all told him he was crazy." He turned to grin at his brothers.

"Yeah, we keep saying she needs someone who's gonna put her over his knee and keep her in her place every day. I don't think she's met that man yet," Matt chimed in.

"Enough teasing, boys." Her mother stood with her hands on her hips. "A lot has happened while you were gone. This is not the kind of talk your sister needs to hear right now." She glared at her sons, and no one dared argue with her. Samuel scratched his head, and tried to look demure. Matthew shuffled his feet. Zach coughed.

Sarah's eyes filled with tears, and she gritted her teeth. Dammit, why did she have to cry in front of them? She'd never hear the end of it. Samuel's smile faded. Everyone stared at her. If only the floorboards could open up and swallow her.

"Well." Her mother clapped her hands together, breaking the tension. "I think we do need to get this turkey prepped. Sarah, can you give me a hand?"

Glad to get away from her brothers, Sarah headed for the workbench to start the tedious task of de-feathering the bird.

"Actually, Sarah, I need your help with something else."

Sarah turned to stare at her father. "Samuel, go pluck the turkey for your mother," he added.

Samuel shot Sarah a disgruntled look. Sarah turned away from him. Any other time, she would have gloated that her brother was asked to take over a chore he didn't relish doing. There was no satisfaction this time.

"There's a stray dog in the old cabin. I thought you could take a look and see if you recognize him. You know all the dogs that belong to the villagers. Perhaps you can help this one find his way home."

"Sure, Papa," Sarah stammered.

What an odd request. He obviously wanted to talk to her brothers alone. He handed her his buffalo robe, which was still warm from his body heat. She slipped it on, and wrapped it around herself. It was much too big for her, but it would keep her warm in the freezing cold.

"I hope you don't mind, Mama," Zach's voice faded in the background as she opened the door. A cold blast of air hit her in the face. ". . . a friend along. Nice fella we met in Fort Raymond . . ."

Sarah pulled the door shut, drowning out her family's chatter, and wrapped the coat more tightly around herself. She pulled the fur up over her face and braced herself for the cold gust of wind that burned every exposed piece of skin. Keeping her head tucked low, she pushed through the deep snow, stepping in the tracks that her brothers and father had left. She trudged on. The company of a stray dog was preferable to her at the moment than facing her family.

CHAPTER THIRTY-FOUR

y the time Sarah reached the little cabin, her nose and cheeks were numb, despite having them buried in the heavy coat. She quickly opened the door, and slipped inside. If the dog darted out, she'd never catch him.

Her eyes slowly adjusted to the darkened interior of the cabin. It was freezing cold in here, too. Her breath looked like steam when she exhaled. A shuffling noise behind her that could not have been made by a dog made her turn. She gasped, and her hand reflexively went to her belt.

A tall figure stood in the shadows, wrapped in layers of furs. Only his eyes were visible. Green eyes. Eyes that had haunted her every day for the past five months. Her hand flew to her mouth. Tears rolled halfway down her face and stung her cheeks and froze in place.

"Hello, Sarah." The man said softly, pulling the fur covering away from his face.

"Chase," she whispered. Her hands flew to her belly.

"How are you, Angel?" He took a tentative step toward her, and she backed away. Her mind raced. How was he here?

He didn't have the time travel device. Her father had said he disposed of it in the Hell Mouth.

He looked different. His heavy winter clothes were fashioned from buffalo hide and fur. On the ground by his feet lay a hornbow and flintlock. His hair was much longer than she remembered, almost to his shoulders. The most noticeable change was in his face. The boy in him was gone. In his place, before her, stood a man who projected confidence.

He held out his hand. Sarah backed up some more, bumping into a wooden trunk. She shook her head. All these months, all the heartache . . .

"Let me explain, Sarah. Please, I--"

"How are you here?" she interrupted, steeling her voice. Her heart and mind raced out of control. All the feelings of loss, anger, and pain jumbled together.

"I came by the usual mode of transportation, Angel. On horseback."

Her eyes narrowed. "You didn't go home to the future?" Renewed jabs of pain ripped through her heart. He had remained here, but left her? After everything they'd shared. After she . . . Her baby . . . their child.

What would he say when he found out? All the feelings of humiliation and shame she'd endured over the last five months, of being a fallen woman with a child and no husband.

Chase shook his head. "There was never anything for me to go back to. Heck, I'm just another statistic in the future. Just another lost hiker in Yellowstone whose body is never recovered." He paused, and rubbed the back of his neck. "Elk Runner told me that from the start, that I was already home. It took me a long time to realize he was right."

Sarah's entire body trembled. Whether from the cold, or the shock of seeing Chase standing in front of her, she didn't know. He took another slow step toward her. Her hand shot out, and she shook her head.

"Don't come any closer," she said, her teeth chattering, despite all her efforts to set her jaw. He stopped, but his eyes remained on her, intense and full of longing.

He sighed, and turned away. "You're freezing cold. Let me get a fire going." Without waiting for an answer, he knelt by the hearth. Rooting with his hand inside the layers of fur he wore, he produced a flint, and gathered some kindling from the wood box. Sarah watched the efficiency in which he worked. In no time, a glowing blaze roared to life. Memories flooded her mind of the first time she had taught him how to build a fire.

"Come over here, Sarah. I know you're angry, and you have every right to be, but you don't need to stand in the cold." He held his own hands to the flames momentarily to warm them, then rose to his feet and faced her again.

"Here, I'll move." He backed away. "Come stand by the fire."

Sarah eyed him warily, but did as he asked. She was freezing cold, and the fire promised warmth. She had to think of her baby. Neither of them spoke for a while. His intense perusal made her uncomfortable. He wouldn't take his eyes off her. Sarah lowered her head. Maybe she couldn't keep him from staring at her, but she didn't have to look back at him.

"You're as beautiful as I remember," he said quietly. "In fact, you're more radiant than ever. There's something different about you."

Her head shot up, and she glared at him. Did he suspect something?

"Why?" she demanded, her voice raised. "Why did you leave, Chase?" She bit her trembling lower lip.

He inhaled deeply. "Because I needed to prove something

to myself. I was living between worlds, Sarah. I didn't fit in here, and I knew I didn't want to go back to where I came from, back to my old life. The thought of leaving you . . . never seeing you again . . . I wasn't the kind of man who could take care of you. You deserved someone better. I needed to be better."

"You left me, Chase. You left, after . . . after I gave myself to you." The tears flowed freely now. She wheeled around and turned her back to him.

He sucked in a big gulp of air. "I'm sorry, Angel. It had to be this way." She stiffened. He stood right behind her. She felt the heat coming off his body, and his breath in her ear.

"Why? Why did you have me believe you returned to the future?" She turned to stare up at him.

"If I had said to you that I needed to go out on my own, tell me now you wouldn't have tried to talk me out of it, or would have wanted to come with me." He gazed intently into her eyes. "This is something I had to do by myself. And if I didn't survive, if something happened to me, well . . . I wanted to spare you the pain of potentially losing me twice. If you thought I was gone for good, you could be angry with me, and go on with your life, in case I didn't make it back to you." He stepped away from her.

Sarah blinked away her tears, and sniffed. She wanted to run from the cabin, but she couldn't. Something held her back. She needed to know more. It still seemed so unreal that he was here. Part of her wanted to throw herself into his arms. The other part wanted to stay angry for all the hurt he'd caused. She had to tell him he would be a father. She wouldn't have to face raising a child without a husband after all. But could she use this baby as an excuse to bind him to her? Did she want to force a marriage on him?

"When did you decide to do all this? Where did you go?"

"It had been on my mind for a while." He looked at her,

then sat down by the hearth, his elbows resting on his knees. "Elk Runner was always talking crazy to me, saying I needed to go on a vision quest, to realize right here was where I belonged. I didn't pay any attention to him at first." He rubbed the back of his neck. "I was torn between what I feel for you, and needing to get back to my own time. Your father was so patient with me, trying to teach me survival skills. You have no idea how inadequate I felt, next to him."

Sarah inhaled deeply, and sat down beside him. He looked at her, hope in his eyes.

"After Hawk died, I made my decision. I couldn't live feeling like a failure anymore. We took his body back to his family, and I had a long talk with your dad, and with Elk Runner. Your father wanted to find the time travel device, get rid of it for good to make sure it wasn't found again. He asked for my help. I could show him exactly where I had been when it sent me here. It would make his search easier. When we found it, we parted ways."

He reached out and tentatively touched her hand in her lap. She didn't pull away. The warmth of his touch radiated through her. All the old feelings that she wanted to forget came rushing back. She still loved this man more than anything. She met his eyes.

"I met up with Elk Runner," Chase continued. He took hold of her hand, entwining his fingers with hers. "He sent me on a vision quest first. It made me see clearly all the things that were holding me back, all the self-doubts I had. He taught me things I needed to learn to survive, and what it took to be a man in this time. I've been out hunting and tracking, and trading with some of the tribes over the months, then headed to Fort Raymond. That's where I met your brothers." A slow smile spread across his face.

"You met my brothers?" Sarah stared, wide-eyed.

"Great bunch of guys." Chase chuckled. "Didn't take me

long to figure out who they were. Twins that look so much like your dad, and Samuel is the spitting image of you, but with blonde hair. They were going to stay until spring, but when the weather let up, they decided they wanted to try and make it through the pass and be home for Christmas. I came back with them, although I would have come back on my own had they decided to stay."

The fire crackled softly behind them. Sarah's back warmed. Minutes passed and neither one spoke. She tried to absorb everything he'd told her. He had done all this to prove himself? So he could remain here and be with her?

Chase brought her hand to his lips, and kissed each finger. Sarah closed her eyes, savoring the sensations coursing through her.

"Let me see if I can get this right," Chase said quietly, and cleared his throat. Sarah opened her eyes to look at him. *"Tsao suwangkun, Aibehi Imaah ba'a".*

Her vision blurred anew at his words, and she could barely breathe. He knelt before her, reaching for her other hand. His eyes did not leave hers.

"I love you, Angel." He wiped the tears away from her cheeks with his finger. "And I have one more confession to make." He smiled softly. "On our way back from the village, after we returned Hawk's body, I asked your father for you."

Sarah couldn't hold back a gasp. "You . . . what?" she asked, breathless.

"He consented. I admit, asking for you, knowing I would be leaving, was my selfish little piece of insurance that you wouldn't go off and marry the first trapper who came along after I was gone. I asked your father to give me six months. If I didn't return in that time, if you found someone else, you would be free to choose then, but your father would refuse any man before then."

Chase stood. He pulled her up with him, and wrapped his

arms around her. "These buffalo robes are really bulky," he chuckled. "I can't even hold you." He released her and removed his heavy robe. "It's getting pretty warm in here."

Sarah smiled softly, and slipped out of her robe as well. Would he notice? He bent and kissed her lightly on the lips. She held her breath.

Chase cupped her face between his hands, his eyes staring intently at her. "Sarah, when you came to me . . . in the customs you grew up with, your father had consented to the match already . . . you came to your husband. I made love to my wife that night."

Sarah's arms shot up and she wrapped them tightly around his neck. Chase inhaled deeply, and pulled her to him. Sarah sobbed, and finally cried tears of joy rather than sadness. Everything would be all right now. She had a husband, and a father for their child. Chase stroked her back and held her. After countless minutes, she reluctantly pulled back, and wiped her face on her sleeves.

Sarah silently removed the belt from around her waist, letting it slip to the floor. Chase stared at her, a slow smile on his face, and one brow rose. With a pounding heart, she reached for his hand, and held it in front of her. He had given no indication that he noticed a change in her size. Her wider appearance could be attributed to her layers of winter clothes.

Sarah held his eyes and slowly guided his hand up her shirt to her abdomen. Her heart drummed fiercely in her throat. How would he react?

"Angel, what are you doi . . ." Chase didn't finish his question. Abruptly, his hand pulled away. Surprise registered in his wide eyes. "Sarah?" He swallowed, and looked toward her belly.

Sarah blinked away the tears that threatened in her eyes. It wasn't the reaction she had hoped for. He didn't seem pleased. She lowered her head, and stepped away from him, a sinking feeling in her gut. Was Chase about to reject his own child?

Just as quickly as his hand pulled away, he snaked his arms around her to prevent her from moving further away from him. A fierce and determined look came over him.

"Sarah . . . Angel," he whispered. "Had I known, I would have come back sooner." His hands trembled, and he felt his way up her shirt, and along her slightly protruding abdomen. His lips curved in a slow smile.

"You're . . . not upset?" Sarah asked hesitantly.

His brows furrowed. "Why would I be upset, Angel? I . . . words can't describe what I'm feeling right now." He leaned forward and kissed her, his hand still on her abdomen. Sarah stepped closer, and she heaved a sigh in relief.

"Junior here gave me quite a surprise. I wasn't expecting this," Chase said. His face sobered. "I'm sorry, Sarah. I can only imagine how difficult the last few months must have been for you. If I'd have known—"

"You're here now," she said, sniffling. His hands moved around to her back, and he pulled her to him.

"I love you, Sarah. I'll tell you that every day for the rest of our lives."

"I like your hair short," she said suddenly, smiling up at him.

"I'll cut it," he responded without hesitation.

His hand came up and stroked her cheek. Then he claimed her mouth in a slow kiss that made her want to melt.

"Sarah," he panted, pulling his head back, "you've redeemed me from my old life. I didn't know what living was, until I came here and found you. All the hurt I've caused, I will make up to you somehow. I still have a lot to learn, but I'm confident in my abilities now."

Sarah cupped his face in her hands. "I love you, Chase," she whispered. "I never stopped."

"So, will you accept me as your husband, and father to our son?" he grinned.

"From now until forever," she said, "but don't be disappointed if we have a daughter." She pulled his head down, and pressed her lips to his.

"Whoa! What is going on in here? Do I need to defend your honor, Sarah?"

Sarah broke away, startled by the loud voice. She looked up to see Samuel standing in the door. His eyes narrowed on Chase.

Chase grinned. "That's my job from now on, *Uncle* Sam. Have you met my wife?"

Sarah laughed at the open-mouthed expression on her brother's face. For once, he was speechless. Finally, he shook his head, and said, "Does Papa know about this?" Without waiting for an answer, he looked at Chase. "I don't know how you two know each other, but I sure hope you realize what you're getting yourself into." With a broad grin on his face, he turned and left the cabin.

Chase wrapped his arms around her. "Ready to see your family?"

"Zach and Matt will be in here in a minute if we don't show up, after Samuel's done telling them what he saw."

"I'll make sure and put a lock on this door," Chase replied, and kissed her one more time. Holding her arms, his face turned serious. "Make me one promise, Sarah."

"Anything," she whispered, breathless.

"When our baby is born, I want to be there. Don't make me wait a month before I get to meet and hold him."

Sarah smiled. "I wouldn't want it any other way, Chase. You will be the first to hold *her*."

He reached for her coat, and wrapped it around her,

before grabbing for his own. "Whatever the future brings, from now on we're facing it together."

"You are my future, Chase." Sarah gazed up at him.

Chase looked into her eyes. "And you are my redemption, Angel."

THE ADVENTURE CONTINUES with a companion story to Yellowstone Redemption, called **Yellowstone Reflections**. Where was Chase and what was he doing during his five-month absence?

If you enjoyed the book, please consider leaving a short review.

DEAR READER

I hope you enjoyed the second installment of the Yellowstone Romance Series. While I try my best to stay true to the general history of the Yellowstone area, and to the beautiful landscape, I choose to use literary license with some dates, locations, and events of the area.

The mountain man and fur trapper era in the Rocky Mountains encompassed only about twenty years, from the 1820's to the early 1840's. These mountain men traveled through the mountains in large groups, most of them working for various fur companies. Only a few operated as free trappers, sort of like independent agents. The annual trapper rendezvous took place in different locations throughout the Rockies each year, but not near Jackson Lake at the base of the Grand Tetons, as I have depicted it in this story.

Trappers spent spring and fall trapping beaver. They did not actually live in the area, and very few entered the area that is now Yellowstone National Park. None lived there year-round. The only permanent inhabitants were the Sheepeater Shoshone. Other tribes migrated through the area that is now the park, but due to harsh winter conditions, they chose not to live there.

Fort Raymond was a trapper outpost built by Manuel Lisa in 1806 at the confluence of the Yellowstone and Bighorn Rivers. It was abandoned in 1813. For the purposes of this story, the fort was still a thriving stronghold for trappers in 1835.

John Colter, a member of the Lewis and Clark expedition, is credited with being the first white man in the Yellowstone area. Whether he actually saw the geysers there is debatable, but Colter Bay on Jackson Lake in the Grand Tetons is named for him.

Chase's experience with the Blackfoot tribe is loosely based on what is known as "Colter's Run." While trapping with a fellow mountain man, Colter was ambushed by a group of Blackfoot. His companion was killed, but Colter was stripped of his clothes and weapons, and given the chance to run for his life. He miraculously lived to tell the tale.

Please join my list of awesome readers, and get exclusive content, such as the unpublished Prologue, and first three chapters that were cut from the original manuscript for Yellowstone Heart Song just for signing up! Find out about Aimee's encounter with Zach before she time traveled.

You'll also be kept up-to-date with the characters from the Yellowstone series in my popular exclusive monthly "Aimee's Journal" entries, sneak peeks, free book offers, behind the scenes info, latest releases, and much more!

Go to: http://www.subscribepage.com/j3x0h0 on your web browser to sign up.

Many of my readers have asked for a timeline for both the **Yellowstone series** as well as the **Teton Trilogy** and the **Wilderness Brides Series**, since the three series are related (by setting and time period) and characters from one series make cameo appearances in the other. Please email me, and I will get you a download link.

peggy@peggylhenderson.com

Without the constant support and help from my critique partner, Carol Spradling, this book would not have been written. Sometimes I think she knows my characters better than I do, and doesn't hesitate to point out to me what works, and what doesn't. So, thank you, Carol, for keeping me going on this journey, and helping me bring these characters to life.

Also, once again, thanks to my husband Richard, for supporting me in my writing efforts, and continued advice about basic survival skills.

Editor: Barbara Ouradnik

Cover Design: Carpe Librum Book Design

ABOUT THE AUTHOR

Peggy L Henderson is an award-winning, best-selling western historical and time travel romance author of the Yellowstone Romance Series, Second Chances Time Travel Romance Series, Teton Romance Trilogy, and Wilderness Brides Series. She was also a contributing author in the unprecedented 50-book American Mail Order Brides Series, contributing Book #15, Emma: Bride of Kentucky, the multi-author Timeless Hearts Time Travel Series, and the multi-author Burnt River Contemporary Western Series.

When she's not writing about Yellowstone, the Tetons, or the old west, she's out hiking the trails, spending time with her family and pets, or catching up on much-needed sleep. She is happily married to her high school sweetheart. They live in Yellowstone National Park, where many of her books are set.

Peggy is always happy to hear from her readers!

To get in touch with Peggy:
www.peggylhenderson.com
peggy@peggylhenderson.com

ALSO BY PEGGY L HENDERSON

Yellowstone Romance Series:

(in recommended reading order)

Yellowstone Heart Song

Return to Yellowstone

A Yellowstone Christmas

Yellowstone Redemption

Yellowstone Reflections

A Yellowstone Homecoming

Yellowstone Love Notes

A Yellowstone Season of Giving

Yellowstone Awakening

Yellowstone Dawn

Yellowstone Deception

A Yellowstone Promise

Yellowstone Origins

Yellowstone Legacy

Yellowstone Legends

Teton Romance Series

Wilderness Brides Series

Wild Mountain Hearts Series

Blemished Brides Series

Second Chances Time Travel Romance Series

Burnt River Contemporary Romance Series

Made in the USA
Middletown, DE
08 June 2021